Also by Amy McCulloch

The Oathbreaker's Shadow
– the first part of Raim and Wadi's story –

WITHDRAWN
FROM
COLLECTION

THE SHADOW'S CURSE

AMY McCULLOCH

flux
Woodbury, Minnesota

First U.S. Edition
First Printing, 2016

Originally published by Corgi Books, an imprint of Random House Children's Publishers UK, London, 2014

Book design by Bob Gaul
Cover design by Kevin Brown
Cover illustration by John Blumen
Interior shield graphic by Llewellyn art department
Map illustration by Elisabeth Alba

Flux, an imprint of Llewellyn Worldwide Ltd.

Library of Congress Cataloging-in-Publication Data
McCulloch, Amy.
  The shadow's curse/Amy McCulloch.—First U.S. edition.
     pages cm
  "Originally published by Corgi Books, an imprint of Random House Children's Publishers UK, London, 2014"—Copyright page.
  Sequel to: The oathbreaker's shadow.
  Summary: With war looming, sixteen-year-old Raim must rescue Wadi, the girl he loves, from his former best friend Khareh, the tyrannical new Khan of Darhan, all while attempting to solve the mystery of the oath he broke.
  ISBN 978-0-7387-4512-1
  [1. Fantasy.] I. Title.
  PZ7.1.M434Sh 2016
  [Fic]—dc23
                                                              2015032029

                              Flux
                    Llewellyn Worldwide Ltd.
                      2143 Wooddale Drive
                    Woodbury, MN 55125-2989
                        www.fluxnow.com

              Printed in the United States of America

For Sophie, mapmaker extraordinaire

PART ONE

1

RAIM

Raim snatched at a long blade of grass and released the seeds from their cluster at the top of the stem. They dropped like stones from his hand to the ground. The air was still, and the grass here was so tall it covered the men with ease. The perfect place for an ambush.

He caught his grandfather's eye and Loni nodded once, his forehead wrinkled in concentration. They had spent many hours poring over Dharma's visions. Raim's younger sister had woven them into an intricate carpet, which predicted where the wagon would pass. The wagon destined for the prison where Khareh kept his most dangerous enemies, guarded by both man and shadow. The wagon that Raim believed was carrying the most important person in his whole world: Wadi.

Wind whistled by Raim's ear. He looked up and saw his spirit-companion Draikh settle down amid the grass. Even Draikh had to hide here. With this wagon in possession of its own shadow-guard, Draikh was vulnerable to being seen. Only oathbreakers could see the true figures of shadows—to everyone else, they appeared as patches of swirling dark, like ominous clouds.

"Oyu has seen them," whispered Draikh.

Raim craned his neck to the sky and saw the garfalcon wheeling overhead. *How far?* he thought in reply.

"They're traveling quickly. Ten minutes, at most," said the spirit.

Raim locked eyes with his grandfather again and signaled with his hands: *Time to go.*

Getting into position, the group barely moved the grass more than would the gentlest breeze, and for a moment Raim allowed himself a touch of confidence. They were going to do this. And who would have known it from looking at them? The group was made up of old men, long banished from their tribes, awaiting death in groups of yurts known collectively as "cherens," not even worth the knowledge they could pass on to their grand or great-grandchildren. But their new mission had drawn purpose out of the most cobwebbed minds. What they lacked in energy, they made up for in experience.

Then doubt. Were he and Draikh ready? Any physical combat with the guards was going to be up to them to win. They had practiced. They had trained. But what if they failed?

Raim didn't want to think about losing Wadi for a second time.

Then, there was no more time to think. Raim's head filled with the pounding of horse hooves, and the grating of iron wheels slicing their way through the field. Dust, rising and pluming in the air, stung his eyes. It happened so fast, he wondered if his muscles would move in time or if he would remain rooted to the ground like another of the blades of grass, bending and breaking in the wagon's wake rather than holding firm, rather than leaping forward to attack...

A screech broke through the cloud in his mind and he answered with a cry of his own, raw and almost primal.

He leaped forward, stringing an arrow and releasing it almost immediately, striking down the driver.

Simultaneously, the old men of the cheren reacted, one man spearing a gnarled branch between the spokes of the front wheel. The horse, already spooked by the sudden loss of the man behind the reins, jumped forward. A loud crack filled the air as the branch snapped and splintered, and as it broke, so did the wheel. The wagon lurched and toppled, coming down hard on the corner where its wheel had given way.

The door on the far side flung open, almost horizontal, and immediately the space was full of swords as the human guards sprang out.

Raim was there to meet them. He swung his first strike with abandon, a wide arc that gave plenty of time for his opponent to leap clear. He cursed loudly.

"We will get to her!" shouted Loni. "Keep the guards away from us!"

That was it. Raim needed to keep his concentration, and then the others would rescue her. He stared at his enemy with sharper focus, slashing with purpose. In a few strokes he disarmed the man, and Draikh was at his side to collect the fallen weapon. Raim kicked the man to the ground and leaped over his prostrate body to find a new target, as another of his group trussed up the fallen enemy with rope.

One of the oldest cheren men cowered in fear, a battered old axe in his trembling hand, his eyes wide, as a much younger man approached with menacing slowness. But the old man wasn't staring at his opponent directly ... because he was unable to see him.

"Draikh!" Raim screamed and pointed at the soldier—who was, in reality, a shadow. "Haunt!"

Draikh swooped down as the haunt attacked. Raim heard a scream, but was instantly distracted as another guard leaped toward him.

Raim was so close to the wagon now, he could almost feel Wadi's presence. Strength imbued his every move in a way he had never experienced before. The next guard, already weak in the shoulder from the crash, was no match at all. He fell quickly to the ground.

Raim jumped onto the wagon and looked inside. It was empty.

"Escape! Escape!"

Raim jerked his head up at the sound of the cries and saw a guard dig his heels into the side of his horse. There was a struggling prisoner, bound with his head covered by a sack, thrown roughly on the horse's back.

Raim strung another arrow, and shot. It whistled past the guard, missing him and, crucially, the prisoner, but flew close enough to the horse's ear to make it rear. The prisoner, still wriggling to break free, rolled off the back and hit the ground with a thump.

The panicked guard looked down at the prisoner, back at the ambush, and gave his horse rein, disappearing fast across the grassland.

Raim ran toward the writhing bundle on the ground.

"What of the guard?" shouted one of Raim's men.

"Leave him," replied Loni. "We have what we came for."

Reaching his target, Raim flung himself down, skidding on his knees in his haste. He grabbed the edges of the rattan sack and ripped it from the prisoner's head.

But it wasn't Wadi. It was Vlad.

RAIM

Vlad's wrists were ravaged red-raw, the edges blackened and blistered. His face, already so lined and drawn from his years in Lazar, seemed older by a decade. Raim found Vlad's haunt too, in the remnants of the wagon, so weak he was almost transparent.

There was no sign of Wadi. Raim kicked at the broken body of the cart, the wood splintering with a satisfying crack. He could blame no one for the assumption but himself.

Dharma's vision had been of the wagon, not the prisoner. Raim had let his hopes soar, and now they'd come crashing down, brought down by yet another of Khareh's arrows.

He swallowed down his disappointment and walked over to where his companions were bandaging Vlad up as best they could with their meager healing supplies. He was barely conscious through all of it, only a low moan escaping his lips.

"You know this man?" asked Loni when they had finished, although it was more of a statement than a question.

Raim nodded. "His name is Vlad. He accompanied Wadi and me from Lazar. We thought that he was just helping us to reach Darhan, but in reality, he wanted revenge."

"Revenge?" Now Loni was confused.

Raim's voice broke, the sudden wave of memories hitting him hard as a lightning bolt. "On Khareh."

He looked up into his grandfather's face. This man had raised him on the steppes. He was grandfather to Raim's two adopted siblings as well: his older brother, Tarik, and his younger sister, Dharma. Raim didn't know how Loni was going to take the next news. "Vlad is Dharma's father."

As ever, Loni's expression remained stoical, though he tugged at his beard with twisting fingers. "And how could you possibly know that?"

"He was Baril, once. Like Tarik is now. He and his wife, Zu, were exiled from the Baril when they broke their oath. They used their Baril knowledge in Lazar to help me, and they said they once had a daughter named Dharma."

"A name means nothing," Loni scoffed, releasing his beard from his nervous hands.

"The scarf," Raim continued. "Zu gave her daughter her scarf as a token just before they were sent away. The same one that Dharma gave to me, before my ..." He didn't need to finish. During his exile, that scarf had been his lifeline back to the home he never wanted to forget. He blinked back tears that had risen behind his eyes. "When Vlad found out what Khareh did to Dharma, he wanted to kill him. He thinks she's dead, but even if he just knew how Khareh injured her, he'd still have wanted vengeance. Obviously, he didn't succeed." He looked over the man's scars again. "Who knows what he must have suffered."

Finally, after a pause that seemed to last a lifetime, Loni nodded. "We need to get away from here," he said, his gaze fixed on the empty plain ahead of them. "They might come back with reinforcements."

Raim nodded, not trusting himself to speak again. He hoisted Vlad to his feet, and with the help of another they carried the broken man away from the site of the ambush, the long grasses obscuring their path. Vlad barely weighed a thing.

They set up camp a few miles away and established a vigilant watch, but no one came; the only shadows on the horizon were the dark peaks of the Amarapura mountains. Still, Loni insisted they couldn't risk a campfire, not even to boil water to help sterilize Vlad's wounds. The air felt so still, though, Raim couldn't imagine anyone approaching without them knowing about it. Not that he thought Khareh would be particularly bothered by the ambush. They hadn't come away with the real prize.

Vlad drifted in and out of consciousness, babbling meaningless words. Raim cringed, looking at him. He was a shell of his former self—the arrogant former Baril priest Raim had met in Lazar. Some of Vlad's wounds were older—scars fading to white, cracking, healing poorly. His haunt was silent and docile. Raim tried to talk to him, too, but received nothing in return. His stomach turned at the thought of what the man must have endured.

Of what Wadi might still be enduring.

"Look, you didn't know. Couldn't have known." Draikh sat cross-legged in front of him.

Raim shrugged. "But what Dharma saw … "

"She saw a wagon. Carrying a prisoner. She didn't see the prisoner. We all just assumed because they had shadow-guards that they were carrying someone important. You hoped it would be—"

"Of course I hoped it would be her! The fact that it's not means that she's still there with him. That I've still abandoned her to whatever fate he has in store for her." Raim stood up, stretching the cramp from his leg. "Gods, this is so frustrating."

Dharma was never wrong. Everyone was awed by Raim and his sage powers, but he was in awe of his younger sister. She had endured terrible pain at the hands of Khareh, but in blinding her, Khareh had inadvertently unlocked the girl's gift. She could see into the future, and what she saw, she wove into carpets that prophesied the future. It had been Dharma who had shown Raim that Wadi was still alive in the first place—when he thought she was dead.

He had seen with his own eyes the knife Khareh had thrust into Wadi's chest. But Dharma knew otherwise, and had set him on the path to rescuing her.

Those who knew of Dharma's gift called her the Weaver. Vlad didn't yet know the wonder his daughter had become. Raim would tell him when he woke up; it might go some way toward relieving his pain.

"Khareh is playing you," Draikh said to Raim. "He knows you too well. He knows you will come after her."

"And surely *you* should know Khareh better than anyone!"

"Raim!" Loni stormed over. Whereas before, when Raim appeared to shout at a dark cloud, his grandfather would look at him as if he was going mad, now he understood what was happening: Raim was having a conversation with a spirit—or, in this case, an argument. "How about channeling that energy into something more productive?" Loni asked. "You've neglected your sage training ever since we came on this expedition."

Raim cursed under his breath, but he knew his grandfather was right. All his focus had been on rescuing Wadi, and he had set aside the progress he and Draikh had been making. The more they worked together, the stronger they became. The first month after his brutal clash with Khareh had been about recovering, for both of them. Khareh had broken them of both physical and mental energy. Raim still had flashes of memory: the expression of sheer joy and cruelty on Khareh's face as he'd looked down on the men and women from Lazar; the fear that had gripped his throat at seeing his likeness—a part of his *own* spirit—empowering his greatest enemy; Khareh's cool demeanor as he'd punched the knife through Wadi's chest.

It was a miracle Raim had escaped with his life. Without Draikh, he wouldn't have. Besides Khareh and his soldiers, he had also been fighting against members of the

Yun—the elite guard of Darhan, the best anywhere in the world, and the order that Raim had once been apprenticed to. At one time, Raim had dreamed of nothing more than joining the Yun and becoming the Protector of the Khan himself. The fact that Khareh, his best friend at the time, had been the heir to the Khanate seemed to make it all the more clear that it was his destiny.

But destiny had other plans for Raim.

In an involuntary twitch, Raim's eyes flicked down to his wrist. Where once there'd been a string bracelet, now there was a bright red scar, a brazen reminder of his betrayal. In Darhan, vows were sealed with knots and carried for ever by the oathtaker. Broken promises were seared into the skin, like brands, when the knots burned away. Even worse, a dark shadow would arrive to haunt the oathbreaker, who would henceforth be shunned. There was no escape from their final fate: banishment across the Sola desert, to the city of exiles—Lazar. Oathbreakers were considered too wretched even to deserve an honorable death at the blade of a sword. Either they would perish in the unforgiving sands of the desert, or they would become Chauk: residents of the city of Lazar, unable to return to their homeland.

At least, that was the legend that Raim had grown up with, the legend that had engendered a deeply rooted hatred for all oathbreakers—even himself, now that he was one.

Yet the truth, he discovered, was a little more complicated. The scars were bad, yes, but worse were the shadows—or haunts, as they were known by the Chauk. As only an oathbreaker could know, the haunt was actually the spirit of the person they had betrayed, who could berate the traitor until the oathbreaker was driven mad or entered the city gates. Yet for most oathbreakers, reaching Lazar signaled the end of their punishment. Their haunt would forgive them and disappear back to wherever they belonged. The forgiven oathbreakers then lived out the rest of their lives in Lazar, still not believing themselves worthy of returning home.

However, children who had not yet reached Honor Age—sixteen—were not supposed to suffer this consequence for their broken promises. Or so Raim had thought. But when, at age sixteen, he'd made an Absolute Vow to protect his best friend Khareh's life, he unwittingly broke an old promise sealed within a knot bracelet around his wrist—a promise he didn't remember making. The bracelet had burned, and he was scarred. Strangely, though, there had been no sign of a shadow from breaking that unknown promise. It was still the greatest mystery.

Raim did later gain a shadow: Draikh, his current haunt, who was part of the spirit of Khareh. But Draikh's presence was nearly as inexplicable as the absence of a shadow from his broken vow—given that Raim had not broken the vow he'd made to Khareh. Rather, Draikh had come to save Raim's life when he was being attacked by a lethal swarm of behrflies in the desert. Maybe Draikh was the only part of Khareh that was good, Raim figured. Most definitely, Draikh was a haunt unlike any other.

Raim had made his first big mistake with Khareh when he'd let his best friend vow to take care of Dharma in his absence. In his determination to become the new Khan of

Darhan, Khareh had chosen to break this vow, branding himself an oathbreaker in an effort to unlock a hidden power of the haunts: the power to make an oathbreaker a sage. If an oathbreaker could gain dominance over, or cooperation from, his haunt, he could harness all the haunt's power—from levitation, to healing, to flight. In this way, Khareh could become both khan and sage.

Now Khareh had learned how to use oathbreakers' shadows to form a shadow-army—one that would aid him in his quest to rule over all of Darhan—and Raim had no idea how to stop him. Khareh was a raging tornado, causing havoc wherever he went with his army.

"Brooding is just as bad as arguing."

Draikh's voice shook Raim from his dark stupor. He shrugged his shoulders back a couple of times and stretched the cricks from his neck.

"You're right." He looked up at Draikh. "We should train. What do you feel like doing today?"

Draikh brandished a stick he had picked up. "How about some hand-eye coordination?"

"Yes, anything!"

"Pick up that rock and I'll pretend it's Khareh's head."

Raim did as he was told and chose a jagged shard of rock from the ground, then launched it as hard as he could toward Draikh. Draikh batted it away with the stick, releasing the same pent-up frustration that Raim was feeling over not finding Wadi. They spent an hour tearing across the plain, practising coordinating their movements until they felt like one unit. Working with Draikh seemed so much more natural now, and with each session they discovered more and more about one another's capabilities, and how each was strengthened by the other.

Raim threw a stone, but Draikh missed. The stick dropped from Draikh's hands and landed with a thud on the ground.

"What is it?" Raim asked.

"It's Vlad. He's waking up."

RAIM

Raim spun round and sprinted into the camp. As he approached, he heard Vlad let out a low groan. Loni was already there, dripping water into Vlad's mouth.

Slowly, Vlad's eyes opened. "Where am I?" His voice cracked.

"Vlad?" Raim knelt down beside him. Despite the disagreement they'd had as they escaped Lazar, Raim was still glad to see him alive. "It's me, Raim. We ambushed the wagon that was taking you to—"

"To the prison." His voice was so weak, Raim had to lean in close to hear him. "I had outstayed my welcome." Raim thought he heard a hint of amusement in the man's voice, but then Vlad slipped back into unconsciousness.

Raim looked up at his grandfather, whose face was creased

with concern. "It's a good sign he spoke. It means he may yet recover more of his strength." He craned his neck back, scanning the sky for something—although Raim wasn't quite sure what. "Enough time has passed, I think. We haven't seen any sign of reinforcements coming to retrieve the prisoner. Pola, Mali," he barked at two of the other elders, "let's have a fire tonight. I think it's time we had some real food." He turned to Raim and raised an eyebrow.

Raim jumped up and nodded, glad for the task. He placed two fingers in his mouth and whistled loudly. Within seconds, he felt the wind rush toward him, a tornado in miniature, and in the center of it flew Oyu—the garfalcon he had acquired in the desert. Oyu was the reason Raim could not simply stroll into Khareh's camp and kill him for what he had done: Oyu had swallowed the promise knot Raim made when he'd vowed to protect Khareh, and now Raim could not break that promise even if he tried.

And gods above, did he ever want to try.

Oyu landed on his arm and let out a loud screech in his ear. Raim laughed even as he shied away in surprise, and then ran a hand over Oyu's silky black feathers. The bird had also been instrumental in saving his life, fighting off a hawk that Khareh's Yun army had sent to attack him. The Yun were renowned for their skill with animals, and their hawks could be their deadliest weapons.

Training Oyu was another task that had helped Raim focus his mind over the past month. "Time to find some rabbits, right, Oyu?" he asked. Oyu lifted off his arm, and Raim had to duck to avoid being hit by the bird's enormous wings.

Later that evening, they all sat around a crackling fire, searing a brace of rabbits over the open flame. Raim tucked into a skewer, the meat tender and pink. It was the most restorative meal they had had in months. The cheren was situated in the most barren part of the steppes, where there was little game to hunt. Why did the old people need proper meat, when they were only sent to a cheren to die? Sometimes Darhan logic was twisted.

"Raim—a little help?"

Raim turned around, a dribble of meat juice running down his chin. He saw Loni approaching, struggling to support Vlad. Raim leaped up, dropping his food in the grass, and moved to take the weight off his grandfather's shoulders. Together they made their way into the circle, and Raim helped Vlad settle onto the ground near the fire. The man shivered, and another elder threw a second cloak around him.

Vlad began attacking the meat Raim gave him with a fury that belied his apparent frailty.

"Enough strength to eat is enough strength to talk, don't you think?" Draikh said.

Vlad threw the haunt a scowl—being an oathbreaker, he could see and hear Draikh—but then he swallowed his mouthful and rearranged his expression into something more placid. "I thought you were dead," he said to Raim. "It's good to see you. Can I ask ... how did you find me?"

Raim hesitated. "We have a seer among us."

Vlad couldn't hide the look of surprise on his face. "Truly? A real seer?"

Raim nodded. "Yes. But first, Vlad, I have something

even more important to tell you." He gripped the old man's shoulder. "Dharma is alive."

"What? But I thought Khareh ... " Vlad attempted to scramble to his feet, but his legs gave way from under him. "I have to see her. Where is she?"

"We will take you to her, don't worry. And no, Khareh didn't kill her. But he did break his promise to me."

"So he did still hurt her." Vlad's shoulders slumped.

"He did. And he will pay for that. But—and these are Dharma's words—he also helped her to see. She is the seer. And Vlad, you would be so proud. She is amazing."

"*My daughter* is the seer?"

"Dharma is the seer," said Loni gruffly.

"I want to go to her now," said Vlad. "What are we waiting here for? Where is she?"

"At the cheren. We will return there in the morning," said Raim. "And in the meantime, I will tell you anything else you want to know about her."

"A cheren? What, a place for withered old men and women, good for nothing?" Vlad's nose wrinkled in disgust. "What is she doing there? A true seer should be celebrated! She should have her own tribe of followers!"

"She is where she is safe," Loni snapped. "What would you know about keeping her safe, when you abandoned her in the first place?"

"Don't talk to me like that, old man."

"Oathbreaker!"

"Stop this!" said Raim, throwing his arms between them. "Vlad, we will take you to her. Soon. But now, you must tell us what happened to you. And you need to tell me what you know about Wadi."

Vlad glared at Loni and chewed another morsel before speaking. He threw a bone onto the fire. "I was mostly kept in the Camp of Shadows."

"Khareh's spirit-army," Raim said, his eyes wide.

"Not just spirits—but the oathbreakers live in the camp too, poor wretches," Vlad said. His hands shook, and his chewing became both more frantic and sloppier. "He's a clever khan, I'll give him that much. He uses the spirits and keeps the oathbreakers weak and desperate inside the camp. He thought he could use me too—Garus informed him that I was both a former member of the Baril and a high-ranking Shan, so I knew much about sagery." The Shan were the governors of Lazar and the guardians of all knowledge relating to sages. "But I would never give that monster anything. Not after what he did to my daughter." Vlad took a shuddering breath and clutched his side. Then, slowly, he lifted the edge of his tunic, all the way up to his armpit. Dozens of cuts littered his side, some of the scars puckered and gnarled.

Raim had heard of this form of torture, but never seen it in the flesh. Every hour, a different part of the body was sliced with a sharp knife, causing an endless stream of agony. Eventually, when all the skin was scarred or marked, they would start removing limbs. Luckily—if any luck could be found—Vlad's torture hadn't reached that point yet. Raim's stomach turned.

"The Khan gave me to Garus to see what information he could extract from me." Vlad dropped his tunic. "After

Garus failed to learn anything, Khareh gave up and sent me to the prison. I think he disliked having so much blood on the floor of his yurt."

Raim winced. "But I thought Garus was the most advanced sage the Shan had ever known—what could you know that he didn't already?"

Vlad shut his eyes and took a deep, shuddering breath.

Loni looked up at Raim, concern deep in his eyes. "Don't make him relive it. Not yet. Ask him again when he is stronger."

Raim couldn't help himself. "Tell us about Garus later. But what about Wadi? Is she still with Khareh?"

Vlad managed to nod, and Raim's heart beat loudly in his ears. "Did you see her? Is she safe?"

Vlad only let out a groan in response, and Raim wanted to shake him in frustration. Loni put a gentle but firm hand on his knee. "We can learn more when we get back to the cheren. He needs an experienced healer—and so do our wounded men. We're like sheep on a plain here, waiting for the wolves to find us. Wait until tomorrow."

"Grandfather, I cannot wait." Raim bit his lip. A plan had been forming in his mind for some time now, but he hadn't had the opportunity to voice it. Now was the time. He looked out at the steppes, in the direction that the last of Khareh's guards had ridden away. "I don't think I will come back to the cheren with you. I can't have traveled all this way without even attempting to rescue Wadi." He had felt so sure that this was going to be the moment he would get her back. Not having accomplished that felt so wrong.

"What if he's torturing her too? What if I'm leaving her to this same fate?" He gestured at Vlad. "I have to find her."

"I don't think that's a good idea," said Vlad, one eye cracking open.

"And why is that?" snapped Raim.

"She's being held by Khareh himself. Surrounded by every haunt and human guard you could imagine."

"But I can't just return without even trying. Not when I'm already halfway there." A hint of desperation crept in at the edge of Raim's voice.

"No, that's right. You cannot go back to the cheren—you cannot waste any more time there," Vlad said.

"Then what?"

"Raim, you are the only one close enough to achieving the kind of sage power Khareh has mastered. Working with Draikh, you are the one who could be powerful enough to overthrow him. But you will never be able to do that with your scar. No one will follow an oathbreaker."

Raim's fists tightened into a ball, but he knew it was true.

"Garus was right about something," Vlad continued. "I—and Zu—both know things about sagery that no other Shan knows. And we know something of the significance of that scar around your wrist that we never shared with you."

Raim looked up sharply.

"Have you heard of a group called the Council?"

Raim shook his head, and instinctively moved his opposite hand over his wrist to cover his mark of shame. It was a habit born of instinct, and one he couldn't shake.

"Zu was a high-ranking Council member based in our

Baril sect in the Amarapura mountains—although they have outposts throughout Darhan. She was bound to not share all its secrets with me, but I know where you can find others who belong to it, who can grant you answers: the Baril. Go to the Amarapura mountains." He gestured to the shadows of the mountain range in the far distance. "You have a brother there, no? Go to him, and ask him about the Council. He might be able to help you. The Council can put you on your true path, and you will be able to rid yourself of that scar—and rescue Wadi."

Raim gazed over at the Amarapura mountains. *Is the answer really there? Could I finally find a way to rid myself of this scar, once and for all?*

"Worth a try," said Draikh, in his mind.

But Wadi has to come first. I can't leave her to Khareh's torture.

"Agreed."

"I'm sorry, Vlad, Loni," Raim said aloud. "I'm going to Khareh's camp to free Wadi. That comes before everything—even my scar. Even if it means fighting against Khareh, and his entire spirit-army and the Yun. Draikh and I can do it. I will not leave her to suffer whatever he has planned for her."

Vlad stared at Raim for a long time, sending an uncomfortable shiver down his spine. Then the man attempted to stand, waving off the helping hand that Loni offered him. He placed one hand on a shaking knee to support his weight, then with a groan pushed himself to his full height.

Raim had forgotten what an imposing figure Vlad struck

when he wanted to. But he resisted taking a step back, standing as tall as Vlad, the grass of the steppes waving all around them.

"Go to the Baril," Vlad repeated. "Discover the origins of your scar. Rid yourself of that burden. Become whole again, in the eyes of the people. Then you can carry out your mission for revenge."

"No. I want to rescue Wadi."

Vlad looked Raim dead in the eye. "But what makes you so sure that Wadi wants to be rescued?"

4

WADI

Wadi sat at the hard wooden desk in the yurt and stretched the cramp from her fingers. The circulation had returned to her hands since they had last been bound, but it had been a long time since she'd written for such an extended period of time. In the desert, there wasn't much need for correspondence.

She was grateful that her father had taken the time to teach her to read and write as a child; he was one of the few Darhanians who knew how. She knew that meant he must have been Baril at some point in his life, but not once she was born.

Throughout all that time learning, she had never envisaged using her skills to become a scribe to a ruthless khan.

It saved her from being just a prisoner, at least.

A tug at her ankle as she attempted to cross her legs reminded her of that fact. A thick, coarse rope tied her ankle to a stake firmly embedded in the ground at the center of the yurt. She had free rein within a predetermined perimeter. Long enough to get to the desk. Long enough to reach the jug of water that had been left for her. Long enough to reach the pile of cushions she slept on. Not long enough to reach the candles, which provided her a little light after the sun went down. Not long enough to reach the doorway.

Sometimes she imagined picking up a cushion and throwing it at the candle, setting the place ablaze. But then either she would be beaten as punishment, or burned alive. Neither of those options was appealing.

Her task had been Khareh's idea, even though Altan— his vile adviser—had argued persistently against it. Wadi had quickly learned to avoid the scrutiny of the beak-nosed Altan, who had once advised Khareh's uncle, before turning traitor to him and throwing his support behind Khareh. The only person in the entire camp worse than Altan was Garus—the sniveling, weak sage who had taught Khareh the secret of his craft: breaking vows. Where Altan was like a vulture, circling the carnage until it was safe to feed on the remnants, Garus was a rat, scurrying for Khareh's scraps on the ground. It was Garus who had convinced Khareh to break his oath to Raim.

For most of her first month in captivity, Wadi had heard a man's screams on the other side of the yurt's thick felt walls. More than once, it had been enough to make her heave the contents of her stomach onto the carpets, imagining what the man must be going through, although she never gave Khareh the pleasure of seeing her discomfort. One night, she had heard the man scream a name—"Zu"—and realized it was Vlad being tortured. From the cackle that followed, she recognized his torturer: Garus.

She had tried to break through the walls that separated them, then. She had kicked at the frame of the yurt, trying to break off a splinter of wood and hack through the felt. But Khareh's guards had been on her immediately, shortening her rope and securing it more tightly than usual.

Last night, there had been silence. No more screaming. Wadi almost cried tears of relief, but then her stomach filled with dread. The lack of noise could only mean one of two things: Vlad was dead, or he had been sent away. She would never be able to help him. And he would never be able to help her.

Her last connection to her former life was gone. Raim was her only hope. But she didn't know where Raim was, or if he was even in Darhan anymore. The last time she had seen him, he had been underneath falling rocks as a cave came crashing down around him.

Pain blossomed beneath her ribs, reminding her of Khareh's brutality and recklessness—the memory of Khareh plunging the knife into her chest almost as painful as the moment itself. The wound could have killed her, but he had reassured her later that he had always known his shadow could heal her before she lost too much blood. Khareh played with life like it was a toy he could discard at any moment.

It had been the second time she had been brought back from the brink of near-death by a spirit. Once by Raim's spirit-companion, Draikh, after she'd fallen from the tunnel exit of Lazar. And once by Khareh's haunt—who was the spirit of Raim.

She wasn't keen to try the trick a third time.

She reached instinctively to the pendant at her neck. One of her haziest memories of her time in captivity was just after she had been stabbed. Khareh had brought her to his yurt, where spirit-Raim had performed the healing. Khareh had tried to take the pendant from her then, but Garus had stopped him. Even through the cloud of pain, she heard Garus explaining the oath contained within the pass-stone: that any person who possessed the stone was sworn to return to Lazar. "Let the girl remain bound to that cursed place, like I am, your Eminence. You do not want that burden to bear."

Since then, Khareh had rarely let her out of his sight. He had her trapped. She couldn't just take off the pendant and leave it behind, and he knew it. Any attempt to abandon the pass-stone would make her an oathbreaker to the spirits within the stone. And that was something she could never allow. The taboo bothered her still. Even if the person who occupied her thoughts the most was an oathbreaker.

Raim. Had he made it back to Lazar? Or had the cave-in at the tunnel entrance wounded him? All she could remember was her fear as rocks came crashing down around her, her shock at seeing Raim hurtling through the sky off the tall cliff to be with her, her relief that he made it safely—and finally, the searing pain of Khareh's blade through her chest. After that ... she remembered nothing else but the yurt.

A flash of bright light interrupted her train of thought

as the curtain into the yurt lifted. Wadi shielded her eyes and dropped her quill at the same time.

She recoiled as she recognized the silhouette of the man who entered: Khareh.

He slumped down on some scattered cushions opposite her. His shadow followed him inside and took up his place at Khareh's right-hand side.

"Wadi, I can't tell you what a day I've had." Khareh reached up and massaged his temples before releasing a huge sigh. He then lifted his enormous jaguar-fang crown from his head and cast it aside as if it were nothing. The crown rolled on the floor, until one of the fangs snagged on the carpet. "Being a khan is really tiring."

"You mean being a tyrant is."

Khareh put a hand over his heart. "Wadi, you wound me."

She rolled her eyes.

"How are those letters going?"

"Fine."

Khareh's request had baffled her. He had asked her to copy out letters that were to be sent to all the warlords in Darhan—most of whom likely couldn't read. She might have risked putting in a line or two of warning, but Khareh had been clear about the consequences if she tried: she would be the one screaming in endless agony for a month.

Khareh's eyes darted to his shadow. "Seriously?" he said to it. "He's coming now?" He paused. "Well, stop him. I don't want to be disturbed."

It disconcerted Wadi so much to know that the haunt Khareh was speaking to was the spirit of Raim. Part of Raim was in that very room with them. But she didn't know if she had ever "met" that particular part—she couldn't imagine any side of the Raim she knew willingly helping Khareh achieve his plans.

Spirit-Raim hadn't managed to relay his message fast enough, as the curtain moved again and from behind it appeared Garus's pinched, wrinkled face. His head was wrapped in an elaborate turban, and his long robe was made from fine silk and embroidered with luxurious golden thread.

Obviously, Garus wasn't missing Lazar one bit. There was no hint of the shabbiness Lazarites took a strange sort of pride in. He grew fatter every day that Wadi saw him, a second chin gradually filling out under his long beard, and occasionally he had the glassy-eyed look and hiccupping wobble of a man who was indulging too much in fermented mare's milk, although today his gaze was clear.

"My Khan, your Great Eminence," he started, his head bowed.

"GET OUT!" yelled Khareh from his position on the cushions. "I told you I didn't want to be interrupted! Just give me a few minutes, you spawn of an oathbreaker."

Wadi flinched from his anger, and so did Garus, who scurried from the yurt like a rat chased by a feral cat. Watching him, Wadi raised an eyebrow despite herself. It was a small comfort that Khareh treated his closest advisers as badly as he did his prisoners.

"Sorry about that," Khareh said. "I'm just so tired of his bleating." He rubbed his fingers against his temples. Wadi had to admit, he did look tired. Worn, even. Served him right. "At least the days of traveling should be over soon."

Wadi sat up straighter at that, and Khareh noticed. He smiled. "I know—it's taking us for ever, isn't it?"

She let her curiosity get the better of her. "Where are we going?"

"We're nearing Yelak. There is a walled city there—Samar—have you heard of it?" Wadi shook her head, but Khareh continued anyway. "It's a dirty place, not much bigger than Kharein, but the tribes of Yelak are strong. They are ruled by Mermaden, the warlord of Samar." Khareh cracked his knuckles, the sound turning Wadi's stomach. "He refuses to pay me tribute, so I must pay him a visit. Moving an army this size is more of a challenge than I'd anticipated. But I suppose that's what happens when you call all your promised warlords and their tribes to your side."

"World domination is tough?" she said, injecting as much venom into her voice as possible.

"What would you have me do? If you're so smart in the ways of ruling, smarter than any of my advisers, smarter than me, tell me what I should do? I've spent my whole life training for this, learning how to rule and how to keep the peace, even if my wretched uncle was planning to strip me of my right to the Khanate." Khareh stopped and narrowed his eyes at her. "So, tell me—you, who are just an ignorant desert savage—you think you know more than me?"

"I know that you'll never inspire true loyalty if you just go around killing everyone!"

"Oh really? My uncle's method of diplomacy worked

really well, didn't it? Do you know how many times neighboring tribes attacked us during his reign? At least once a month, sometimes back-to-back, without a moment for our people to rest. Each time required soldiers and horses and resources that Darhan just doesn't have to beat them back. If we amassed as a single people, united under one knot, do you know how much stronger we would be?"

"Your uncle united more knots in a single rule than all of his predecessors put together."

"But not enough, and he was losing them." Khareh approached Wadi then, his cloak sweeping the floor. "And there's another threat. Have you heard of the Golden Khan?"

She held her ground, trying not to recoil from his presence. She didn't want to give him the pleasure of her fear. "The myth of the true leader of Darhan."

"The myth, yes. What does it say?"

Wadi swallowed hard. "It says that the Golden Khan stands as leader over all of Darhan, with a golden carpet laid at his feet."

"The golden carpet, that's right. The Sola desert. If a khan has the desert under his rule, he is the one true leader of not just Darhan, but of all the lands of this world—with Kharein at its center. But did you know that there's another myth—the myth of the Golden King?" He grimaced at the last word, as if it was foreign in his mouth.

Wadi shook her head.

"I wouldn't expect you to know of it. It's a legend from the South. The Golden King is the king who rules with a crown of gold on his head. You can guess what that is, right?"

She narrowed her eyes. "The desert."

"Exactly. And the legend goes that he will control all the land and people of the world too, but his center is in Aqben. Now, when I was just a prince, I thought that we were completely cut off from the South. But now, as Khan, I know that isn't true. There are still some—especially in the Baril—who maintain a line of communication there. News and messages pass barely once a year, if we're lucky, but my uncle couldn't have cared less about what was going on at the other side of the great desert. But I care a great deal. Because I know for a fact that the Southern King has grand ambitions, and he is strong. He has an army with thousands more men than mine, armed to the hilt, better disciplined, more experienced. He has an army designed to conquer. He believes himself to be the Golden King. But while I am Khan, I will never let him conquer Darhan and threaten my people."

Wadi laughed bitterly. "The Golden King, the Golden Khan … call yourselves what you will, but it's all just words. I might be an ignorant desert rat, but it means that I know one thing: *No one* controls the desert. To believe that it is possible to march *an army* across it is suicide. Other khans have attempted it, long before your time, and they failed."

"If it's possible that he has figured out a way, I cannot risk it. Do you understand my frustration now? The South has so much more knowledge than us, simply because they actually have a way to *share* knowledge. It's not just the elite who can read and write. They value their engineers and their men of letters. They have disgusting habits too—they not only treat the land like a slave, but they have *actual* slaves, who serve them. You might think I am evil, but I do not have slaves. Which is why I will gather all of Darhan under my knot, and then I will head to Lazar. I will crush the Southern King's army before it has a chance of reaching Darhan's borders." As he spoke, he leaned over and picked up his ludicrous crown, placing it back on his head.

A sick feeling returned to Wadi's stomach as she remembered how quick the Chauk had been to return to Darhan once they thought Khareh might be a ruler who would forgive them. And how he had treated them in return?

"What do you want with Lazar?" she asked. "You hate oathbreakers. You've said that yourself. I've seen how you hate them. And besides, you'd have to *get* to Lazar first. The Alashan will fight you, and they are the blood and soul of the desert."

Khareh rubbed his chin and stared at Wadi. "Maybe they will, maybe they won't. I have my own theories about the Alashan."

Wadi opened her mouth to protest, but Khareh continued. "Besides, you are forgetting about my spirit-army. I've learned that there is a use for oathbreakers after all. I have an army of shadows that requires no food, no water—what is the desert to them? This is what sets me apart, Wadi. This is what makes me the Golden Khan. I am a sage. The only true sage in Darhan!"

"But you're not the only true sage. There is Raim."

"Raimanan is weak and in hiding somewhere."

"But he's not dead. And you need him alive."

With a sigh, Khareh placed both his hands on the coarse

wooden top of Wadi's desk and leaned forward. "It would be easier if you would cooperate. I wish you would help me."

Wadi wished for a weapon, but all she had was her quill. Her quill and an inkpot.

She snatched the inkpot from the desk and threw it at Khareh. He ducked to the side, avoiding the pot, but ending up with a diagonal spray of black ink across his cheek and his bright green tunic. The pot landed with a thud on the carpeted floor, spilling the remainder of its contents into the knotted rug in a thick, black pool.

Wadi gripped the edges of the desk as Khareh's eyes met hers.

But surprisingly, his tone was calm. He wiped his cheek with the cuff of his tunic. "How long has it been since you have seen the sun?"

She couldn't answer. Fear paralyzed her.

"Come on. I'll cut your bonds. I have something to show you."

5

WADI

Outside, there was chaos. Khareh picked his way through the camp, the mishmash of tents and cooking fires, stopping every now and then to talk with one of his soldiers. Wadi couldn't help but notice how they cowered in fear as he approached. They bowed their heads low, anxious to avoid any breach in etiquette. Khareh spoke to them as if he hardly noticed their discomfort.

Now that Khareh was outside, Garus dared to approach him again. Wadi's stomach turned as he came near. The years of degradation in Lazar seemed to cling to him as he crept up to Khareh's side like a spider, his eyes constantly shifting from side to side. This was a man desperate for power. And when he couldn't have power for himself, he latched on to those that had it.

"Garus, you may explain yourself now," said the prince-turned-khan. "What was so important that you felt the need to interrupt me?"

The old man bowed several times, and Khareh crossed his arms, tapping his fingers against the rich fabric of his tunic.

"Khareh, Your exultant Highness," simpered Garus, "I fear I have bad news—two-fold."

"Ach, not near the soldiers." Khareh clasped Garus on the shoulder and walked him to where Wadi was lingering, by the entrance of the yurt she had been held captive in. "What is it?"

"With all respect, my Khan, we have been moving too quickly. The majority of the caravan has fallen behind. They are a day's march away."

Khareh threw his hands up in frustration. "What is taking them so long? Do they not know the meaning of 'keep up'? Not exactly a difficult command."

"Maybe they're just tired," interjected Wadi.

Khareh looked at her sidelong, and Garus gripped his chest as if he was about to have a heart attack, but Khareh didn't react to Wadi's antagonism. "You said there were two pieces of bad news. What's the second?"

Garus tugged at his beard. "Well, my Khan, I'm afraid Mermaden has heard of your approach. He's decided, as you predicted, not to sit behind the safety of his walls in Samar. Our scouts say he is sending an advance party to meet you. An advance party that is three times the size of our front battalion."

"Only three times? He underestimates me," Khareh joked,

but he rubbed his chin in thought. "I don't want to face him here. I want the city."

Wadi studied Khareh's face. He was looking at Garus, but not—he seemed to be staring beyond the man, through him. Wadi felt a frisson of excitement. Maybe, in the chaos of warfare, she would be able to escape—make a run for it.

She was confident in her ability to survive in Yelak. The land was green, rich, and lush, which meant plenty of water—and water meant survival. The desert had prepared her for anything.

She almost jumped as Khareh's expression changed, and for a dreaded moment, she thought he could read her mind. But as a grin spread over his face, it became very clear that he'd had an idea. Khareh was never so pleased as when he impressed himself with his own genius.

"Round up all my generals. Inform them that tonight, every man in the camp will light a fire—every man, without exception. Use up all the firewood if we have to—no matter, we will have a city to raid tomorrow night. Spread the fires out. Let's make Mermaden's men think that while his scouts say we are a thousand, our camp seems enough for ten thousand. He won't come near. Mark my words."

"Oh, Great One, no one can doubt your genius." Garus bowed several times, so vigorously Wadi imagined he might come apart at the waist.

"Quit your pandering, Garus, and just spread the word. Then tomorrow, I want three generals sent to ask Mermaden to back down and surrender. Maybe we can avoid this siege after all." Khareh turned to Wadi. "Do not let it be said that I don't offer a fair chance first, before I crush my opponents."

Wadi rolled her eyes.

Garus coughed. "Oh, Your Eminence, that reminds me. We have the, uh, new tribe to deal with. They have agreed to your terms."

Khareh's eyes lit up. "Ah, excellent!" He gestured for Wadi to come closer, but she remained rooted to the spot. "I won't have to take you to see my shadow-army after all—I can take it one step further!"

Dread lined Wadi's stomach. "What do you mean?"

"You'll see," he said, his eyes widening. He snapped his fingers at Garus. "Let's get moving then. I want their oaths before nightfall."

Khareh spun on his heels and followed his rodent-like adviser. Wadi prayed that if she stood still, she would just be forgotten. She had no desire to witness whatever Khareh was about to do.

She had no such luck. Two of his burly guards came and stood either side of her, penning her between them, forcing her to move—or be moved.

She threw off the hand of one of the guards who dared to touch her, and willed her legs into action. *The more you know, the more weaknesses you can find,* she reminded herself. *He will regret the trust he has placed in you.*

As she walked further from her yurt prison, Wadi grasped the sheer size of the camp. Groups of soldiers loitered in every corner, huddled around fires, mending their arrows or tending to their mounts. She walked quickly through them, self-conscious as their eyes slid over her strange clothing—she was still wearing the looser, more billowing clothes of the desert, rather than the leather-and-coarse-silk tunics of Darhan. They did not look at her with lust, but rather with wariness and unease.

Nevertheless, she was a child of Sola, the harshest master in the known world. She was not going to be afraid of a few lowly soldiers.

She turned her attention to the forest beyond the camp, and what she saw there took her breath away. She couldn't remember seeing such a place in her lifetime. Impossibly tall trees rose high in the sky, their trunks thin but straight as an arrow shaft. Their leaves, too, reminded Wadi of the plumes of an arrow, bristly rather than flat. The ground underfoot was trampled, but beneath the trees she could see it was covered with a rich carpet of moss and wild flowers.

Of course, the vast forest played its part for the army. The army used the trunks to tie up hammocks, for it was plenty warm enough to sleep outside rather than cooped up in a stuffy tent. In that way, Wadi was lucky. The yurt she slept in was airy, erected in a large clearing. Khareh could have treated her a lot worse.

An ear-splitting crack filled the air and Wadi almost dropped to her knees in shock.

Khareh looked back over his shoulder. "They're felling some of the trees deeper in the forest."

As he spoke, Wadi heard the anxious shouts of men, and saw the treetops shake as one of their number came down.

"They're for my siege engines," Khareh continued. "Battering rams, catapults, that sort of thing. This forest is perfect for some of my new inventions. Not that I'll need them if things go to plan." He pouted, like a child denied his toys. "No matter. With the knowledge I'll gain from Samar, I'll be able to perfect all my weaponry."

Wadi took a deep breath. Even though she knew Khareh would never abandon traditional weapons of warfare for his new shadow-army, seeing it coming to life in the forest around her was frightening. When Khareh's attention was distracted, she turned around to one of her guards. "Why do you follow him? Why do you—" But before the words could even leave her mouth, the soldier shook his head furiously and moved his hand to his sword hilt.

At first, she was confused. But then it became obvious. Although she was a prisoner, she was also being kept in Khareh's inner circle; they thought she might be looking for a way to turn Khareh against them. She was a foreigner too—they could tell that by her accent, her mode of dress and the very color of her skin. No, these soldiers would not talk to her. She was alone.

Her mouth set in a firm line, Wadi resigned herself to silence.

RAIM

What if Wadi doesn't want to be rescued?

Vlad's words echoed in his thoughts, making him shudder.

"You don't mean that," Raim had replied. Of course Wadi would want to be rescued. She wouldn't want to spend any more time than was necessary with Khareh.

"I heard them talking about her, when they thought I'd passed out from the pain. They're not torturing her. They want her pass-stone."

"They might have just been saying that to confuse you." Raim folded his arms across his chest.

Vlad shook his head. "No. She can read and write too, can't she? Khareh was using her to write orders to other warlords, and she obeyed. She's not in any danger. They need her."

"*I* need her," said Raim. "Just because they're not torturing her doesn't mean she should be kept there against her will."

Vlad's hawk-like stare softened for a moment. He turned to look at Loni, then at the other men of the cheren who were around. A gentle steppes wind swept through the wiry strands of hair on his head; he closed his eyes and let the breeze caress his tired features. He looked at peace.

"You were right to wait here," he finally said. "This place is perfect for an ambush. You know the steppes well, and the wind would have brought with it the smells and noise of the wagon long before the guards could spot you in that long grass. They didn't stand a chance." He opened his eyes slowly and settled his gaze on Raim. "But to ambush Khareh's camp, you'll have to sneak past the legions of warriors pledged to him. Even if you succeed there, you'll need to get past his personal guard, made up of the very same elite Yun soldiers you know all too well. And if you defeat them, Khareh will call up his shadow-army, and they will be led by *your own spirit*. And then there is the Absolute vow you made, which prevents you from hurting Khareh— but he would have no such problem killing you. No, Raim. There is no way for you to do this."

Raim hung his head. "I can't give up," he said, although the words came out as barely a whisper.

Vlad stepped forward and put a hand on Raim's shoulder. "You're not giving up. You have to give yourself a chance, for Wadi's sake. You'll find a way to get her back. But not with this." He reached down and grabbed Raim's wrist, then shook it in his face, so all he could see was the hideous scar.

"He's right," said Draikh. "I hate to say it, but he is. When we're stronger, we'll get her back."

"Before anything else."

"Before anything else," Draikh repeated.

And so, even though it went against every fiber in his being, Raim agreed.

That had been three days ago, and then Vlad, Loni, and the rest of the ambush crew had returned to the cheren. Raim was left alone, with just Draikh and Oyu, as his path took him in a different direction: north, toward the Amarapura mountains.

Raim shivered in his thin shirt, the night air having taken on an increased chill as he drew closer to his destination. He took in a sharp breath, the cold air filling his chest giving a sharp jolt to his senses.

He needed it. His mind felt like it was wrapped in sheep's wool. Vlad had outlined the route in the dirt, a winding trek through the mountains that would take him further north than he had ever been. Vlad had made it clear that if he—a branded oathbreaker—stood any chance of being allowed to speak to a Baril, he had to find the one person there who might listen to him: his brother, Tarik.

Raim dropped the pack he'd been carrying to the ground and rooted around in the top, pulling out a sheep-skin cloak to ward off the chill. He hadn't prepared for this journey, and though he'd borrowed the warmest clothes the others could spare, he worried it wouldn't be enough.

From afar, he could see smoke rising from near the base of the mountains. With a pang, he realized he was looking at the very village his tribe had camped in before his brother's wedding. He felt like he'd traveled all the way to Lazar and back, only to come full circle.

He had to avoid the village, one of the few permanent settlements on the steppes. If he was spotted and his scar revealed to the villagers, they would drive him away. Or worse, they would kill him on the spot. He adjusted the angle of his path away from the village, but not so far that he lost sight of it completely. At least if he could see the dwellings, then the Baril couldn't be too far away.

The cloak was enough for now, and Raim relaxed into the warmth. He slung the pack back over his shoulder and started walking once again.

"Why do they live in the mountains? Surely there are better places," said Draikh. "It's already cold enough on the steppes in winter."

Raim rolled his eyes. "You don't feel the cold."

"True, but I remember it." The spirit shivered for effect, rubbing his hands on his shoulders.

"The remoteness of our location is our pride." Raim imitated Vlad's solemn voice and expression, lowering his voice while stretching his neck up high and looking down his nose.

"Like the Chauk," said Draikh. "Cut from the same skin, those two clans."

Raim laughed, dropping the act. "Whatever you do, don't say that to their faces."

46

"Might do them some good to hear it." Draikh swooped down low so he was level with Raim. When they walked like this, Raim found it difficult not to think it was Khareh next to him. Just the two of them out exploring, like old times. Despite himself, he missed his friend. *That friend is gone,* he reminded himself, and he clenched his fists at his side.

"How do you think you will find your brother?" Draikh said, glancing sidelong at him. Draikh would know what he was thinking.

"I'm not sure." Raim shrugged. "Vlad said he might not be in the main temple, as he's probably still a novice."

"How do you think he will take seeing you again?"

Raim bit his lip and continued to plod, one foot in front of the other, staring down at the laces of his boots.

"Come on," said Draikh. "You can't avoid it for ever. You'll be seeing him soon enough."

Raim shrugged, but his heart beat wildly. When he'd last seen Tarik's back retreating into the cave, he had thought it would be the last time they would ever meet. Under any other circumstances, it would have been. Tarik had shed his previous life as Loni's grandson, as brother to Raim and Dharma, and adopted a new clan: the Baril. That was the Darhanian way, just as Raim would never have expected to see Dharma and Loni again once he had joined his chosen clan. The Yun.

The Baril, and the Yun. One, masters of words, the other, masters of swords. Tarik and Raim had never been close, certainly not as close as Raim and Dharma, but they had one thing in common, and that was the desire to join the most elite clan of their chosen fields. And while Tarik had achieved his goal, Raim had failed at the first hurdle.

Tarik might enjoy that. Raim had always been the stronger one, the one who naturally excelled at games: racing horses across the steppes, shooting arrows and spears through narrow targets, wrestling. Tarik was the one often left eating dirt, having fallen from his horse or been shoved to the ground.

"He never liked asking for help," Raim remembered. "He thought it was beneath his intellect."

"Then maybe he won't be surprised you're asking him for help," Draikh said.

"What do you mean?"

"Because your intellect is nothing to be proud of."

Raim swatted the air in front of Draikh, sending him wheeling away in a fit of laughter. It was only then that he looked back up at the mountain range and stopped in his tracks. For so long, it had loomed like a shadow on the horizon. Now it was right in front of him, so immense his mind could barely take it in. He didn't remember feeling so overwhelmed when he'd been here last—but those were different circumstances. This time, he was going to conquer the mountains, not just sit at their base.

He took a few deep breaths, then carried on walking.

A violent thud sounded from nearby. Raim spun on his heel and immediately dropped into a crouch, using the long grass as shelter. White plumes of an arrow shaft protruded from the ground a few feet from where he had been standing.

He looked in the direction of the shooter.

And there, quivering with fear, his hand releasing the bow and letting it fall to the ground, was Tarik. His brother.

7

WᴀDI

The atmosphere changed as they drew close to the limits of the army camp. Gone were the legions of hardened
men, the trained warriors tending to their weapons or
their armor. Instead, they were moving through tents that
housed the newest tribes to join Khareh's campaign. Unrest
was evident in the wary glances shot at Khareh's entourage.
Clearly not all of the tribes were comfortable with their new
ruler. But where the army went, they followed.

Still, Wadi's attention was drawn to something far
stranger. There was a gulf, a stretch of emptiness two yurts
wide, separating these tribes and another group of tents.
Everywhere else, tribes mixed and intertwined, many tribu-
taries merging into Khareh's great river of war.

But beyond this particular tributary, there was an island.

She looked over at the yurts on the other side of the divide, and felt unease settle deep into her bones. The army camp was hardly the epitome of neatness and cleanliness, but the yurts over there displayed a shabbiness that Wadi found eerily familiar.

It reminded her of Lazar.

Most ordinary Darhanians took great care in their homes, but these yurts were badly patched together and poorly maintained. One even had a rip in it big enough to let in a significant amount of water when it rained. The bands of cloth that held the yurts together were frayed and splitting. It was as if the inhabitants took a strange kind of pride in the degradation of their homes.

In Lazar, they purposefully chipped away at any object of beauty—their carvings, statues, their homes—because they did not feel worthy of creating anything of value. The hatred against their own kind was ingrained too deep.

She suddenly realized where they were. This was a moving city of Lazar, the tent city of oathbreakers: the Camp of Shadows.

Wadi pulled up just short of walking into Khareh's back. She shuddered at how close she'd come to touching him. They had stopped in a small clearing, in between the mysterious camp and the main army.

"Bring forth the captives!" bellowed Garus.

A group of four men and two women, their wrists tied by a long piece of rope, shuffled forward. Wadi gasped. Hovering around each one of their hunched figures was a dark, swirling shadow. She could feel the wave of revulsion flow over her as they approached. Oathbreakers.

Their heads hung low, their eyes cast down to the ground. Khareh drew himself up to his fullest height, observing the prisoners.

"Name yourselves to the Khan," said Garus.

None dared to speak until Garus tugged on the rope, sending them tumbling forward. The oldest man found his tongue and said, "We are oathbreakers of Yelak, Your Highness."

"You are now the captives of Khareh-Khan, His Great Eminence, High Sage and Lord of Darhan," said Garus.

Wadi bit down on her tongue to stop from scoffing. Khareh was no better than an oathbreaker himself.

"Two nights ago, you were found deserting your tribes in battle, breaking the solemn oaths you had pledged to your clans," Garus continued. "You are the lowest of the low, and your punishment would be exile to the Sola desert, never to return to your homes again." The oathbreakers winced at his every word. "But our khan, in his great wisdom, has offered you a choice: exile, or join his spirit-army and remain in Darhan."

"We want to join the army," said the oathbreaker, his voice struggling to remain steady.

Wadi frowned. She couldn't believe that Khareh was offering the oathbreakers a chance to avoid their exile. She narrowed her eyes, surveying the scene, looking for something she was missing.

"You understand what the Khan has asked you to do?" probed Garus.

"I think so," said the man.

Khareh stepped forward from behind Garus. His normal smug expression was gone, replaced by something altogether more serious. His mouth was set in a firm line, and creases appeared on his forehead. In his hand, there was a length of golden thread. "Do you have your promise string?" he asked the oathbreaker, who was now visibly shaking.

Wadi knew what it was like to be approached by that enormous, jaguar-fanged crown—and the boy wearing it. She would be shaking too.

Khareh took the man's promise string and tied it into a loose knot. He gave one end to the man. Wadi noticed that Khareh's shadow-companion—spirit-Raim—hovered close by, a swirling gray cloud. The man's eyes darted between Khareh and the shadow, and Wadi knew that he, as an oathbreaker, would be looking at Raim's face. He would see this proof that Khareh was a powerful sage, that he was able to control his shadow. Wadi also knew that the man's own haunt would be screaming abuse in his ear. It was why all oathbreakers fled into exile, driven away not just by their shame, but also by the constant berating from the shadow. They would only have the chance to be released from the torment once they reached Lazar.

She'd heard stories of oathbreakers who didn't head straight for Lazar. Despite the torment of their haunts, they tried to sneak back to their tribes to beg forgiveness of the person whose oath they broke—or worse, tried to kill the oathmaker to free themselves of the burden. But with the presence of the haunt and the scar, they were easy to spot in Darhan. And if they were caught heading anywhere other than the desert, they were often killed on sight—stoned to death by those too terrified to do anything else.

Oathbreaking was the ultimate Darhanian taboo. But now here was Khareh, changing the rules again. Wadi's stomach felt like it was full of lead. She could see where this was leading, and she didn't like it at all.

"I promise you, oathbreaker of Yelak, that you will be able to return home after my war is won. I promise this as your khan."

"I accept your vow," said the man, and pulled the string tight. But he did not seem pleased by the vow he had just made. His shoulders remained slumped, his chin down by his chest.

Khareh went down the line, making the same vow to each one of the oathbreakers, until he held six knotted promise strings in his hand. Then he spun around and signaled to his guards. "Take them away," he declared. "They will all be prisoners in the Camp of Shadows until their deaths."

"No!" cried one of the oathbreakers.

Wadi couldn't tear her eyes away from Khareh. Or, more specifically, away from Khareh's hands, which were engulfed in fire from the promises he'd just broken. The flames danced in his eyes, reflecting orange on his face. But he didn't cry out. He didn't wince in pain. He just stared at them, and Wadi couldn't help but think he was mad.

Then, just as quickly as they appeared, the flames flew toward Khareh's torso and went out. Dark holes were singed in his tunic. Garus threw a cloak over his shoulders and

Khareh pulled it tight across his chest. Now Khareh winced in pain, closing his eyes tightly and clenching his fists around the fabric.

Wadi blinked, and Khareh was engulfed in shadows. Six of them, she realized. Six shadows, for the six oaths Khareh had just broken.

"Make the haunts obey me!" commanded Khareh, his eyes still closed.

Khareh's Yun guard drew their swords, pointing them at the six oathbreakers. But they didn't have to use them. All six dropped to their knees and began to whisper prayers— or, more likely, pleas—into the ground. The shadows swirling around Khareh speeded up, faster and faster. Wadi bit her lip. She didn't think this was going as Khareh planned.

Then Khareh began to rise. At first, it looked as if he was pushing up from the ground with his toes. But as the distance between his feet and the ground grew from the width of a finger, to a palm, to an arm's length—she knew he had exactly what he wanted. Absolute power. The haunts of the promises he had just broken were now his to command. Part of his spirit-army. The oathbreakers themselves looked defeated.

When his feet touched the ground again, his eyes flew open, and a huge smile was on his face. He snapped his fingers. "What are you waiting for? I told you lead them to the Camp of Shadows," he said to one of the guards. The oathbreakers dutifully followed, still tormented by their own haunts.

They wouldn't return home, but they wouldn't be exiled to Lazar either. *Was that any better?* Wadi wasn't sure.

Khareh turned to her. "And now you see how I formed

my shadow-army. Imagine this"—he gestured to the six shadows that now obeyed his every command—"but now imagine thousands of them."

Wadi could. Her stomach tightened, and she thought she might be sick.

"I almost pity oathbreakers. They think the burden of their broken promise will be lessened if they can at least stay in their homeland. They think I might somehow have the power to free them from their haunts. They cannot see that they are a means to an end. That it would be better for them if they accepted what they deserved. If they went into exile."

"You are offering them hope, and then you snatch it away for your own gain. You are despicable."

His jaw tightened at Wadi's words, the skin pulling tight across his sharp cheekbones. "I am doing what is necessary to win. I am using every resource at hand. Including the filthy oathbreakers."

"You are an oathbreaker too," Wadi spat back. "You are the worst of them all."

His eyes darkened and he raised his hand. Wadi winced instinctively. But Khareh only adjusted his crown and let out a sharp breath. "I know," he said, not loud enough for anyone else to hear. Then he marched off, back toward the center of the army camp.

Wadi was marched back after him by the guards. Once they reached the royal yurt again and she was installed inside, Khareh and the human guards left, but his shadow lingered.

He drifted to Wadi. Even though she could only see a shadow, she knew it was Raim's spirit. A part of Raim that she had never really known. "Please," she said to the shadow. "Please stay away from me."

The shadow hesitated. But it did as it was told and didn't come any closer. It lingered for an instant, as if studying her, then in a swirl, a rush, it swept through the yurt wall—surely to find Khareh again.

Wadi let out a breath. And with it came the first of many tears.

RAIM

Tarik was running. Raim took off after him like a shot, knowing that he could absorb the shock of seeing his brother *after* he caught up with him. *Draikh, can you help?* Raim asked in his mind. Tarik still wasn't the quickest runner, but on this unfamiliar ground, he had the advantage over Raim.

"Tarik, wait!" he shouted out. His brother's head bobbed almost out of sight. Then Raim caught sight of him again, heading upwards, toward the hidden heights of the mountain.

Draikh, however, had no hindrances. He didn't have to worry about the rocks underfoot or keeping a sense of direction on unknown ground. He simply flew up to Tarik and held his hand out. Tarik ran chest-first into Draikh's outstretched palm. He let out an anguished cry and beat at the air with his hands, but Draikh had disconnected again, so his fists flailed at nothing.

Raim used those few seconds to scramble up to the same level as Tarik. Still his brother tried to run from him, but now Raim was able to pick up his pace. He reached out and grabbed his brother by the edge of his tunic. Tarik pulled away, shaking and twisting his body as hard as he could, but Raim didn't let go, and they both tumbled to the ground. Still, Tarik struggled.

"Tarik! It's me!"

"Raim?" Tarik stopped struggling. It was as if his eyes had opened and he was seeing Raim for the first time. "But what are you doing here? Last I heard, you had been exiled from Darhan to the desert!"

Raim studied his brother, still holding him tightly by his tunic. He wasn't certain he could trust him, not after seeing the way he'd run away. Finally, he let out a long sigh and let go. He was going to have to trust Tarik if he was going to get answers. And, in turn, he somehow had to find a way to get Tarik to trust him.

"I was in the desert, you're right. But not for the reasons you think. I'm not an oathbreaker," he said.

"Then what are you?"

"I'm … " Raim hesitated. He hadn't ever spoken the words out loud before. "I'm a sage."

Tarik stared. "What did you say?"

The words had barely come out a whisper. Raim cleared his throat and spoke more loudly. It was the truth, after all. "I'm a sage."

Raim had expected shock, or at least surprise, from Tarik, but all he could see in his brother's eyes was curiosity. Tarik looked from Raim to the shadow-form of Draikh. "That isn't possible," he said.

"It is," said Raim. "I control this shadow," he added, following Tarik's gaze as it continued to flicker between them.

"That's not strictly true," said Draikh, in Raim's mind.

I know, but our situation is too difficult to explain just now. Will you cooperate?

"For you, I suppose," the spirit replied.

"Can you prove it?" asked Tarik, his voice edged with excitement.

Raim nodded. He made a show of swirling his hands in front of him, and in response, Draikh flew in circles around him, so it looked to Tarik as if Raim were engulfed by shadow. Draikh picked up several shards of rock for effect, so it looked as if Raim were able to levitate the stones. Then Raim raised his hands to the sky and Draikh flew straight up in the air.

Sagery.

Or so it would have looked to Tarik.

Then, that curiosity turned to something else. Tarik sat up straighter and stared wide-eyed at Raim. "You've taken a big risk coming here. Are you alone?"

Raim nodded. He had no choice but to be completely honest with his brother. "I have questions, and I need your help."

Tarik shook his head, but there was a small smile on his face. "I'm not sure I will be able to help you. I'm just a novice. But if anyone has answers, then Qatir-bar, my master, will have them. I can take you to him."

"Thank you," said Raim. "It is good to see you, brother." He suppressed the urge to pull him into an embrace. Although they had never been close, it still filled Raim's heart with warmth to see him alive and looking well.

But the gulf between them remained wide.

Walking beside his brother, Raim looked at him more closely. Tarik's head was shaved, but he still didn't have the signature flattened forehead of the Baril, said to be formed by hours of intensive prayer. Tarik was the most pious person Raim had ever known, so it surprised him that he hadn't spent every second he'd been in the Baril with his head bowed to the floor.

Maybe he was too busy running chores to pray. Raim bit at the edge of his fingernail as they walked. Tarik looked the same as the brother he had known, but there was something different about him. In the Moloti tribe, Tarik had been the most intelligent one—the one who could read and write, the one who was destined to be a Baril master. Ordinary tribespeople both feared and were in awe of the Baril. The secretive monks spent their days devoted to exploring life's mysteries, while most tribespeople were too busy simply living to spend much time pondering.

Tarik's intelligence meant he had often segregated himself from their tribe, but it also gave him an edge—an authority. He used to walk with his head held high. But all signs of that quiet authority were gone now, replaced with a curved slump of his shoulders that suggested something else: servitude, maybe. He looked defeated. Something must have happened in the few months to effect the change, but Raim couldn't think what.

Raim had never been in awe of the Baril, but as they climbed, his awe increased at the place they'd chosen to live. On the horizon, he could see a line of mountains so huge their snow-covered caps were visible above the clouds. The air was sharp and crisp, every breath searing his lungs and sending shivers running down his spine.

There was a clatter of stones nearby, which attracted Raim's attention. He looked up the sheer cliff on their right-hand side and spotted a scrawny goat making its sure-footed way across the rock face. Beneath its chin, the goat had a soft beard, something considered very precious in Darhan—it could be spun into high-quality promise string. Such goats were supposed to be quite rare. Raim wondered if the people here hunted the goats for their hair. Even as he was thinking this, a bit further along the mountainside he caught sight of a young Baril woman edging her way toward the goat.

He imagined that would be a pretty good source of income for the Baril.

"Watch out," said Draikh, a moment too late to be useful. Tarik stopped, and Raim ran straight into his back.

Raim was expecting a temple to appear ahead of them, but as of yet, as far as his eye could see, there was nothing more than the same craggy boulders they had been crossing. Despite the Baril's pledge to lead simple lives, he could imagine that a lot of them needed a little bit more luxury than the inside of a cave.

"This part is a bit tricky," said Tarik. "You might need my help."

Raim almost laughed—the Tarik he had known would have never offered help to him. But then he saw what Tarik meant. At the base of the cliff face, a very steep set of steps had been cut into the rock, with iron handholds bolted in at some of the trickier junctions where the steps switched directions. Even as he marveled at the workmanship, he dreaded the prospect of the climb. But seeing his brother scale them as easily as if they were the big, wide steps up to the palace in Kharein filled him with confidence. Or, at least, if not confidence then the desire to prove that he could do anything his brother did.

Do you think they get avalanches here? Raim thought to Draikh. *Rockslides?* He craned his neck and looked up at the mountains around them. They were tall and silent; it did not look like they were in any danger of dumping a load of snow on the stairs.

Raim's thick boots didn't provide him with the right grip, and he wished for a second that he could take them off and go barefoot, where he could at least feel the surface with his toes. But as he pressed his cheek against the stone, the coldness of it almost froze his skin—his toes wouldn't have stood a chance.

His brother looked down at him. "How are you doing?"

"Fine!" said Raim, with more confidence than he felt. At a difficult switchback, Tarik waited for him, and guided him round it as he held on to an iron bar. "Thanks," Raim said.

"No problem. Just keep your head up in about ten steps time. You're not going to want to miss this."

Raim's feet felt like they were inches from slipping, and each step was narrower than the last—too well worn by the passing of hundreds of Baril to really be safe. But he kept his eyes on where Tarik had disappeared, over a ledge and to what he assumed would be the destination.

When he finally reached the last of the steps, he gripped the handhold and practically ran up the last few. And he wasn't disappointed. At first, he could only see cloud, but then the mist dissipated enough to show a flash of gold. The cloud continued to part like a curtain, unveiling the roof, then the terrace, then the walls, then the windows, then the steps leading up to the enormous temple.

Now this was more like what he expected of a great Baril dwelling.

The sight of the gold-painted temple surrounded by majestic mountains was something he thought he would never see in his lifetime. In fact, ordinary people just never came here. Only Baril.

Raim rubbed his palms against his tunic. He was glad there was no one else around. He could feel little beads of sweat accumulating around his hairline.

"Nervous much?" asked Draikh.

You have no idea.

"Come on," said Tarik. "I will take you to see Qatir-bar."

The temple doors burst open, and out came a stream of Baril monks—but different from any Raim had ever seen before. These men had muscles bigger than most Yun, with expressions that made Raim believe he was about to be pummeled into the ground. There was no escaping it either—behind them were only the sheer steps, and Raim didn't fancy going down them in a hurry.

One of the biggest monks stopped and pointed a finger at Raim. "There! There is the oathbreaker. Take him!"

"Raim, what do you want to do?" asked Draikh.

I don't know—we've come so close . . . I can't go back now.

Raim turned in desperation to Tarik, who held up his hands. "I'm sorry, Raim—I thought I could avoid this. I will speak to Qatir-bar and explain everything."

Raim's only choice was to trust his brother as the burly Baril monks grabbed him roughly by the arms and dragged him toward the temple.

9

WADI

The night passed without incident, which meant that Khareh's plan with the spread-out fires had worked. Early scouting reports said that Mermaden's men were holed up behind their city walls and would not attempt a nighttime raid. Khareh sent his generals to negotiate a settlement with Mermaden as the next step. As they waited for the emissaries to return, Wadi spent the night listening in as Khareh learned about the great fortress city of Samar. It would be the young khan's first proper test. He and his army had overrun numerous other villages and small towns in Yelak, but none of them had the sophistication of Samar's defenses.

Yet Khareh didn't seem to care much for Altan's lessons on siege engines and warcraft. He was far more concerned with two other things: the infrastructure of Samar's water supply—which Wadi was having trouble wrapping her head around—and something Garus had mentioned called the "Temple of the Undying Women," which sounded far more interesting to her. Although her eyelids felt heavy, she didn't want to sleep while Khareh and his advisers were talking strategy. Any snippets of information she could garner might one day prove extremely useful.

"And that's where I will find it?" asked Khareh, rubbing his eyes. None of them had slept a wink.

Garus nodded, his eyelids drooping.

"So that will bring our total to three out of seven."

"Yes, my Khan." Garus's words slurred into each other, and his chin slumped against his chest. He jumped with a start.

Khareh rolled his eyes. "Go back to your yurt, Garus. All of you, clear out and get some rest. Tomorrow will be a big day. Tomorrow, I conquer my last enemy in the North."

At his words, the yurt emptied of everyone except Khareh, his shadow, and Wadi.

"The palace in Samar has water that runs through the walls, can you believe that? We could use that technology in Kharein. I don't know why my uncle never insisted on Mermaden sharing his knowledge."

Wadi couldn't be sure if Khareh was talking to her or thinking out loud. When she hesitated in replying, he leveled his gaze straight at her.

Wadi swallowed but refused to back down under his scrutiny. "I met a few people from Yelak in the desert. From what I heard, Mermaden has never pledged allegiance to a Darhanian khan. He proclaims Samar a free city."

"You're right there. He won't even pledge to me, and you know well enough the rumors people spread about me," said Khareh. "He was one of the warlords my uncle never dared to put pressure on. Unfortunately for Mermaden, I do dare."

"Samar has held against many sieges. It's thwarted many armies, some bigger than yours. That's why Batar-Khan didn't try."

"I am not my uncle."

"That's for sure. You are far worse."

Khareh studied her for a few unnerving moments. "That's why I like our little chats, Wadi. You're never afraid to tell it to me straight."

She narrowed her eyes, but in a way, she didn't want to lose Khareh's misplaced sense of trust in her. She needed to learn. She changed the subject. "What is the Temple of the Undying Women?"

"Ah, now that is interesting. It's the real reason I'm going after Mermaden now. Otherwise I might wait ... "

He is afraid, Wadi realized with a shock. Mermaden was not some lowly warlord of a tribe of fifty people, a few felt yurts, and a herd of goats—he had ruled over a fortified city for more than thirty years. Khareh's loyalty was newly won through fear. Mermaden's rule was sealed by fear too, but it had also withstood the test of time. He had experience, and Khareh was little more than a boy. A boy with a spirit-army, but a boy nonetheless.

She only hoped that Mermaden didn't underestimate the boy-khan. Then maybe he would stand a chance.

"The Temple of the Undying Women is run by a weird

subsect of the Baril—maybe the only sect not under Qatir-bar's control," Khareh was saying. "They call themselves 'The Council.' Every generation, the Council selects a woman to become 'the Undying.' Of course, these women do die—often while they are still young, as if they are struck by some kind of mysterious illness—and when that happens, they just choose another to take her place. What links them is a special stone necklace that is passed down to each new Undying Woman. I used to beg my old tutor to tell me about them."

"You probably hoped the story was a key to immortality," said Wadi.

Khareh shrugged. "Probably. But it wasn't until I interrogated Garus that I understood what it truly could be. You see, I just couldn't understand how Garus had escaped Lazar without crossing the desert. And that was when he told me about the tunnels—and how they were sealed by seven pass-stones, only two of which were left in Lazar. Or one, I suppose, after he stole the other. The rest were lost out in the world..."

Wadi gripped her own pass-stone, and Khareh nodded. "Yes, exactly like yours. When I heard the story of the Undying Women again, something clicked. Maybe the necklace that the Undying Woman must wear is a pass-stone too? If I'm right, that will bring me one step closer to owning all the stones—and unlocking the underground path to Lazar for good."

Wadi's mind exploded with questions, but she was unable to ask them. There was a loud commotion outside the yurt, and a mud-streaked hand pulled open the curtain that barred the entrance. It was Lars, the Yun who Raim had beaten in a duel. But Wadi had learned that since Raim had been exiled as an oathbreaker, Lars had been given a place with the Yun.

"The general has returned, Your Excellence," said Lars. He looked pale, as if he had seen a ghost.

"One general? I sent three." Khareh stood up.

"Yes, my Khan." Lars pulled aside the curtain.

Wadi screamed. She couldn't help herself. Even Khareh staggered backward against the desk. The general stepped into the yurt, but around his neck were the heads of the other two emissaries, tied together by their long hair.

"Mermaden did this?"

"He said he would never accept a settlement with you, my Khan." The general trembled with every word.

"Lars, get those wretched things off the man's neck and get him some help, for Sola's sake. Are the troops ready?"

"Of course," said Lars.

"Then we will move as soon as possible." Khareh balled his hands into fists. "Mermaden will not get away with this." The yurt filled with movement, dozens of servants materializing seemingly from nowhere to dress and ready Khareh. Wadi remained in her corner, watching everything with careful eyes. She didn't know what would be asked of her now that they were preparing for battle. She wouldn't fight, although Khareh knew she was more than capable of it. He wouldn't be foolish enough to give her a weapon. She knew exactly where she would use it.

Khareh was going fully fledged into battle—his ridic-ulous crown on, his two Yun swords, their curved edges twisted outwards, at his side. The blades were hung that way just for show—Khareh could never use them practically in battle. If it wasn't so horrific, Wadi might even find it funny. Instead, it just demonstrated the extent of Khareh's tyranny and power—that he could be as ostentatious as he wished, and no one dared to challenge him.

Wadi's hand went to the pendant around her neck, and her fingers absentmindedly ran over the lines engraved into the stone. From what she had been able to glean, Khareh had not been so evil and terrifying when Raim knew him. Suddenly he had gone from Crown Prince—a spoiled brat, yes, but not a tyrant—to ultimate ruler, with no limits to his power and ambition. That was not a transformation that he could have undergone overnight. Or had Raim been right? Had Khareh lost the part of his soul that was reasonable to Draikh, and all that was left was the power-hungry, tyrannical ruler Khareh-Khan?

A voice calling her name snapped her from her thoughts.

"Wadi." She looked up, and Khareh was staring at her.

She immediately felt her shoulders tighten, her breath catch. She wished he didn't have that effect on her, but he was so unpredictable.

"Come with me," he said.

She hesitated. "I won't fight for you."

"I'm not asking you to," he said. "But you can't stay here. I need to put you under a different kind of protection. You will be kept close, but hopefully not involved in the action. At least, that's the plan. So there's only one place you can go."

"And where is that?"

In his infuriating way, Khareh didn't answer immediately. Instead, he waited as his servants finished lacing up his supple leather boots, which reached all the way to his knees.

Then he turned his back on Wadi and strode out of the yurt, followed closely by Altan, Garus, Lars, and then the rest of his contingent. The final two guards took Wadi roughly by an arm each, and dragged her out.

10

WADI

Outside, Wadi was shocked. Compared to the evening before, there was almost no one around. Smoke still rose from the campfires, but the coals were dark, the ashes damp. They had been put out some time ago. Every man and woman was needed for this attack, and sent to the front lines.

Wadi hurried to keep close to the group, so she could keep track of their conversation.

"We'll send the newly taken Yelak tribes out first. The ones who aren't oathbreakers. Maybe Mermaden will be less likely to want to hew down his own people."

"I strongly doubt that, Your Excellence. They are converts to your side. They turned over their villages to you rather than fight. Mermaden will consider them traitors."

"They are traitors," said Khareh. "Another reason why

they should be in the front line. If they survive then the gods have spared them, and they will have proved themselves useful in my eyes. Let them take the first volley of arrows for me, the first wave of burning pitch poured down from the city walls. Then we will move."

Altan nodded, then barked a word at Lars, who sped off as if a whip had been applied to his back rather than just a tongue.

"Wait—" cried out Khareh, and Lars skidded to a halt, bowing his head low. "Remember what I said. When you breach the city walls, take anything you want, but leave the people alone. Spread the word."

"Of course, my Khan." And Lars was off again, this time beyond Khareh's earshot.

Wadi raised an eyebrow. Khareh caught the expression and shrugged. "What? You can't trust the soldiers to tell the engineers from the enemies. I need everyone useful to be taken back to Kharein—alive."

They continued to walk until they came to another yurt that was almost twin to Khareh's. In fact, Wadi had to blink sleep out of her eyes to be convinced they hadn't just walked in a big circle. But no—as they drew closer, she could see that this was slightly smaller in size than Khareh's tent, and displayed a slightly different pattern on its woven walls—although it was just as ornate.

Behind it, the trees here cleared, and a vast plain spread out in front of them, leading up toward an enormous walled city. The pale stone walls, partially obscured by smoke from smouldering fires, blended in against the dawn sky. Looking over at it, Wadi thought it looked strangely serene—the calm before the storm that Khareh was set to bring.

She tore her eyes away from the city Khareh was about to invade and pushed down the pity in her heart for the lives that were about to be overturned, uprooted—and, likely, destroyed. There was nothing she could do.

Instead, she returned her focus to the new yurt. Why she needed to be moved from one to another, she had no idea ... until the curtain was drawn aside and a girl not much older than her stepped out, a look of thunder on her pretty face.

The Khan's wife. The Seer-Queen. Erdene. She was beautiful, dressed in an intricately embroidered overcoat that covered her from neck to boots.

"Khareh," she said. "You are here, finally. I thought for a moment you weren't coming. I have been ready and waiting for your call for hours. Remember, I am your Protector. I should be with you at all times, not hidden away without you."

Khareh reached out and grabbed her by both hands.

"Erdene, we've been over this. Your duty is to do what I ask, and today I want you to protect my prize. This is as important as my protection now. And plus, I have my spirit-guard."

The Seer-Queen bristled, a shudder that brought her shoulders tightly together. "I am Yun—I am one of the best fighters that you have. Leave your 'prize' with one of your regular soldiers. I will be of more use to you on the battlefield. I am not weak."

"You're not weak, but don't test me today, Erdene."

Khareh dropped her hands. He gestured to the guards, who pushed Wadi forward. She almost stumbled into the other girl's arms, but managed to pull up in time. "This is now your most important task. I say that as your khan." Khareh then spun on his heel and walked away.

The tightness around Erdene's mouth made her anger as obvious as if she were shouting. She looked Wadi up and down. "So. You are the important one."

Clearly, that fact riled Erdene.

"You can let me go if you want," Wadi replied with a shrug.

Erdene tutted, then swept back into the yurt. Wadi followed; there wasn't much of an option to do otherwise.

"You'd think he'd want me by his side; I am his Protector, after all! I am not the protector of his pet projects." She looked sidelong at Wadi. "I didn't think the savages of the desert spoke Darhanian. Let alone wrote it too. I've heard about the tasks he's been giving you. Things he should entrust to a true Darhanian."

Yes, Wadi thought. *If any of them could read or write.*

She kept her mouth shut.

The inside of this yurt was plusher even than Khareh's. Silks trimmed with sparkling gold cloth draped the walls; soft furs covered the ground and the seating areas. A blazing fire warmed the whole tent from the center. Wood, at least, was plentiful in Yelak.

"Oh, come on. I know you're not mute." Erdene threw herself down on one of the fur-covered, cushioned surfaces, letting her arm drape across her forehead. Melodrama she must have learned from Khareh—unless it came naturally.

Wadi snapped back before she could think. "I didn't think you'd want to talk with...what was it? Khareh's pet project."

"He's the Khan to you. Or His Excellence." To Wadi's surprise, Erdene then laughed. "Plus, you're one of many projects Khareh has ongoing. Even I might be one of them."

Then, like a flash of lightning, her expression turned more somber. "I should be out there with him."

Wadi raised an eyebrow. "I'm no stranger to a fight, but all-out war...that's something different."

Erdene shrugged. "It's what I trained my whole life for!" Then she slumped. "But he doesn't need me now he has his sage powers." She held up her knotted necklace. "He could have had any of the older, more experienced Yun as his Protector—once he'd proven his strength to them, of course. But he picked me. I don't think this Protector role means anything to him anymore, not since Raimanan disappeared."

She noticed that Wadi visibly stiffened at Raim's name.

"You knew Raimanan, didn't you?" Erdene's eyes narrowed.

Wadi tried not to answer, but her pained expression gave her away.

"You did!" Erdene laughed. "Oh, you liked him? Don't try to deny it, I can tell. How funny."

Wadi didn't smile.

"I could have had Raim if I wanted," Erdene said, staring at her fingernails, although she sneaked a glance at Wadi, who tried her best to remain impassive. "He used to run around after me like a little puppy. It was sweet, really. But why have the bodyguard, when you can have the Khan? Seems like Raim has resorted to picking up scraps in the desert instead."

Wadi couldn't believe that Raim had ever liked such a horrible person, but then, his former best friend was Khareh. Maybe Raim wasn't the greatest judge of character when he was growing up.

Silence filled the air between them, Wadi biting down on her tongue so as not to respond to Erdene's barbs. She sensed that Erdene was on edge. She didn't want to antagonize her, but her curiosity was too strong.

"What does Khareh want with me, if I'm just a scrap of the desert? Why not just kill me?"

Erdene shrugged. "He doesn't tell me much. All I know is that I'm to bring you to the temple in the city once they have conquered it."

"So we could be here a while." Wadi had overheard enough of Altan's lectures on sieges to understand that you didn't just walk into a city and take over. There were strategies. Tactics. And the city always had the upper hand over the invading army.

For a moment, it was as if Erdene's dark brown eyes drained of color, like a cloud had passed over them. She was blinking back tears. When she spoke, her voice was low, barely a whisper. "No. Not if he unleashes the shadows."

The thought sent shivers up and down Wadi's spine. Although she hadn't grown up in the North—where the stigma against oathbreakers was strongest—she still had experienced the revulsion and horror the shadows inspired.

She could imagine the terror of the people of Samar when they saw an army of haunts bearing down on them. Khareh would seem invincible.

She thought of the Camp of Shadows, and what Khareh had asked of those people. "All those broken oaths. How can you follow him?"

"He has all these plans. He rants and raves all night about everything that's wrong with Darhan. The fact that our cities are so small—but who needs big cities when we are traveling all the time? He hates that no one can read and write. He hates that about me, you know that? He hates that while I am Yun-trained, skilled with sword and bow-and-arrow, I can't read any of his damn papers. That's probably why he likes you best."

At that, Wadi grimaced. Erdene rolled her eyes. "Well, why he prefers your company. He says even the savages teach their youth to read—what does that say about us?"

"You don't agree with him?"

"I don't see what's wrong with our society. It's been functioning fine for so long. The Baril preserve our history. That is enough for me."

"You have to admit, some of the Darhanian traditions are more than a little strange. What about this Seer-Queen stuff? Are you a seer?"

Erdene studied Wadi for a moment. Then, there was a moment—a crack in Erdene's veneer. "You are a savage," she said. Wadi was about to protest, but Erdene continued without noting the other girl's shock. "So I suppose that means I can tell you—I don't know what a seer is. I thought they were legends. There hasn't been a true seer for an age. If there has ever been one … a person who can see the future? It's impossible."

"Although they said the same thing about sages," said Wadi, filled with caution.

Erdene paused, mulling that thought over in her mind. "That they did." She let out a long breath. "Well, if there are seers out there, I'm not one of them. But I'm strong in other ways. I can help Khareh. He will see that in time. He never used to be like this, you know? Raim's betrayal broke him. Changed him. He became … " She didn't finish the sentence, but her eyes passed over Wadi's form and turned hard.

The slight warming Wadi was beginning to feel toward the girl froze in an instant. Now there was ice between them. For a person born and bred of the desert, it was not a pleasant sensation. "Khareh is a monster," she said, and shuddered.

"Yes," said Erdene. She dragged the tip over her tongue over her top lip. "But he is my monster."

RAIM

He was on his knees on a hard wooden floor. The man who stood over him had a nose like a beak, and a flattened forehead so pronounced he could have balanced an entire tea set without spilling a drop.

"Is this the oathbreaker?" the man said.

Raim recognized him. Even through the sting of the bruises that were rising all over his body from the handling of the monks, his mind was clear. This was Qatir-bar, the head of the Baril, the man who had married Tarik to his wife, Solongal, so long ago, before Raim's exile. All around him, other Baril monks were gathered to watch the spectacle.

Tarik rushed forward and prostrated himself at the man's feet, bowing as low as he could without burying his head in the floor.

"Oh, great and wondrous Qatir-bar. This is the one, Raim, who possesses the shadow. In my previous lowly life, he was my brother under Loni, my guardian in the Moloti tribe. As soon as I saw him, I knew to bring him to you."

Qatir raised an eyebrow. "And who are you?"

"Tarik, my lord. One of your humble novices." He spoke into the ground, still not daring to look up.

A visible shudder ran through Qatir's body. "A novice? So you are the one responsible for bringing this dirty oathbreaker to our lands? I should cast you out of the Baril for this!"

"No, please, Qatir-bar. He says he is not an oathbreaker. He says he is a sage. I have seen his powers with my own eyes."

Qatir turned his attention back to Raim. "A sage?"

Raim remembered what Vlad had said. He had to appeal to the Baril's greatest strength and greatest weakness: their thirst for knowledge. That was his only opportunity.

"Qatir-bar," he said. "I can tell you something known only to the Shan. Although all you see in front of you is a shadow—and only oathbreakers are haunted by shadows—there is more. Sages *control* the shadows. That is the source of their power."

Qatir stroked the bottom of his chin. "Why have you come here?"

"I need help," Raim said.

"And why should we help you?"

"Because if you can help me, I will teach you everything I know about sages and promise magic."

"If we refuse?"

"If you refuse, or you can't help me, then I will leave here and find someone who can." Raim wiped his hand across his brow, feeling a lump rise where one of the Baril monks had hit him across the head. He had not fought back. If the Baril refused to help, he would fight back with all his might—and they would not stand a chance.

A long moment of silence followed, during which Raim refused to look at the floor. Instead, he stared straight at Qatir-bar, allowing the man's piercing gaze to wash over him. He had been in worse positions before. No one could scare him, after Khareh. And he had nothing to lose.

There was a large commotion from behind another door to the temple. The door swung open, clattering against the wood and disturbing the otherwise peaceful scene. A woman dressed in black, with long, dark hair, strode in.

"What is this, Qatir? Something you are hiding from us?"

The Baril who had gathered around Raim all moved so that they stood between him and the woman in black.

"The boy and his shadow were found by one of my novices," snapped Qatir. "He is mine to deal with. Get back in your hovel."

The woman managed to catch Raim's eye through the crowd of people, and he felt her stare burn into the deepest recesses of his soul. He squirmed—uncomfortable under her scrutiny. He wondered who it was that could cause Qatir to become so flustered.

"As you will, Qatir," she said. "But why don't you ask your new prize what he's hiding under that fabric around his wrist." She left, without any sign of a bow in Qatir-bar's direction.

The color drained from Raim's face. *Draikh?*

The shadow drew closer to Raim, ready to defend him at any moment.

"How did she know?" Draikh's anxious voice rang in Raim's skull.

I have no idea! What should I do?

Qatir looked back down at Raim, then with a sharp gesture of his head, signaled for two of his guards to grab Raim by the wrists. One of them held his arm aloft, while the other took a knife and sliced the fabric that was wrapped around his wrist. The pieces fluttered to the ground, revealing Raim's crimson scar to the entire room.

There was a sharp intake of breath, and the man holding his arm released it as if it had burst into flames.

"You lied to me," said Qatir-bar. "You are an oathbreaker."

"No, I'm not—let me explain—"

"The time for explanations are over! The evidence is clear. And you—" He turned to Tarik. "You brought this oathbreaker into our midst. How dare you!"

"I didn't know!" whimpered Tarik.

"I'll deal with you later," said Qatir, his voice as cold as the snow on the mountains. "Take the oathbreaker to the cells."

RAIM

The cell was little more than an empty room with thick stone walls and a bolted wooden door. In the freezing darkness, Raim shivered on the floor, tucked in close to the far wall on a thin layer of straw, beneath a thin blanket—the only comforts he'd been offered. His sleep was fitful, interrupted by nightmares of creeping red rope entwining itself around his body and threatening to strangle him. When his nightmares scared him awake, all he could see was the crimson of his scar around his wrist, as bright as if it was glowing in the dark, still tormenting him with the fact that he was an oathbreaker. What was he thinking, coming here? Why would the Baril wait for him to give an explanation?

When he closed his eyes again, he tried to put the thoughts out of his mind. Nothing would be accomplished by dwelling on his predicament. He needed all the rest he could get.

"Raim."

He wasn't even sure if the word had been spoken aloud, or whether Draikh had just spoken deep in his subconscious. It didn't matter either way: in an instant, he was wide awake. The urgency in Draikh's tone meant he had no choice.

"Lie still. They think you are asleep."

Raim had tensed under his blanket, but apart from that he made no other movements. He tried to keep his breathing even, as if he were still in deep sleep.

How many? he asked Draikh silently. He could hear people slipping across the floor, despite the fact that they were obviously trying to be silent as ghosts. The air around him had changed too—it was warmer; the sudden influx of bodies and the smell of nervous sweat was something even the quietest attacker could not hide. But Raim had Draikh, and that was an advantage no one could compete with.

"Three, with two more outside the door," the spirit answered.

The door?

"They've unlocked it, but you won't be able to get past. Oh, gods, no time. Go!"

Raim pushed off from the wall, rolling across the floor, just as the air above his head was sliced by a cudgel wielded by one of the attackers. Wood smacked against stone, missing him by inches, the sound only mildly dulled by the rough straw bedding he'd been lying on.

The Baril swore loudly. Raim stopped rolling as soon

as he felt the edge of the man's boots. He threw a numbing chop at his ankles. The man yelped in pain, and as he fell to the ground, Raim pushed him hard against the far wall.

The room was suddenly a swirl of motion. Raim's eyes rapidly adjusted to the darkness, but he remained crouched low. He heard one of the attackers go down behind him—Draikh working fast. But there was still one Baril left, plus the two who were coming through the door—and they would no longer have the element of surprise on their side.

If Raim thought that the Baril monks were all muscle and no finesse, he was wrong. This became increasingly clear as the other Baril gathered his senses and leaped for Raim.

Raim didn't react in time, and the monk slammed him back into the ground, one hand on his throat, the other keeping him pinned down. Raim scrambled and squirmed beneath him, but the man was strong. His face was covered by a mask. Raim could only see the man's eyes, which were dark and full of hatred for him.

Raim reached out with one hand, scrabbling across the stone tiles, coming up with only fistfuls of straw and blanket—not helpful in this situation. His lungs burned in his chest as the monk pressed down, then slammed his elbow down onto Raim's stomach, knocking the air from him.

The blow caused Raim's arm to jerk to his side, dragging with it the remnants of his blanket. As a result, Raim found what he was looking for tangled in the blanket—the cudgel the first Baril had tried to use to smash his head in.

He grabbed it and smashed it at the Baril on top of him. The weapon was too long for the man to receive the full force of it, but it was enough to make him to release his grip as he tried to block the blow. This was all the encouragement Raim needed. He took a lungful of breath, then brought the cudgel back down, this time with both hands. It cracked in two across the man's back, sending him shuddering to the ground, one half of the stick flying across the room.

Raim spun around to confront the two other men. They stormed in through the door, and Raim watched as Draikh took them on, weakening them so that Raim could throw them to the ground.

"Good teamwork," Draikh said when the men lay silent. *Is that everyone?*

"For now." Draikh sounded solemn, but he looked solid—which was a relief to Raim. Their training had paid off. Draikh was able to fight for longer without fading from the physical world. "But we should get out of here. Quickly."

Agreed. But where will we go? Raim had no idea where in the Baril temple he was, and for all he knew, every corner would take them deeper into disaster. He'd have to disguise himself. He looked down at the men they'd incapacitated. He tried to eye up if he could take their clothes, but...

"Hurry, there's no time. We'll figure it out later," said Draikh.

Raim ran toward the door—and freedom.

But then, from behind him, came a grating noise: stone being dragged along stone.

Raim spun around and stared at the wall of his cell as it shifted in front of his eyes.

"Oh gods," said Draikh. "There's someone coming down the hall now too."

So we're surrounded?

"Looks like."

"Raim?" A voice—more like a hiss—came from behind the moving wall.

There was a grunt of effort, and finally the piece of wall shifted completely. In the hole behind, a woman's face appeared. It took Raim a second to realize it was the woman who had confronted Qatir-bar.

"Quickly! Come with me," she said, gesturing behind the wall. "Before the others get here."

"Who are you?" asked Raim.

"We don't have time for that—I'll explain on the way."

"Raim—there's someone approaching the door," hissed Draikh. "I think it's your brother."

Raim spun round, and sure enough, his brother's voice sounded from further down the hallway.

"Hello? Raim? I've brought food."

Tarik appeared in the door to the cell, then dropped the bowl of soup he was carrying. The gloopy yellow substance sprayed everywhere, mingling with the blood and straw. He stared wide-eyed at the bodies littered across the floor.

"What happened?" His eyes adjusted even further, and he caught sight of the woman in the cell with Raim.

"Aelina-bar?"

The woman pulled herself up to her full height and Tarik quaked in his boots. "The leader of your faction tried to kill Raim," she said. "These are his men, no?"

Tarik stole a glance at the men and whimpered.

"Qatir wants you dead," the woman said to Raim. "He wants to destroy what he doesn't understand. However, we can help you. Because we know who you are. And who you made that promise to."

"Don't trust her, Raim!" Tarik found his voice at last. "She is the head of one of the rebel Baril factions."

A sick, uncomfortable feeling took over Raim, his palms sweaty. "How do you know?" he asked the woman.

How could she know? He wanted to trust his brother, but there was an expression on the woman's face that was impossible to ignore.

"Because Mhara told me," she said.

"Mhara?" Raim's mouth went dry. "Who is Mhara?" he whispered.

"I think you know."

"But that's impossible. The Mhara I know is dead."

He knew that. He hadn't found her body, but she'd fallen so far, and he'd searched for so long. He'd carried the weight of her death with him since that moment. He had been responsible.

"She is here."

"I—I don't believe you."

"She thought you might say that. Maybe this will convince you." From behind her back, the woman produced a ring with a curved hook that protruded from the thick silver band. Raim took it from her, feeling like his hands were moving through air that was as thick as water. It was an archer's prize bow ring.

The ring was heavy in his palm, far heavier than it should

be. It carried with it the weight of Raim's memories. Of training with an amazing Yun warrior, who taught him how to ride, how to shoot, how to wield a sword. He had spent a long time coveting a ring just like this. A ring that was forged especially for its owner. There was no mistaking it—the ring belonged to Mhara. His old Yun mentor, and the woman he thought he'd killed on his way to exile in Lazar.

With a *whump*, Tarik landed on the floor in a twisted heap. "I had to take him out," Draikh said with a shrug. "He was about to run away. He'll be fine."

"Take me to Mhara," said Raim, closing his fist around the ring.

Aelina beckoned over her shoulder and disappeared through the wall.

Raim looked back at the mass of bodies he'd left behind, some still groaning in pain, others suspiciously still. It was the proof that Baril factions were fighting for control of him—or to kill him. He wasn't going to leave Tarik to whatever punishment Qatir would deal out to him. *Take his feet,* he said to Draikh, positioning himself to carry the unconscious Tarik under the arms.

He shoved aside his guilt and followed Aelina through the wall.

WADI

Wadi and Erdene spent the rest of the day and a night cooped up in the yurt, the air between them cold as mountain snow. Every so often, the noise and stench of war would reach them inside the tent, and neither of them slept a wink.

An ominous shaking of the ground, so violent it threatened to topple the yurt's wooden frame, shocked them both. Erdene looked up sharply. "What was that?"

"I'm not su—"

Erdene cut her off with a sharp chop of her hand. "Gods take Khareh's orders. I've had enough of this. I'm not sitting in here any longer like some lamb waiting for slaughter." She leaped up from her cushioned perch, tearing off her richly embroidered overcoat to reveal full leather armor beneath. She was dressed for war. "Khareh said I had to look after you, but he didn't say I had to stay in the yurt." She walked over to one of the trunks stored at the edge of the room and pulled out a leather jerkin, which she threw at Wadi. "Put that on," she said. "Last thing I want to worry about is some stray arrow taking you. Come on! Hurry!"

Wadi grabbed the jerkin and stared at it for a moment. She didn't want to stay holed up in the yurt any more than Erdene did. As Erdene sliced through the bonds around her feet, she pulled the jerkin on over her silk tunic. "Hands out," Erdene said.

"What? You're joking—I can't go out there with my hands tied!"

"*Hands out,*" repeated Erdene, before yanking at Wadi's wrists herself. She bound them with rope. Then, with a sharp tug on it, she led Wadi out into the fray.

Wadi hoped—prayed—that someone would spot them and send them back to the yurt.

She was afraid. Fighting didn't scare her; in hand-to-hand combat, she felt confident in her skill. But out here on the battlefield, terror gripped her like a vice. Arrows whistled through the air high above her and the clash of swords rang in her ears. Her leather jerkin felt thinner by the moment. Her hands were tied, and Erdene pulled at her bindings whenever Wadi dropped too far behind: a skittish donkey being led by its master through a raging battlefield.

Of course, no one would send them back to the yurt, because no one had more authority than Erdene except the Khan himself. As the Seer-Queen stormed through the army ranks, a scythe slicing through blades of grass, the soldiers cleared a path for her. Ahead of them, thick, black smoke obscured the sky; the city was an enormous campfire. Wadi couldn't make out which were Khareh's men and which were the city's defenders, but almost everyone she could see was engaged in combat in a tight perimeter around the city walls. They weren't yet being pushed back, which Wadi took as a good sign for Khareh. But he hadn't seemed to have entered the city yet, either. The longer that took, the more the city had the upper hand.

A tall, broad-shouldered soldier spotted them and came scurrying over. The mask on his face and the cruel, glittering blade in his hands made it clear that he was Yun, like Erdene. He raised his mask as he came close; it was Lars.

"Tell me what's happening," said Erdene.

"Mermaden's front line is defending the city."

Erdene frowned. "So he hasn't broken through the walls yet?"

Lars shook his head. "The lead battalion tried, but Mermaden poured burning pitch over the walls. We can't raise the ladders without them catching fire."

A soldier running past them toward the city let out a loud cry of alarm. Instinctively Lars and Erdene raised their shields, which only moments later shook with the thuds of arrows hitting the wood at full force. Their shields protected them, and Wadi too—but the soldier was not so lucky. He fell at Erdene's feet, two arrows at his back.

"Mermaden's not concerned that it's his former people making up the Khan's front line, then?" Erdene ignored the fallen man, continuing her conversation with Lars. "Of course he's not," she said, answering her own question. "He's not stupid." She tugged on the rope, hard, and Wadi stumbled and fell to her knees. Erdene rolled her eyes.

"The Khan is in trouble," said Lars, his voice low. "Mermaden knows how to defend his city—he's ruled over it for thirty years, and he's been stockpiling food and resources ever since Khareh-Khan took power. He knew this was coming."

"He's not in trouble," Erdene countered. "He still has the shadows. Enough dawdling. Take me to the Khan."

Down in the mud, Wadi was face-to-face with the realities of warfare: the dead soldier's eyes were open and staring at her. Accusing. She swallowed down the revulsion rising in her gut, and even though her body was shaking, she had to focus. That's when she saw it. The blade in the dead man's hand. Keeping her movements slow to avoid alerting Erdene, she reached for the blade and teased it out of the man's grip without touching him, ignoring the fact that the liquid churning the dirt around them to mud was more likely blood than water. She twisted the blade's hilt in her hands and prayed it was still sharp.

It was.

She sliced through the rope and her hands were free.

Wadi tried to keep her head. She looped the newly loose end around the man's wrist and tied it off just as Erdene gave her another tug on the rope.

"Come on, get up," she said, without even looking down at Wadi.

Wadi took her moment and bolted. Erdene yelled out in surprise, but Wadi didn't stop to look behind. She was too busy concentrating on not tripping over the bodies and broken bits of metal armor that littered the ground. She still had the sword in her hand, and she ran *toward* the battle. Losing herself in the chaos was her best opportunity for escape.

Except that she ran straight into a cloud—one that solidified in front of her. She beat at it with her arms, but it wrapped itself around her so that she couldn't move. When she heard Khareh's voice, she stopped struggling.

"Wadi, you can't leave before the best part!"

She looked up to see him riding across the battlefield on horseback, looking every inch the powerful Khan. Lars had given the impression that Khareh was at a disadvantage in the siege, but she wouldn't have known it by looking at him. He still had the same cocky, self-assured grin.

"Tell your haunt to let me go," she said through gritted teeth. She struggled hard against it, even though it was useless.

Khareh waved his hand and the shadow moved away from her, taking her weapon with him. He turned his attention to Erdene and Lars, who had sprinted over after Wadi's escape attempt. Khareh didn't acknowledge Erdene at all, and Wadi could see the hurt in her eyes. Hurt that turned to contempt as she stared at Wadi.

"Lars, it is time. Sound the horn." Khareh turned to his shadow. "You know what to do." The shadow disappeared toward the line of yurts that signaled the beginning of the camp—where Erdene and Wadi had just come from. Lars blew the twisted bone horn with all his might, and the sound echoed across the battlefield.

"This won't take long," Khareh said.

Far in the distance, another horn sounded. Khareh's soldiers began retreating from the city, leaving the Samar soldiers confused. A cry rose up from behind the city walls.

The Samar soldiers were *cheering*. They believed they had won.

A knot of dread formed in Wadi's stomach. From deep in the camp, a cloud was building—an approaching storm. Only this cloud moved with purpose; with intention.

"Just wait," said Khareh, listening to the cheers. His lips were set in a determined line, the cocky smile gone. His knuckles went white, gripping onto the reins of his horse.

"Nervous?" Wadi asked.

He shook his head. "No. The shadows will take them. How can they defend against an enemy they can't see?"

He was right. The shadow-army swept up, over the heads of Khareh's army. Lookouts still barricaded behind the Samar city walls spied the great cloud's approach, raising the alarm in the city once more. They hurled rocks, slung arrows, and jabbed spears into the cloud, but nothing stopped it, and the rest of Khareh's army had moved far out of range.

The shadows swept through the city, the wails of Samar's soldiers louder than any of their cheers had been.

The battle had raged for hours, but this part lasted only minutes. Khareh snapped out of the stupor he'd fallen into while watching the shadows do their work and signaled to Lars and Erdene.

"Find your mounts—and make sure there is one for Wadi," said Khareh. "It is time I took my city."

14

WADI

There was so much death.

It struck Wadi as soon as she entered the city on the back of a tall, chestnut-brown mare. Erdene and Lars sandwiched her between them so she could not escape, but she was glad for the protection from the brunt of the view. It wasn't even that she hadn't been around death before. The Sola desert took people all the time—men, women, babies. She'd seen a young girl with her skin blackened and burned off her body. She'd seen a man taken by behrflies, their poisonous bites covering his skin in welts that had swelled and burst.

With those deaths, Wadi had felt the grief wrap its hands around her heart and throat. She had felt enclosed, suffocated.

But this was different. The scale of this death made her feel detached. Removed. Soldiers' bodies lay bent and broken over the city walls, from where they had been tasked with pouring burning pitch on Khareh's army—only to be at the forefront of the attack by the shadows. Some had fallen to their deaths, blood staining the gray stone in dark pools. Flies buzzed in thick swarms around the dead; no one had yet come out to move their bodies.

There would be many graves to dig around the city soon.

The tips of her fingers turned cold, even though the air was warm. Her body was shutting down from the pain of—from the pain of what? Of witnessing? Of understanding?

She stole a glance at Erdene's face. *She was trained for this,* Wadi reminded herself. Or at least, trained not to look bothered by it. Erdene could remain stoical and unaffected in the wake of the death and disaster. Well, maybe Erdene didn't look so happy about it after all. Her skin had turned a sickly gray and a sheen of sweat lay on her skin; her mouth was set in a firm line. But she looked determined not to show fear. It made Wadi feel ashamed at her more visceral response. Had she really been so sheltered by a life in the desert? She'd always assumed that in Darhan life was better than life in the desert. But if life in Darhan only meant more war, then maybe she had been lucky after all.

She centered herself.

Khareh did this. Remember that. Maybe she could remind Erdene of that fact too. The Seer-Queen could turn into a powerful ally.

Or a worst enemy.

They rode through the city's narrow stone streets toward the temple, where Khareh would be waiting for them.

Despite being surrounded by lush forests, there was not much greenery in the city. Not like Lazar. In fact, Wadi's main impression was one of poverty and disarray—at least in this part of the city. There was hardly anybody in the streets, although she could see a few pairs of eyes staring out at them from windows and doorways, and down one alleyway she spied a young girl, clothes ragged, covered head-to-toe in dirt, her thumb propped listlessly between her lips. A woman—her mother, presumably—stepped out of a nearby doorway and grabbed the girl brusquely by the upper arm, dragging her indoors. Wadi thought she heard the girl squeal, and it made her wince.

But at least it meant that Khareh hadn't killed everybody. It was a small comfort.

The streets opened up as they headed toward what Wadi assumed was the temple—the only place that looked as if it had been built with any degree of care and attention. They passed underneath the temple gates, which were intricately carved and the only thing of beauty Wadi had yet seen in the city. Inlaid into the stone arch were tiles of bright blue and green. A large metal disc of concentric circles hung in the very center of the gate—the symbol of Samar.

Khareh was waiting on foot, just inside. They dismounted and walked toward him. "Is the city ours?" Erdene asked as they approached.

The Khan nodded. "Except for Mermaden himself." He spat into the ground. "The supposedly great ruler is a coward after all. He escaped with some of his generals before we could reach his palace. I lost my horse from an arrow—one of Mermaden's men making a passing shot. It would have crushed my leg if my shadow guard hadn't returned to protect me."

There was a long rectangular clearing behind the gates, dominated by a shallow pool of water. The temple itself was at the far end of the pool. It was almost too picturesque for the shabbiness of the rest of the city, built of stone and covered in mosaic patterns—which even spread onto the floor. The mosaics made the large, square walls beautiful. Some of the tiles spelled out words—prayers to the gods, predominantly Sola. It calmed Wadi to know that she was in Sola's presence—even here, so far away from the desert itself. It was good to know that even from afar, the desert goddess was feared and awed.

Wadi was glad despite herself when they moved inside. Anything to get away from the sight of the city, and the stench.

Khareh's guard met them just inside the temple doors, and guided them through several hallways until they reached what must have been the temple's main room. The floor was polished until it shone, and Wadi had to watch her footing after she almost slipped on the slick surface.

Unfortunately, Khareh didn't miss anything. "Be careful," he said to her. "I know you think I'm heartless. But if I'm right, then there is another pass-stone kept within these walls. Doesn't that intrigue you just a little bit?"

It did. Reluctantly, Wadi followed Khareh out of the large room and down a set of stone steps that led far beneath the temple.

When she got to the bottom step, she stopped in shock. There were twenty girls down there, in a long line, each with a veil over her face and wearing a pendant identical to the one Wadi wore around her neck.

Khareh walked right to the end of the line of girls. A trembling priestess stood there, held between two of Khareh's guards. A cold chill descended Wadi's spine until fear rooted her to the floor. Under her tunic, her pendant burned. The two sensations made her feel like she was suffering from a fever, and sweat broke out on her forehead. Something here was deeply wrong.

"We will never tell you who wears the rightful stone," the priestess said, tossing her hair back and holding her head up high. She had rows of braids wrapped in concentric circles around her head, but they were in complete disarray.

"I could just take all of them, you know. That doesn't matter much to me. But let's do this the easy way, shall we? Wadi?" He gestured her forward. "Which of these is the real stone?"

The chill came again, because the answer stood out to her plain as day. But for Khareh, she tried to control the shake in her voice as she said, "Why should I help you?"

Khareh rolled his eyes. "Don't put us through this, Wadi. By force or by pain, I won't leave this room without it, so you might as well tell me."

"That just makes me want to give it to you less. At least tell me what you want with it!"

Khareh clicked his fingers, staring at Erdene. Immediately, Erdene drew a dagger from her side. Despite herself,

Wadi flinched. Her eyes darted around the room, looking for something she could use as a weapon. But there was nothing but the smooth stone walls and the terrified girls. Maybe if she could disarm Erdene, but she was well-trained...

To her utter distress, Khareh just laughed as he stepped forward to take the dagger from Erdene.

"Don't be stupid. I'm not going to torture you. I need you." He spun around on his heel, reached out and grabbed the arm of one of the girls, making her stumble. He slipped the knife up against her trembling neck. "No, but I can torture every single one of these girls, until either they break—or you do."

The girl let out a piercing scream, amplified within the enclosed space, as Khareh pushed the blade against her skin, splitting it, drawing blood. "Don't you think they've suffered enough?"

"Fine!" shouted Wadi as the girl's screams increased. "You are a monster, Khareh."

The knife pulled away; the screaming stopped, replaced by quick, panicked breaths.

"It's none of them," she mumbled.

"What?" said Khareh.

"I said, it's none of them."

Khareh was deadly still. "Then where is it?"

Wadi gritted her teeth. Then she walked slowly through the line of girls, through the gap Khareh had created, and began running her hands along the wall.

There was another sharp cry from the girl behind.

"Come on, Wadi. I know you know exactly where it is.

Why are you insisting on wasting my time? Unless you just enjoy causing this girl pain."

Wadi grimaced, then placed her hands more firmly against the wall. One stone shifted beneath her palms. She pulled it out and there, buried deep within the wall, was another pendant.

She reached in and prised it out. Once in her hand, it grew warm, as if it burned with an inner fire. She looked back at Khareh and raised an eyebrow. "What do you want with this? Owning one of these stones can only mean one thing."

"And what's that?" Khareh asked.

"It's a curse. Whoever holds this stone is cursed to return to Lazar. But most would rather pass the burden on to their descendants than go back there. The legend of the 'Undying Women' . . . it makes sense now. It's just a lie to explain why these poor young 'chosen women' die unnaturally early deaths, desperate to leave their city and pursue a destiny they never chose for themselves. Why would you want that?"

Khareh stepped through the line of girls, who parted quickly as he passed. He stood in front of Wadi, so close to her she could smell the remnants of crushed mint leaves on his breath.

"Wadi, all this time you've spent with me, and still you misunderstand me. I want to go to Lazar. No—more than that. I want to go to Lazar, and then I want to go South, to Aqben, to fulfill my dream of being the Golden Khan. I want Darhan to be the greatest empire under Naran's great sky. And he who owns Lazar owns the desert. And he who owns the desert owns the world."

RAIM

The Baril. Layers within layers within mysteries. Was there anything simple about these people? There was certainly nothing simple about their temple. As they slipped through the narrow passageways, Raim was shocked by how much he could hear from the other side of the temple walls. At some point, the stone of the walls seemed thinner than paper, and the occasional pinprick of light belied the position of tiny peepholes into what Raim presumed were private rooms. The Baril, protectors of culture? More like liars and spies and manipulators—a web of factions that waged war with words. The politics here were more complicated than between the warlords and the khans. At least those battles were won with the sword—not with the mind.

At one point, Raim heard his name being shouted from

a hidden room beyond. He didn't recognize the voice, and he couldn't quite make out all the words, but the intention was clear: they were searching for him.

Raim was glad when the passage finally widened, because carrying Tarik, even with Draikh's support, was becoming increasingly difficult.

"We're almost there," murmured Aelina, still keeping her voice low.

The muscles in Raim's shoulders twitched—from supporting the dead weight of Tarik, but also from the tension. Could he trust this woman? It didn't seem like a good idea. The only thing that kept him following her was the thought that Mhara was somewhere close by. Mhara had been his mentor—a person he would have trusted with his life. Just like Wadi.

The muscles of his jaw tightened as he thought about Wadi. The more time he spent with the Baril, the longer she remained Khareh's captive. Vlad might have been convinced Khareh was not torturing her, but what was to prevent the Khan changing his mind? Even though Raim had reluctantly agreed to Vlad's plan, he would never forget his real aim: to rescue Wadi from Khareh.

Aelina stopped ahead of him and began tapping on the wall in a deliberate pattern. After a few moments, the wall opened, and Aelina stepped through.

Raim followed, but just as he did, Tarik stirred in his arms.

"Come on, brother," said Raim as Draikh dropped Tarik's legs to the ground. "Let's enter this mess together." Tarik's feet just about caught his weight, and he wobbled slowly to standing, groaning loudly.

Raim pulled Tarik's arm over his shoulder while Draikh supported him on the other side, and the three of them stepped into a cavernous room full of women standing in a semicircle. And at its center: Mhara.

She was really there.

And she looked ... surprisingly well for a woman Raim had assumed was dead. She was not dressed as he'd left her, in her Yun army gear, but in a long, almost floor-length tunic more typical of the Baril. More shocking was that her long, dark hair had been shorn close to her head. All Yun wore their hair long, and so to see her like this—like an apprentice not long finished their final test—took some getting used to.

Down one side of her face, she now bore a raw, jagged scar—not the mark of a broken promise, but the result of a brutal, painful trauma.

Like plummeting hundreds of feet from a cliff.

"Mhara ... what? How?" Raim left Tarik propped up against the door and stepped toward her.

"Raim—it's really you," she said.

"Mhara, I don't know how I can tell you this, but—I am so sorry." Tears welled up behind his eyes. Ever since the encounter on the cliff, he'd believed that he had killed her. He had borne that weight, and had tried to honor her memory with his actions. But now he didn't have to mourn his mentor. She was standing right in front of him.

"How ... how come you are here?" Raim wanted to know everything. It must have been a miracle that allowed Mhara to come back alive—and well.

She waved off his question. "It's good to see you. I will

tell you all, I promise. But from what I hear, you are in a lot of trouble. It seems you attract it ... "

Raim nodded and raised the arm that bore his scar. "It is the same problem."

Mhara unleashed a string of curses from her mouth that shocked Raim into stunned silence. "You still don't know who you made the promise to?"

Raim shook his head.

"And that shadow that follows you—that is not the shadow from this broken vow?"

"No—the shadow is different. The shadow is Khareh," Raim said. "But I call him Draikh. I thought he was a dream at first. Dream-Khareh ... " His voice trailed off.

Mhara exchanged a look with Aelina, who stood behind him. Then the tall Baril woman moved so she stood next to Mhara. "What do you know about the person who you made this promise to?"

Raim's forehead crinkled into a frown. *Can I trust her?*

"I don't know," replied Draikh. "But do you have any choice?"

"Raim, this woman might be able to help you," Mhara said. "Tell her what you know."

Raim took a deep breath. "Not much. There have been several times that I thought I saw her."

"Her," said Aelina, jumping on the word. "So you know it's a woman?"

Raim nodded. "I think so. When I was with my grand-father, we used memory tea to try to unlock my recollection of that moment. It didn't work, but I remember seeing her hands—a woman's hands. And since then I've seen fleeting glimpses of her." His hands clenched into a fist, his nails digging into the flesh of his palms. "Normally it happens just before I'm about to get hurt—like when I tried to save my friend from falling and suffering the same fate as you, Mhara. Or when I almost fell myself, and Draikh wasn't strong enough to help me. I looked up and saw her white dress. But I've never seen her face. I suppose she has saved me on several occasions. Although it never felt like it."

Mhara tapped her finger on her lower lip. "So she only appears when you're in danger? I think I know who the woman is. And how you can meet her."

"You do?" asked Raim, hope exploding in his chest. But just as he spoke, Draikh's voice filled his head.

"She won't come."

What? How do you know? Have you known who it is too? All this time? Raim felt betrayal stab in his chest.

"No!" Draikh reassured him. "She hides from me."

Mhara continued, oblivious to their conversation. "Raim, the only way I can convince her to reveal herself is if you send the other shadow away."

Raim shared a look with Draikh.

"I don't think you should do that," said Draikh. "It might be a trick."

I trust Mhara. If she thinks she can convince the other spirit to come out, if I can find out what my promise was once and for all ... that has to be worth it.

Draikh was agitated. He shook his head and swirled

around Raim. "She has never protected you when it was needed. I don't trust her."

I'll be all right. I can defend myself. Take Tarik with you.

"Are you sure?"

Do it.

Draikh flew to where Tarik was still propped up by the wall.

"If you follow the tunnel further down," Aelina said to the shadow, "you will find another room, run by the Council. They will be able to heal Raim's brother."

Draikh took Tarik, who was too dazed to protest, away. Raim caught sight of Mhara watching them leave with a strange expression on her face. He tried to see it through her eyes: Tarik would look as if he was being supported by a swirl of darkness.

When Draikh was gone, Raim felt sick to his stomach. It was as if a limb had been removed, and it made him feel vulnerable and alone. He was suddenly much more alert to the fact that he was wearing nothing but his loose-fitting tunic and trousers. No armor. No weapon.

Mhara would not be pleased with me, he thought. No good Yun would ever be so unprepared. He had been leaning on Draikh and his own sage powers like a crutch.

And suddenly, he knew that Draikh was right. This had been a trap. And he was going to pay for his recklessness.

Before Raim could react, every woman in the room started moving toward him. There were bright flashes of light as metal objects appeared from behind their backs. Long objects, with sharp tips. Spears.

In unison, they pointed their weapons at Raim. And then they walked toward him.

"Draikh!" Raim roared out loud and in his mind, in case the shadow was still close enough to hear him. He retreated toward the hole in the wall they had come through. But Aelina blocked his path with a small dagger and an apologetic look on her face. The women pressed upon him with their spears, tightening the circle around him.

He turned and ran at Aelina, hoping she was not trained to fight. But she stood firm. He dodged the knife she was holding and grabbed at her wrist, causing her to drop the weapon. But the other women were also closing off the retreat to the passageway. "Draikh!" Raim screamed again, and he looked around frantically. His shadow was too far away.

Above the fracas, Mhara's voice echoed around the room. "His life is in danger! We will kill him!"

Raim pivoted round, hopeless and helpless as the spears surrounded him, a sea of metal and wood. He took a step backward, only to feel the tip of a spearhead dig into his spine, so sharp it split his skin and drew blood; when he tried to move forward, there was another spear at his neck. He stood stock-still. He barely dared to breathe. *They're not going to kill me,* he kept saying to himself. *They want something from me.*

"Still not enough? This is not a bluff."

He had no idea what Mhara was trying to accomplish, but whatever it was, it wasn't working.

"Kill him," Mhara said.

The woman holding the spear against his neck snarled, and she started to thrust forward with all her might.

Raim's eyes were wide open and his heart pounded in his chest. Only one face flashed in his mind's eye: Wadi. He would never see her again now.

"No!" There was another scream, another voice. There was a flash of white and Raim saw the woman who'd been about to kill him go down in a crumpled heap. Panic broke out among the other women. A blur of white sped around the circle, disarming the women, twisting their arms until they cried out in pain and dropped their spears. One brave woman attempted to thrust at him from the side, but the blur of white was there in an instant, jamming the butt of a spear it had stolen into the woman's stomach. The shadow then sped toward Raim, picked him up, and flew him above the women, so close to the ceiling that Raim could almost reach out and touch the rafters. He had been saved.

Mhara began a loud, slow clap. "See? That wasn't so hard," she said.

"How dare you do that? How dare you provoke me!" said the shadow holding Raim.

But, it wasn't a shadow. It was the form of a woman—the woman in white he had spotted on several occasions before, but had never fully seen. The mysterious other shadow he had always known had been there, but who had never appeared to him. He could look into her face now, and he recognized it.

"Tell me, Raim, who do you see?" asked Mhara from the floor below.

"I know her from Lazar," said Raim. "They have a statue to her there. Her name is ... Lady Chabi."

Mhara's expression softened. "A statue? How fitting. Well, Raim. That is the woman who gave you your scar." She held her hands up to the shadow of Lady Chabi. "You can put him down now. I won't harm him."

Raim couldn't help the frown that appeared on his face. "You ... why?" Who was this woman who had caused him so much pain and torment when he should be at the pinnacle of his life?

She turned to him, her face young and beautiful. The statue had not done her justice. "I had to."

"Raim," said Mhara, and he turned his attention reluctantly back to her. "Say hello to your mother."

PART TWO

RAIM

"Bar the doors. I want no one from outside the faction to find us here," said Aelina.

The shadow of his mother had brought him down to the ground, where Raim now rested on a single bended knee, his knuckles against the ground. He wanted to pound the stone beneath his fist, cause some kind of scene, but he knew it would do no good.

Raim looked up at the shadow-woman, the Lady Chabi—his mother. He had waited such a long time for this moment: the moment when he would finally discover what his promise was, and why he had made it.

But now that he was in front of her, he found himself speechless.

It was Mhara who spoke first. "I'm sorry, Raim, but I

knew I had to put your life in real danger for her to appear. It was the only way."

"I don't understand," Raim said to the woman. "All this time, you've been here... you could have told me what I needed to do."

"No, I couldn't," said his mother.

Draikh burst through the wall at that very moment. "Raim! Are you hurt?"

"And *that* is the reason why," she said. "Not when you have *him* whispering in your ear, corrupting you every moment!" She pointed an accusing finger at Draikh.

"Me? As you are perfectly aware, *I* am the one who has saved Raim on many occasions when *you* couldn't be bothered. Remember the behrflies? I am more loyal to Raim than anyone."

"More loyal than to *yourself*?" she spat. "I hardly think so."

"Enough!" Raim shouted.

Mhara stared at him in alarm. "What's happening? Tell me what they're saying!"

Raim threw his hands up in the air. "She says she won't tell me anything because of Draikh—she doesn't trust him."

Mhara raised her eyebrows. "Well, of course she doesn't."

Now it was Raim's turn to feel surprised. "What do you mean?"

"I think it's time you heard the entire story, Raim. And Aelina can help me fill in the blanks, as she knew your mother too."

"You did?"

Aelina nodded. "She was one of us, once."

She gestured to a low table in the far corner of the room. Raim didn't want to sit—he wanted to stand, fight, anything but sit around and listen—but he knew that it was vital for him to do so. He gritted his teeth and followed Mhara and Aelina to the table.

"All this time...what does she want from me?" he asked, slumping onto the bench. His head fell into his hands.

"The woman you know as Lady Chabi—the spirit behind your scar—was born into our Baril faction known as the Council," began Aelina. "The Council was formed for a single purpose: to restore the rightful leader of Darhan to the Khanate."

Raim lifted his eyes to Draikh, who looked uncomfortable, his mouth set in a firm line. "But even though I hate him, Khareh killed Batar-Khan's only son, so he *is* the rightful heir of Darhan," said Raim. "And he was confirmed by the warlords."

With surprising swiftness, Aelina stabbed the tip of her dagger into the wooden table. The spirit of Lady Chabi glared at Draikh, her eyes saying far more than words could. "No. That is what Darhanians have been led to believe, but it is not true. Even Batar-Khan was not a rightful ruler. The last true Khan of Darhan was also the last true sage—Hao."

That name rang a loud bell in Raim's brain. Puutra-bar had told him about Hao in Lazar: he was one of the final sages to use his *own* spirit to provide his sage powers, not relying on a broken oath. "He was the one who sealed Lazar with the pass-stones," said Raim, rubbing his chin.

"Yes. After the great battle in Lazar, which saw it burn to the ground and the passage through the mountains sealed by magic, Hao returned to Darhan. That's when he discovered someone else had risen to take his place. Oghul-Khan. The great-great-grandfather of Batar-Khan. He lay in wait to ambush Hao when he emerged from the tunnels, and Hao was killed. His people never knew what happened to him, and no one was able to avenge his death.

"The Council was formed at that moment by Hao's former Protector, a great Yun warrior. She knew a great secret that not many knew: that Hao had a child, and that his bloodline had to be protected at any cost, until the moment when Hao's descendant could take back what was rightfully his."

"There was a problem, though. Hao's Protector did not know where the child was, and she died before she could find him. But before she died, she passed the knowledge of Hao's secret child down to another woman in the form of a promise knot. The Protector's vow became the next woman's oath, and so the generational promise was born.

"Ever since that moment, one woman has been chosen to guard that generational promise and to continue to search for Hao's bloodline. And we, the Council, have grown up around that woman to support and protect her from harm."

Raim stood up quickly from the bench, the sound of wood grating against stone echoing in the large, cavernous hall. "If I can accept this—and I'm not sure I do—I still don't understand what this has to do with me."

Mhara jumped up too. "Your mother—she was the last woman to bear this promise."

"And she was the one who carried the promise when we thought we had found the bloodline," said Aelina. *"Generations* of searching were finally coming to an end. But the only way we could really know we had found the right blood was if we also found the stone: the pass-stone that Hao had with him when he left Lazar. Your mother entered the tribe we had identified as holding the bloodline, befriended them, and found the stone.

"That was where she found your father."

"My father?"

"Yes. If Sola had ordained it, he might be the Khan right now. But we were unaware that Batar-Khan's people were tracking us the entire time. They hatched a plot to slaughter the tribe."

"I was able to get a warning to your mother before it happened," said Mhara. "She had once been my friend. I owed her that."

"The rest of the tribe was not so lucky," said Aelina.

"The last blood of Hao was wiped out in an instant. Or so we thought. But your mother knew better."

"You cannot hear this." Lady Chabi spoke then, and his eyes darted to her face. Aelina noticed Raim staring at the shadow and stopped talking.

"I have to hear this—this is answer I've been searching for!"

"No, you don't understand. *He* cannot hear this!" She pointed at Draikh. "He will kill you if he finds out the truth. He's treacherous and ruthless, just like the rest of his kind."

"*My* kind? How many times have I saved Raim's life?" Draikh asked. "I am the one who has been keeping him safe!"

"Wrong! Twice I have had to save him when you could not or *did not*. You keep trying to get him killed!"

"Enough!" Raim cried out, tired of being caught between the two bickering haunts. Whatever his blood was, it boiled with rage at the woman's accusations against Draikh. He turned to her. "If you had appeared to me in the first place and told me what to do, this never would have happened!"

"It wasn't supposed to happen!" The anger Lady Chabi felt agitated the entire room, and even Mhara and Aelina shied away from the spirit. She closed her eyes, and when she spoke again, her voice was calmer. Softer. "My plan had been to raise you myself to be the khan Darhan needed—there was no need for you to make a vow. But despite Mhara's warning, Batar-Khan's men caught up with me. You were just a baby! I had to protect you and your bloodline. So before they could find you, I made you promise me that when you came of age, you would do everything in your power to take up your rightful place as Khan of Darhan."

Raim's mind swirled with the news, but still one thing confounded him. "But how could I make that vow, if I was just a baby? My honor age was so far away . . ."

Lady Chabi frowned. "I wasn't sure if it would work. But this kind of vow—this generational promise—is the most powerful kind. By forcing you before your honor age to take it, I had to give up my entire spirit. My body is empty. All of me is here, to guard this vow for you and make sure you fulfill it. All I needed was for you to make one vow at age sixteen to *anyone*—other than Khareh."

Raim gritted his teeth, his fingers curled into tight fists. "So you always meant to make me an oathbreaker."

"Yes, but I would have been able to explain everything—just not when you had *him* as a spirit guide!"

"So explain now!" shouted Raim. "What does it mean? That I'm some descendant of Hao?"

Aelina interrupted then. "No, Raim. Not some descendant of Hao. *The* descendant. The only one. The rightful Khan of Darhan."

"What?" Raim was momentarily speechless. Then the anger built again as the news sank in. "But I'm an oathbreaker!" he yelled, his rage exploding out of him like a volcano spitting fire, all directed at the woman who had caused this pain. The woman who had forced him into exile, who had played with his life and expected him to follow a destiny based around a promise he never even knew he'd made.

He jabbed the sleeve of his tunic up over his elbow, revealing the twisted red scar. He held it in front of the spirit's face. "This is what you have left me with. No Darhanian in their right mind will follow me while I have this!"

"I know that," she said, her voice calm and smooth as a lake at dawn. "And that is why I will tell you one thing: how to rid yourself of that scar."

"How?" Raim said, his voice still shaking with anger, his face wet with tears he couldn't control.

"You must make the vow again, to me."

"And how do I do that?"

"First, you must go to the South. Seek out the Council women there and find my sleeping body. I will join you once you reach it." And then, she disappeared.

17

WADI

The weight of two pass-stones now hung around her neck.

Khareh had forced her to keep the one they had taken from the temple. "You will wear this, Wadi, and take the curse upon yourself, to add to the one you already own."

"Why not give it to Garus? He is your adviser," Wadi said.

"No, I don't trust him with this," he admitted.

"And yet you trust me?"

"I can keep you under my control," said Khareh with a shrug. "But also, my shadow trusts you. That's good enough for me."

Wadi stared at the swirling shadow, and the hair rose on the back of her neck. She half believed she could see the shadow staring back—but then cursed herself for getting carried away by her imagination.

She wondered, not for the first time, if Khareh missed Raim as much as she did.

His reliance on his haunt companion overshadowed all his other relationships. Even Erdene, who was his queen, hardly spent any time with him.

Maybe Khareh knew that Raim would come for her one day. She wished she could get a message to him. *Stay safe. Stay strong.* Coming to rescue her would be a suicide mission. She hoped he was not that stupid, but she also knew how stubborn he could be.

In the meantime, while Khareh was keen to keep her close, she would learn all she could. Even if she was only bait to draw Raim out of hiding, at least she could be useful bait.

Like now, for instance. She was standing, chained, in the shadow of a tall pillar in Mermaden's former throne room. She tried to melt into the darkness so that they would forget her presence and perhaps reveal a secret worth knowing.

Khareh and Altan were in the middle of an argument.

"You must spend the night in the city, my Khan. Your new subjects will expect it," said Altan, his voice cool and calm.

"Fine. One night." Khareh threw his hands up in the air and slumped down on what had previously been Mermaden's throne.

Wadi was bemused that Khareh wanted to run back to the yurt when he had worked so hard to take the city. She had assumed he'd want to stay in it at least one night. But then, he had what he wanted—the pass-stone, and the allegiance of the city—so maybe that was enough and he was just going to storm off, leaving this city leaderless and blood-ied, before heading to whatever his next conquest would be.

"But no feast!" Khareh added, as Altan opened his mouth to continue. "I won't celebrate while Mermaden is still alive. Besides, I think the people of Samar have had enough of rulers who celebrate every minor event with a feast, drowning their spirits in drink while they go hun-gry. Did you see the state of the city outside? This is why warlords like Mermaden are fools and need to be removed from their post. Leadership is earned on the steppes, not bestowed. It's time the people were reminded of that."

There was a crash from the hallway outside the throne room, and several shards of pottery came dancing through the open door and across the tiled floor. Erdene was by Khareh's side in a flash, her Yun sword drawn, but when the culprit emerged, her sword-arm dropped.

It was Garus. Under his arms, he carried two barrels, and he swayed from side to side under their weight. "Rago wine, my Khan. Of the finest quality."

"Are you drunk?" Khareh asked, his face screwed up in disgust.

Altan sensed that this might send Khareh over the edge—and back to his camp again. "One night, my Khan."

Khareh hesitated. "But I should be back with my men, my horses—ready to pursue Mermaden in the morning."

"You will still be ready to pursue him, but you must secure the city first."

Khareh sighed and rubbed his temples. "Just get *him* out of here." He gestured to Garus.

This was a battle that Wadi wished Khareh had won. She didn't want to stay in the palace any more than he did. But she and Erdene were forced to stay wherever the Khan stayed. Wadi yearned for the warmth of the yurt—for the comfort of a rug at her feet, the smell of incense mingling with sheep's wool. Even though she was a captive there, it was better than this cold stone palace that reeked of blood and ashes. The hall they were in—Mermaden's old throne room—was bare and empty of almost any decoration, except for six decorated stone pillars.

"Did the men do as I asked? Did they secure the engineers, the men of letters, the artisans?"

"Yes, my Khan," said Altan.

"Bring one of them to me. Take Erdene too, so there isn't trouble."

Erdene straightened and immediately protested. As if in response, spirit-Raim swirled to Khareh's side. Erdene threw a scowl in the shadow's direction. Wadi was impressed. At least she wasn't appearing scared of it. Erdene turned on her heel and followed Altan out of the room.

Wadi was now alone with Khareh. And his shadow, of course.

"I'm surprised at you," said Wadi.

"What do you mean?" Khareh feigned insult.

"You saved those people."

"Of course. As I told you, who else but engineers will help me transform Kharein?" Khareh's face had such an expression of earnest wonder on it that Wadi found herself momentarily speechless. "And the artists?" Khareh continued. "Have you seen some of the stonework in here? We have nothing like this in Kharein."

Wadi raised an eyebrow and found her voice. "I didn't take you for someone who appreciated fine art."

"I appreciate genius," said Khareh.

There was, in fact, something of genius about it. The pillars of the great hall were engraved with beautiful flowing Darhanian script. It must have taken some skill to carve those rounded letters, the delicate links between words. She tried to read it, but it was difficult as the script was old, worn away in places, and written in archaic language. It wasn't worn in the same way that the scripts of Lazar were—artificially, so as to destroy the beauty before it even had a chance to be called beautiful. This was just the telltale decay of age.

The script told of the history of the city, that much was clear. As Wadi's eyes traveled from the ceiling to the floor, the script became much clearer, as if the words toward the bottom were much newer than those above it. Suddenly, she laughed.

"Something funny?" said Khareh.

"You don't want the artisans for the beauty of their work. This bit here tells the story of Mermaden 'the Great.' It's just exaggerating his conquests—and from what you've told me yourself, they weren't that great at all. You said he's just a drunkard and a braggart, not a mighty warrior. This is just his ego carved into stone, and now you want something like this for yourself. You only want the artists so that they can write of your genius, not so you can use theirs."

"History will remember what it remembers. We need works like this in Kharein to immortalize our history."

Wadi scowled. *"Your* history, you mean. But you can't just rewrite everything. There will be those who remember the truth."

"Like who? Please, tell me of them. I will be sure to put them on my list of people to kill."

"You are despicable."

Khareh just laughed.

A series of sharp knocks on the door made them both jump—although Khareh concealed it better than Wadi. He replaced the crown on his head; it wobbled slightly as he adjusted it, then settled, the two fangs of the jaguar skull on either side of his eyes. It was ridiculous. But ironically, it was an impressive sight too. That much was impossible to deny.

"Enter!" said Khareh, putting on his most khan-like voice.

A man in the sky-blue turban of a messenger entered. Dust covered his boots and dirt marred his face in thick streaks. His legs were shaking slightly as he stood before them, and Wadi knew that meant he had been riding hard for several days. Darhanian men—bred from birth to ride—rarely felt the discomfort of the saddle.

"I have ridden seven horses to get here as fast as possible," he said.

"Where have you come from, messenger?" asked Khareh. There was a bench in the center of the room, which the man could sit on if Khareh gave him permission. Wadi saw the man glance sidelong at it. Khareh did not give him permission.

"From the steppes between the river Tyr and the Amarapura mountains, my great Khan. Your men were transporting the captive to the prison at Genar to be tortured. They were ambushed in the steppes by—" The man rasped a dry cough.

"By whom?" said Khareh, stamping his foot impatiently.

"Please, my Khan, if I could just have some water..."

"By whom?" Khareh repeated, louder.

"A band of old men from a cheren."

Khareh burst out into laughter. "You are saying a group of wrinkled grandfathers ambushed a wagon of mine? That my soldiers couldn't handle some decrepit old men?"

"One of the men had a spirit-companion."

At that, Khareh stopped laughing. "He was an oath-breaker? Why hasn't he been rounded up to my camp?"

"No, my Khan. He was no old man—and no ordinary oathbreaker. He... controlled his spirit. He managed to free the captive. We think he was a sage, my Khan."

"Why did you not deal with him? You had spirit-guards with you!" Khareh exploded, and the man cowered in response.

There were several moments of tense silence, until Khareh spoke again, in quiet anger. "How many of my guards survived?"

"One, my Khan."

"And where is he now?"

"I... I believe he is receiving care with a tribe in the east."

"No, no, no. He should have been brought straight here. That is not good." He said the last words to the ground, as if more to himself than to the room. He looked up at the messenger, finally remembering himself. "Wadi, bring this man a cup of water."

Wadi could only just reach the man within the confines

of her chain. Her hands were trembling. *Raim. It has to be Raim.* He was not only still alive, but he was still fighting. She tried to stop herself from sloshing the water everywhere as she took it to the man. Before she handed it over, Khareh asked another question of the messenger.

"Who did you tell about this on your way here?"

"No one, my Khan. I traveled from tribe to tribe, collecting horses in your name, stopping nowhere, to reach you as soon as possible with this news."

"That is good. That is very good indeed. Wadi?" He gestured to her, and she handed the man the cup. He immediately took a long draught.

"Your lordship is most graci—" But before he could finish the final few words, there was a knife buried deep in his chest.

Wadi screamed in shock, then spun around to stare at Khareh. "There can be no other sages in Darhan," he said, his eyes wide, his hand shaking.

"You're just scared! You're scared of Raim because you know he is a good man who can inspire the people! Because he is a better man than you could ever be!"

Khareh's face didn't change. "There can be no other sages in Darhan but me."

RAIM

"She's gone," Raim said, his voice cracked. He looked all around the room, but there was no sign of her. *Can you see her?* he asked Draikh.

"No," the spirit replied. "She won't come back while I'm here. She doesn't trust me. But it doesn't matter. I'm not going anywhere."

I don't want you to. I'd rather have you than her, anyway.

"What?" said Mhara, a confused frown on her face. "What did she say? Tell us everything."

"I need to get out of here," said Raim. Mhara and Aelina recoiled.

"No, not to escape," he added. "I just need some air. Please." Even though the hall was large and cavernous, Raim felt the weight of everyone's eyes on his back—the expectation of the Council, Mhara, Draikh.

Mhara studied him for a few moments, then pointed to the far end of the room. "The door there will lead you outside."

Raim had to breathe deeply to keep from bursting into a sprint. He was used to making his decisions under the great clear sky—whether it was here in the mountains, or before, in the vast desert. If there was ever a time that he needed clarity, it was now.

He had an answer to a question he had long asked: what was the vow sealed within his promise knot? He had promised his mother he would take his rightful place as Khan of Darhan. Now he knew, but he felt even further from the truth than ever before. Every answer seemed to pose a hundred more questions. Knots within knots. Promises within promises. Secrets within secrets. What was it that Zu had said to him once? That he was a maze of mysteries. That was what it felt like: he had been dropped in the center of a maze with no points of reference, no sense of direction. Every corner he turned required yet another choice. Choices he wasn't sure he wanted to make.

For a moment he let himself yearn for the simpler time, the simpler vow. There was a time when he thought his life would revolve around a single knot: a vow to protect his best friend with his life. No ambiguity. No questions.

Nothing was that simple.

Up here in the mountains, it felt like he was glimpsing the magnitude of the world. Up here, he could see jagged crags spread out for miles around him. Those that looked small from this vantage point, he knew stretched for many lengths higher than where he was standing now. Here, tiny trickles spread and grew to great rivers. Here, flakes of snow amassed into devastating avalanches. Here, mountain lions could feast in caves, while just next door goats perched on cliff faces so sheer he would have thought them impassable to those on two feet, let alone four hooves. Life here was complicated, and dangerous.

And was it so different on the steppes, where he grew up? The terrain, perhaps, was simpler—but it was not simple. If anything, it was subtle. He had learned as a boy to tell the difference between the wind blowing through the grasses and the near-noiseless patter of a wolf making its way toward one of his goats. He learned which clouds brought life-giving rain, and which brought fierce tornadoes. He learned the ways of the steppes and how to live on them; now he had to learn something else…the ways of people, and how to lead them.

Once again he thought, *Khareh is far more interested in this than me.*

The night air blew cold against his fingers, and he stuffed them deeper into his tunic, where the pockets were lined with soft fur. Though his toes had turned numb in his boots, he wasn't ready to turn in just yet. He let the wind sweep through his dark hair, blowing what felt like cobwebs from his mind.

The Lady Chabi spirit's words came back to him, along with the enormity of what she asked. *I need to remake my vow to her. Draikh, what have I agreed to? Can I even do it? What about my Absolute Vow to Khareh?* He placed his hand on his chest, over the place where the mark of permanence was seared.

"You vowed to protect Khareh's life, not his throne," Draikh replied. "You can promise to fulfill your destiny as Hao's descendant—as long as you aren't the one who harms Khareh."

So you won't kill me if I try?

"Only if you try to hurt Khareh."

Raim nodded. After a few moments of amiable silence, Raim looked up at his spirit. *Draikh, I need to be alone. Completely alone. Just for a bit.*

Draikh had taught him a trick back in the cheren, something he hadn't really thought would be all that useful—until now. It was the ability to block the flow of his thoughts from his spirit. It hadn't seemed to matter when it was just him and Draikh. But now that he knew about Lady Chabi, it suddenly seemed much more urgent.

Even as he thought about doing it, Draikh tried his best to distract him. "Try blocking *this* out! How are you ever going to become Khan? You've never led a camel properly, let alone a nation. You're just a lowly goatherder boy."

They were all thoughts he'd had himself already, worries that ate at his brain. They were the perfect distraction—so Raim tried to focus on something else. He thought back to the one face that always kept him grounded: Wadi. He built her in his mind's eye from the chin up, focusing on the details he'd had only such a short time to memorize.

She was the first person who had really believed in him, and she'd had to see him through his scar.

Each piece of Wadi's face that he built up in his mind was like a key to a series of locks, closing his mind off from Draikh. As he moved past her dark brown eyes, to the smooth expanse of her forehead, he felt the last walls go up, and suddenly he heard his mind go blank.

Or maybe—he *didn't* hear, was the point. He'd been so used to having voices in his head, this sudden silence was like a new sound for him. *Draikh?* he said tentatively into the darkness of his mind.

There was no answer.

I renounce my bloodline and I'm going to run off this mountaintop right now—you won't be able to stop me!

Nothing.

He was truly alone.

He let himself open his eyes. Draikh was still there, floating not far from him, and he looked uncomfortable. Raim unlocked his thoughts. *Please leave me,* he said to Draikh. *Don't worry, I won't do anything stupid.*

"You'd better not," said Draikh, but he floated backward until he disappeared from view. Raim closed down his mind again.

He was alone now. He was free. He let out a loud whoop and started running, feeling his feet pound across the mountain paths, dodging rocks and shrubs. When he'd finally exhausted himself, he fell with a slump against a large rock, allowing the coolness of the surface to penetrate deep into his muscles. From his vantage point, it felt like he could see the whole world. He even imagined that far off on the horizon he could see where the green turned to gold—the start of the Sola desert.

But of course, that wasn't the entire world. It might have been his world, sure—but there was still so much he hadn't seen. Somewhere, across the never-ending desert that did end somewhere, was Aqben. That was where his mother, the Council, Mhara, even Draikh wanted him to go. But how could he? He knew nothing about the South, and he couldn't see how there was anything there for him. If he was supposed to be the rightful ruler of Darhan, then he was needed in Darhan. And the people of Darhan did not want an oath-breaker for a ruler.

"Do you hear that, world?" he shouted into the open air from the top of the mountain. "I am an oathbreaker. I can't be your khan. Not yet."

Just then he felt a sharp pressure on his mind. It was Draikh trying to work his way back in. Had he been listening all along? Did he know his plan?

Tentatively, he let the wall down again, his resolve like Yun steel.

What is it? he asked Draikh.

"Mhara is coming to you. I think you should listen to her," Draikh said, his voice gently insistent.

Raim spun around to see Mhara standing at the top of the path he had run down. She walked slowly down to meet him, joining him on his perch at the top of the world.

"I still have this," Raim said, to break the silence. He held out her ring in his hand.

She took it from him and rolled it between her fingers. Then she threw it, as hard as she could, from the mountain. "A remnant of my old life. I don't need it anymore."

Raim could keep it in no longer. "How are you here?" he asked. Now that she was close to him, and they were alone, he could see the trauma of the scar across her face, saw the edge of it disappear down her neck and beneath her tunic.

"I thought you were dead," he added. "I searched for you. For so long."

Mhara turned to look at him, and the corners of her lips rose in a smile. "I know you did, Raim. The fall from the cliff... it did kill me. Or—almost." Her eyebrows knitted together in a frown. "My memory of the event is confused, as I know you can imagine. The pain was blinding, until it wasn't. It felt like I had lain down in a deep patch of snow, even though I was on the edge of the Sola desert. I felt nothing in my limbs. I knew that death was coming to take me.

"But I was lucky—if you can call it that. A passing Alashan tribe found me and took me in. They tried to heal me themselves, but I knew they did not think I would survive long. The agony was unbearable. In fact, I think they debated finishing me off. It would have been merciful of them. But then, somewhere far away in Darhan, Khareh was taking his place as the Khan—by killing Batar-Khan.

"That was when Batar's spirit brought me back from the brink of death. He healed my wounds, so I could fulfill my Absolute Vow: to avenge his death. That is what I was sworn to do."

Raim's mind buzzed with questions, but he knew they

would have to wait until later. "How did you end up here with the Council?"

"Because of your mother. Because of our friendship. I had to leave the Alashan—I wasn't going to get my vengeance from there. I knew that the Council would take me in and heal me to full strength. I was broken in many ways by that fall, Raim—not just physically. It took longer than I anticipated to rebuild, and Khareh was growing stronger by the day.

"But when Aelina came to the Council claiming she'd seen a boy with a scar around his wrist he claimed not to understand... I realized it had to be you. And your predicament has haunted me for a long time. I had to find out if my theory was right: that it was Chabi who had forced that vow on you."

"She should never have done that," said Raim, pounding his fist into the rock. It hurt, but not as much as the knowledge that he had been used.

"No, she shouldn't. I don't think she really understood the consequences, either. Her body lies in Aqben, unconscious. She gave up her entire soul by forcing that promise on you. I'm not sure she expected that. She is not the type to want to give up her spirit so easily.

"You would think that a people who have to suffer so much from their broken vows would care more about the consequences, the boundaries. But fear is a powerful thing. Before all this happened to you, when have you ever thought to question what a promise truly meant? Have you ever questioned why the punishment for oathbreaking is so harsh?"

"Never," said Raim. "Well, no, that is a lie. You told me

to question. You told me to think before I made an Absolute Vow to Khareh. Now I wish I had listened to you." He laughed bitterly.

"And now? Now what do you think?"

He thought of the people in Darhan who had to live out their lives away from their family because of one bad decision. No chance to beg for forgiveness. No opportunity to change their fate.

At least he was trying to change his. But it was so hard.

"I think you were right," said Raim. "I don't think I can do this." His voice choked as he made the admission to Mhara. "She told me to go to Aqben. To find her."

"Of course you can do that, Raim. You are Yun. What is past is past, and we make the best of what we have now. Just concentrate on what you can control. Concentrate on what is most important to you. Like getting rid of this." Mhara picked up his wrist and placed it so that the scar was all he could see, all he could think about it. "While you have this, you cannot do anything else. You cannot save your friend. You cannot live in Darhan."

"And I definitely cannot be the Khan."

"Exactly. Now come back inside. We need to plan this route south."

Raim's ears pricked up. "We?"

"Of course. I'm coming with you. You think I would abandon you now? Never."

RAIM

Tarik was led back into the room, looking worse for wear with a large lump rising on his shaved head, at the same time Raim and Mhara returned. Aelina wanted to send Tarik straight back to Qatir, but Raim refused. "He knows too much now. If you send him to Qatir, he will be punished!"

"He will kill me," said Tarik matter-of-factly.

"And what about your wife?" asked Aelina, her arms folded across her chest.

"Solongal? She will have been informed of my treachery already. I am sure that they are preparing her to be moved to another monastery, with, I assume, the rest of the Qatir faction. Have you taken Amarapura?"

"Yes," Aelina replied. "We have control of this monastery now, and I am the leader of the Baril."

Raim put a hand on his brother's forearm. "I'm sorry, brother. For dragging you into this—literally."

Tarik shrugged. "If you hadn't dragged me from the cell, my fate would have been the same. At least here I can learn—and maybe, I can help. These people are telling you to go south. But do you know what you are even looking for there?"

Raim glanced at Aelina and Mhara. "I am looking for my mother, the Lady Chabi, who gave me my first vow."

"And when you get rid of the scar, what will you do then? How can you hope to overthrow Khareh? You have no army, no weapons, and no support. You are just a boy and a shadow."

Raim bristled at the word *boy*, but he couldn't disagree with anything that Tarik said.

"Not to mention the fact that you have to *get* south to begin with," continued Tarik. "A journey that is said to be nigh on impossible. Your ancestor Hao made sure of that by sealing the passage to Lazar. There is more than just a desert separating North from South. There are other things too." His eyes opened wide. "Monstrous things."

"How do you know all this?" snapped Aelina.

"My studies," said Tarik. "I have been studying the history of relations between the North and the South."

"Qatir may have led you to believe that he knew all things, but there is much that the Council has kept hidden," Aelina said. "Firstly, we have a secure passage to the south: a ship."

Raim stood up so abruptly he knocked over the bowl of food he had been given, sending it flying over the floor. "You mean—across the water?"

The only ships he'd seen were the ragged collection of timber planks that made their shuddering way across Lake Oudo. They didn't look like they were made to last for more than a day on a quiet lake—let alone a long journey across the fierce ocean. Not that Raim had ever seen the great salt water. He had never wanted to.

"How have you managed to hide a ship?" asked Tarik, picking his jaw up off the floor.

"The ship anchors near the Temple of Bones."

A shiver ran down Raim's spine. The Temple of Bones was a legendary Baril temple, somewhere across an enormous wasteland that most people believed to be abandoned. Raim had never been there on his nomadic travels. Nor had anyone he knew. There was no pasture there for animals, no game to hunt or plants to harvest. Only death. Nothing lived in the desert, but this wasn't the same. The Sola desert had raw, natural power. The Baril had burned the land around the Temple of Bones to ash so that no one would have reason to travel there. It kept the temple isolated from the rest of Darhan—just as the Council wanted.

"We need to get you there quickly," Aelina said to Raim. "The ship will leave at the next full moon—only five nights away. The captain only has a short window in which he can make the journey safely, before the storms become too dangerous on the open ocean."

"And when you get to the South, what then?" said Tarik, like a dog with a bone he was unwilling to drop.

Aelina threw him an icy glare. "That is the second stage of our preparations. The Southern King has been raising an army to conquer the North, awaiting the arrival of the rightful heir of Darhan to lead his campaign. There are Council members in the South who have been preparing this for far longer than you have been alive, Baril novice! We have waited and waited for the rightful heir to appear, and now that he is here, we are ready to help Raim take back what is his."

"You are ready, but is Raim?" asked Tarik, his voice steady. He turned to his brother. "Do you even know the Southern King's name?"

Raim swallowed. "No."

"King Song," said Tarik, his voice quiet.

"There is plenty of time for Raim to learn everything he will need to know on his journey," said Aelina.

"What are we waiting for then?" said Mhara, still in possession of her Yun impatience for action. "We must leave."

"Tarik must come too," blurted out Raim. Tarik might not have been part of the Council, but he was still the smartest person Raim knew—and he wanted him there. "He knows about the South. He can be useful."

Aelina frowned, but after catching Mhara's eye, she nodded. "We will gather the necessary supplies."

There was a flurry of movement around Raim, the women of the Council each dropping into a bow as they walked past him.

"My Khan," they all said.

It was enough to turn Raim's stomach. He was no one's khan.

WADI

"My Khan—" Altan stopped abruptly as he entered the chamber just moments after the messenger had been killed. The man's body was still splayed on the throne-room floor. "Are you all right?"

"I'm fine. We need to send men and spirits to the steppes between the Tyr River and the Amarapura mountains. One of the soldiers who accompanied the prisoner is injured there. The prisoner has escaped. We need to get him back."

Altan's facial expression didn't change. The man was hard as desert earth. "Was it the other?"

Khareh nodded. "I want him captured, Altan. I need him where I can control him. How could we not find him yet? The messenger said that old men had accompanied him, from a cheren. Did we not search the cherens?"

"I'm not sure that we thought those communities were capable of doing anything."

"I bet it's his grandfather—that old man was always crafty. And after … the incident … Loni just disappeared from the Moloti tribe. I bet it was to that cheren."

"By *incident*, do you mean the fact that you killed a little girl he considered his granddaughter?" shot Wadi, remembering Raim's pain in Lazar. The entire time they spoke, she had barely been able to tear her eyes from the messenger. Her body shook with revulsion.

"I didn't kill her." Even Khareh had the decency to sound pained. "Just … injured her."

"Well, that makes it all better then. Just injuring someone. I see you're getting better now at the killing part!"

"Khareh-Khan, you don't have to listen to this!" said Erdene, who had come in behind Altan. "I will silence her for you."

"No need." Khareh shrugged, took a moment to shake himself of his guilt, then turned with a confident look to Altan. "You have brought people here to see me?"

"Yes, Your Highness." Altan snapped his fingers, and two men were brought forward, one clothed in battle gear, the other in a long white tunic. "These are the last two of Mermaden's men—one of his generals, Imal-yun, and his chief engineer, Regar. The rest fled with him."

Imal-yun stared straight at Khareh, Wadi noticed, his gaze unwavering. By contrast, Regar's eyes kept flickering from Khareh to the shadow behind him—but not with fear, as most people looked upon them; rather, in curiosity. "So it is true," the man muttered.

"Why did you two not join Mermaden in his flight?" Khareh asked.

The engineer spoke first. "I was put in charge of the defense of the city in his absence."

"A brave post, I should imagine, and surely one he should have held himself?"

Regar did not answer.

"And you?" Khareh turned to the Yun warrior, Imal.

"This morning, you suffered a setback, did you not, Lord Khareh?" Imal asked.

"It is Khareh-*Khan,* and what setback did I receive?"

"Your horse was cut from under you by a well-placed arrow."

"It was," said Khareh, eyes sparkling with amusement.

"I shot that arrow." Imal dropped to his knees. "I will happily accept any punishment you see fit to give me, under the watchful eyes of the Undying Women."

"You are a good shot. Not good enough to take *me* down, of course. Surely a Yun should be able to take down a man on horseback—or has Mermaden allowed you to go soft on your skills?"

"Your reputation precedes you, Khareh-Khan," said Imal. "I thought your shadow would catch the arrow, then from that arrow create a hundred more and send them flying back at me, guided by its spirit hand to enter my heart. I gambled that your horse might not have such protection."

Khareh threw his head back and laughed. "That's a good one; I want that recorded in the account of my life.

My spirits catching and duplicating arrows. There's a tale that will inspire fear."

"Very good," said Altan. "What punishment do you wish for the Yun?"

"Punishment? For what? He obeyed the command he was given; he did not betray his leader, nor more importantly did he abandon his city and his people. That is the kind of man I would like in my service. I always need more Yun." He turned to Imal. "Will you join my army?"

Imal-yun was silent for a moment, then carefully looked over Khareh's company—from Erdene to Altan, then finally to Wadi. "My last leader abandoned his post and is running scared like a dog with its tail between its legs. I will join you." He untied the length of string from around his waist. "I will even knot for you, if you will let me."

But Khareh held up a hand. "No. Your word is enough."

"My Khan?" Imal could not hide the shock from his voice. Wadi was shocked too, but she saw that Erdene and Altan were not. Erdene even looked vaguely embarrassed.

"Only one person now holds a knot of loyalty to me. That is enough. Even my new Protector has not knotted— her words hold her. Isn't that right, Erdene?"

"Of course, my Khan," she said, her eyes not leaving the ground.

"You see? So your word will be enough. You are Yun. Your loyalty will not come into question."

Imal continued kneeling, seemingly paralyzed by the events. But Khareh gestured for him to stand by Altan. He recovered and got to his feet, while Khareh addressed the other man.

"As for you, Regar, you are also proven to be loyal to your master, and as you can see, that is a trait that I value highly. You must also be well known to these people if Mermaden sought to put them into your care while he fled. So, I require that your people feed and water my soldiers and their animals. I require that you allow half of your workforce to accompany me back to Kharein. I require that you give me half of Mermaden's wealth, to continue to fund my campaign. If you do this, I will accept your city under my rule and I will be lenient with your people. If you do not accept, I will loot your treasures and set my men on your town, and there will be no city left for you to rule over. Is that clear?"

"As the waters of Lake Nebu, Khareh-Khan."

"Good. Now, you both know Mermaden well. Where will he have gone?"

"Northeast, my Khan," said Imal. "He will try to find sanctuary with the Baril who are friendly to him."

"Where?"

"The monastery of Pennar."

"That settles it then. One night in this blasted palace—one night to get our men rested and fed—and then we will hunt down that traitor." Khareh clicked his fingers, and the group followed him out of the room. As he reached the throne room's great doors, Khareh stopped and gestured at the dead body of the messenger. "Oh, Regar—your first duty as warlord of the city. You might want to clean up that mess."

Wadi fought down the urge to slap him.

21

WADI

They had traveled from sunrise to sunset on Mermaden's tail. They moved at a hurried pace, dogged in their pursuit of the old warlord and his envoy. Khareh wanted to capture him before he reached the Baril temple. Even Khareh wanted to do his killing out in the open air—not in a holy place.

That night, once again for reasons out of her control and comprehension, Wadi was summoned to Khareh's yurt. Even though she had been with Khareh for some time now, every one of these private meetings scared her, as if one day they would turn violent—or, possibly worse in her eyes, intimate. But they never did. It was always the same: Khareh would welcome her like an old friend, and invite her to sit on the cushions in his yurt while he sat opposite.

"I have sent the guards after Raimanan. They will find him and bring him here. Wouldn't you like that, Wadi?"

Wadi didn't say anything. What was there to say? He was most likely planning to kill Raim in front of her.

In the awkward silence that followed, Khareh stared at the two pass-stones around her neck. It made her want to touch the design—it was the habit that always calmed her—but she forced her hands to stay down in her lap.

Normally Khareh's tent was filled with heady scents of incense and sweet perfumes, but today it was earthy, damp—the way a yurt should smell. Wadi was glad, as the other perfumes gave her a headache. But it also set her on edge. Anything that was different always made her nervous.

"These are strange times, you know that, Wadi?" Khareh said, although still he didn't look at her. "Sometimes I wish I had been born earlier—in the time of my grandfather, maybe—when things were simpler. A time when there were no sages but in legends. And I say that even as a sage myself."

"You probably wouldn't have conquered so much so quickly," she said.

"That is true. But I would have got there." Abruptly he turned his gaze away from the stones and slumped onto more cushions. Now this was more like the Khareh Wadi was used to, and she let out a long breath of relief.

"Did you know that there are rumors that a seer has emerged in the East?" he continued. "Not a seer like the fakers who have sat on the throne next to every khan for a generation—so-called Seer-Queens like my uncle's wife, or Erdene, who mysteriously 'passed' the test despite the fact that I know that girl can see nothing past the end of her robe. A *real* seer. One who can see into the future and read the events that are going to take place. And how can I doubt that there might be a seer, when I am a sage? If one legend can come true, why not another? I should find her."

"If she really could see the future and saw you coming, I hope she would kill herself rather than let you find her," Wadi said.

Khareh chuckled. "I know you hate me, but I like talking to you, Wadi. It's because my shadow likes you a lot. He tells me to listen to you, and I trust him."

"You should never have betrayed the person who made that shadow."

"I know." Khareh chewed his lip thoughtfully. "And maybe that's why I like having you around, really. You remind me of that. Not only with your words! Just with your presence. You remind me of where I have come from. Even more than this scar." He gestured to his palm. "This, I can cover up. But I can't cover up you, no matter how hard I try."

"You hurt a little girl to get that scar." She was so tired of listening to Khareh's excuses, his explanations. There was still a fact that remained: he had gained his power at the suffering of an innocent child.

"That is my biggest regret," Khareh said, and Wadi looked up sharply. Khareh's voice was different from how she'd heard it before. It was breaking in a way that his normally confident voice never would. "Raim loved that little girl so much. She was special. She was a great weaver too—so talented for one so young. When Raim asked me to promise to protect her, I didn't even think what it would mean. I just said 'done' and made the knot.

"Then, after Raim fled, I was so blind with rage at the thought that he'd betrayed me only hours after making his Absolute Vow to me that I went straight back to Garus. He was pleased to see that I had taken a vow, and then he reminded me that all I needed to do was break it, and I could be a sage too. That's when it hit me: what I'd agreed to do. I'd vowed to protect Dharma. That meant that in order to break the vow, I'd have to let harm come to her.

"But who would harm her? No one. Only me. I could have summoned Dharma to me—the Yun were searching for the family, after all, in case Raim headed to them for help. But I knew Loni wouldn't have stayed near the city; he would have taken Dharma away as soon as Raim was first jailed. He knew he couldn't help Raim if he was locked up in the city."

"You knew Loni well."

"Of course I did. Raim and I were practically brothers! Loni scolded me almost as much as Altan, and I learned much about 'normal' life from him. Just the ordinary stuff that even Altan can't teach because he's never *lived* it. But Loni is a man of the steppes, through and through. So I knew he would try to run.

"Then Garus told me another hideous thing, which I believed at the time to be a lie but now I know it was true. The Seer-Queen was pregnant, and I was to be stripped of my heirdom whatever happened.

"Needless to say, that made me angry again and I agreed to Garus's plan. We sneaked out of the prison tent, his shadow following us and making me shudder, and stole two horses from where they were hitched at a nearby post. I sent Garus on ahead, then I found the nearest Yun and told him about Pennar—where I had sent Raim. That would at least keep them busy, and send them away in a different direction to me. Then I set off after Loni and Dharma."

"I wish to all the gods that you had never found them," spat Wadi.

Khareh had the decency to look ashamed. "They couldn't have escaped me. I was on a mission now—maybe the most important mission of my life. Garus and I rode North, where I knew Loni would be heading. If Raim had had the choice to go anywhere on his own, it would have been back to the Amarapura, where Tarik, his only other relative, lived. So Loni was heading there too. It was obvious.

"We pursued them for well over two nights and a day. On the third night, they obviously thought they were far enough from Kharein to have eluded capture. They even lit a fire—why would you do that if you weren't confident you were safe? We hitched the horses nearby and approached silently. Doubt still raged across my mind, this way and that, but every time I really doubted what I was about to do, I looked across to Garus and I knew that I was doomed unless I became a sage. Then I could fulfill my ultimate ambition: I could lead the Darhanian people to be the greatest tribe in the known world! I could bring them all the things I had seen in my time as prince that they didn't even know they were missing—education! Culture! Architecture and sophisticated war machines!

"Still, a voice inside me kept telling me how wrong it was. I wanted to listen to that part of me. This was *Dharma* I was thinking about! This was *Raimanan* that I was about to betray—my best friend in the entire world. Was that worth nothing to me?"

"So you have a conscience then? I didn't think that was possible for you," Wadi muttered.

"That's … that's just it. I don't think I do anymore. I lost it, that day that I disobeyed it. I went into the tent first, and the surprise on Loni's face was incredible! He didn't know whether to looked pleased or horrified to see me, but then he looked down at the blade in my hand and knew the correct emotion was terror.

"He railed at me, and came at me, but I pushed him backward and he tumbled to the floor. Dharma didn't look scared, though. She put her hand on her grandfather's arm and told him not to be afraid. Then she turned her face to look at me, her beautiful, round, innocent face and told me to do it.

"I called Garus in and told him to take Loni away. He couldn't do it on his own, but with the help of his shadow he managed to drag the weakened old man out of the tent. As he did so, Loni spat on my shoes. 'You will pay for this,' he said to me. 'But it's for the greater good,' I told him, but without conviction. Still something raged at me inside. *Don't do it!* it said. *Think what you will become … think what you will have to live with! Raim will come back for you and you can build your empire together!*

"That part of me didn't understand. I didn't want to wait any longer. I wanted to be Khan, Khan and sage in one! The thirst was so strong that I... I walked slowly over to Dharma and took her by the wrist. She was still so calm. I held the knife up against her throat.

"That's when I heard another voice. It was Raim's voice, asking me what I was doing. I said, 'Raim, I'm sorry.' Then I tried to use the knife. But I couldn't do it. I couldn't kill her.

"I was angry then that I was too weak to do it. Can you believe that? I thought maybe I could just hurt her... but it had to be hard. It had to be permanent, or else the shadow it made would be weak. And in the end it was Dharma I listened to, not either of the other two voices—my own and Raim's—that were still raging against me in my skull. She said, 'Take my eyes. Please. I don't need them.'

"She was so brave. She acted like she wasn't scared, but I could see that she was crying. I think I was crying too. But then my true purpose flashed through my head. I'd helped a prisoner escape, I'd lost my heirdom to the Khanate, I was nothing—but if I did this, I could have everything. Then everything in my head went silent, and... I did it.

"The tent filled with noise. There was so much screaming—from her, from me—and from my new shadow. As I finished I could feel something within myself ripping, tearing, like my soul was being wrenched in two. Then I felt the sharp edge of a blade against my own palm and looked down in horror to see Raim slicing at me, the ugly crimson-red scar of an oathbreaker appearing on my palm. My mind was a blur—how was it that Raim was here, in the tent with me? He was on the run in Pennar...

"I was pushed aside by Loni, who had broken free of

Garus when he heard Dharma's screams. He tried to kill me himself, but I pushed him away and stumbled out of the tent. Loni picked up Dharma in his arms, bundled her onto one of our horses—since they had none of their own—and fled. Garus asked if he should try and stop them, but I said to let them go.

"I could see better then. I saw the spirit of Raim floating above me, screaming hideous curses in my face. 'What is this madness, Garus?' I shouted at him, and when I looked over at him I saw—not his shadow behind him, but the figure of a young girl. 'The shadow is the spirit of the one you betrayed,' Garus explained to me. 'You must win your shadow's trust back to become a sage!'

"I didn't know how I was going to do that, when I had betrayed Raim so deeply, when I had committed the most heinous act in the world. Why would this spirit ever forgive me?"

"Obviously he did," Wadi said. "I don't know whether to be more disgusted with you or with your shadow. I wish he had continued to haunt and torment you, just like any other oathbreaker! I don't understand how he's come to serve you."

"One day you will. If I didn't have him as a shadow, I wouldn't be a sage, and I wouldn't have control of my sage army."

"Your so-called sage army is just an example of how much of a monster you are. You're just lying to them! They still believe that you will one day set them free."

"Set *them* free? Wadi, is there something you don't understand about being an oathbreaker?"

She hesitated. "What do you mean?"

"I need them to set *me* free."

"I don't ... "

Khareh untied the strings on his tunic.

Wadi sat up straighter and pulled her legs into her chest. The ankle chain stopped her from retreating too far.

"What are you doing?" she said, unable to keep fear from quaking her voice.

"I'm showing you the true consequences of my shadow-army," he said.

As he pulled the ties of his tunic apart, she stopped moving. Jagged red lines crisscrossed his chest where his tunic flapped open. He pulled the tunic over his head, and Wadi gasped.

His entire upper body was covered in promise scars. He turned around, the muscles in his back flexing, making the promise scars move and shift across his skin.

"You see?" Khareh said, putting the tunic back on again. "Leadership requires sacrifice."

"But Khareh ... " Wadi was speechless. Seeing their greatest taboo written all over Khareh's chest and back was too much even for Wadi to feel revolted. Her mind thought her eyes must have lied to her. No one could commit that much betrayal and survive—but the evidence had been before her all along. Her mind had just refused to comprehend it.

"Our biggest test is coming," Khareh went on. "From what I've heard of the Southern King—the mad King Song—he's planning to march on us soon. Do you know what will happen if he reaches Darhan? He will enslave all of us. He would enslave Naran if he could!"

"And what will you do when you reach the South?" Wadi asked.

Whatever moment of softness had come over him, whatever fragility she had momentarily seen in Khareh, it vanished with his next piercingly hard look. "I will take my place as their Golden Khan and make sure they never threaten the North again."

....

Back in her yurt, Wadi slumped down next to the post she was tied to. Erdene had brought her from the Khan's tent. She also gave her a bowl of dried meats, softened by a sprinkling of mare's milk. Wadi wasn't hungry, but she ate anyway. As she did, she studied Erdene. The girl was tall—taller than the average Darhanian, a bit like Raim, and slender. Yun were rarely over-muscled—they were trained in close combat and sword-fighting, but also to be great strategists, expert bowmen, and accurate throwers of knives.

Erdene was wearing a fine robe of silk, pale and delicate against her olive skin. The clothes accentuated the softer, gentler side of her, although Wadi had seen enough of the girl's fierceness not to be deceived by outward appearances. Since becoming the Seer-Queen, Erdene wore a thick layer of red stain on her lips, made from the juice of Rago berries; her eyes were lined with kohl, accentuating their almond shape—make-up that could just as easily become warpaint.

Erdene stared into a piece of mirrored glass, wiping away stray kohl from beneath her eyes. "So, what did the great Khan share with you this time?"

"He is despicable. I don't understand how you can follow him."

"It is not the way of the Yun to question their leader," Erdene said, without meeting Wadi's eyes.

"Even if he is stupid and cruel?"

She laughed. "He is far from stupid. But even if he were ... loyalty is not something you can pick and choose. Once you promise to serve, that's it."

"You said he was not always like this, though. That once he was different."

The other girl paused. "I thought he was different. I mean, he always had this wild ambitious streak, you could tell that, but when he came back with the shadow, he had changed, and we were all afraid.

"He needed supporters, though. I thought if I could show him from the very beginning that he had my loyalty, he would reward me. And in a way, he did. After we overthrew his uncle, he was the undisputed Khan of Darhan. He needed a queen, and he chose me."

Wadi bit down on her tongue. She didn't want to say what she thought about being the queen of a tyrant. But when she looked back at Erdene, she was surprised to see that the girl had tears in her eyes.

"Do you ... do you love the Khan?" she asked, finding it both an impossible thought and an explanation for Erdene's outburst of emotion. "Do you think he loves you?"

"I don't think he loves me. I'm not even sure he likes me." Then Erdene fiercely wiped away the tears and took a deep breath. "But of course I love him. I'm his queen. And

Khareh will protect us." She swept out of the room, leaving Wadi to her thoughts.

There was someone else out there who could protect and rule Darhan. Someone else who was a sage, but who had not done something terrible to gain his power.

Raim.

Wadi thought of his face, and, for a moment, the sense of utter loneliness passed.

22

WADI

"Pennar, home to the monks." Khareh was standing with his hands on his hips, facing the monastery at Pennar across a long, narrow lake. He narrowed his eyes. "Not a great place for Mermaden to stop. We have him trapped." Still, anxiety poured off Khareh like wind from the Amarapura mountains.

It was strange that Mermaden would choose to rest here, Wadi thought. Everything about the situation felt wrong. The whole army had worked itself up into a frenzy throughout the hunt. They were like dogs that came across the rabbit sitting serenely in the woods as if it wasn't about to face its impending doom. It was as if the rabbit knew something the dogs didn't—like that the wolves were on their way.

Unlike dogs, though, Khareh had enough sense to stop. Evaluate.

He gestured to Erdene. "You go ahead to the monastery and check if Mermaden is really there. And take Imal with you." The two bowed stiffly and left to fulfill Khareh's command. "Altan, prepare the rest of the camp."

Once they had all left, Wadi asked, "Why do you always send her away?"

Khareh shifted awkwardly. "I sent her away so she can report back the truth."

"But she just wants to keep you safe. To do her duty as your Protector."

Khareh shrugged off his doubt. "Once I had my shadow guard, it didn't matter whom I chose to be my new Protector. They just needed to be Yun. She didn't ask questions—even once she saw my broken oath. She knew I had power. She was afraid, but I proved my strength to her. I showed her which side was the winning side and, like a smart girl, she chose correctly."

With a rough jerk of his head, Khareh gestured for Wadi to follow him. Wadi restrained the urge to shudder or refuse. If she couldn't escape, then this is exactly where she wanted to be. Close to Khareh. Compiling information she could use against him. Learning his weaknesses—and his strengths—so that when the time came, she knew precisely where to hit him so it hurt.

And the time would come. She clenched her fists. Khareh noticed. "Wadi, you look tense."

She shook herself. Khareh appeared relaxed, but she noticed that his shadow moved closer than normal. "How can you be tense on such a beautiful day, in such a beautiful place?" He flung his arm out wide in a dramatic sweep.

And he was perfectly right. It was beautiful. Wadi could not believe how different the landscape could be from Yelak, after only a relatively short ride. Yes, she had grown up in the desert, which was her home and her first love. The desert could have a million subtle differences, but at the end of the day, you could ride for days and it would still be just sand and rock and the sun's harsh rays. This place ... it could not be more different from Yelak than from Sola. In place of the close forests, there was an endless stretch of grassland as far as the eye could see. The vast blue of the sky melted into the steppes at the horizon. Even though she knew there were mountains and forests nearby, she might believe that the world stretched into eternity.

Directly in front of them, a sparkling lake broke the line of green. This was, of course, the reason that the monks had chosen to build a monastery here. It was a route marker for nomads, a known place of rest. The sunlight danced off the windswept waves, glittering like the jewels on Khareh's crown. Across the water was the monastery—and Wadi was instantly reminded of Raim's story. It was the place that would have been Raim's sanctuary—or, more likely, his tomb. Wadi felt strange being here, like she was walking in his untaken footsteps.

The monastery itself was built of wood—wood that must have taken an age to carry across the grassy plain, likely on wagons pulled by oxen. From Wadi's vantage point, it was a strange mix of sturdy and fragile: big, thick beams that curved softly as they reached up toward the open blue sky, and delicate carvings as intricate as a spider's web. The roof was painted white, so when looking at it from afar it appeared like clouds floating in the sky.

"Pitiful, isn't it?" said Khareh, looking over at Pennar.

Wadi grimaced. "Actually, I was thinking the opposite."

He waved his hand dismissively. "Oh, I know it's the best we can do. But one tired old monk, drunk on mare's milk, knocks over his candle and ... poof! The whole place goes up in flames. Happened three times already. They just keep moving it to a different location on the lake."

"Let things change," said Wadi. It sprung to her mouth before she could stop it: something she remembered her father once saying to her.

"I hate that phrase. Yes, things should change. But only if they're growing, learning, advancing. What's the point in changing if you're just going to repeat the same mistakes again somewhere else?"

Wadi did something she did not like to do. She tilted her face upwards and stared at Khareh. She searched his face, the smooth oval of it, searched his dark eyes, the curl of his lip that, at times, could appear the cruelest mouth in the world.

She stayed focused on his eyes. "And this is what you see as the problem in Darhan?"

He looked straight back at her. "Yes."

Both their attentions were wrenched away by a commotion across the lake. Dust plumed in the air as two horses came riding out of the monastery. Khareh's standard was fluttering wildly in the wind behind them. The same wind picked up the stray strands of hair around Wadi's face. She relished the coolness of it. She had a feeling what was to come would result in a very long night.

Imal and Erdene soon came into view. Altan hurried over as well, a young boy trotting behind him holding the reins to other horses. Imal did not dismount when he reached Khareh and Wadi, but spoke from the back of his mount: "The traitor Mermaden is in the monastery. The monks refused him sanctuary. They have been holding him, waiting for you to come, my Khan."

Khareh's face lit up. "Ah, the monks have been loyal for a change! How nice. Very well." He snapped his fingers and the boy jumped forward, tugging one of the horses with him. Khareh quickly mounted. He turned to Altan. "I think you will need to find another horse."

"But my Khan, there are four horses, and four of us. The savage should stay behind."

Khareh leveled his gaze. "No, there are five of us." He clicked his fingers at Wadi. *"Savage,"* he said, his voice dripping with sarcasm—although she knew it wasn't directed at her; he was mocking Altan. "Get on that other horse. Altan, find another mount and come after us."

Once Wadi had mounted, she scowled at Khareh. "Why do you do that? You know you only make him hate me more."

"He needs to understand his place. And right now, yours is higher than his, whether he likes that or not."

23

RAIM

That evening, under the cover of darkness, their route was due to take them past the ancient Baril monastery at Pennar. It had been a fraught journey so far, their nerves frayed to breaking as several small groups of Khareh's army came within inches of finding them. None of them had dared to sleep, especially once Mhara identified the groups as search parties. Raim guessed that news of Vlad's rescue had finally reached Khareh's ears.

"They're looking for you," Mhara said, as the last group moved out of earshot.

Raim shivered. It had been a close call. "At least they don't seem to expect me to be going south."

As they approached the monastery, Raim pondered the journey he had come on. Pennar had once meant a place of sanctuary, of safety. It was where Khareh had said to meet him so they could solve the mystery of Raim's scar together.

A meeting that never happened.

Now he was going to Pennar, but not with Khareh; instead, he was going with Draikh.

"What are you looking at?" asked Draikh.

I'm worried.

Draikh scratched. "I know what you mean. I'm worried too, and Mhara definitely senses something wrong."

Mhara's demeanor had changed since they'd left Amarapura; a dark glower was permanently etched on her face.

The atmosphere felt too charged, like the calm before a storm. They had chosen the route that went past Pennar specifically because they expected it to be calm. The bulk of Khareh's army had last been spotted far away—in Yelak.

It quickly became clear that they hadn't stayed there. The area around the temple was illuminated by lights from campfires dotting the shore of the lake—enough campfires to indicate an army.

Khareh was at Pennar.

The tension was so thick, Raim could almost eat it.

"We have to change our route," hissed Tarik, as it became increasingly clear that they were heading straight into trouble.

"No," said Mhara. There was a dangerous glint to her eye, something more than just the reflection of the campfires. "We must keep going. This is the quickest route to the Temple of Bones. Khareh won't be expecting us. And the Baril here will shelter us for the night."

"It's too dangerous!" said Tarik.

If Khareh is here, then maybe Wadi is too. What do you think, Draikh?

"She could be," he replied.

Then we have to find out. If there's a chance, even a remote one, I have to try.

Mhara was still talking to Tarik: "You're right, it is too dangerous—for you. Don't come with us into Pennar. You will head around the perimeter, and you will wait one night and day, then meet us at the fork of the river between Pennar and the Temple of Bones. Have horses and supplies ready for us there. Do you think you can do that?"

Tarik looked ready to protest.

"We won't be any more than one night," said Raim, jumping on Mhara's plan. "Take Oyu—you know that I would not willingly go anywhere without him. And if you don't see me when you should … go and find Loni and Dharma. They will take care of both of you."

Tarik hesitated for a second, but then nodded. Raim whistled into the air and Oyu flew down from the sky, landing on his outstretched arm. He slipped the hood over the bird's eyes, and Oyu calmed immediately, allowing Raim to shift him onto Tarik's trembling arm.

When Tarik saw that Oyu's sharp talons weren't going to rip his arm to shreds, he visibly relaxed. He whispered "good luck" to Raim and scurried off, making a wide circle around the temple.

In the darkness, Raim noticed a figure moving toward them.

"He's Baril," said Draikh.

How do you know?

"The light occasionally shines off his bald head."

"Baril?" said Mhara. Raim nodded.

"Good. Let's find out what's going on."

The priest looked as if he was about to retreat, but Mhara drew her Yun sword. "Baril man. You know this sword—this means I am Yun, and I can be trusted. I am a friend of the Council. We seek to stay with you for one night. We won't bother you long."

The whites of his eyes flickered as he stared at the sword. Finally, he bowed his head and gestured for them to follow. Raim's mouth was set in a firm line. Most people did not want to argue with a Yun sword. He was glad the Baril weren't so foolish as to forget that.

The priest led them through a back door of the temple. Luckily, it didn't seem like Khareh had entered the temple yet—but it was unnerving to know he was only a stone's throw away. Once they were inside, the Baril lit a large bowl of straw, which reflected light into the room. It was sparsely decorated, with woven straw matting on the floor.

"Naran take me!" the Baril said as their faces came into proper light. "You are Mhara-yun."

Mhara's hand did not leave the hilt of her sword for an instant. "Yes."

"But you are dead!"

Mhara's silence was enough of a reply. The Baril looked over at Raim but did not recognize him. Only Mhara.

The Baril wrung his hands. "Mhara-yun, I'm afraid you have come at a difficult time."

"Tell me."

"It is Mermaden. He is here, and he is claiming sanctuary."

"And you cannot give it to him."

"No. Khareh-Khan and his entire army are camped outside our doors. They will enter the temple at dawn."

"So he hasn't taken Mermaden yet?"

The priest shook his head, and it was then that Raim noticed the man's entire body was shaking. He was terrified. He wasn't surprised—not with Khareh lurking on their doorstep. Or maybe it was from the presence of Draikh. Sometimes Raim forgot the effect the shadow had on people, even though Draikh wasn't dark and menacing, as ordinary shadows might be.

"Good, that means there is still time."

"I can lead you to a place you can rest—but I'm afraid you won't have long."

"We only need one night," she replied.

The priest took them one level below the ground. Raim's room stunk of damp. There was a tiny window almost at the ceiling that let in the smallest sliver of light and air, and a low wooden cot with blankets. Raim gratefully took the bowl of rice and meat he was offered, then shut the door on the world. Once he had eaten, he crashed down onto the mattress, only carrying one thought in his head as he let sleep take him: tomorrow he would find Wadi.

WADI

The Baril waited for Khareh in a long line, one bald, flattened forehead after the other, occasionally broken up by the occasional Baril woman, who all wore their hair cropped short—but not quite shaven. It distinguished them from the ordinary women of the steppes, who kept their hair long. Khareh stayed on his horse as he traveled through them, regarding them all with suspicion and distrust. Wadi was the second-to-last in the convoy, with Erdene maneuvering herself so that she was behind her. Wadi huffed inwardly at this. As if she was stupid enough to try to escape within sight of Khareh.

Still, the power of the beast she was riding was tempting. She felt the familiar itch in her fingers, the desire to take to the wind while everyone was so distracted.

She quelled that thought. Instead, she concentrated on the faces of the Baril as she rode past them. With the exceptions of Vlad and Zu in Lazar, she had never been so close to the legendary monks before. She was curious to learn where those two had come from, what kind of society produced people who were so intelligent.

These Baril seemed to be much more subservient in attitude than Vlad and Zu had been—but then again, Vlad and Zu had been oathbreakers. They clearly had a rebellious streak. Here, the Baril monks' heads were all bowed as Khareh passed, their eyes lowered to the ground. Wadi was about to turn away, when suddenly one of the Baril women raised her eyes to look at her.

Wadi had never seen so much hatred there. It was written all over the woman's face, in the snarl of her mouth, the flare of her nostrils. Wadi almost pulled up her horse in shock. The mare clearly noticed the sudden tension in her body and began to fret and shudder. Wadi placed her hand on her horse's neck, calming her, and when she flicked her eyes back to the woman, she was gone. Melted away as if she had never been there. Wadi looked over her shoulder at Erdene, but Erdene's gaze was on the other side of the line-up. She stretched up in her saddle to try to see over the heads of the Baril, but even though there was nothing but empty space beyond, she couldn't see where the woman had gone.

Wadi's stomach churned.

She thought about telling someone. But then, whom would she tell? In front of her was Khareh, behind her

Erdene—neither would listen to her. Then there was Imal, who thought she was only plotting to escape. She kept her mouth shut and her eyes focused on the chestnut mane of her horse. Nothing good could come of saying that a random Baril priestess had frightened her. And why wouldn't they hate her? She looked like she belonged to Khareh's inner circle. If she saw herself, she would probably feel the same surge of hatred. They wouldn't be able to see, from their vantage point, that her wrists were still bound together by a length of rope. That she was Khareh's prisoner, albeit a privileged one.

But there was something about that woman's gaze that felt like something stronger than hate. It haunted her as they approached the gates of Pennar and entered the magnificent temple.

Wadi was reminded of the temple in Lazar, although everything here was wood rather than stone. Lacquered wooden carvings ran along the top of every door frame in a web of interconnecting lines. There was a small pool of water in the very center of the first courtyard, with a wooden island in the middle of that. A miniature tree grew on the island, with branches that spread like the wisps of clouds.

Once Erdene entered the courtyard, two Baril closed the gates behind them and Khareh dismounted. The others followed suit, although Erdene came over to help Wadi down without breaking her neck. She hated needing anyone's help, but while her hands was bound, there was no real way for her to do it safely.

"Khareh-Khan, welcome to Pennar. I'm sorry that it has to be under these circumstances—"

Khareh didn't let the priest finish. "Bring me the prisoner."

"He's locked up inside, Your Grace. If you would come in..."

"I have no desire to see inside. Bring him out here."

"Do as your khan says!" said Erdene, drawing her Yun sword. The Baril threw up his hands, clasped them together in front of him, and bowed.

"Right away." He disappeared back into the temple.

"Erdene?"

"Yes, my Khan."

"Find somewhere in Pennar that will serve as a cell."

"For Mermaden?"

Khareh laughed. "No, not for Mermaden. Mermaden is going to get a much more public incarceration, back at our camp. No, I mean for Wadi. The events today are going to make the camp chaotic and frenzied. I won't be able to keep as close an eye on her as I would like, and I don't want that to result in the loss of my most precious prisoner."

Wadi wished the ground would open her up and swallow her whole. She had been lulled by Khareh's attitude—letting her, instead of Altan, ride the horse here, talking to her like she was someone he trusted. Now she was going to be locked away—in a proper cell—for the first time since she had been taken captive.

Erdene stepped over and placed her hand firmly on Wadi's shoulder. She squeezed it in a movement that was meant to be either reassuring or dominant—Wadi wasn't sure. She was in no position to protest, though. Erdene pushed her, and she stumbled toward the entrance of the main temple building.

"You brought this on yourself, you know," Erdene said once they were out of earshot of Khareh.

"I know." She gulped. She caught a glimpse of a lavishly decorated room beyond one of the doors, but that's not where Erdene was directed to take her. Instead, a monk showed them down a flight of stairs leading deep underground, and the smell of damp and rot invaded her nostrils. Khareh had been right—this temple, for all its beauty, had not been well constructed. "Do you think he's going to leave me here?" she said, panic suddenly welling up in her throat. If Khareh imprisoned her for good, she could do nothing to thwart his plans.

"Somehow, I think not. He needs you, doesn't he?"

"I suppose so." For once, she felt grateful for the pass-stones around her neck.

"I think he just wants you out of sight of what is to come. More for your sake than anything else. I somehow doubt he is going to be merciful to Mermaden."

"Will you tell me what he does?"

Erdene set her mouth in a firm line, but only so that she could prevent herself from grinning. The corners of her mouth pulled upwards. "Only if Khareh-Khan doesn't ask me otherwise."

At the bottom of the stairs, they came to a long hallway, with wooden doors placed at even intervals on both sides. Wadi swallowed, hard. "Are these the cells?"

Erdene shrugged. "I've only been here once before, but

this is where some of the more junior monks live. Pennar isn't exactly a prison—it's not built for housing captives—but they have a few barred cells for badly behaved monks further along."

She continued down the hallway. As they passed one door, the hairs on the back of Wadi's neck stood on end, and her palms suddenly becoming clammy inside their bonds. An involuntary shudder rocked her body. It was a familiar feeling ... of shadow.

She looked from side to side, but there was nothing in the narrow hallway. She looked up at Erdene, who was showing no sign of anything amiss except for a bead of sweat that had appeared on her forehead. They were underground, and it was cool.

What is behind those doors? Wadi thought.

They turned down yet another hallway and through a heavy wooden door with a small window in the top. It opened onto a corridor with a lighted torch hanging on the wall. The flame glinted against something: the iron bars of a row of cells. Erdene took a set of keys from beneath her tunic and undid the lock on the first cell. Wadi shuffled inside. It was an empty room—with nothing that even closely resembled a bed, or a chamber pot. She turned around.

Erdene shut the door behind her. Wadi put her hands around the iron bars and gave them a weak tug, even though she knew it was futile.

This time, Erdene really grinned at her. "Here," she said. She took her cloak from around her shoulders and passed it through the bars. "At least have something to lie on."

Wadi took it, surprised at the girl's generosity. Then Erdene spun on her heel and was gone.

Wadi was alone.

RAIM

"Are these the cells?"

The words sent chills running up and down his spine. Raim recognized that voice. He rushed to the door of his room and pressed his nose to the wood, his eye to a crack, but it was so dark he could hardly see a thing. He wanted to open the door, but as the people moved past, he didn't want to draw attention. He saw the flicker of a torch rounding a corner, and the retreating figure of a tall woman, though he couldn't see her face. Her cloak swept up as she turned the corner and Raim thought he caught a glimpse of a shimmer at the woman's side. The shimmer of a Yun sword. Mhara had warned him there might be Yun presence here too. He just hadn't expected to see it so soon.

Not long ago, maybe an hour, if that, Mhara had come

in to wake him. Despite all the anxiety, he had slept longer and deeper than he had in an age. Somehow, though, it made him feel even groggier than usual, sleep clouding his thoughts as Mhara spoke in insistent whispers.

"Khareh is nearby. He sent two Yun to make sure the prisoner was here: the girl, Erdene, and a Yelak Yun, Imal. Both would recognize me."

Raim blinked sleep from his eyes and waited for his sight to adjust to the semi-darkness. "I'm not so sure Erdene would, not with your new hair." He didn't want to mention the fact of Mhara's gaunt face and the new scars that crisscrossed her body. She looked like a woman brought back to life, which was exactly what she was.

Mhara nodded. "But Imal would. We trained together as apprentices. I must be careful. Khareh will come next."

"Was there sign of Wadi?"

"You say she would look more Alashan than Darhanian?"

"Yes."

"I saw no one of that description, but as I said, Khareh only sent a small entourage this way. She may well be kept prisoner deep within the army camp."

Raim cracked his knuckles. "I will get to her." He stood up and pulled on the fresh tunic that Mhara offered him.

"No, it's too dangerous right now. When Khareh comes, he will have this entire place locked down. But once he has the prisoner, he'll want to put on a public display for his execution. That's when you make your move. Amid all the confusion and revelry. Find Wadi, then get out of here to meet Tarik. Nothing else."

"When I make my move . . . what about you?" Raim asked. Mhara avoided his eye. "I won't be with you."

"What do you mean?" Suddenly his heart stopped at the thought of his old mentor not being with him. "You said you were going to come south with me."

"I have my own promise to fulfill," Mhara said. Her eyes flicked to his. "If we plan it just right, then you will be able to get out, and I'll be able to—"

Draikh moved to Raim's side and put a ghostly hand on Raim's shoulder. Raim understood. "No, stop, Mhara. I can't know. If I know, I might try to stop you. I won't be able to help myself. But—will I see you again?"

Mhara shook her head. "I don't know. But Raim . . . be careful." Mhara swept aside the cloak, which rested over her shoulder, to show Raim the holster of her Yun sword. She put her hand on the hilt, and held it there for a second. Then she drew the sword. The magnificent weapon seemed to fill the entire room with light with its brilliance. Encased within the glass-like sword was Mhara's promise knot to Batar-Khan. "Maybe it would be better if you went straight to the South without looking for Wadi. There is still time. You know the place where you can meet Tarik—go there."

"No."

Mhara stared at him, but Raim was no longer her apprentice to be quelled with a glance.

"You might not have a choice," he said. "But I do. And I choose to try to rescue Wadi. Don't worry, my plan doesn't involve getting caught. Plus, I have Draikh, and—I guess, somewhere—Lady Chabi, who will do everything in her power not to see me die before I go south. But if there's an opportunity to find Wadi, then I have to take it."

Mhara still stared at him, but he thought—or maybe he hoped—he saw a measure of respect in her eyes.

And then she had left him, to await his fate.

Hearing Wadi's voice outside his door only reinforced Raim's belief that he had made the right decision. His heart swelled at the thought of seeing her again. This must have been ordained by the gods.

"That was her, wasn't it, Draikh?" he asked. He couldn't really believe that he could be so lucky.

"I'd know that voice anywhere," the shadow replied, and Raim was glad to hear he sounded as determined as Raim felt.

He pumped a fist in the air. Once Wadi was free, they could both escape in the mayhem of Mermaden's likely execution, get to the ship, and go south: together. Once he was free from his scar, he could return to Darhan and try to win the hearts of the people. Part of him wished he and Wadi could leave to find their own place in the world—to have destinies not dictated to them by a strange Council or bound to them by oaths neither of them wanted: the knot around Raim's wrist, and the stone around Wadi's neck. But if that wasn't possible, then he'd settle for them just being together.

It took all of the willpower he possessed not to rush out there and take down the woman with Wadi and free her then and there. He had his Yun training, as well as the power of surprise.

But then—just few moments later—the woman came striding back down the hallway. Raim could hear her heavy boots as she thundered around the corner. His heart stopped for a moment as the boots stopped in front of his door. His fingers closed around the hilt of the sword, ready to strike at any moment, but the woman only sighed and then moved on. Wadi wasn't with her. That meant she had to have been left close by.

Raim let out a long breath.

He waited a few seconds, then pressed his hand against the door and inched it open. The hallway was silent. He slipped out, and Draikh followed. He crept in the direction the women had gone, his boots making just a soft shuffle on the stone floor. He rounded one corner, and then another, and then he saw the flickering of a light up ahead, through a small window in a wooden door. His breath quickened.

The door was not locked. He pushed it open to find a long hallway lined with cells, and another door at the far end.

He heard the sound of an iron bar rattling. "Erdene?" said a female voice.

Raim ran down the hallway. "Wadi!"

"Oh, Sola ... Raim?" Her hands came shooting through the iron bars as Raim approached. They pulled each other into an embrace, the cold iron forming a barrier between them. "What are you doing here?" she cried.

"I've come to free you!" said Raim, taking a split second to relish the sound of her voice.

"Thank the gods!"

They eventually separated and Raim ran his fingers along the gate until he found the lock. "I should be able to break this..."

"How did you know I was here?"

"I've been looking for you for so long, and then I stopped here on my way south with Mhara and my brother...oh gods, Wadi, Mhara is alive! So is Dharma! There is so much to tell you, so much to catch up with. I'll be able to tell you everything on the journey. We need to get to the Temple of Bones, where a ship is waiting for us." He took a dagger out of his belt and flipped it over so that the handle was facing downwards. He then smashed at the lock, trying to get it to spring open.

"South?"

"That's where I can finally get rid of this scar. The woman who gave it to me was my mother—she said that I am the rightful heir to the Darhan Khanate. If I go to her and make that promise to her again, then I will no longer be marked as an oathbreaker, and I will use the Southern King's army to return to Darhan."

"And then you can beat Khareh and take your place as the true Khan." Her eyes opened wide.

Raim blushed. "Well, yes..." He hit the lock again, but it was surprisingly stubborn. The power of the blow resonated through his wrist and up his arm.

Wadi grabbed his hands through the bar and held them tight. "You have to succeed. Please."

A sudden noise from further down the hallway made them jump. "Oh gods," Wadi whimpered. "They've come back to check on me. What if someone knows you're here? They can't catch you, Raim. You have to get rid of your scar. You have to come back here with an army, take back the throne. Then we can change things. Together." She put both her hands on his face. "The people will follow you. I know it."

"I'm not leaving you here." Raim stepped back to the entrance to the cells and slammed the door shut. He took his dagger and jammed it into the lock, to make it more difficult to open.

Then he drew his sword and hacked at the lock on Wadi's cell again. But no matter what, it wouldn't budge. If only he had a Yun sword—that would cut through anything. Plans raced through his mind. Could he get Mhara here? The bird call? *Draikh? Can you do anything?*

Draikh swooped in front of him, sliding through the bars of the cell. He put his spirit-hands to the lock and tugged. But nothing happened. "I don't think there's anything I can do," he said.

"It's no use," said Wadi. "You have to get out of here. Leave me. You have to fulfill your destiny."

"No, I'm not going without you."

"Raim, you have to. But wait...let me make a promise to you."

Raim stopped mid-strike. "What?"

"Let me make a promise to you. Then if I break it I can have a piece of you with me, just like Khareh does. Just like you have Draikh."

"Wadi, you're out of your mind. I could never do that to you. I could never make you an oathbreaker. You don't want that." He hesitated then. What if *he* took a piece of her? He looked at Draikh. If had one spirit, then why not another...

There was a loud bang as something—Khareh's men, most likely—shuddered against the door.

Wadi shook her head, and her voice changed from desperate to insistent. "Go—there's no time! Khareh will bring shadows; you'll be caught and killed. You're outnumbered here. Come back when the fight is more even."

"But, Wadi—"

"Go! Just come back to Darhan."

She spoke the last sentence using her hands, in the desert language of the Alashan. Then she changed the final symbol by moving one of her fingers. The meaning changed to *Come back to me.*

Raim clasped her hand one final time.

And then he started running.

26

WADI

The dagger flew out of the lock, and the door crashed open. Raim had been gone mere seconds—disappearing down the hallway and into the darkness. Wadi prayed he had fled fast enough, even as her heart ached for him to have stayed.

"Why was this door jammed?" asked one of the guards. They raced up to Wadi's cell. She needed to distract them. She tried to act like there was someone with her, and that she was using her body to hide them. The soldiers fumbled with the keys to the cell rather than continuing down the hall. Raim had dented the lock, so they had trouble with the key.

They swung open the iron bars and kicked at the cloak that lay in a heap beside Wadi; she'd bunched it up with her feet to make it look more human. But there was nothing there.

By then, Khareh had caught up with his guards. He strode into Wadi's cell.

"He's here! He's been here! Have you seen him? Where is he?"

Wadi stared up into his face. "Who?"

"You know who!" he shouted. "Raimanan! He's been here." He looked down at the cloak, then at the stupefied faces of his guards. "You idiots, he's getting away! Follow him down the hallway...come on! Go! Go!" He rounded on Wadi. "Where is he? What did he say to you?" Khareh was pacing the cell, yelling the questions at Wadi, but not waiting for answers—not that she wanted to give him any.

"He's been here! You've seen him!" he yelled at her again—statements, not questions.

Finally, tears welled up in Wadi's eyes, despite the fact she tried her best to keep them down, and all the emotion of the past few moments came crashing in a huge wave over her. "Yes! Yes, I have!" she blurted out.

Raim had been there. He had been so close to her. They had...they had kissed, and it had all happened so quickly that she could barely remember if the touch of his skin had been just a dream. Maybe she had hallucinated his appearance. That had to be less insane than the thought of him actually being here, with her, and then leaving without her by his side.

And if he had any sense, he would be heading south without another thought of her. The likelihood of her seeing him ever again...

Staring at Khareh's wide-eyed, bright red face, Wadi realized that Khareh was the only person who cared about seeing

Raim as much as she did. She wanted to love Raim; Khareh wanted to kill him. She spoke her next words quietly, but Khareh was listening. "I tried to get him to make a vow to me too, but he wouldn't."

Then she regained her senses and remembered whom she was talking to. She flew at Khareh and began pounding at his chest before his shadow swept down on her and pulled her away. "He wouldn't let me have a part of him!" she sobbed. "He wouldn't let me have any of him because you already have too much! It's all your fault."

She launched herself at Khareh again then, but it was half-hearted, the emotion already leaching her muscles of their power. The shadow let her loose, and Wadi collapsed against Khareh. She beat at him with her fists, but to her surprise, he just held her until she stopped, too weak to continue. Too surprised, maybe, to feel the tenderness in his touch.

She pulled away from him and looked up into his face.

"I know," he said. "I know what it feels like. I just wanted to see him too. I just want him to be here."

There seemed to be an intense war of emotion struggling on Khareh's features: anger, sadness, betrayal, hope. Wadi tore away, disgusted with herself. She withdrew into the corner, curling up into a ball in the ground, not even caring that the shadow stood between her and Khareh. A part of Raim stood between them.

Finally, an emotion won on Khareh's face. Anger. It would always be anger, because Khareh knew almost no other feeling. "And now he has left me for good," he snapped. "He could have stayed here and explained himself, but he chose to leave.

Again. He will pay for his foolishness. My guards are after him. He won't escape me again." He looked down on Wadi in the corner. "Get up."

"What?"

"I said, get up! You're not staying in this cell any longer. If you had been with me then I would have seen him too. Then we would both be in the same position."

Wadi considered resisting, but the thought of being kept in the cell any longer while Raim was out there made her stomach heave. She scrambled to her feet. Two guards stepped up to rebind her wrists. She stumbled after Khareh, who was striding back upstairs.

Altan was waiting for him at the top.

"Has he been found?" Khareh asked. Desperation tinged his voice.

Altan shook his head. "There's no sign."

"We're on the steppes, for Sola's sake! No one just disappears on the steppes. I'll send spirits after him. I'll send the army! If we found Mermaden, we can find Raim."

"My Khan, may I speak freely?"

Khareh gestured his agreement with an impatient wave.

"Mermaden still needs to be made an example of. He is a threat to your reign by his refusal to acknowledge your leadership. On the other hand, Raim is a traitor on the run. He has no followers to speak of; he is weak and dumb as an ox. You have all you need of him in your spirit-guard, who has already proved more useful to you than the boy himself. He can run, but no matter where he runs to, we will find him. Tonight, let your priority be Mermaden."

Wadi could read the confusion warring on Khareh's face.

"Don't let him—or *her*—distract you," Altan said, with a pointed look at Wadi.

As if a mist cleared from Khareh's eyes, his shoulders dropped and his breathing calmed. "Fine. I won't." He turned to look at Wadi, and she could see that any trace of another side of Khareh had gone. "You hear that? Raim is nobody. He can run around the steppes like some poor lost sheep if he wants, but you should remember that I am the wolf. And the wolf always wins."

WADI

The party was wretched. Raim was not mentioned again, and Khareh seemed too busy being entertained by twirling fire dancers, dancing women, and horse games that tested each rider's skill to care about his friend on the run.

They were sitting on a low platform of wooden planks, raised up just off the ground by small boulders. Great spits of roasted goat hung over open fires and vats of fermented mare's milk and Rago wine were being passed around the hungry horde. Even though the Baril had been loyal to him, Khareh seemed to have no qualms about raiding the Pennar monastery's stores of food to feed his army.

For all the merriment that spun itself around her like a web, Wadi retreated behind a wall of solitude. She wondered if Khareh was being extra cruel, extra ruthless, for her sake. He was so intent on being that person—the cruel one, the evil one—it was impossible to believe he could be anything else.

Or maybe he was doing it to make sure that she would think of nothing but what was happening in front of her eyes. And Khareh was clever, so of course—he was right. She had never seen anything more horrific, but she couldn't tear her eyes or mind away.

In front of them was Mermaden, the former ruler of Samar. He was stripped to the waist, bound to a post on his knees, his forked beard matted with dirt and sweat. He was not allowed to eat, but all the food was passed in front of his face, torturing him. Still the old warlord refused to show a hint of discomfort, and held his head high. Wadi was almost impressed. Khareh munched on a leg of meat, ripping at it with his teeth. He should have looked so undignified, but somehow he succeeded in looking powerful.

Wadi felt a low rumble in her own stomach.

"Wadi, eat something! You're allowed," Khareh said, in between mouthfuls.

She didn't look at him, and didn't reply. Her treacherous stomach rumbled again anyway.

He laughed and waved a meat-laced bone in her face so that she had to pull back and away from it. She was hungry, but she wasn't going to give Khareh the satisfaction of seeing her participate in the feast.

Eventually, to her relief, the food was cleared away. Khareh was red-faced, but while men around him were near to lolling on the ground—sated on too much food and too much fermented milk—he wasn't close to drunk. That would involve him losing too much control. "Look at them all," he muttered, half to himself and half to her.

"Disgusting."

Then he stood and raised his hands up to the sky. It took a moment for the merriment to die down and for the men to notice that their khan was demanding their silence. Mermaden noticed, though, and his eyes glared at Khareh. *Mermaden should be more careful,* Wadi thought.

Khareh clicked his fingers, and two of his shadow-guards, looking like swirls of gray smoke to Wadi, floated up onto the low wooden platform, carrying between them a large carpet. A few of the eyes around her bulged. Strange sights like a carpet moving of its own accord were still so unusual—even though they were becoming more commonplace under Khareh's rule.

Mermaden, at least, managed to remain unmoved. He would have only heard rumors of Khareh's power, since he had never seen it for himself—nor had he witnessed the attack on his city. He had gone straight into hiding, and then fled. *Coward.* Wadi felt a surge of anger toward him. *You should have stayed and fought.*

"Mermaden, formerly Lord of Samar, do you recognize this?"

Mermaden stared from Khareh to the carpet and back, but did not reply.

"You should. Look closer."

His command was to Mermaden, but the strange tone of his voice encouraged them all to look more closely at the rug. Thousands of tightly woven threads formed intricate patterns that looped and swirled across its surface. Yet what immediately stood out was the fact that the rug had a hole in the center of it—as if a portion of the pattern had been sliced out. Looking even closer, Wadi could see that Khareh's own seal appeared at the top, a jaguar surrounded by a hexagonal green pattern. At the bottom was the symbol she had seen above the gate to Samar. The symbol that used to belong to Mermaden. This was the rug that was supposed to seal Mermaden's promise knot to Khareh. Even she knew that. She had spent many hours staring at the other rugs of fealty in Khareh's possession, often the best alternative to having to look at the man himself.

Mermaden's face lost some of its color, and Wadi thought his impassive exterior was cracking ever so slightly.

Khareh noticed. "Ah, so you do recognize it." He raised his voice so the rest of the crowd could hear. "This is the carpet that I had specially commissioned from the Una tribe, to bear this man's oath to me in the most honorable way possible." He looked down at Mermaden. "I am going to give you a rare opportunity, Mermaden. Pledge allegiance to me now, and I will spare your life. You can return to Samar and live out your days as my vassal, but with your freedom. What do you say?"

Mermaden struggled to his feet then, every muscle in his shoulders and back straining against the bindings of his wrist against the pole. He kept his gaze locked on Khareh's, never breaking contact, and Wadi got a glimpse of the warlord who had ruled over Samar for so long.

"I will never knot with you, you oathbreaker khan!" Mermaden's voice was a low rumble that built to a thunderous shout. "Your uncle should have killed you as soon as he knew he'd have his own heir. It's the only way to deal with treacherous pretenders like you."

"I am not an oathbreaker, I am a sage!" Khareh roared back, his voice louder than Mermaden's. It was amplified as shadows swirled around him, raising him up above the platform, his arms outstretched and his head thrown back, cloak billowing in the wind. Wadi felt the breath leave her lungs, felt any warmth in her blood desert her as she observed Khareh's enormous display of sagedom.

Even Mermaden cowered, his knees buckling beneath him.

Khareh descended again, and when both his feet touched the ground there was absolute silence.

"I offered you the choice," he said, his voice barely above a whisper—but no ear missed it. Then he turned to his army. A feverish buzz swept over the crowd as they all began to talk about what they had just seen. "Every soldier here has witnessed that Mermaden has refused my knot. Should I show him mercy?"

"No!" cried the crowd.

Wadi was watching Mermaden. He was sinking now, sinking down into the floor—his former display of pride cracked and broken. His long beard was trembling, his mouth mumbling meaningless words.

Khareh looked down on the pitiful man. "Since you were a warlord, I will do you one honor. I will not spill your blood upon the ground."

"Thank you." The man's voice sounded like it was being scraped across muddy ground, or as if his tongue had been stung by behrflies. Every word was preceded by a ragged breath. "May...may the gods shine down on your boundless mercy."

"Mercy? Who said anything about mercy? In my opinion, it would be a shame to see such a beautiful carpet go to waste. Now, at least, it can go some way to demonstrating the true extent of my justice. What could have been your salvation...now will be your tomb."

The reality of what was happening finally dawned on Mermaden. "No. No. Do not do this. I will promise whatever you would like. You may take my city, my oaths...please."

"I already have your city. I have your people. I have your lands, and your animals, and your forests. And as for the oath? I gave you the chance, and you refused it. A knot from you now would be worth less than nothing to me. No. You shall die."

The shadows moved the carpet so that it was flat behind Mermaden's back, encompassing his bound wrists and the tall wooden stake. Then they rolled it around him as he screamed. Khareh signaled with his hands, and drums began to play, and even their low vibrations grew to overtake the sounds of Mermaden's protests. Wadi didn't take her eyes off the warlord's face as the carpet closed around him, encasing him in its knotted tomb.

Human guards secured it with ties used to strap down cargo onto camels' back. Then they lifted one of the planks that formed the makeshift stage. They lay Mermaden down on the ground, and replaced the heavy wood on top of him, as if he were a boulder rather than a man. Khareh brushed his hands together. "Now that the coward has been dealt with, let us feast again! People of Darhan, I am your Khan! More than that, I am the Golden Khan! I will make our people the greatest under Naran's great sky. I will control the world we live in. I will ensure that no one but a true Darhanian warrior rules these grasslands, and the lands we have yet to discover. This is our world!"

Cheers went up from every corner of the camp, and even more as word of Khareh's speech spread to the outer reaches of the crowd. Khareh was cruel, but Khareh was powerful. And power was attractive. Power was magnetic. Power made people forget.

Wadi did not forget. Not as Khareh moved all of his entourage off the platform, and invited the main act of the night up: a pair of women who danced on the back of an enormous elephant wearing a headdress of elaborate crimson and gold, its gray hide decorated with thick ropes entwined with gold thread. The dancers wore lightweight tunics that flowed around their bodies like water around a stone. They were a graceful duo, using the elephant's vast size to balance and perform feats of daring that shocked and awed the crowd. The elephant was trained to perform its duty perfectly, lifting its feet in time with the hypnotic beat of the drums. As it stepped across the platform, the wooden planks creaked and splintered under its weight, but it never once lost its balance. A second elephant joined the first, and as the two enormous beasts performed their elaborate dance, the platform dipped and eventually broke, the snapping of wood joining the music like another instrument.

But all Wadi could think about as the elephants performed was the man trapped in a carpet underneath the central wooden slat of the stage, being trampled to a bloodless, and yet far from painless, death—and all at the hands of a merciless man.

RAIM

Come back to me.

Not for the first time, Raim felt his heart twist inside his chest. Not for the first time, he thought about turning back.

Not for the last time, Tarik had to convince him to keep going. Raim had run from Pennar so fast that his feet seemed to fly over the ground. *I will come back to you, Wadi. But not like this. I'll come back when I'm no longer an oathbreaker.* The words hardly convinced him.

Tarik had been waiting for him, just as they had planned, and Oyu too. Tarik had bartered for two sturdy steppes ponies, which had carried them right to the very edge of the blackened, scorched wasteland that led to the Temple of Bones. They let go of the horses, and watched as they galloped off across the steppes in search of greener pastures.

Raim wished he could join them. Instead, he dropped down to one knee and picked up some of the scorched earth in his hands. It ran through his fingers, so dry it barely stuck to his palm. It was different from sand, though—this was burnt soil, devoid of any moisture. Here should have been more grasslands, more greenery, something for the ponies to eat. But instead there was nothing but death.

Why would the Baril do this? They must have had a lot to hide—like the Council with their ship. For any Darhanian, the sacrifice of grassland was almost inconceivable.

He pounded his fist into the ground.

She's my life, Draikh. What have I done, leaving her behind?

The shadow swirled in front of him. "You heard what she said. You have to come back stronger. You have to come back ready. What are you to her now anyway? An exile? A fugitive?"

An oathbreaker.

"Exactly. Come back to her a khan. That is, if she hasn't crowned herself Khan first."

Raim laughed. *She would do better than either of us.*

"That's for sure," said Draikh. Then the shadow shuddered and swirled in the air. "She might have help, if Mhara has her way."

It was the same thought that had been lurking in the back of Raim's mind. His former Yun mentor hadn't told him her plans, but it wasn't hard to guess. Mhara had been brought back from the brink of death for a single purpose: vengeance for Batar-Khan, whom she'd sworn to protect. She wasn't going to miss that opportunity when the culprit in his death was right there. And there was no better shot in

Darhan than Mhara with the right weapon. *Mhara is following her own path.*

"Come on," said Tarik, mistaking Raim's silent conversation with Draikh as hesitation over continuing their journey. "We can't be far now."

Raim reached over and put his hand on Tarik's arm. "I know I haven't been the easiest companion, brother. Thank you."

Tarik stared at him. "I can't go back. I can only go forward. But you and the Council have offered me the chance to learn more about the world than Qatir-bar ever did."

"Well, thank you, anyway. Do you miss the Baril?"

"Miss what? Waking up at daybreak to scrub the floors with blades of grass? Scuttling along a cliff face trying not to slip to my death while trying to shear fur off a mountain goat? Copying page after page of books on the ancient history of butterflies? No, being a Baril apprentice wasn't exactly what I expected."

Raim thought back to his brother's wedding day, and the years of preparation he had completed for that moment. "You seemed happy," he said with a shrug.

"Solongal and I used to compete to see who could copy the most pages. Those were the most fun moments." Tarik smiled ruefully. "It wasn't much. This, though, is real discovery!" He reached into the folds of his tunic, and to Raim's surprise, he pulled out a thick fold of paper. "I've been writing down what you and your shadow can do. It's fascinating! And tell me how many Baril have been to the South in the past century. I can document it all. If I can learn from this, I could come back the most learned Baril, and see if they dare treat me like an apprentice anymore." Tarik's eyes flashed, and Raim smiled at the fire racing in his brother's blood.

Yet Tarik also saw the tightness in Raim's shoulders that belied his worries about what he was getting into. "Look," Tarik said. "You have a right to be nervous. Serving Khareh is all you've ever known. Trust me, you could talk of nothing else growing up. But if you want to do the best thing for yourself, your family, your way of life, your people ... you have to learn to think like a leader. And that's going to take time."

Raim had never before rebelled against things he *had* to do—duty was drilled in to him as deep as any vein—yet this opened a fear in him he wasn't sure he could easily ignore. He knew how to follow, not how to lead. And he was afraid of how much this journey south felt like he was running away from his problems, when what he wanted to do was stay in Darhan and fight.

That was when Draikh came and floated in front of his eyes. He wouldn't let Raim look anywhere but directly at him. "Fight. Yes, Raim, that's what we all want you to do. But fight when it is fair. Fight when you can win."

He understood.

They kept walking. He could sense eyes around him, as could Tarik, who glanced nervously in all directions.

No one approached, even as they continued to walk further into the barren land. The place grew stranger as they progressed. The wind picked up, tossing the thick black strands of Raim's hair. He licked his lips and tasted the sharp tang of salt—the air seemed to cling to his skin. It stung the inside of his nostrils.

That was when Tarik let out a loud cry.

"What is it?" asked Raim.

But then he saw it too, even without following Tarik's outstretched finger. In front of them, the horizon rose and fell, swelling like a beast taking a breath. It shimmered in the dying light of Naran's rays.

The sea.

Raim had never seen it before—neither of them had. They approached the edge of a steep cliff that fell straight down onto a rocky beach. Of course, there would be a cliff here. Sharp cliffs broke the land across Darhan, marking the border of the Sola desert.

The view from the top of the cliff brought other wonders too . . . like the Temple of Bones itself, on a headland jutting out into the waves, almost as if the sea was eating away at the land it had been built on. Raim wondered if it had always been like that, or if the sea had crept closer with every passing year.

From his vantage point, the temple looked like any other he had seen—built of layers of wooden planks, though the side facing the sea was covered in barnacles. For some reason he had expected the Temple of Bones would be made of just that—the bones of the damned—but perhaps it was just another story designed to keep curious people away.

And just beyond that, the most unbelievable sight of all: a ship. A proper ship. Bigger and more terrifying than anything else he had seen sitting atop water. It filled his lungs with fear, and that fear threatened to drown him. He took a breath, to remind himself he still could.

A voice sounded from just beneath their feet. A Baril priestess stood below him, on a pathway cut into the cliff face. "Come on, then. Let me take you to meet the captain. There isn't much time."

WADI

Wadi tilted her head back against the wooden post in the center of the yurt. It was funny how in a way this had become her safe place in the center of the maelstrom. Khareh could be ravaging the world around her, and she could just shut her eyes to it for a few moments.

Her memory would let her think of nothing except the night's events, overpowering even the joy of seeing Raim again. She had witnessed Khareh at his most brutal, but also at his most powerful. She remembered Mermaden's message to Khareh before the battle began—the sickening heads of Khareh's emissaries, who had only been messengers, slung around the neck of the only survivor. These men should have been protected. But brutality ruled on the steppes, and Wadi understood that.

But not cruelty.

There was a burst of commotion and Khareh strode into the yurt. He looked drawn and tired, with dark circles like bruises underneath his eyes. Wadi shifted against the post.

"Don't stand, Wadi, I think we're beyond that now."

Wadi swallowed hard. She had to seem normal. "Tired, are you?" she said, trying to appear defiant again rather than scared or shocked. She hoped she was hiding the shake in her voice better than she felt.

Khareh's eyebrows rose, and she clamped her mouth shut.

"You're acting strangely. I suppose you think Mermaden's death was too much. You understand that I had to show him—or rather, show the tribes—who is in charge?"

"What, so you think having someone brutally trampled to death is the way to prove your strength? Please." This time, Wadi didn't need to pretend to be defiant.

"It's what they expect. They need to see their leader as powerful."

"You're not powerful; you're cruel. You enjoy it."

"I don't."

Wadi's lips formed a thin line. But something in Khareh's demeanor changed. He placed his head in his hands. "I don't enjoy it," he continued. "I have no choice. If I show weakness, that will be the end. Altan says already I show too much weakness."

Wadi scoffed. "How could that be? I could call you many names, but weak would not be one of them."

He shrugged. "Because of you. Because I haven't had you killed or locked away. Because I let you talk to me like this."

Wadi didn't respond to that. She knew Altan didn't like her, but she hadn't realized how much poison against her he was pouring in Khareh's ear. Maybe even more surprising was that Khareh was ignoring it. She looked over at the young khan and took in the gray tint to his skin, the sheen of sweat on his forehead. She had to admit that he looked genuinely distressed. "What you did to Mermaden was unnecessary—and cruel."

Khareh nodded. "I know. He was a bad ruler, though. He ran from his people when they needed him most. He vowed to protect that city, and he failed in his duty."

"I'm not saying he was a good ruler. He deserved punishment. But it's a fine line..." Even Wadi didn't know how to continue. She knew nothing about how to rule a nation.

"A line I crossed, but trust me—it is not easy to see where it is. Maybe I got it wrong." Khareh stood up then and began pacing the perimeter of the carpet. "Do you know how long I've been preparing to be a khan?"

Wadi just stared at him.

"My whole life," he continued. "When I wasn't studying old Baril manuscripts with Altan, I was being trained to fight, or I was sitting in on meetings with my uncle. Every moment of my life has been about manipulating me, shaping me into a great leader."

"I don't think any amount of training can prepare you for this," Wadi said, gesturing to the yurt, but meaning the entire situation. "And no great leader would have betrayed his best friend like you did."

"I realize that now," said Khareh. "Raim was my *only* friend. He was the one who distracted me from my training, but also the one who pushed me to be better. He would have been loyal to me to the very end. But don't you see, Wadi?" Khareh came right up to her then, grabbing her hands in his own. She tried to pull away, but he held on tight. "That's why I have to make this work. I can't have broken my vow to him for nothing."

A tear rolled down his cheek, streaking the ash on his face from the campfires. "I am not always cruel," he said.

The curtain to the yurt flew open, and both turned their eyes to the bright light. Wadi could just make out a tall, shapely silhouette.

"My Khan, I have a surprise for you." The words died inside her mouth. It was Erdene. Her eyes darted from Khareh's face to Wadi's, and then to their hands, which were still clasped together.

Wadi snatched her hands away.

Erdene's face turned a bright shade of crimson.

"What's..." Then she remembered herself. She clenched her fists at her side and adopted her normal, sneering expression. "Well, doesn't this look cozy," she said.

Khareh stood up slowly and turned his back to Wadi. He walked over to Erdene and kissed her on both cheeks. The girl stood as rigid as a board. "You said you have a surprise? What have you planned for me?"

Erdene bowed her head. "It's just a small thing, my Khan, but I have arranged a tournament for you, like the games held during the Festival. A tournament of Yun."

One of Khareh's eyebrows rose. "I thought Yun didn't fight each other, except on the battlefield?"

"We have made an exception for you, my great Khan."

"Well then, what a treat! This should be a sight to see." He swept past Erdene and out of the yurt.

Wadi braced herself for Erdene's wrath, wondering what vile barbs would be thrown her way by Erdene's sharp tongue. But none came. Instead, Erdene narrowed her eyes into a look so deadly and full of hatred, Wadi felt her throat constrict and her heart pound at full speed in her chest.

Then Erdene left, following behind Khareh. But Wadi knew it was not over between them. Another reason to have to watch her back.

She tilted her head back against the pole again.

WADI

They were outside again, and it seemed to Wadi as if Khareh's army had doubled. More of the nomadic tribes had traveled to see the mad—but brilliant—new khan, and to pledge their allegiance to him so that he would not move to attack their people next.

Khareh was back to his normal self—a different man in front of his army than the boy Wadi knew in the yurt. He sat up on his makeshift wooden stage and made Wadi and Altan sit just off to one side, watching as the tribes made their pledges.

The warlords presented him with gifts, from rich pelts of fur to stunning varieties of promise string, and necklaces made of teeth from rare animals. One of the most impressive gifts was a set of throwing knives, their handles carved out of bone.

It made Wadi's fingers itch—not just for the revenge she could wreak, but also for the sheer pleasure of fighting with knives. It had been her speciality in the Alashan tribe, and made her yearn for home. The desert was a harsh mistress, but the one who had made her into the woman she was. With the knives, she was as dangerous as a sand snake, lightning fast and deadly accurate.

Khareh caught her expression and teased her by placing the knives in a woven basket almost within her reach. With all the Yun and the guards around, though, any attempt by her to reach them would likely result in her death.

Khareh let most of the warlords make their presentations without too much fuss or interrogation, sending them back to their tribes with all their limbs and most of their dignity intact. Maybe he was learning. Wadi dared to dream.

Erdene was as good as her word, and once the tribe leaders had made their pledges, she announced the start of a Yun contest. As darkness descended around them, and the moon rose to hang high in the sky, a hush fell over the army that only something truly awe-inspiring could cause. Wadi craned her neck to look. At first, she couldn't see anything. But then the crowd parted in a smooth motion, like scissors through cloth.

Even once they came into sight, Wadi couldn't really tell what she was looking at. She wasn't sure she could even believe her eyes.

The Yun were in their ceremonial garb: long, midnight-blue cloaks edged with gold, tied with a thick leather belt, and breastplates of boiled leather pieced together like snakeskin, which allowed them both freedom of movement and protection. Each had a leather shield lashed to their left arm, and they carried their dazzling Yun swords straight up and pointing at the sky. The swords bent and dispersed the light from the fires and the moon, looking as if each sword took the light and drank it in, then pumped it through its blade like blood through veins.

But the swords didn't compare to the final element of the Yun garb: the mask. The masks were cast from the face of Malog, the very first Yun, whose face had been brutally disfigured by a rival khan. Dressed in that mask, all the Yun looked the same, distinguished only by their heights and body shapes. But even so, it would be hard to tell them apart from each other. Wadi knew Lars and Erdene best, but she couldn't pick them out from the line-up of Yun. Even their boots, trimmed with silver fox fur, were all the same.

They paired off and fought, one by one. The sight of them was mesmerizing, like watching two people dance, not fight with swords. None of them lacked any training; not a single one had slacked off in their duties. As they were dueling, Wadi kept noticing something else—the knots encased within the translucent material of the swords.

There were dangerous moments too. One Yun's sword came down across another's shield so hard that the leather snapped and blood spilt from an arm wound. The Yun cried out in pain, and the other stopped his approach.

"Keep going!" shouted Khareh. "There's no reason to stop—he's not going to die from that!"

But when the wounded Yun pulled the face mask off,

it was Erdene. Khareh bit back a protest of annoyance and waved her off. She left the field, her head hanging in shame.

Khareh wasn't the same after that, and no longer enjoyed the contest the way that he had previously. *Good,* thought Wadi.

The other Yun were unsure how to proceed now that Erdene was not there to lead them. They didn't want to continue fighting each other if they didn't have to.

Then one Yun stepped forward. Wadi wasn't sure whether it was man or woman, but whoever it was, they were bold. They pointed their sword straight at Khareh.

Wadi tilted her head to one side and tried to guess. The Yun looked the same height as Imal, and stood with the same easy confidence.

"Khareh-Khan, would you agree to a duel?" The mask distorted the Yun's voice so that Wadi still couldn't be sure.

A stunned silence descended once again, as all eyes turned to Khareh. There was a cry of protest from Erdene to break the moment, but Khareh stood up, a smile on his face. "I think I will." He removed some of the more elaborate rings from around his fingers and dropped them in the basket next to the knives he'd been given.

Wadi rolled her eyes. As if any of the Yun would be stupid enough to offer up a *real* fight against the Khan. And then there was the matter of Khareh's shadow. His haunt— the main source of his sage power—would not let him come to any harm, and besides, could heal him instantly if he did.

The haunt must have caught her staring, because he drifted over in her direction. The closer the shadow came, the more she felt like there was a hand constricting her heart. She knew the shadow was part of Raim, but she couldn't fully understand it. In the prison cell, that moment of madness had possessed her to ask Raim to make her a promise—if she broke it, she could have a piece of him with her. She thought maybe she would have actually done it, even if it meant potentially becoming an oathbreaker, but time had slipped away from them.

The haunt was in front of her now, the gray shadow swirling before her eyes. She held her nerve and looked at it, wondering if she looked hard enough whether she could see the outline of Raim's face in the nebulous cloud, the broad set of his shoulders, the delicate slant of his eyes.

Behind the shadow, Khareh descended the wooden steps from his platform toward the makeshift arena. He had yet to even draw his sword. Erdene had been bundled off to one side while her arm was being bandaged. The rest of the Yun had melted back into the crowd. Even Khareh's other guards seemed distracted.

And his haunt was distracted by Wadi and did not follow Khareh down into the arena. The shadow seemed to reach out to her, like a ghostly hand outstretched. She braced herself as the shadow touched the skin of her cheek.

"Raim?" she whispered.

The Yun who had challenged Khareh reached up and pulled off the mask, throwing it down onto the ground.

"I have been searching for you, boy."

Wadi's eyes opened wide. It was a woman. Not just any woman, but the woman she had seen in the Baril line-up.

216

The woman who had looked at her with so much hatred. But her shock didn't even come close to mirroring the shock on every single other face around the arena—including Khareh's. In fact, Khareh looked more horrified than shocked. His mouth dropped open, his sword-tip nearly scraping the ground before he remembered himself.

"Mhara?"

"That's right, Khareh. I have come for vengeance."

Khareh spun around, searching for his shadow. "Not possible..." he said, looking every bit as young as his eighteen years.

The other Yun, Imal, and Erdene even with her injured arm had started moving, rushing toward them, but the distance was too great. Khareh's shadow, the spirit-Raim, flew away from Wadi then too.

Mhara had a snarl on her face that was more wolf than person. Her cheeks were hollow, her skin deathly pale, her eyes fierce and fixed on one goal. She thrust the sword in Khareh's direction.

And nothing, not even Raim's spirit, could have come between Mhara's blade and Khareh's heart at that moment, except that Wadi had launched herself toward the box of throwing knives and snatched one out of its casing.

Without even waiting a beat for rational thought to take over, she let her instincts guide her and flung one of the knives in Khareh's direction. It flew over Khareh's shoulder and stuck into the Yun woman's heart.

Mhara's sword clattered onto the ground and she dropped

down onto her knees. "I'm sorry," were her final words, until the light left her eyes and she slumped to the dirt.

Erdene came to a screeching halt. "My Khan, are you all right?" she cried. But then she followed Khareh's gaze up to the source of the thrown knife—to where Wadi trembled by the platform, wondering what in Sola's name she had done.

RAIM

The boat anchored out to sea was vast and hideous. Raim thought back to the last time he had seen a boat, when he and Khareh had spent time lounging on the shores of Lake Oudo.

The memory brought a smile to his face until he caught himself. He thought how much Khareh would have loved the journey he was on. Raim had experienced so much—from how to find water in the desert, to the tunnels of Lazar, the Baril mountains, and now a great vessel that could cross the ocean between the North and the South. Khareh would have known exactly what questions to ask to understand everything. Raim just felt like tumbleweed being blown around by strong winds—the twisting tornado of exile, and now, the hurricane of his supposed destiny.

They would never have those moments again. They were

on opposite sides now, and Raim could not fulfill his destiny and be friends with Khareh at the same time.

At least he had Draikh, who let out a low whistle. His shadow-friend was staring out across the waves, watching as the boat gently rose and fell with the swell of the tide. The ship had three tall masts with enormous sails like bat wings. Lit up by the dying sun, they appeared a burnished red against the darkening sky. It didn't look right that something so enormous should be able to stay afloat.

How is it possible? Raim thought.

"They must have some wondrous ship-builders in the South," said Draikh. "Far more sophisticated than anything we have."

Raim shuddered. *I'm surprised anyone would want to experiment out over the salt water. I only hope I don't have to swim.*

Even though Mhara and Aelina reassured him several times that this boat—and only this boat—had made the passage to the South and back several times, he wasn't filled with confidence. It was easy for them to say—they weren't the ones who had to clamber on board and survive the journey. He was comforted to look over and see that Tarik had turned a sickly shade of green.

But now so much more made sense. He had always heard Khareh talk about the South with a kind of reverential tone—and he had been convinced that there was far more to the South than met the eye. Had Khareh ever seen the true extent of the power they had there? If they could make ships as big as a temple float—what else could they do? They were like sages themselves...

But if these items existed in the South, why were they not in the North? Why didn't the rest of the Darhanian population have access to them? He could imagine the tribes along the Zalinzar river trading much more briskly with ships like these, but not even the richest warlord had one. Not even Khareh-Khan.

Once they reached the beach, made up not of sand but of millions of crushed shells, the priestess of the Temple of Bones introduced him to the captain of the ship, a grizzled old man with blackened stubble on his face. His face was lined with wrinkles, his hands calloused with rope burns, his skin weather-beaten and leathery.

"Raim, meet Shen-quo, captain of the *Zuan*," said the priestess. "To be honest, we thought you would never come."

"We came as fast as we could—far more quickly than I wanted," replied Raim. His knees still felt shaky from the steep walk down the narrow cliffside path. At some points, he had felt like a strong breeze would have easily blown him over the edge to a rocky death on the beach below. Even Tarik was more sure-footed than him, but then he guessed that he had had more practice in the mountainous Amarapura region.

"Aye, and I stayed already a day longer than I had intended. Does that make us even?" Shen-quo spat a wad of chewing tobacco on the ground. "I come to this godsforsaken North only once a year. That's all the Council can afford, plus I wouldn't brave the passage across this sea at any other time of the year. I'm the only man mad enough to do it at all, so you'd have been a long time waiting for anyone else. Until next year!" The old sailor chuckled, although it sounded more like a gag. He eyed up their meager possessions. "Get in the rowboat. We leave as soon as you're aboard."

This was it. The moment Raim stepped on the deck of the ship, he would be on his way south and there would be no turning back.

As if sensing his hesitation, Draikh said: "What are you waiting for?"

This is it.

"Yes. And?"

I don't know if it's the right thing.

"What do you think is best for Darhan?" asked Draikh.

"Not to have Khareh in charge," Raim said, although it came out like barely a whisper.

"Exactly," said Draikh. "And with his spirit-army, he is unstoppable. But there is *one* person who can stop him."

Me.

Draikh raised an eyebrow.

Me, but without a scar.

"You, without a scar, and with an army. That is your answer."

Raim nodded and turned back around to face the rowboat. The captain was there, looking at him strangely.

"The shadow that surrounds you ... I have never seen anything like it. Do you control it?"

"Yes," said Raim, as he stepped into the boat. "I am a sage."

The captain's eyes widened, but he said no more. Once they reached the ship, they climbed up a shaky hemp-rope ladder to reach the deck.

This would be Raim's home for the foreseeable future. Straightaway, his stomach churned, and his first few steps forward sent him swaying across the deck. He threw himself against the rails and gripped tightly.

Draikh laughed at him, as did the other sailors. Luckily, Tarik was exactly the same.

"You Northerners will get your sea legs soon," Shen told them. "Either that or this will be a very long journey for you all." The captain's steps were sturdy, his legs adjusting to the ship's every movement. He appeared like an extension of the ship rather than a passenger on it. "Boy?" He gestured to Raim. "Let's see it then. On board ship, there can be no secrets."

Raim swallowed hard and balled his hands into fists. He wanted to be strong, but the motion of the boat kept threatening to take his legs from under him.

"Come on, don't be shy. We were informed that one day we would carry a dirty Northern oathbreaker to the South. We must see the scar."

All eyes on the ship were turned toward him, and the back of Raim's neck burned. Even the sailors who were previously engaged in fixing the sails or swabbing the deck turned to look at him.

Finally, he could bare the scrutiny no longer. He pulled up the sleeve of his tunic so that it revealed his twisted red scar in all its cruelty. It was enough to make Shen shudder.

"And then there is this other," Raim said. He showed the captain just the edge of it, the tip that crept out of his tunic at the base of his neck. "This one is the Absolute Vow I made. That vow is not broken."

Shen's eyebrows lifted. "Why is that one dark like a sailor's tattoo, while the one on your wrist is that hideous red?"

"Because of this creature." Raim pointed up into the sky, where Oyu was delighting in the strange new currents that blew across the water, his enormous wingspan casting a shadow on the deck. "My garfalcon. When he consumed my promise knot to Khareh, he made it even more permanent. Indelible. So that I cannot break the promise even if I want to, and Khareh himself cannot remove it from me."

"You mean the prince."

"The Khan."

"Oh yes, khan, sorry. A bird that eats men's promise knots." Shen rubbed at the beard on his chin, deep in thought. "I've heard legends of sea creatures that are the same. With you on board, though, my bargain with the Council will be over and I need never come to the blasted North again if I choose not to. And yet, I wonder if the new khan will be interested in my ship? Somehow, I bet he would pay more than the old monks do."

"You would not want to deal with him, trust me," Raim said.

"Trust you? You're an oathbreaker, so why would I do that?"

Raim trembled with shame, but Shen put a hand on his shoulder. "You know, you Northerners are a strange lot, but I understand you better than any other of my countrymen. I'll tell you why. You tie knots to bind your promises, and when you break a vow your knot burns. You value honor, I'll give you that much. Maybe because I'm a man of the sea,

I understand. Every day I have to tie knots in my ropes, and I entrust that they will keep me safe. Every knot needs to do its duty, to know its role in this process, or else the whole thing will fall apart. I make those knots promise to hold even when the foulest winds blow at them and the rain drenches them and the rats chew on their threads. If one of those knots breaks, it spells disaster on board a ship. So maybe I know a bit more than I let on about their significance. And the significance of someone who willingly breaks one."

Raim swallowed, trying to keep his voice as steady as possible. "I did nothing willingly."

"And hence the journey."

"Hence the journey. By the end, I will be rid of this scar."

"As you say."

There was a loud clap of thunder, and Shen's attitude changed almost immediately. He shifted from his laid-back stance to a man on high alert, his muscles going from sluggish to tense in an instant. At first, Raim couldn't tell what was causing the change in the captain's demeanor, which shed years from the man just in the alertness in his shoulders. But then he felt the difference himself—a kind of spark in the air that made the hair on the back of his neck stand on end. He looked up at the sky and realized that the sun had been obscured completely by clouds hanging in thick clumps. It looked ominous.

"Men, jump to it. Raise the anchor. We need to get out of here, and fast." Shen turned to Raim. "You two'd best get below," he said, gesturing to Tarik. "You'll learn the ropes soon enough, but your first night is not the night to do so.

You'll suffer enough downstairs without getting under my feet all the time." Then he spun around, turning his attention back to the crew, who had gathered on the deck. He set each of them to work, flinging his arms out in each direction, and men scattered where he pointed. The sea beneath them lifted and swelled, and Raim could see men at the far end struggling with the heavy anchor. He wanted to do something to help, but then Draikh was in front of him.

"Get below decks," said Draikh. "It's a lightning storm. I learned about these in my studies. Once the season for them hits, there will be no going anywhere in this ship. Oyu will be fine," he added, seeing Raim's eyes shoot up to the sky.

"But I can help—" protested Raim.

Shen overheard. He spun around, and the anger etched on his face was enough to send Raim scurrying below deck. He stumbled against the sides of the ship's thin corridors until he found an empty berth. There was a hammock of stained hemp rope suspended from the ceiling, which he tumbled into. He felt useless, but he was aware that he could easily be the source of more annoyance than good. He knew nothing about how a ship worked. He had no idea even how they got a ship this size moving. Maybe a great wave would lift them up and smash them against the cliffs—then he would have no hope of reaching the South, no hope of overthrowing Khareh, no hope of returning to Wadi. *Definitely* no hope of being the Khan.

He didn't feel much like a leader of anything sitting in that tiny room that stank of mildew and salt and sweat and fear. He cowered in the hammock, letting the rope dig into his skin, not even bothering to move to find a blanket or anything that would make him more comfortable. The ship seemed to lurch, and so did his stomach. He reached over the side of the hammock and retched into the bucket that had been provided just for that purpose.

Now the smell of sour acid and old water added to the mix.

All he could do was wait out the night, and see if he was still alive in the morning. There was no going back now.

RAIM

The initial storm passed quickly, and when he felt well again, the next morning, Raim clambered back out onto the deck. That first moment of seeing the open sea in its entirety was a sight that would never leave him for the rest of his life. There was no sign of land on the horizon, just mile after mile of dark blue water, crested here and there by the white caps of sea foam on the waves. It was only matched by the feeling of looking out over the desert for the first time. In fact, if the waves stayed stationary, they could be sand dunes. But these sands dunes rolled, rose and dipped, and this boat was no more master of the waves than he had been of the dunes. And while sand-worms and garfalcons and great snakes lived in the sands, Raim was terrified to think of what must lurk beneath the waves.

Raim's stomach heaved. He swung back to face the mast and sunk to his knees.

Another man burst out of the cabins below—Tarik. He spotted Raim and stumbled across the deck to get to him. Together they both sat, their backs against the wooden railing of the ship, their heads between their hands.

"How much more of this do we have to go?" Tarik said, his voice shaking.

"Too long," said Raim. The captain had been vague about certain details—like the time he thought the journey would take.

"I haven't even been able to write anything. Every time I get the quill out, I end up feeling sick again."

As if their conversation had conjured him, Shen loomed over them, snapping them both from their reverie.

"Boys, this is the easiest part of this journey. Trust me, if the seas were like this more than they were not, you'd see plenty more ships venturing out onto these waters. Maybe even King Song himself would send his fleet rather than attempt to cross the Red desert to get north. There, boy, that should give you an indication of just how dangerous this crossing is! The king would rather cross the desert than the sea, and he owns the finest fleet in the world."

Why in Sola's name did we agree to this? It's a suicide mission! thought Raim to Draikh.

"At least one of us is enjoying it," Draikh replied. As if on cue, Oyu dived into the water and came back with a fat, juicy fish in his beak.

"Is that normal behavior for a garfalcon?" asked Tarik,

although he knew no one could answer his question. He slipped his scroll of paper out of his tunic pocket and began to scribble down notes while observing Oyu.

Raim laughed. Tarik could squeeze learning out of any situation.

"The sea spares us because we bring nothing back from the cursed North," said a voice. It sounded as if it was coming from above them. Raim looked up to see a man swinging from the rigging like a monkey. He jumped down next to the captain, landing with a dull thud. He might've been the thinnest man that Raim had ever seen; his skin was the same windburnt, leathery brown as Shen's, but without the prodigious beard he just looked shriveled like an old prune. The man's eyes were set so far back into his skull, they might as well be gone completely.

"This is Bayan," said Shen. "He's my first mate, and a superstitious old sod if I ever knew one."

"They shouldn't be here," said Bayan. He drew out the "sh" in "shouldn't" like the rattle of a snake's tail. "The gods allow us passage to bring things north—not south. Not to bring these twisted spies to our shores, to contaminate our lands and our peoples!"

Shen laughed. "We bring nothing south except gold, don't forget. The northern monks give us just enough of that to make this journey worthwhile. And now they've given me more gold than I know what to do with, all just to guarantee the safe passage of these two souls and one hideous shadow to Aqben. Who am I to argue? I can't guarantee anyone safe passage over these waters, but I will guard against anything in man's control. Including you, Bayan. Now, to your duties, man."

"They shouldn't be here," Bayan repeated. He threw one sharp look at Raim before shuffling off and disappearing below deck.

We'll need to keep a watch on that one, Raim thought, reaching out to Draikh.

"Absolutely," said Draikh. "I don't think I've ever seen anyone shiftier in my life."

But where is everyone else? There was just a skeleton crew on board, and they scurried through the ship like rats—avoiding him and Tarik as if they might carry the plague.

There was still one other thing Shen had said which caught Raim's attention.

"Tell me about the Southern King's army . . ." Aelina had mentioned it, but she hadn't known any details. Maybe Shen would know more.

"It's the biggest army the South has ever seen. Some of the men on this boat, they joined me just to avoid being conscripted into the army. Though why he cares about the North is beyond me. The North keeps my wife in silks and me out of her bed—that's why she keeps sending me up here when I could just be doing easy sailing trips to the Jewel Isles, filling my boat with rich spices, relaxing on sand beaches, staring at beautiful women . . ."

"The Council warned the king that I would be coming," Raim said. "I will need that army to become the rightful Khan of Darhan, as my promise knot foretold." Even as he spoke, he couldn't stop doubt from creeping in.

Shen narrowed one of his eyes at him in a way that came off more curious than threatening. "I don't know what you and your monks believe, but you'll have trouble wrestling away that army from King Song."

"But I must," said Raim. "It is my destiny."

"Hmm, so you have been told. It's just I wouldn't be surprised if others had different beliefs about this supposed 'destiny,' King Song included. But come on then," Shen said to Raim and Tarik. "No use having you both lazing around all day. If you're feeling seasick, I know a good cure for it: hard work and exhaustion. I've heard some pretty fantastical stories about you—especially you," he said, looking directly at Raim. "Let's see what you're truly made of, then."

He snapped his fingers and Bayan came back with two mops and pails. He dropped the mop handles, and they landed with a clatter at Raim's feet. "There you go. Swab the decks if you must do something."

Raim picked up his mop, then looked up at Draikh, who was floating around the mast. *Well, are you going to help me? Show Shen what we can do?*

Draikh raised an eyebrow. "You're joking? You're on your own for this one. I'm not cleaning up for you."

Raim sighed, and with Tarik next to him, dragged the mop across the wooden deck.

It was going to be a long passage.

WADI

She had been aiming for Khareh.

She tried to convince herself of that fact. *Hadn't she?*

The memory of it flashed before her eyes. She had lunged for the knife. She had seen the target in her eyes. She had thrown it.

It had hit the woman square in the chest.

She had been aiming for Khareh.

No, she hadn't. If she had aimed for Khareh, she would have hit Khareh. Instead, he had been in danger and she had saved him.

There was chaos in the moments right after. Erdene had ripped herself free from the healers and thrown herself to Khareh's side. Imal was there too, his sword drawn, standing over the crumpled form of Mhara, who was lying dead—

there was no mistaking it this time—on the packed dirt of the makeshift arena. Blood from the open wound dripped down into the dirt, turning it into mud, albeit crimson-tinted. The bone handle of the knife Wadi had thrown still remained embedded in Mhara's chest.

She had thrown that knife with deadly accuracy. *To save Khareh's life.* She left that thought hanging in her mind. *How could I have done that? I didn't want that. I wanted him dead.*

I wanted him dead, she repeated, trying to get herself to believe it. But she hadn't. She had wanted to save him, even from Mhara. Wadi knew that name—she had been Raim's former mentor, the one he thought he had killed. The one he had tortured himself with guilt over. Wadi had killed her now.

She had been turned to Khareh's side. Khareh had won. With great reluctance, Wadi lifted her head. She found Khareh's eyes just where she expected them to be: boring a hole deep into her skull with their piercing gaze, so deep she swore he was finding out things about her that she didn't even know about herself. He didn't break eye contact even while Erdene fussed over him, even when she called out to Altan for help, even once a healer wrapped the wound he had received in falling to the ground. He just stared at Wadi.

Then, with a gesture, he ordered her back to the yurt, and she knew that at any moment he would follow her back and thank her. *Thank her for saving him.*

Her mind raced and her palms began to sweat as two ordinary soldiers began to lead her away. Wary of her skill, they kicked away the other knives and knocked over the basket, a shiny object rolling out and catching her attention. It was one of Khareh's rings that he'd removed before his duel. Wadi palmed it and slipped it in her pocket.

She had seen enough to know what he was capable of. It was time to remind him of what *she* was capable of.

The soldiers accompanied her back to her yurt, where her chains awaited. They hadn't chained her feet while she was walking from the festivities, because, after all, she had *saved* their khan and now they didn't know how to treat her. A mistake on their part, if they thought she could be trusted.

In the dark shadow of her yurt, as one of them released his grip and stepped away to find the keys to her chain, she threw all her might up at her other captor, her fists colliding against his jaw. There was so much noise from the surrounding yurts, she hoped no one would notice their satisfying squeals.

There wasn't much time to savor the victory. The other soldier fumbled the keys, dropping them onto the ground as he charged back at her to secure her. She grabbed the body of the soldier she had smashed in the mouth and threw him hard at his companion before kicking out at the man's groin. He crumpled into a heap, his companion on top of him.

Wadi grabbed strips of cloth from where they had been drying on the lines securing her yurt and used them to bind and gag the two soldiers, then she dragged the men deep inside, so their inert bodies couldn't be seen, and chained their ankles together as a last-minute idea. It wasn't subtle, but it might buy her a few extra minutes.

Every single one of her senses was on high alert—but no one came to investigate the noise she had made incapacitating the guards. Everyone was still too focused on what had happened at the tournament.

But it wouldn't be long until Khareh came along, so she needed to be quick. The army camp was set up in a long column formation around the lake, so Wadi scurried toward the outer edge, trying to find the narrowest point of exit. It would be hard to run away into the steppes—but as only one woman, she could do it.

She could go anywhere—she could try to find Raim on his journey south—but he would likely be on the ship already. Or she could go to Sola, find her old Alashan tribe, and warn them of Khareh's plans to invade the desert. She could do anything—as long as it wasn't staying here any longer and spending any more time under the hypnotic influence of Khareh.

Wadi tried to act as if she belonged—and as she walked past one of the yurts, she grabbed a strip of leather that had fallen to the ground. She convinced herself she was just an ordinary woman tasked with repairing some uniforms. She kept her face hidden by a scarf thrown over her head. Her dark skin—darker than any natural-born Darhanian—would mark her out in an instant. There weren't many people of Alashan descent in the tribe.

Luckily, no one looked at her face—barely anyone looked at her at all. There was a strange energy in the air as word of the attempted assassination spread though the camp. Yet most seemed happy that Khareh had survived. Khareh had two things in his favor: his natural charisma, which gave him ability to inspire despite being despicable, and the desire of the Darhanian people to win. So far, Khareh had yet to lose a battle he had led his armies into.

To beat Khareh, to bring him down, was going to require a leader who possessed everything Khareh did—charisma, the ability to motivate people, the ability to spot talent and use it to his advantage, his sagery—but without Khareh's cruelty. Wadi hoped that Raim was up to the task. She knew she could help him get there.

Finally finding a suitable place, Wadi burst out of the camp and into the grasslands. She tried to slow her pace despite the fact that she wanted to run. The beating of her heart sounded so loud, it was like the pounding of a war drum in her ears. *Just act like you have every reason in the world to head away from camp.* She kept her pace even, and occasionally stopped to look around as if she was missing a child or a friend. When she judged she was far enough from the camp for the lights of the fires to no longer reach her, she dropped down onto her knees. Then she started crawling through the grass, as quickly as she could.

The grass here was long and lush after a wet spring and offered plenty of cover. She just needed to stay low, to stay quiet; to be quick and move away from here.

She saw no one then but a falcon, wheeling high over-head. The steppes were wide and cold and empty compared to the desert. But there was plenty of life around: soaring birds, scurrying rodents and grazing animals. But there was only one animal Wadi was interested in: the steppes pony.

One allowed her to approach, curious and unafraid of humans. Wadi spotted the brand on its haunches and knew that it was one of the army ponies, built for stamina over long distances. The horse would be able to survive on little sustenance as well.

"We'll be in this together, little one," she said to it, in her most soothing tone. She stroked its velvety soft muzzle, allowing it to become accustomed to her scent. She was grateful that she would smell like the smoke and incense of Khareh's camp. She was not unfamiliar.

When the moment felt right, she took a fistful of its mane and hoisted herself up onto its back. She clicked with the back of her tongue and dug her heels into its side until it sprang into action.

She was going to regret the lack of saddle by the end of this journey, that was for certain. But as she glanced back over her shoulder at the camp, an eerie calm came over her. She was free.

And she would accept any pain in the world as a price for that freedom.

WADI

Wadi rode until her fingers cramped from gripping the pony's matted mane, until her thighs ached and foam rose on her pony's back, but to her relief, no one pursued her. She rode until she came across a braided river, twists of it running through the steppes like the plaits in her hair.

She dismounted and fell, knees first, into the river. The water was shallow—only a few inches deep—and icy cold, but she didn't care. While the horse drank upstream, she lay in the river and let the water rush over her, cleansing her body and clothes of the dust and sweat of her journey.

In the vast wilderness, completely alone, she let herself break down. Her tears joined the river with the dust. She didn't know where she was going, or how she was going to find Raim. Her stomach rumbled with intense hunger; she hadn't eaten since long before the Yun tournament.

"Help me," she whispered to the river, hoping the words would somehow find their way down to the sea and get carried to Raim's ear on a rogue wave.

She snapped back to her senses, cursing herself for being so foolish, and began to clean her legs where riding had caused blisters to swell and burst. She took long draughts of the clean, fresh water, then washed her hair and rebraided the long dark strands. The practical things she could think about. Small steps.

Survival first. Plan second.

Eventually, Wadi dragged herself from the river and sat on an island of crushed rock, silt, and mud in the middle of the water. Her mount still drank happily, and she needed a moment to reassess.

She needed food, and a safe place to rest, but she could not hope to seek hospitality from the local tribes. She was too unusual, too different, too strange, and in a time when "war" was on everyone's lips, hosting an obvious foreigner was a risk few would be willing to take. Without the generosity of the nomads, though, she did not know how she was going to find the help she needed.

A deep pit opened in her stomach that had nothing to do with hunger. Maybe this had all been a big mistake. She could have stayed with Khareh. Now she had truly lost any trust he might have had in her, despite the fact that she had just saved his life.

The sound of laughter drifting out over the water chilled

Wadi to the core. She scrambled backward into the river, but there was not enough water to cover her. She was helpless to whoever was approaching.

The laughter stopped abruptly. It was a young girl, approaching the edge of the river with a pail made of animal skin. She didn't look older than ten; her hair tied back in two plaits that framed her face, her skin burnished bronze by the sun. She stared at Wadi, the strange woman in the water who had interrupted her game. But she was alone.

They stared at each other for what felt like an age, and Wadi could see the girl analyzing her as if Wadi was a wild animal whose danger she was judging. Then the girl shrugged her shoulders and kept approaching the water, leaving Wadi relieved but bedraggled, and still sitting in the river.

She now had a choice: to run away, in case the presence of the girl meant that others were nearby too. Or she could approach.

"Hello?" Wadi said.

The girl perked her head up, like a rabbit about to flee. Wadi couldn't stop herself now that she had started. "Wait, please, do you understand me? My name is Wadi. What's your name?"

There was a slight hesitation, but to Wadi's surprise, the girl didn't have any fear in her eyes. This was a daughter of the steppes, a nomad child who fiercely protected her animals against all dangers. She could be miles from her home now, but her parents wouldn't fear for her.

"Shanna."

"Shanna, can you help me? Do you have any food?"

The girl didn't reply, but she didn't run away either. Wadi stood up and moved closer to her, trying to keep her movements slow and nonthreatening so as not to spook her. "I'm a long way from my tribe," Wadi said. "I haven't eaten for a long time."

The girl's eyes opened wide. "I have some dried meat."

Wadi could have cried. "Really? Will you let me have some?"

"You're not from here," the little girl said, and Wadi's heart stopped in her chest. "The Weaver told me you would be from the great golden ocean, but I didn't believe her. No one can be from Sola."

"The Weaver? Who is that?"

"My grandmother says she is a seer. A true seer, like the ones in the old stories. Well, are you from Sola or not?"

If she hadn't been so terrified by the girl's words, Wadi would have laughed at her boldness. "I am from Sola. But how would your Weaver know that?"

The girl pointed downriver. "She says if I find you, I'm to bring you to her straight away. Are you coming?"

Wadi hesitated. It could be a trap. But what choice did she have?

The girl took Wadi to where she had set up her own little camp to watch her goats. They slept out under the stars, on a beautiful carpet woven in unusual shades of blue and gray—so different from the normal bright reds and oranges that made up most tribal carpets. But as Wadi looked even closer, she saw that the blue formed streaks of a river, and in that river was a dark-skinned girl sitting there.

"Who ... who gave this to you?"

A little frown appeared on the girl's forehead. "The Weaver gave it to me. That's why I knew not to be afraid of you. I knew I would meet you eventually."

The Weaver had seen Wadi coming.

35

RAIM

"Ready!"

Raim drew back the bow, his shoulder blades squeezing tightly together, both his eyes open and staring at the tip of the arrowhead. He leaned to the side, his body bending into almost a triangle, his feet firmly planted on the deck. Shen-quo had been right—he had found his sea legs, and now he was putting them to the test with old weapons the captain had dug up from one of the multitude of watertight storerooms beneath the deck.

"Aim!"

The world reduced for him to the tip of that arrowhead. He felt the muscles in his thighs adjust to the motion of the boat; even after only a week on board he felt his body adjust to the new sensations. He hadn't used a bow and arrow properly in too long. He could feel his fingertips tremble against his ear, the uncharacteristic shake in his arms. So slight, but also so big that it could make the difference between striking the target dead-on and missing it completely. He took a deep breath to steady himself. This was why he was doing this. So he could be ready.

"Now!"

A sailor hurled a shard of broken plate into the air. Raim aimed ahead of it along its trajectory and released the bow-string, the familiar twang vibrating through his entire body. He had attracted a crowd again, and he heard their collective gasp as the arrow struck its target and the shard smashed against the backdrop of a clear blue sky.

"Again! And make it more difficult for him."

Raim grinned as several more shards flew out over the water, this time flung from different parts of the ship—some from the prow, some from the rigging, some from the very top of the mast. He thought a word—*Draikh*—and wasted no more time. He drew the arrows rapidly, firing as fast as he could draw. Draikh flew about in the air too, smashing any plates Raim missed, and between them they broke every bit of pottery before it smacked the water.

Tarik stood next to Shen, a few feet behind Raim, marking down every time Raim hit a target. His eyes bulged in his head; he clearly could not believe what he was seeing, despite knowing what Raim could do.

"No wonder the Khan is afraid of you. I'm surprised you're not dead already," Shen commented.

Raim smiled. "I'm surprised myself, most of the time."

"You might have a chance with King Song after all—even he won't fail to be impressed by your abilities. Maybe I should just keep you on board and take you to someone who will pay even more for you. You might be a sage, but I know you can't swim." He winked.

Tarik looked up from his tally then. "We had your word you would bring us safely to the South!"

Shen raised an eyebrow. "Aye, and soon you will see why I could never live in the North, with your magic-imbued morals. I thank our gods every living hour of the day that it is only your cursed place that binds oaths with magic." He shivered. "A man should be free. That means free to break his oaths as well as keep them.

"Oh, but before you open your gobs to protest too much, I'm not going to tell anyone about you. I need that gold, and I want to keep relations sweet with those northern monks. Your passage is safe with me." He cast his eyes up to the sky, and furrowed his brow. "Well, as safe as I can make it."

Raim followed the man's gaze. It had been a surprisingly calm day—the blue sky seemed to melt at the horizon, so that Raim could hardly tell where the sky ended and the sea began. Shen had been right; he was even starting to enjoy his time on board.

The captain muttered something under his breath.

"What was that?" Raim asked.

"I said, we're never going to get beyond the Xel rocks at this rate. Bayan! To me!"

"The Xel rocks? What are they?"

Shen's eyes narrowed. "They're home to the most dangerous creatures in this ocean. Don't you go listening to stories about sharks or jellyfish or any of that nonsense. If we're not beyond the rocks when the storms strike . . . "

Bayan announced his presence by slapping down the mop he was carrying. It hit the deck with a resounding thwack. "Aye, captain?" He still wouldn't look Raim in the eye.

"How fast are we going?"

"Not fast enough. I've never known winds like this."

"Or *no* winds like this, more like." Shen cast an eye out to the sky, as if he could conjure the wind with a foul look.

Bayan shrugged. "Maybe this is the year we don't make it. I told you bringing the Northeners on board was a bad idea. The god of wind has turned against us."

Shen waved his hand impatiently. "That kind of talk is not helpful."

"Not a lot would be helpful, except wind."

At that, Raim felt a gentle breeze on his cheek. "There's a bit of wind around."

Now Bayan turned to look at him—and so did Shen. They both looked at him like he was crazy.

"Did you not just feel that?" More gusts came, enough that Raim could feel his hair being lifted.

"There is nothing," said Shen, but even he hesitated, looking at Raim.

Raim spun around, in the direction of the wind. He could see nothing—obviously, it was just air—but then he spotted Draikh, floating near the prow of the ship. He had a strange look on his face, one that Raim recognized all too well.

He left the captain and Bayan to stare after him, confused, and climbed the steps up to the prow, running his hand along the railings as he did so. They had once been painted and varnished, that much he could tell—every now and again there would be a patch of wood that was shockingly smooth, or marked with a splash of bright color, like a bruise. Despite its rough, battered appearance, the ship had the feeling of longevity: it had been through a lot, and would suffer much more before it succumbed. It was comforting that the ship was old. Very comforting.

Draikh was on his own. Raim was glad. It had been too long since it had been just him and Draikh, alone.

"Raim, when you used to hear stories of sages, what did you hear?"

Raim pondered for a second. "The usual. That they had powers that no one could believe: they could make objects fly, they could levitate, they could heal themselves. They helped destroy armies, they built tribes."

Draikh made a noncommittal noise, and tapped his finger against his lips. Raim knew that gesture. Draikh was on to something.

"What is it? Why do you ask?"

Draikh flew closer to him, almost as if he was perched on the railing. "What if we had even more power?"

"More power? What do you mean?"

"I'm not entirely sure. It's been something I've suspected for a while now. Look." Draikh seemed full of purpose, and his excitement drew Raim closer. "Hold your hands out. Good. Now wait a second..."

Draikh shut his eyes for a moment and tilted his head back. It looked almost as if he was praying. But who did Draikh have to pray to? It wasn't as if he could talk to any gods. He wasn't a person. He was a spirit. Then Draikh swirled his hands around in the air above Raim's hands, but without making contact with them. It was strange, because Raim could see Draikh's hands moving, but he could not feel the buffeting of the air against his skin.

Until suddenly he could. It wasn't like he could feel the air being moved by Draikh's hands—it was as if there was wind blowing all around his hands, like a breeze concentrated in that one area.

"Are you doing this?" Raim asked, astonished.

"It's the air—it has its own energy. Its own spirit. I can reach out to it and … join with it. Manipulate it." To prove his point even more, Draikh swirled his hands and the wind moved around Raim's hands faster and faster, until a small tornado rested in his palm. It spun and spiralled as Draikh moved it, until he commanded it to die away.

"That's amazing!"

Then without warning a fierce gust of wind nearly blew Raim off his feet. Draikh held his palms up, and Raim felt a surge of energy run throughout his entire body. For a moment, he felt his own spirit reaching out toward the air. He tried to focus on the sensation. Maybe this is what being the descendant of Hao meant. Maybe he could externalize his own spirit, become a sage in his own right …

He hit the deck of the ship with a resounding smack.

He cracked one eye open, his head throbbing. He tried to sit up, but Draikh pushed him back down again.

"I'd rest for a moment if I were you. You hit your head pretty hard."

Raim did as he was told, keeping his eyes tightly shut as he waited for his vision to stop spinning. *What happened?* he thought to Draikh.

"I'm not sure... you tell me?"

I think I almost released my own spirit.

Draikh was silent.

Do you think you could do that with other elements?

"What do you mean?"

What you do with the wind... could you do it with water, or fire?

Raim opened his eyes, and Draikh's spirit-form came into focus. He was chewing on his lower lip, exactly what Khareh used to do when he was in deep thought. His eyes were wide, like he was only just coming to terms with the magnitude of the revelation. "There's no harm in trying," he said.

Raim struggled to a sitting position, and Draikh pulled on his outstretched arm to help him to stand. *If you can summon enough wind, we could get this ship moving and save it from the Xel rocks or whatever the old captain is afraid of,* he said to Draikh. *Regardless, it will get us south quicker, so we can return north sooner too.* He eyed the spirit, full of nervous energy. *Are you up for it? Do you think you have the strength to do it?*

Draikh nodded. "We've been training, haven't we? What do you think we've been training for, if not for something like this? I can handle a bit of wind."

"I guess you have been blowing wind most of your life," Raim said, with a wink that belied his excitement.

"Just don't you try anything—don't want you to hit your head again. You might lose what little brain you have left."

Raim made a rude gesture with his hands, then grimaced. "I don't think I'll be doing that again any time soon." He rubbed the back of his head.

Draikh swooped up to the top of the main mast, where each sail hung limply in the still air.

Raim ran to find the captain, whom he spotted at the enormous wheel. Shen had told him that in bad weather, it required at least three men steer the ship. The man regarded him with an expression that mixed surprise with annoyance.

"What is it, boy? This is no place for an inexperienced..." But his words drifted away on the sudden wind—or maybe shock stole them away. Raim had faced the sails and raised his arms, directing Draikh behind the largest. Immediately Draikh raised a wind, conjuring a gust so strong that the sails snapped and the ropes whined in reluctance at having to stretch themselves to the full. The ship lurched into motion, picking up pace where before it had floated close to motionless.

Raim laughed as Draikh commanded the air, filled with a joy he could barely contain. His heart swelled as the wind swirled around him, the sails fuller than he had ever seen them. He had never felt like this before—like suddenly every opportunity in the world was open to him, his for the taking. His spirit was—literally—soaring.

The entire crew gathered on the deck. Shen gripped the wheel with white knuckles. They all stared at him. Tarik was there too. His jaw was open so wide, his chin could have picked up splinters on the deck.

Raim could imagine what they were seeing. His arms wide-stretched, controlling the wind. It looked like *he* was doing it, even though it was far from the truth. For a second, he could taste what Khareh obviously fed off of every day. The sweet—the intoxicatingly sweet—taste of power. He could feel his blood surge through his veins at the thought of it, like lightning through his body, hair standing up on end, his mouth dry with anticipation and fear—so much fear. But he closed his eyes and lowered his arms. Draikh took it as a sign and stopped his manipulation of the air.

He was just Raim. He wasn't yet the leader of anyone. Even this addition to his arsenal couldn't change that fact.

He curled his fingers into a fist, but not out of anger. He wondered if he squeezed tightly enough, he could keep all that ambition, all that thirst for power, deep inside until he was ready.

Shen's gruff voice cut through his thoughts. "That was you?"

Raim opened his eyes, reluctantly, and nodded.

"Well, do it again, will you? We've got a lot of ocean to cross, and not a lot of time."

36

RAIM

Draikh's trick with the wind set the ship sailing—and sent Raim's esteem among the other sailors soaring. Even Bayan approached him with a very different sort of attitude, one that bordered almost on reverence. As they sailed through the night at a constant and secure speed, Shen muttered a kind of mantra under his breath: "We do not have people who can do *this* in the South."

Eventually they had sailed into a place where the wind blew strongly on its own, meaning Draikh could rest. It was like when they had first explored their sage powers back in Lazar—Draikh was not yet strong enough to sustain the manipulation of the wind for long, and they would have to train in this new skill to make themselves stronger. Raim felt himself drained of energy too, and he dragged himself down the wooden steps to the galley to find food.

As he ate, his mind drifted back to Darhan. He thought of Wadi and couldn't wait to show her this new discovery. But then he thought of Khareh, and wondered whether he had realized that the spirits could wield this strange and awe-inspiring power.

He doubted it. It had been Draikh who had made the discovery—Draikh, who was always pushing the limits of what they could do. He didn't think his own spirit—the part of himself that was accompanying Khareh—would be that inventive. Creativity had never been Raim's strong suit, whereas Khareh had always been experimenting, ever since he'd been a little boy.

As Raim looked over at Draikh, he found it hard to reconcile the spirit with the real boy-turned-khan. The Khareh he'd known had been too intelligent for his own good. He'd had all the training and learning that Raim could never dream of as a simple tribesboy; even as a Yun apprentice, Raim would never have been educated beyond the lessons needed to do his duty. Khareh had been a quick learner, and once he grew smarter than his teachers, he was never willing to obey authority. But he'd never been cruel. Draikh was never cruel either.

Draikh is not Khareh-Khan, he thought.

"No, I'm not," said Draikh.

Shen came down to join him in the galley. Raim rarely saw the man below deck—he guessed that part of the reason he captained this mad ship was because he was insane enough to want to keep an eye on it all the time. That was probably why they had survived so many journeys. Shen ladled soup into a crudely carved wooden bowl and sat down on the bench opposite Raim.

Tarik stumbled in not long after, hanging a little too long in the doorway. His complexion had taken on a permanent green hue. Raim really hoped that the weather didn't get any worse for him—he wasn't sure that Tarik would be able to cope. He wished now that Tarik had stayed behind. He'd always been a better student than adventurer. He remembered the first time he'd seen his brother take up arms for a raid against an eastern tribe. He'd never seen a person shake so much.

"How much longer until we reach the South?" Tarik asked.

"If this wind holds, maybe another two, three days at most. But we have the most difficult part of the journey ahead of us now. The Xel rocks. If I were you, I would get as much strength in your bones as possible. We're going to need every hand on deck if we want to get through in one piece."

"I'm not sure how much help I will be," said Tarik. "Maybe I should just stay down here and keep a record of our journey…"

"Nobody will be allowed below deck," said Shen. "Eat up."

That night in his hammock, Raim couldn't sleep. Something about the air had changed, become closer, more suffocating. There was a tension in the way the crew moved. A heaviness had set into Shen's brow. Even Bayan didn't seem to want to waste his energy in insulting Raim.

Two days. Two more nights, maybe three. And then he would be South. The place that had loomed large in his mind since he was a boy—but as the source of everything to be looked down upon. If Lazar was the home of disgraced oathbreakers, Aqben in the South was the home of disgraced *people*. The legends told of a place where people worked the land until it surrendered, where they kept their animals confined no matter what the quality of the grass that surrounded them, where they refused to leave their homes even if the walls crumbled. One word stood out among all others when it came to Aqben and the South in general: *lazy*. And if there was anything that Darhanians hated almost as much as oathbreakers, it was sloths. People who never moved.

On the steppes, if you were lazy, you died.

Yet Lazar had also taught him how wrong the old stories could be. He had seen some wondrous things that had originated in the South: like this very ship. He couldn't let his old prejudices dominate. He had to keep an open mind.

Two days passed, and the tense atmosphere in the ship managed to lift.

Of course, that was their mistake.

It started with Raim being thrown from his hammock. It took his brain a few seconds to catch up with the events: at one point, he was asleep, safe, calm, peaceful—the next, he was on the ground. He tried to stand up, but as he did so he was thrown against the door. The weight of his body flung the door open and he found himself, once again, on his knees on the hard wooden planks, but this time buttressed up against the opposite cabin. The door smacked shut again behind him, the slamming sound barely registering against the sudden clap of thunder overhead.

Ahead of him, Tarik stumbled out into the corridor, his hands gripping the walls, arms and legs outstretched.

"What's happening?" Tarik managed to shout out, and Raim just caught his words before there was another rumble of thunder overhead.

"Let's get on deck!" he tried to shout over the noise, but when all he got in return was a blank stare, he pointed upwards. Tarik nodded, but the fear in his eyes meant Raim would have to lead the way.

He stumbled past, pulling at Tarik's arm, trying to transfer some of the courage he wasn't even really feeling himself. He had to act courageous, a game of pretend. Really, he had no idea what he was doing. But doing something felt better than being cooped up down below, with no sight of the sky.

They burst out onto the deck, ejected from the lower decks like the ship was throwing them up. Heavy rain pounded Raim's face and arms, like arrowheads sent down from the sky. Little balls of ice skittered along the deck, even though they were *south*, for the sake of the gods! But the sky above them looked like no sky Raim had ever seen before. Thick black and gray clouds swirled around them in a hypnotizing pattern—lit up by flashes of lightning.

The waves seemed to join the sky, equal in their gray, roiling darkness. Raim put his arm across his face to shield it from the rain, but it did no good. He found himself flung up against the bulwarks, clinging for his life. As his sight cleared, he spotted sailors running around on deck, brows furrowed with purpose.

"Look out there!" shouted Draikh.

Where? Raim craned his neck, trying to spot what Draikh was referring to. His hair was plastered over his eyes by the rain, and he let go with one hand to push it back. That's when he saw it.

A twister. A spinning spiral of water and wind, snaking its way from the waves to the clouds.

"Not that!" said Draikh. "In the water—look."

Raim was mesmerized by the twister, which looked as if it was about to make its way toward the ship at any moment. But finally he tore his eyes away, down to where Draikh was pointing.

Just below the twister, under the water, there was a flash of red. Raim watched, wide-eyed and trembling, as the red object breached the ocean's surface, and he could see that it was the body of a serpentine creature—half as wide as the ship but many times as long, judging from the rolls of its body as it undulated beneath the waves.

"What on Sola's great earth is that?" shouted Tarik above the wind.

"No idea!" said Raim. But when the creature's head finally emerged, Raim felt all rational thought leave his body. It had an enormous head, like an oversized camel, but with the tusks of a boar and horns like a deer. As it opened its mouth, row after row of sharp teeth gnashed together, water pouring out of the corners of its gruesome smile. Long filaments dropped on either side of its nostrils like an old man's beard. The creature's eyes flashed, lit up by lightning.

But most terrifying of all was that its eyes were fixed on Raim.

"It's a seadragon!" shouted Bayan, his legs wrapped around the mast where he clung like a monkey, his arms outspread despite the ferocious wind. "She has come for the oathbreaker! We should give up the boy as a sacrifice!"

With a speed that belied its enormous size, the creature's head dived under the water, the rest of its body following, although it never seemed to end. The ship lurched and tilted, sending Raim and Tarik scrambling backward, sliding along the slippery wooden deck.

"Oh gods, it's gone underneath us!" said Tarik.

Sure enough, the seadragon emerged again on the other side of the ship. It raised itself up, revealing its pale yellow underbelly in contrast to the dark red scales of its back. Raim didn't have long to contemplate it as the dragon flung itself across the prow of the ship, holding the ship hostage within a loop of its enormous bulk. It began to squeeze the ship, and a resounding crack signaled the buckling of the structure under the sea serpent's weight and muscle.

"She's going to break the ship in half!" shouted Shen. "All men gather arms!"

The sailors reluctantly followed his orders, scrambling around for weapons—but they didn't have many options. The captain thrust a pitchfork into Raim's hands, but he didn't know what good that would do against the dragon's scaly hide. Now that he could see it up close, he saw that each scale shone like the rubies in the Khan's crown. They shimmered brighter with every twist of its body, the coil tightening, splinters of wood flying off the ship and into the sea.

He stepped forward, the pitchfork in his hands, and immediately was thrown off-balance by another enormous wave. Anyone who had managed to reach the serpent found their weapons turned aside by the scales. Shen, who had a sword, swung his blade hard against the creature's back, only to have it break on impact.

"Fire!" Another man burst from the galley below, thick black smoke pouring out onto the deck—as if they didn't have enough to worry about. Raim turned his head to see red and orange flames dance in the doorway.

"It's no use!" said Bayan, who was still so calm it made him appear all the more crazy. "This is our punishment for bringing the oathbreaker aboard." He cackled with the laugh of a madman.

Draikh, we have to do something! thought Raim.

"I know. I have an idea!" Draikh replied. "We need the fire!"

I'm coming! Raim dragged himself hand over hand along the rail to get closer to the door down to the galley. Despite the biting wind, he could feel the heat from the flames on his face. A roar came from behind him, and Raim didn't know whether it was from the storm or the seadragon.

"Raim, look out!" His brother's warning made Raim fling his body down onto the deck, and only just in time. The seadragon lashed out at him, its long fangs only just missing their target. Instead the dragon ended up with a mouthful of wooden planks, which only seemed to anger it.

"Draikh, I need you!" shouted Raim. The seadragon lunged again, and this time it was more accurate. Raim managed to jab his pitchfork up into the roof of the creature's mouth, but it released a sulphurous roar of pain that singed Raim's face and clothes and made him release his hold of the meager weapon.

His clothes were torn and tattered, the dark tattoo of permanence on his chest and the crimson scar around his wrist clearly visible and open to the elements. The dragon arched back for another strike, but Oyu bought him some time, swooping from the sky and pecking at the creature's eye to distract it.

One quick glance at the ship told Raim all he needed to know: if the dragon wasn't defeated soon, the whole ship would go down. All the sailors were working to push a section of the serpent's body off the prow of the ship, but the creature was hardly bothered about that. Tarik's face was white with fear and he was shaking like a leaf.

All these people would die because of him, Raim thought. He could jump into the water now and try to lead the creature away from the ship, to give them all a better chance. The fact that he couldn't swim was just a minor flaw in his plan.

Luckily, Raim didn't have to make that decision. A column of fire burst from below the deck, followed by Draikh who, with his palms spread, directed it toward the beast. It hit the scales and spread, like the base of a fiery waterfall.

Another roar from the dragon signaled that Draikh had definitely attracted its attention.

The sailors began to cheer as balls of fire began to attack different parts of the seadragon's body, making it loosen its hold on the prow of the ship. It momentarily forgot its attack on Raim and finally dived into the water to escape the persistent flames.

RAIM

"We have to get the ship moving, now!" said Shen. "If we get beyond the Xel rocks, we'll have a chance of reaching the South before that wretched creature can come back. All men to oars!"

Tarik gripped his arm. "You can do something, can't you, Raim? You controlled the fire—now do the same with the wind again. Steer us to safety past the rocks." There was desperation in his voice.

Raim looked to Draikh, to the place where the seadragon had disappeared, to the crew on the deck, and made up his mind. "Shen!" he yelled. "Shen, I have a plan."

All the sailors made way for Raim as he approached Shen, who was back at the wheel. During storms, they were all equal: oathbreaker, Darhanian, Southerner. Two emotions ruled their faces: absolute terror, and a glimmer of hope. Raim represented the hope. Was this what being a leader of men was about?

He just hoped he could handle the pressure.

Draikh's voice filled his mind. "I don't know if I can right now! I feel so weak from the fire."

"What does the spirit say?" asked Tarik. "Does he agree? Will he help us?"

If we don't do this, we are all going to die, Raim told Draikh. *You're the only one who can help us through this storm.*

Draikh stopped hesitating and swooped up toward the mast and sails. He tried to do the same thing as before, outstretching his arms and attempting to control the direction of the wind. But the moment his form connected with it, the wind blew him swiftly across the prow of the ship. He dropped to the deck and yelled at Raim: "It's too strong!"

"Try again!" Raim said, not hiding the blind panic in his voice. The sky behind them grew even more menacing, if that was even possible. It was as black as night, angrier than the waves. Draikh tried again. But the moment he flew, there was a bright flash of light and a sickening crack. Lightning had forked out of the sky and struck the mast, which bloomed fire. The lightning struck again, and this time the mast came hammering down in fiery splinters.

The waves lifted the ship up, and it listed to the side. Raim found himself dangling almost vertically as he hung onto the nearest rail. A flash of lightning illuminated something even more terrifying: a rock, jagged and immense, jutting out of the ocean like a spear. The ship tilted back the other way and

Raim's feet touched the deck again. "Is that the South?" Raim yelled, not really expecting an answer from anyone.

"Those must be the Xel rocks that Shen was talking about," Draikh said in his mind. "The home of the seadragons."

Raim didn't even have the mental strength to think up an answer. He tried to swallow down his panic, which was growing stronger with every passing moment. *We escaped the seadragon, was it all for nothing?*

Seeing Raim's plan fail, Shen's head was thrown back in maniacal laughter while his hands gripped the wheel so tightly his knuckles were going white. He was trying in vain to control the movement of the wheel, which looked as if it wanted to spin right off its axle. Shen had said the wheel needed at least three people to control it in bad weather. There was no way he could do it on his own.

In fact, from Raim's vantage point, it didn't look as if Shen was in control of the ship at all.

Shen's voice pierced the darkness and the wind. "We've hit the rocks!" he shouted. Raim watched as he let go of the wheel, which spun out of control. He took a run at the side of the ship, and then—to Raim's great surprise—leaped overboard into the roiling sea.

He wasn't the only one. All around Raim, the crew ran to the sides, abandoning ship, bailing out of the storm. The ship lurched, taking in water toward the back. She seemed to be caught on something—the rocks most likely—and the waves and wind and lightning and rain continued to batter her into submission.

Raim was paralyzed—he couldn't face the water ... Sola! He couldn't swim! And neither could Tarik. They would rather cling to the disintegrating ship than risk the water.

Draikh had abandoned trying to control the wind and was attempting to make his way back to Raim. But the ship's tenuous grip on the rock failed, and it came free with an ominous ripping sound.

Only half the ship came away, weakened by the seadragon's attack—the half that Raim was on. For a moment, his half of the ship hung there on the sea, suspended in a moment that he prayed would last for ever.

It didn't.

He let go of the rail and looked over at Tarik. He gave him one firm nod—one he hoped would give him the confidence to follow.

Then he jumped overboard.

His body hit the water with a smack, and then he kicked for his life. But the water overwhelmed him. The darkness swelled into his lungs, so much colder and more powerful than he ever expected.

The water consumed him.

PART THREE

WADI

Apart from Khareh's camp, the Weaver's camp was the biggest group of yurts that Wadi had ever seen. Hundreds of felt-covered, rounded dwellings huddled together on an open plain. There were animals too—not just goats and horses, but oxen and camels, birds with hoods over their eyes, and the odd dog running around snapping at heels.

People turned to stare at Wadi as she entered. She pulled her scarf up over her head to try to hide her face, but it didn't work. Shanna was riding on the pony in front of Wadi, and once they reached the outskirts of the camp, she jumped down, surefooted as any of her animals.

Wadi dropped to the ground as well, trying to ignore the myriad eyes staring at her. She stroked her pony's muzzle and followed the girl into the camp.

There was a peace in this camp that was a marked difference from Khareh's. There weren't large swords, bows, arrows, and axes littered on the ground, no stench of sweat and blood like in a war camp. Here, life was more domestic; the smell of leather drying in the sun, of fermented milk being warmed, and the dusty scent of stretched felt filled the air. That didn't mean that there wasn't a sense of danger too. The women squinted through hooded eyes, large sticks within arm's reach. And there were men too, from the few remaining tribes that hadn't submitted to Khareh's reign. They looked both strong and deadly.

Wadi and Shanna approached a yurt that was very different from the others: tied around the middle with a band of bright blue silk. The girl ran ahead then, but when she got to the entrance, she turned back to Wadi. "She is here, Wadi. Do you want me to tell her you are coming?"

Wadi nodded, her throat suddenly dry. She walked slowly toward the tent, and as she did so, more people came out of their yurts to watch her. When she was just outside, four women swept aside the curtained entrance. They were solemn, dressed in long cream tunics trimmed with intricate gold-thread detail. More than that, though, they all had scarves covering their eyes. They all functioned as if they were blind.

A tiny voice sounded from the dark inside the yurt. "Come in, Wadi."

She entered. She didn't know what she had expected, but it wasn't what she saw. There were almost no furnishings— no cooking stove, no bed, none of the normal accoutrements that would normally fill a home. Instead, there were carpets everywhere, over every surface, dripping from the walls like woven waterfalls in every color and style.

And in the center, looking up from the loom on her lap, there was just a young girl, her long dark hair loose around her shoulders and a silver scarf over her eyes. Wadi's heart pounded in her chest.

She recognized that scarf.

It was the same fabric that Raim had wrapped around his wrist, what felt like so long ago.

Khareh's words pounded in her ears: *I didn't kill her. I only... injured her.* Could this little girl be Raim's sister?

The name slipped out of her mouth before she could stop it. "Dharma?"

"You will address her as the Weaver," a gruff voice said from behind her. There was an old man sitting on the floor, his back bent over a small bowl of food.

"Grandfather, don't be silly," said the girl, who got up from her weaving and ran up to Wadi, embracing her around the waist. Wadi was shocked for a moment, but then came to her senses and dropped her arms around the young girl, bringing her close. "This is Wadi," the girl continued. "She's the one we have been waiting here for."

When their embrace ended, Wadi sheepishly unraveled her headscarf from around her face and turned to face the man. "Are you Loni?"

The man's expression softened, and he stretched out his arms as well. "Wadi? I'm sorry; I thought you were another person asking to buy a vision. So many people come to seek out the Weaver now that her reputation has grown."

271

"So it's true then? Dharma is a seer?"

Loni looked down at Dharma, reaching out to stroke her hair. "It's more than true. She is the most remarkable creature to walk this earth. Everything that she has seen has come to pass. Including your arrival. We've been waiting here for two nights already."

"You had trouble," Dharma said matter-of-factly.

Wadi nodded, blinking back the tears that rushed to the corners of her eyes. Dharma reached out and took her hand.

"I just don't know how to help Raim from here. But I couldn't stay with Khareh any longer. I had to escape."

Dharma stroked Wadi's hand with a tenderness that was almost maternal, even though Wadi was years older than she was. "I'm sorry, Wadi, but I have some bad news."

"What is it?"

"You're going to have to go back to Khareh."

"No, no, I can't." Wadi shook her head. "I have to find Raim, or go to the desert, or … anything but that."

"But Raim is already gone from the North, on a journey where you won't be able to follow him. Instead, you have a different role to play. An important one. Without you, Raim won't be able to win. He won't be able to take up his destiny and become the Khan of Darhan."

Wadi rubbed at the corners of her temples. "But how can I help Raim?"

Dharma's face was turned in Wadi's direction, as brilliant and round as a full moon and, even though her eyes— or what was left of them—were covered by the silver scarf, Wadi felt as if Dharma was staring into her soul.

"It is very stuffy in here," the girl said, fanning herself with her hand. "Shall we take a walk outside? That way, I can tell you what I have seen, and your part to play in it."

"I'd like that very much," said Wadi. She found herself oddly formal in Dharma's presence, even more so than with Khareh-Khan and his advisers. Even though she was just such a little thing—so young, still a child—Dharma spoke with the wisdom of someone far beyond her years. When she talked, people listened.

They stepped outside, to the scent of woodsmoke and roasted goat. Dharma skipped in front, and Wadi couldn't help but laugh. She was glad to still see a playful child buried underneath the wisdom. Her second thought was of worry: there were so many ramshackle yurts, tied down with ropes and weighted with rocks, that she had no idea how Dharma could navigate without her vision.

Loni touched her elbow. "Everyone in the camp sets up the same way for her, so no matter where we are, she knows where she is going."

"They really love her, don't they?" Wadi asked. But the question didn't need answering. It was evident on the face of everyone who came out of their yurt to see Dharma as she passed. Two young women instantly stepped ahead of her and began to sweep the ground to keep it clear of debris. Some even laid down mats of twisted grass, as if in offering to the child. They treated her as if she was a little goddess.

Then Wadi spotted another familiar face in the crowd. "Vlad?" she said, her hand flying to her mouth.

"Oh, you know my father?" Dharma stopped short and turned around.

"Yes. I knew him from Lazar," Wadi replied. She didn't mention that the last time she'd heard Vlad, it had been because his screams came through the thin walls of her yurt as he was being tortured.

Vlad's eyes opened wide and his jaw dropped at the sight of her. "Wadi? What are you doing here?"

"I escaped from Khareh's camp two nights ago. I couldn't bear it anymore."

"Couldn't bear what? All the trust the Khan put in you? Did you get tired of having to listen to the poor Khan's stories?"

Wadi felt as if she had been punched in the gut. "I don't know exactly what you went through, Vlad, but I do know that Khareh was terrible to you. I am sorry for that."

"Just make sure you are ready to do whatever the Weaver tells you. She will be able to make things right."

Wadi nodded. "I will."

"What do you know of Khareh's plan?" asked Vlad.

"Khareh has heard a rumor that the Southern King is amassing an army across the desert. I know Khareh is planning on going to Lazar and using it as a base from which to face the Southern King head-on. Maybe strike before he's ready and use the element of surprise."

Vlad raised an eyebrow. "And how is he planning on crossing the desert?"

"The pass-stones," Wadi said. "He's been obsessing over them. That's why he wanted me all this time. He wants to hunt down all seven, no matter which cities or how many lives he needs to destroy in the process, and then he will return to Lazar. Open up the route through the desert so he can go on and become the Golden Khan."

"But he will never have all seven."

Wadi frowned. "I know. I have two of them. Garus has one, and one remains in Lazar still. The other three are lost in Darhan."

"Is that what the Khan thinks?"

"Yes."

"Ah." Vlad nodded. "It makes sense now. Garus, that pathetic old sage, has been feeding your Khan lies. The last thing Garus wants is to return to Lazar, even as your Khan's adviser. For one thing, he knows as well as I do that one of the stones is in the South. With the Lady Chabi. So Khareh can never have all seven."

Wadi's mind reeled from the revelation. Khareh had been relying on Garus's information. If he ever found out that he had been lied to ...

There was a gasp among the people who had been watching them, and all eyes turned to Dharma.

"Oh no," said Vlad, rushing forward, even though Loni got there first. "She's going into one of her visions."

Dharma was shaking, convulsing on her feet. Her hair swung from side to side and her hands trembled—then began to move in the air in a distinctive pattern.

"Stand back!" said Loni, immediately taking control. Several of the women who'd followed Dharma around stood around her in a protective circle, keeping away curious onlookers—including Wadi. Loni scrambled to find a piece of paper and quill, fumbling in the pouch around his waist.

At an opportune moment, he slipped the quill—already dipped in ink—into Dharma's hand. He held the paper in front of her, backed by a thin stone tablet. Dharma's flailing right hand now created a series of characters on the parchment: beautiful, flowing script that didn't resemble any of the written Darhanian Wadi knew.

Even as her hand moved across the page, Dharma trembled and cried out. She quickly filled up one sheet, and Loni signaled for another to take its place.

Wadi just wanted to leap forward and wrap the girl in her arms, but like everyone else she only stopped and stared.

The fit seemed to stop as quickly as it began. Loni was ready this time, and caught the young girl as she slumped into his arms. A reverent silence descended on the crowd. Vlad gave Wadi a small nudge between her shoulder blades, and she stepped into line behind Loni, walking Dharma back to the yurt.

In the warm confines of the dwelling, Loni revived Dharma with a strong, sickly-sweet-smelling tea. Gradually color began to return to her face, and she pushed herself up to a sitting position.

She turned her face to Wadi. "With you being here, my visions changed again," she said, her voice quiet. "Grandfather, may I have the text?"

Loni nodded and handed her the piece of paper she

had written on. "Do you recognize this language?" he asked Wadi. Dharma showed the paper to Wadi, who shook her head.

"It's the language of knots," Loni said.

"This is the weavers' language?" Wadi stared at the parchment.

Loni nodded. "Used by the weaving clans to make their carpets. This is how the Weaver transcribes her visions."

"What does it say?"

"It says what I've been scared of," said Dharma. "That because you are here, the future has changed. Khareh is looking for you; he's angry that you are gone. But he is also determined to go to Lazar. If he gets there, he will meet the Southern King—who will also be heading for Lazar as soon as he can."

"What about Raim? Do you see Raim?"

"Of course I do. He will soon be with the Southern King, as the Council had planned it. But even with Raim there, if you are not with Khareh, then they will fail."

"But, I don't understand. Why will they fail?"

"Because only you will make sure that Khareh enters the city of Lazar through the main gates. The spirits will leave him then, and he will be weak. Only then can he be defeated."

"But he will kill me if I go back! He will never trust me again," said Wadi.

"You must trust me," said Dharma, her face solemn.

Wadi stared at Dharma for a second, her eyes flicking from the girl to Vlad to Loni. Then she nodded, although dropping her head into her hands. "I will return," she said, although it came out as barely a whisper.

"Go tomorrow," said Loni. "For now, just rest."

39

RAIM

His lungs heaved and burned.

Salt water stung his eyes, and he tried to lift his arms to wipe them. He couldn't. He couldn't feel his arms.

With a wrench of his back, Raim twisted, and with a hideous squelching sound, one of his arms came loose from the mud.

At the same time, his legs felt like they were plunged in the ice from the mountains as water rushed up his body toward his chest, threatening to engulf him. He was so weak, he felt his body lift in time with the water, and then the seductive pull of it as it rushed backward.

He coughed, spluttered, and urged his body forward, trying to get away from the water line. The beach was covered in tiny rocks, over which Raim proceeded to cough up his lungs. When the convulsions subsided, he rolled onto his back. Naran's rays seemed especially bright to him then, and he had just enough energy to shut his eyes to block them out.

He lay there, trying to remember. The creature.

And the storm.

There had been a storm unlike anything he had ever experienced. His heart pounded in his chest just thinking about it. He remembered Tarik and the crew, looking to him like he could save them. He remembered clinging onto the rail for his life, he remembered letting go, his body plunging into the water, and then... and then nothing.

Tarik. The captain. The rest of the crew. What had happened to them all? And Draikh—where was he?

No, really. He opened his eyes. His breath quickened, his fingers tightened over the rocks. Where was Draikh? He was never far from him. He reached out with his mind. *Draikh?*

No answer.

Draikh? Answer me, damn it!

Nothing.

Panic set in. He had to get moving. He had to see if anyone else survived. Since he had, the chances were good. He wasn't about to get stuck in the South all by himself.

But he was just so tired. Maybe he could just rest there a little bit longer...

As if to encourage him to move, water rushed up his legs again, covering his bare feet in foam. Absurdly, Raim wondered where his shoes had gone. He scrambled backward, then tried to pull himself into sitting position. He shouldn't have worried about his boots. The lower half of his clothing was completely shredded, and his legs were covered in shallow gashes, oozing blood—which was why they burned like they were engulfed in fire.

He forced himself to look around. He was in a small cove, on a rocky beach that ran all the way up the shore until it became dunes covered in long, tall grasses. The beach was deserted.

Almost. He heard a caw directly behind him. He craned his neck around and saw Oyu, standing over Draikh's head. Draikh was so transparent Raim could see pebbles through his weakened form. In fact, Raim had pulled himself backward so far that he was actually *in* Draikh's feet.

He immediately rolled to one side, then crawled forward on his forearms, ignoring the pain as the pebbles scraped his raw, salty skin. The thought of standing just yet was impossible.

"Draikh, can you hear me?" he said once he was level with Draikh's head.

Draikh moaned in reply. "Are we alive?" he asked.

Raim would have laughed, but he felt more like crying with relief. "Thought you'd left me."

"I seem..." It took Draikh time to form every word. "Seem to remember...you were the one encouraging *me* to stay away from you."

Raim had forgotten that, but then it all came back to him. Draikh had tried to control the wind, to divert the storm away from the ship. But he hadn't been strong enough, or he hadn't had enough practice. Whatever the cause, they'd lost the ship.

Oyu hopped over and Raim stroked his head. The gar-falcon's black feathers were tinged white with dried salt. They all needed to get away from the wretched sea.

"So what you're saying is, you disobeyed me and stopped trying to conjure the wind."

"And in doing so, rescued you from drowning. You're welcome, by the way."

"I was joking."

"I know. I'm just a bit too weary to joke. I couldn't control that storm anyway."

Raim pressed his fingers hard against his temple. "The creature?"

"It wanted the knot sealed under your skin. It sensed it—just as the behrflies did."

"What about the ship?"

"The ship is lost."

Raim pounded his fists into the rocks, only managing to make his sore arms feel even worse.

He hoisted himself to his feet and waited for his balance to return by placing his hands on his knees. It didn't come quickly. He swayed like a man drunk, like he was still on the ship. He scoured the beach with his eyes again, and there was no sign of Tarik. Or Shen. Or of anybody, not even the ship. There was no flotsam, no stray planks of wood drifting on the surface. Nothing to indicate there had been a wreck close to the shore.

"Can you move, do you think?" Raim looked down at Draikh. It didn't look likely, and Draikh was barely trying.

"We should get off the beach and try to find cover. Anyone who comes by here will see us, and they might not be friendly."

And then what? said a voice in his head—his own voice of doubt, this time.

One thing at a time. First, cover. Then ... work out a new plan.

Draikh wasn't moving anywhere.

"Do you think you have enough strength to become, you know, solid?" Raim asked.

"Maybe," Draikh said after a moment. Raim knew he had done it when the pebbles beneath the spirit shifted under his newly solid form.

Raim stooped, put his arms beneath Draikh, and lifted. He wasn't heavy.

Then he turned and aimed for the dunes.

40

RAIM

He stood up on the hill, looking down along the coastline. A cry from above him turned his head to the sky; his heart leaped to see Oyu making wide circles among the clouds.

There was still a chance of finding other survivors. It wasn't only an altruistic decision. He selfishly hoped that someone else had survived. He had no idea what he was going to do if it turned out he was alone.

The ship could have sailed a thousand miles or a hundred; how close he was to Darhan, to the South, or even to the desert was beyond his knowledge. He knew nothing, and that was terrifying. The thought had driven Raim all the way to the top of the hill, even though his legs were weak and raw and painful. His head hurt and his lips were split and cracking. He was dehydrated, which was ironic considering he had spent so long essentially marinating in water. Just the wrong kind of water.

The longer he stared out from the top of that hill, though, the more it became clear: no one else had survived the storm. At least, not along the coastline that Raim could see. He had hoped that the ship was simply in another cove, tucked away. But as far as his eye could see, there was nothing. The ocean dared to sparkle, as if it were made of the same material as Yun blades. And just like Yun blades, it was beautiful—but could quickly turn deadly.

The shock of this realization was almost too much to bear. *He* had brought his brother into this. Tarik had been living—okay, not *well*, but at least *in safety* with the Baril. Raim had his own protectors, after all. Spirits who were desperate to save his life and who cared for no one else's. Tarik had no such luck. *Raim* was supposed to be the one who took care of the people he loved. And again, he had failed.

He clearly wasn't the protector he thought he was. He fell to his knees and stayed there.

"You were right, you know. We need to keep moving," said Draikh after a while. Already the spirit was looking stronger. More solid.

"Did my mother help you?"

"What do you mean?" said Draikh, but he pulled on his lower lip with his teeth. He was feigning innocence.

"So, she did help you. She came to my rescue once again."

"I couldn't have done it in the condition I was in."

"Then maybe I should have died in the sea with all the rest!" shouted Raim into the wind. Anger—irrational anger—surged up inside him. "I'm tired of being saved all the time. If Sola wants me dead, then let me die!"

Draikh's voice was surprisingly calm. "If Sola wanted you dead, you'd be dead."

"Tell me where to go! Where are you, Lady Chabi?"

There was no reply. In defiance, Raim sat down cross-legged, looking out at the ocean. He wasn't going to miss any movement, any potential survivor, any wreckage or proof that the ship really did go down. So far, he had seen nothing. Surely something would wash up on one of these godsforsaken beaches eventually.

He sat there for what seemed hours. It had been a fruitless watch. But he couldn't stop looking. His body felt shattered, but his eyes and mind were alert. A moment of dropped focus and he might miss something. Miss his only chance.

He looked down at the cuts on his legs, knowing that Draikh was in no condition to heal them. But he didn't want to rely on anyone but himself anymore. The moment on the ship when he had almost released his own spirit had shown him what was possible. He knew he could do it.

He focused on the cuts, on the pain. He channeled his thoughts into feeling the hurt and fixing it, knitting the edges together in his mind. His skin warmed; the tingling sensation returning. *Heal,* he told himself. *Heal.* He felt his spirit rise to the surface. He squeezed his eyes shut even tighter, trying to force the spirit out. Almost … almost …

"Raim," said Draikh, interrupting his thoughts.

The moment disappeared, just as he thought he'd grasped it. "What?" he snapped, unable to hide his frustration.

"You need to see this."

"I'm not turning around. I know your tricks." He really had almost done it again. Externalized his own spirit.

"No, I'm serious. There's someone coming this way."

That got Raim's attention. He spun round, instinct driving him low to the ground. He peered through the tall grass and tried to see what Draikh was seeing. It took a few seconds, and then he placed it: a small figure, hunched over a cane, moving in slow trundle up the hill.

"It's an old man," whispered Raim.

"Could be a young man pretending to be an old man."

Whoever he was, he was moving straight toward where Raim lay crouched on the ground. When it became clear that the old man knew he was there, Raim stood up and brushed his knees with his hands.

He had to pray the old man was friendly. He had no weapons, no shield—no defense except his strength, which had been sapped by the storm. While he was still confident in his abilities, if the man could wield that cane, Raim was doomed.

The old man climbed the hill toward him, stopping a few feet away. Raim half expected a bow and arrow or a spear to appear from behind the man's back, but instead, he just stood there looking him up and down. Then, in a flash that belied his previously slow movements, he spun around and started heading back the way he'd come. He made no attempt to speak, but gestured with one arm for Raim to follow.

Raim looked up at Draikh, who shrugged. "You don't have much choice."

And so, Raim followed.

He looked down at his knee. One of the cuts that had been there was gone.

He had done it.

RAIM

Raim followed the old man inland, away from the sea and the shore. His eyes opened steadily wider as they walked, taking in the new surroundings.

Green, green hills spread for miles around. There was vegetation everywhere, but it didn't seem natural—not to Raim's eyes. The plants grew along neatly ordered, dead-straight lines, as if they had been planted along the edge of a sword blade.

There were so many rows, a seemingly endless stretch of them, heading into the distance as far as his eyes could see. The pattern they created was hypnotic; Raim couldn't tear his eyes away.

These are farms, Raim realized. *This is how they live.*

It was then that Raim had all the confirmation he needed.

He was in the South. This was the place where he would find his mother—and make himself whole again.

He snapped from his thoughts and turned back to the old man—who had meandered a fair distance in front of him. Raim's legs were suddenly full of energy, and he broke into a run to catch up. But his muscles were still weak from his ordeal and began to cramp up, so he slowed back to a walk. The old man disappeared over the crest of yet another hill.

When Raim reached the top, he pulled up short. He had reached his first village of Southerners. He could see the old man waiting at the door of the outermost house. It had a ramshackle appearance—broken boards crudely nailed together, a roof of dried grasses. It was surrounded by weeds. The rest of the village was eerily quiet.

He swallowed down his fear and forced his feet to move down into the village. He had no shoes, but his feet felt like they were encased in lead.

Once he reached the man's home, he was finally able to get a good look at him. He was younger than Raim had first thought, and had the bright spark of intelligence in his eyes.

The man pushed open the door and gestured Raim inside.

The salty tang of meat—cooked meat—wafted out of the door, and Raim's mouth filled instantly with saliva. His stomach growled. Draikh urged him in. "What are you waiting for?" he said.

But Raim wasn't sure. "Where are we?" he said to the man, and he stood rooted to the spot.

The man stared back at him blankly.

"Where are we?" Raim repeated, and tried to swallow down the desperation in his voice. "Is this the South?"

The man did finally reply—in a torrent of words, in a lyrical but fast-moving jumble of sound that Raim could not understand. But he understood something: urgency.

A noise from one of the other houses grabbed his attention. He craned his neck to look, but the old man sprang forward, grabbed his collar, and dragged him into the house.

The door slammed shut behind them.

WADI

The flames cast a warm glow inside the yurt, and Wadi snuggled underneath the furs. Dharma lay with her head in Wadi's lap, and Wadi ran her fingers through the young girl's soft hair.

"Does it hurt?" Wadi asked. "The seeing, I mean." What she had witnessed today had shaken her to the core. She had become—dare she say it?—used to Khareh and Raim and their sage powers. But neither of them, as far as Wadi knew, could see into the future, nor inspire the same kind of fierce, loyal passion that Dharma could.

"Sometimes. But only when I see things I don't like that I cannot change," she said. They lay in comfortable silence for a few moments. "I see Raim often."

"I saw him too," said Wadi. "Although not in the same

way as you. I saw him in Pennar. He was chasing the originator of his promise knot. He will be far across the sea by now. I hope he is safe."

"He would have taken you with him, if he could. I know that was written in his heart, even if it wasn't what was written in his destiny."

Wadi pulled Dharma closer to her. "Thank you for that. I wish I could do more to help him."

"What you are doing will help." The little girl sat up. "I have seen what happens to the South if Khareh succeeds." She traced a pattern on the rug with her finger. "There's a field, swaying with green, and water—so much water— soaking into the ground. The green is in rows, like the wefts on my loom. So neat. It's . . . it's beautiful. There are animals there, little goats and sheep and fat pigs, all kept in pens surrounded by fences. There are oxen, but they're working out in the fields, dragging big blades behind them."

"Blades like swords?" Wadi winced at interrupting her. But so far, Dharma was describing the traditional Darhanian view of the South: that they worked the land like a slave, as if it could belong to them any more than could the wind, or a droplet of water, or a tongue of fire. They did not respect what their animals could do for them—they didn't believe in taking care of them, in finding the best pastures. They believed that animals and the land worked only for them.

Dharma continued: "Not blades like swords. Bigger. Stronger. When the oxen pull them, it breaks up the ground, and the man can plant things in its wake. He grows food for his family, and has happy, healthy children.

"But that isn't what I see if Khareh wins. If Khareh is allowed to take over the South, he will do everything in his power to destroy their way of life. I see fires. I see those same green fields burning. I see animals slaughtered to feed his growing army. I see the people running from their homes, forced to leave everything they know, running toward their death. Men, women, children—he won't discriminate. To him, there is no life in the South that is equal to the North."

"And if the South wins?"

Dharma paused. "Does Khareh know much about the Southern King?" she asked after a moment.

Wadi shrugged, but then realized that Dharma wouldn't be able to see her body language. "I'm not certain. He knows that he doesn't want to have any Southern pretender invading his lands."

"The Southern King—King Song—is mad, from what I can tell in my visions. And mad men are often the most dangerous. His family was disgraced a long time ago, and he is looking for a way to restore his family's pride. He has slaves, and he misuses them ruthlessly."

"So he is no better than Khareh."

"No," said Dharma. "But that is why Raim must rule. He must not only be the Khan, but the Golden Khan, ruling over all the lands Naran touches, and the world will be right again."

"He will do it," Wadi said, although her mind couldn't help but worry at about the difficult journey Raim had to take. He was the key to all this—but he had no one to help him except Draikh.

"He has to," whispered Dharma.

Wadi woke up to the sound of squeals. It took a moment for her to orient herself. Where was she? Nothing was familiar, there were none of the sounds that she had grown used to, and her leg felt too light without its chain...

But beside her, there was the cry again—louder this time—and Wadi rolled over to see the curled-up form of a little girl, limbs writhing in what seemed like great pain. She remembered where she was.

"Dharma?" She reached out and placed a tentative hand on the girl's shoulder. She was like a kettle about to reach boiling point.

The tent door flapped open and Loni stumbled in, concern etched on his face. He carried with him a small bowl filled with water, and a rag. He knelt by Dharma and dabbed the cool, damp rag against her forehead. Her writhing body calmed; her flailing limbs turned still. She still cried out, though, and Loni muttered soothing words until it subsided.

A chill ran through Wadi's body and goose bumps rose on her arms. The night air was warm; it was the sight of the girl in pain—the girl who saw the future in her dreams, in pain—that caused her to shiver.

"It's been like this every night..." said Loni in a quiet whisper once the girl had settled back into a more restful slumber. "Every night since Raim left for Amarapura."

"What does she see?"

"She sees too much...but what causes these night terrors? She won't tell me what makes her cry at night. It distresses her too much to look too far ahead, when the future becomes more and more uncertain."

Wadi looked down into Dharma's angelic face. "The poor girl."

"She is stubborn. I sometimes wonder if she sees things that she won't tell us."

"Like Raim failing on his journey?" Wadi's mouth went dry.

Loni's eyes bore holes into her skull. "Maybe. But that's why she was adamant about waiting for you here. She knew we had to be here to turn you back around. To send you back to Khareh. Raim is going to need all the help he can get, and you are going to have to be there."

"I understand," said Wadi. "I won't let her down."

WADI

They equipped her with a horse, a long sword and a short dagger just in case, and plenty of food for the return journey. She hadn't worked out quite what she would say when she saw Khareh again—she would have to cross that bridge when she came to it. Her brief stay with Dharma had confirmed it: she had to win back Khareh's trust and accompany him on his journey to Lazar.

By whatever means possible.

She cantered across the steppes, the yurts representing all the tribes who had joined to follow Dharma fast disappearing into the horizon. But she hadn't gone far when she thought she could hear the pounding of a second set of hooves coming up behind her. Had she forgotten something back at the camp? Was there another message for her? Wadi's mind raced. What if Dharma had seen another vision that changed everything?

She glanced over her shoulder, but to her surprise she saw a young woman blazing toward her, a bright sword raised high above her head.

"Oh gods," Wadi said, attempting to spur her mount on faster. Her fingers grew slick with sweat around the reigns. *Erdene.* She looked back again and saw that she was catching her up.

"Stop!" The word reached Wadi's ears but she felt no inclination to stop, even if to ignore the command was futile.

A whistle sounded in the air, and Wadi's blood turned ice cold in her veins. Something hit her shoulder, hard, and Wadi cried out in pain. Her horse whinnied loudly, rearing up and throwing her from its back. She rolled on the ground, clutching her shoulder, as her horse fled.

The arrow had hit her shoulder, but luckily she'd been wearing her thick leathers, and a silk shirt underneath, so the arrowhead had not penetrated her skin. If she survived the night, she knew she would have a deep indigo bruise there to match her clothing.

She heard Erdene's horse slow down as she approached. Wadi looked up at the other girl, trying to keep her expression neutral. "Erdene? What are you doing here?"

Erdene's eyes narrowed. "It is my duty protect the Khan. And I don't know what you're up to, but whatever it is … I know it's not in the Khan's interest." She drew her Yun sword, the metallic twang of it slicing through the air.

Wadi's eyes opened wide with fear, staring at the drawn

sword. The ruse she had prepared about being sent away with Khareh's ring would not work with the Seer-Queen. "Erdene... please. Don't do this. I... I don't mean Khareh any harm. I saved his life, remember?"

Erdene threw her head back and laughed, but it was tinged with bitterness. "You saved his life, but you have betrayed him by escaping. He might pretend to be your friend, but I know the truth. I know what he wanted me to do: he wanted me to find you. Find you and kill you."

Wadi swallowed, hard. "Khareh ordered you to come after me and kill me?"

"Khareh-Khan didn't have to order me to do anything! I know what I have to do. Why are you sneaking around here, anyway? I thought your home was in the desert. Whatever you are doing, I know you're trying to bring Khareh down. And I am not going to let you do it."

Wadi looked up at Erdene. She loomed against the sky, a fearsome figure on the horse, her Yun sword held high. Wadi felt like a bug the Yun girl was about to crush beneath her boot. She had the sword that the tribespeople had given her but didn't have the skill to use it. She should have asked for throwing knives instead.

Raim had taught her the basics of how to use a sword, and Silas too. She'd had Yun trainers, but she was not Yun. Erdene—for all her love of fine things, for all her complicated feelings for Khareh—was Yun. She was one of the best.

"Maybe Khareh will never want me. But I know he'd want me to do this." Erdene then surprised Wadi by dismounting. Her hair was hair tied back in a long braid, and she was dressed in her finest Yun fighting gear. She had long boots that reached up to her knees, and a leather striped tunic that acted as lightweight armor. She also had a strip of toughened leather on her arm—a shield like the one Raim had used.

Erdene swung her Yun sword in the air in slashes of figure eights, and the sword dazzled as the light caught it in the air.

Wadi drew her own sword, but it looked blunt and battered in comparison.

Erdene charged at her then, with the fury of a person who was defending the one she loved. Wadi blocked the blow and recovered as quickly as she could—with all the conviction of someone who was fighting for her life. Fighting to survive.

That was stronger.

Or so she hoped. Erdene slashed at her again, and again Wadi was only just able to parry the strike in time. The blow had Erdene's sword right up against Wadi's neck; the only thing preventing it from slicing her head clean off was the pressure of her own blade back against it. She could feel her skin stiffen, stretch and then split beneath the weight. Her breaths quickened, her eyes stretched wide. With a mighty grunt, she shifted all her weight back onto Erdene, giving herself a split second to spin away from the sword.

Blood trickled down her neck. She could feel it running under her tunic; she could smell it in her nostrils.

Fear ignited in her bones now, a fire lit by the scent of her own blood. She unleashed a scream of anger and began going on the attack against Erdene. She was satisfied to see the sheen of sweat appear on the other girl's face, even as she dripped sweat like she'd emerged from a lake of exertion.

Then Erdene seemed to drop her right hand, rolling her wrist in a manner that suggested pain. Wadi was like a fear-soaked animal. She didn't think about whether she had hit Erdene on that side. She only saw an opportunity.

She didn't see the feint.

Erdene retaliated with a blow that knocked the sword clean from Wadi's hands. There was a moment of shock—of panic—a moment that Wadi could not afford. While she scrambled to find her sword again, Erdene put her boot on Wadi's back and kicked her into the dust. With another kick, she spun the sword away from Wadi's grasp. Wadi flipped onto her back, prepared to face her opponent and meet her end head-on.

Erdene didn't take a moment to reflect or brag. She struck down again, with a blow as hard and as accurate as she could manage. Erdene would show no mercy even after being her companion for so long. No mercy for the moments they had spent together. No mercy at all. Not so long as Wadi was on the side opposite Erdene—the side opposite Khareh.

Wadi's reflexes rarely failed her, and she rolled to avoid the blow. It rang against the dusty ground as if it had struck metal. Wadi couldn't imagine how any ordinary blade ever stood a chance.

She didn't know then if it was because she was Sola's child, or whether it was just dumb luck—but the sun came out from behind the clouds just then, striking the sword as Erdene was lifting it. The brightness of the flash scared them both, but Wadi was used to moving with the sun in her eyes. Her hands scrambled against her body, finding the dagger that she had tied around her thigh. She yanked it out, drawing blood along her leg as she did so, but in the heat of the moment, fighting for her life, she didn't notice the pain.

The flash of sunlight on her sword blinded Erdene for no more than a second. But a second was all Wadi needed. In that moment she moved swiftly up and close to Erdene. So close … her hand suddenly grew warm, warm and wet.

Erdene's mouth opened, then shut again, her throat trembling as she spoke. "Don't … don't let … "

But before she could finish, the light went out in her eyes. Erdene dropped to her knees, then to the ground, Wadi's dagger stuck in her side.

44

RAIM

"I'm sorry about that," said the man, in surprisingly good Darhanian.

The inside of the man's house was lit only by the light from a small bamboo stove. Shadows seemed to inhabit every corner, and as Raim's eyes adjusted to the poor light, he saw how simply furnished it was. Heat emanated from the stove, which sat on a table in the corner. On top of it was a small iron kettle, brewing leaves. The smell reminded Raim of his grandmother's favorite tea.

The man pulled a bowl down from the shelf, a deep crack running through the orange-red pottery. "I've been waiting for you." He poured a watery-looking substance into the bowl and passed it to Raim.

Raim sniffed it, and wrinkled his nose at the odd pieces

of … brown gunk floating in the clear liquid. Tentatively he raised the bowl to his lips and took a sip.

"Assuming, of course, you are Raimanan of Darhan."

Raim almost choked on his sip of tea. He coughed as the liquid hit the back of his throat, and he had to steady himself against the table. The man waited for him to finish.

"Can I take that as a yes?"

Raim hesitated for a moment, then nodded. "How did you know that?"

"Welcome to the Southern lands, Raimanan." The man smiled warmly, but then it faded slightly. "I'm afraid you've arrived at a difficult time. This village is very suspicious of foreigners, and someone washed up from the sea beyond the Xel rocks is especially suspect."

"You have been waiting for me?"

"Yes. I am one of the servants of the Council." He gestured up to the wall behind Raim. A painting hung there. Raim swallowed hard. It depicted Lady Chabi, her eyes closed in sleep, but unmistakably her. "We didn't know when or where you would come, but there are servants everywhere along this shore and the borderlands of the desert, awaiting your return."

So they have been preparing for me, thought Raim.

"It would seem that way," said Draikh.

"I sent out a messenger bird as soon as I spotted your body in the cove. Other Council servants should be on their way. I hope they come quickly. I might not have been the only one to see you. With any luck, they will reach us before the sun and the villagers have properly risen…"

The man's erratic tone set Raim on edge. Draikh seemed

to feel it too. His spirit form kept flickering in and out. Draikh was not only weak, he was nervous, and that made Raim nervous.

There was a loud bang on the door.

Now Raim's eyes were truly open. The tiny one-roomed dwelling had no other exit point. One window had been hastily boarded over, rusty metal nails hammered in at precarious angles. The other window was half blocked by a tall chest.

Raim cursed himself. What had he thought when he'd walked in? The darkness. The shadowy corners. Of course, there was no light coming in. All of it had been blocked.

He'd just walked into a death trap.

Worse, now he could hear shouts, commotion outside the door.

"Is there another way out?" he asked the man.

He shook his head vigorously. "I thought we would have more time! I'm sorry; I was following instructions. Find you, bring you here until you can be collected..."

"There's no time," warned Draikh. "They're right outside."

Raim took two leaps to reach the boarded-up window and began ripping at the boards with his bare hands. The man ran over to try and help. A few of the nails pinged back with the first tug, and with the second, half of a piece of board snapped off in his hands. One board down, only two more to go.

It was too late. The door swung open, and in the half-light, Raim could see the outline of a man—tall, broad-shouldered, imposing in silhouette. He stepped inside and dominated the space. There were more men clamoring behind him, but now

Raim was grateful for the smallness of the room—less room to be outnumbered in.

The man carried a large stick—it looked like the damaged end of a piece of farming equipment. Something a Southerner might use to enslave the land, just as Raim had been taught.

That meant the man wasn't a soldier. This, at least, gave Raim the advantage. Raim was Yun-trained. Now was the time to prove it.

He bent down and picked up the broken piece of wood from the window, even as the villager yelled and rushed at him. He had no idea what the man was shouting, but he could guess. He wondered what tales had been told about the North. He imagined they weren't flattering—if the attitude on the ship had been anything to go by.

Draikh? Raim thought as he ducked into a roll, sending the man running headlong into the wall behind.

"I'm useless. Too weak—I can't help at all."

You're kidding?

"Do you hear me laughing?"

He didn't. He didn't hear anything but the sound of his own heartbeat, the anguished shout of the Council servant behind him as the villager bashed against the wall, and the war cries of the other men at the door.

Another villager charged in headfirst, as if he was imitating a bull. An angry bull.

The man's clumsiness was his undoing—his bulk wasn't going to be a match for Raim's finesse. Raim used the momentum of the man's weight as he charged, swinging him around in a circle and knocking down several of his comrades along the way.

In the resulting confusion, Raim turned back to the window. There was barely space between the boards for him to pass. But *almost*. Just one more plank and that might just be enough...

He jammed his own piece of board behind the loosest-looking one and pulled—trying to use it like a lever. There was a bit of movement, the plank almost coming loose, but then Draikh called his name.

The men were back in action.

Raim was shoved against the wall, the entire building shuddering under the force. Maybe the house would topple over and he could make his escape that way. Absurdly, he wanted to laugh. But there was no time for that. The servant of the Council was cowering in a corner, clearly not a fighter, but the villagers were ignoring him: they only wanted Raim. One villager had him by the tunic, and Raim was whipped around into the crowd. But he still had his piece of board. He used the force of the swing to smash the plank into another of his attackers. It exploded into shards of splinters over the man's head and he collapsed onto the ground.

Raim managed to plant his feet firmly and pushed as hard as he could backward. The man holding him stumbled, took a few steps back, and fell, dragging Raim down with him.

The ensuing scream filled Raim's ears with a terror that momentarily paralyzed everyone in the room. The man had fallen straight into the searing hot bamboo stove.

He let go of Raim, who rolled off immediately. The

stench of burning fabric—then flesh—filled the room. The man fell off the stove, but flames licked at his back and his clothing. He ran in a panic against the wall, trying to pat down the flames—but rather than putting them out, the dry timber caught fire. No longer confined to their tiny brazier, the flames ran around the house, as if they possessed life of their own and had finally been set free.

That was all the distraction that Raim needed. The room was rapidly filling with smoke, and the men were confused, distracted, unable to fight. One of them grabbed at his foot, but he pushed him away with a swift kick. He scrambled on his hands and knees to the window, trying to breathe shallowly so his lungs didn't fill with smoke and send him into paroxysms of coughing like the others. He pulled at the plank again, and sent up a not-so-silent prayer of thanks to Sola once it came off in his hands. He pulled himself up and through the window, his tunic snagging and tearing on the broken shards of wood, but at least he was free. He fell with a thump to the ground.

He could hear what must have been the rest of the mob coming around the burning building to reach him. He wasted no time in picking himself up and running. He ran through the town, past other houses, not daring to stop and look to see who might be following him. He didn't know what direction to run in. He just knew he needed to get away. To get out. To get far from there.

He finally risked a glance behind him. A few men were in pursuit, but most were trying to put out the fire.

He kept running. He thought of the burning man in the

house and prayed he would get out alive. There was no way for Raim to turn back and check without being recaptured.

Suddenly, new sounds captured his attention. Voices. Horses. Dust rose from the mud-and-stone road in front of him. Before he could think—before he could act—a figure on a black horse rose over the hill, such a beautiful and blinding sight he could barely believe his eyes. The figure smiled down on him—a young woman with thick dark hair tied in an intricate knot above her head. Behind her, a group of five women crested the hill, all on horseback and dressed in long black robes. They thundered into the village and stopped in front of Raim, blocking his path.

The woman in front opened her mouth and spoke to the crowd that had begun gathering round. Raim turned around and watched as the men who had previously been chasing him—threatening him—turned their anger to astonishment, and then into something that resembled awe.

Then something even more astonishing happened.

The crowd dropped to their knees in front of the women riders. Raim thought back to what the spirit of his mother had told him: *I am a goddess in Lazar.* Maybe not just in Lazar. Maybe here too.

"Come, Raimanan," said the lead woman on the horse. "It is time for you to fulfill your destiny."

RAIM

The woman's eyes ran over his wounds—the cut above his eye, which dripped a steady stream of blood down his face, the splinters and scrapes on his hands from the planks of wood, his ripped tunic, his dirty, shoeless feet. "It seems we have arrived just in time," she said.

Raim had been given a horse to ride, and he plodded slowly beside the woman.

"We have been waiting for you, Raim," she continued. "My name is Mei, and I am a priestess of the Council, and handmaiden to the Lady Chabi. The old man who found you, Wu Li, sent us a message about your arrival. As soon as we received it, we came as fast as we could."

"Before an angry village mob could kill me?"

Mei laughed, and it was a delicate sound, like the tiny

bells Raim used to attach to baby goats so they wouldn't get lost. He didn't see what was so funny about him almost dying, though. "The villagers didn't want to kill you. They just wanted to capture you. Whoever handed you over to us would receive a hefty reward—the notice from the Council only went out a week ago, when we knew the ship was approaching. Of course, we hoped to just meet you safe and sound at the harbor, but things have never gone as planned. No Northerner has made the journey to the South since... well, I suppose since your mother did. Her arrival changed everything. Just as yours will."

Raim swallowed. This was why he had come all this way. "Are you taking me to where she is?"

Mei nodded. "Yes. Lady Chabi is ready for you. We don't have far to go. We must head to Aqben."

Aqben. The home of the Southern King and, if Raim remembered properly, the biggest city in the South. Khareh used to say that it was ten times as big as Kharein, but Raim had refused to believe him. He would soon find out.

As they moved, his ears pounded with blood and filled with the sound of the horses' hooves against the ground, the strange metallic sound they made. He couldn't even focus on what Mei was saying, even though he knew it was important. Everything was too different here. Too strange. And it was only getting stranger as they approached the city.

Raim was happy to spend the rest of the journey in silence, even though his head spun with questions. He concentrated on his surroundings, which steadily filled him with a strange mix of awe and dread. Whereas the little village in the countryside had seemed more or less familiar to him, as they traveled further inland everything changed. Everything.

For one thing, there were just so many *people*. They were on a path so well traveled it was beaten into the dirt, and Raim couldn't think why they didn't go off the path to give the ground some room to breathe. Then he saw the odd person lift their head out of the fields to watch them, and he realized that those people felt they *owned* the land they stood on. People used the path because they simply weren't allowed to walk anywhere else.

The thought baffled him.

Gradually other people joined them on the path, but no one spoke to them. That much, Raim could understand. He wasn't sure that he would want to speak to this group either, who looked particularly forbidding in their long black robes. The people around them were all dressed differently—some in barely more than rags, others in silks so fine he almost pulled up in expectation of being introduced to King Song of the South.

They stopped when they reached the outskirts of a city far bigger than Kharein. The entrance to the city was marked by a big stone archway, and the top of the arch had a roof that reminded Raim of the Rentai, the temple in Kharein. The corners of the roof winged out at the edges like the upturn of Oyu's wings. He reached over and stroked the bird's oily feathers. Oyu had rejoined him once he'd started the journey with the women. He was glad for the company.

"Is this Aqben?" he asked, looking out at the town, where buildings spread in every direction as far as his eyes could see.

Mei chuckled, though the rest of group remained silent. They all dismounted while a puzzled Raim stayed on his horse. "This is just town called Zibai," Mei said. "We'll stay at an inn here for the night, and then we will be in Aqben tomorrow."

Just a town? Raim couldn't believe it. Khareh had been right after all. Strange, too, was the concept of the inn. In Darhan, they would have stayed with a passing tribe, their horses fed, watered or replaced by whichever family had taken them in. Travelers were treated as honored guests, and always with great care and attention.

The group he was traveling with was treated with reverence, and more than a little fear, but Raim was shocked when Mei handed over pieces of gold in exchange for their night's stay. Hospitality would have been free in Darhan— with the expectation that the debt would be paid in kind should the need be reversed.

But here, even the people who served a goddess were expected to pay.

Raim was taken to his room, a rolled mattress of straw covered in a cotton blanket on the floor. But it was far too warm for him in that stuffy room, the heat closing in all around him. The tiny window at the far end of the room let in no breeze—in fact, it seemed to only let in noises that made Raim feel equally claustrophobic, because they were not the noises of Darhan. They were the noises of this strange, new place: the chatter in a strange tongue, the clink of glasses in the room downstairs, the sound of passing wagons. None of it made sense.

In the end, he slept in the stable, with the horses. It was there—surrounded by the one scent that was vaguely familiar to him—that he was finally able to close his eyes and sleep.

46

WADI

Wadi felt sick to her stomach. Erdene had not deserved to die. Guilt wrapped its hand around her heart and squeezed it tightly.

This is the steppes, Wadi, she scolded herself. Erdene would have killed her in a heartbeat. No, she wasn't angry because of Erdene's death—it was kill or be killed. But she knew she'd been lucky.

Erdene had been the more skilled fighter. *If there had been any justice...*

She couldn't think like that anymore. She turned to face the wind, letting it wash over her face and blow through the strands of her hair. Wadi gave herself one breath of wind to feel guilt, to feel sorrow, to feel *lucky*—and then she had to move on.

Inside her tunic pocket, she felt the gold ring she now knew she could use as a ruse to dupe any other of Khareh's followers she met along the way.

She approached Erdene's horse, who shied away from her, the whites of its eyes bright against the dark sky. Of course it would be afraid of her—it had just seen her kill its former master, and Erdene's blood was all over her hands. She felt the revulsion rising again and fumbled in her pack for water, which she sloshed over her skin to wash the blood away.

It almost worked.

She spoke softly to the mount until it let her approach, and then she swung herself up onto its back. She leaned forward and whispered "home" in its ear, kicking her heels into its flank. It jumped into a canter and the steppes began to disappear beneath its hooves.

They rode for a day, but it wasn't until she could see the green banner of Khareh's standard flying high above one of the yurts that a guard came out to meet her. Khareh must have relaxed his defenses since the defeat of Mermaden.

It must be nice to feel so comfortable, she thought. She wondered if he realized that he was about to let the most dangerous person he knew back into his camp.

"I was away on the Khan's business," she said to the guard, once he had drawn close enough to hear. She held up his gold ring between her thumb and forefinger.

He narrowed his eyes at her suspiciously, but once he saw the Khan's seal on the ring, he nodded. Wadi knew he wouldn't risk incurring Khareh's wrath by not bringing her straight to him. In the guard's mind, if she were truly a threat, Khareh would kill her straightaway.

Her heart beat wildly as she walked her horse into the camp. She no longer kept her head covered, wearing the indigo-dyed hood wrapped around her long neck, framing her dark, oval face. She caught the gaze of the soldiers who stopped their work to watch her, and boldly held eye contact. She was not going to be afraid anymore. She was not going to be a captive anymore.

Khareh needed her, and she knew it. She was going to make sure everyone else knew it too.

It was Lars who came out to meet her. She prepared herself to be led to the platform where Khareh received his visitors—prisoners or warlords or messengers—but instead Lars said, "The Khan would like to see you in private."

When she entered Khareh's yurt, he was working at his desk, Altan and Garus standing behind him. If looks could kill, she would have died from both of their glances. Khareh, on the other hand, didn't lift his head to look at her. He continued to sit at his desk, scribbling on a piece of parchment with a quill. For a while, the only sound was the scratching sound of the nib as it etched across the paper.

"So, you came back."

"Yes," said Wadi.

"And without a fight, or so I hear. Good thing my search party didn't find you first." He put down his quill and finally lifted his eyes to look at her. "An *unauthorized* search party, I might add. I told Erdene you would be back of your own accord, but I turned my back on her for a second and she went after you."

Wadi lowered her eyes and stared at the pattern on the carpet. "She did find me."

"Oh." The silence stretched out, once again. "And you made it back." There was a hint of a question in his voice, but Wadi knew her silence would speak volumes.

Khareh slammed his hands down on the desk, standing up so abruptly his chair crashed to the ground, its back breaking in two. "I told her not to go after you! Idiot girl!" With a flying jerk of his hand, he sent the inkpot flying across the yurt. It smashed into one of the wooden posts at the far end, black liquid staining the carpet and cushions.

In one swift motion, Khareh vaulted over the desk. His hand snatched at Wadi's neck, and only her quick reflexes, jerking her head back, stopped him from grabbing her throat. Instead, his fingers closed tightly around her forearm, which she held defiantly in front of her face.

"Why did you leave?" he hissed.

She wanted to cry out in pain, wince, yelp, anything—but she held her expression impassive. "It's not *me* you should be lashing out at, Khareh. It's *them*." With a jerk of her head, she indicated to Altan and Garus. "They've been lying to you."

"And why should I listen to you, savage?" he said, but his grip on her arm loosened. She was winning him over. Despite his harsh words, he was listening.

"The Southern army is coming. You know it's true, Khareh. You need to get to Lazar now, or else he will beat you to it. What are you waiting for? You have everything you need—your shadow-army, your regular army. You are the undisputed Khan of Darhan."

He dropped her arm brusquely. "You know what I'm waiting for. I want to own Lazar, and the routes through the desert. To do that I must have all the pass-stones. Garus said—"

"Well, you will be waiting a very long time."

"What do you mean?"

"Garus has been lying to you all this time, stalling you. He knows full well that one of the stones went to the South! Without it, you will never have the complete set. You could have searched Darhan ten times over and never found it."

Khareh stared at her for a few seconds, and then he spun on his heel and rounded on Garus. "Is this true, old man?"

Garus trembled like a leaf in the wind. Even Altan took several steps back, not wanting to be caught in the wake of Khareh's anger.

Garus stroked his long beard, running it through both hands. "You would trust this savage over me?" he stuttered out. "She has already proven to you that she bears you no loyalty— she tried to run away, she murdered your Protector, she is a dirty Alashan—"

"She saved my life!" Khareh growled. "I asked you a simple question. Is this true?"

"Please, my Khan, I have always served you..."

Khareh looked up at his shadow, who was swirling a dark gray. They seemed to be having a conversation that only Khareh and Garus could hear, as Khareh grew even more angry (if that was possible) and Garus lost more of his color and began to shake his head and mutter the words "no, no, no" over and over. "I just thought if you would stay in Darhan a little longer, you would become stronger, my Khan," he said.

His excuses were weak, Wadi knew. Garus just didn't want to return to Lazar under any circumstances. He knew what his reception would be once he got there.

"Enough!" said Khareh. "Garus, you have lied to me. For anyone else, the punishment would be death. But for you ... you deserve something worse than death. A punishment you have experienced once before. Exile."

"No—" Garus dropped to his knees.

"Stripped of title. Stripped of this clan. Stripped of everything you own. All of it shall pass to me—including your pass-stone, and the pathetic excuse for a spirit that you possess. You shall make her join my spirit-army, and your name will be less than dirt throughout Darhan."

"You cannot do that to me! I have not broken any vow to you—I am no oathbreaker!" Garus tried to stand his ground as Khareh's spirit approached him, but he was beaten down by the shadow. Wadi knew the shadow had won once Garus's pendant began to lift from around his neck, seemingly of its own accord. The spirit brought it over to Wadi. She tentatively reached out and grabbed it, then put it around her neck—adding to the two that were already there.

Khareh continued: "You are worse than an oathbreaker to me. You were my teacher. My adviser. Now ... go!"

But Garus stood firm. "No! If you want me to leave this camp, you will have to drag my dead body out of here. Kill me if you want to be rid of me."

"What, so you can spend your final moment in a position of privilege? No, I want you to crawl out of here with nothing. And I want everyone to see it. Outside—now!"

It was as good as a death sentence. With no clan, and no title, Garus was nothing. He would never survive out on the steppes.

"My people!" said Khareh, as he stepped outside. "I pronounce this man an exile of Darhan. Anyone caught harboring him will be put to the sword. Anyone offering him kindness will see their hands cut off. He has betrayed me, and he has betrayed Darhan. Now, march!" Khareh stamped his foot on the ground. When Garus didn't move, he stamped again, and again.

The crowd picked up the cue from their leader and a steady beat began to rise. Wadi felt an itch in her foot to join in, but she did not. She just watched as Garus was forced to stumble through the crowd and out, out beyond the edge of the army camp and into the wilderness of the steppes beyond.

The beat grew, until it became a thunderous roar.

Khareh stood in the center of it, allowing the noise of the crowd to wash over him.

This was the storm, and when Wadi stood next to Khareh, she stood in the very center of the hurricane. Khareh turned his face away from Garus then, and looked in the opposite direction: south.

47

RAIM

They reached Aqben, and Raim saw how wrong he had been to mistake the last town for this.

Rooftops sprawled in front of him as far as his eyes could see, and they kept going. They piled on top of each other, a jumble of brick and tile. And the people! Raim had never seen so many in one place. Normally, he would be glad to be out under Naran's sky. But he felt less comfortable out in the open in the South than he ever had before. Something about the sheer number of people just set him on edge. When he had been part of an army as a child, or as part of his Yun apprenticeship, there had been many Darhanians in a single place—but they didn't feel as crammed in as they did here.

Raim had never known claustrophobia before. He had never known a place where he couldn't ride for a mile and find a stretch of open grass—or even open sand. Here, not even people's eyes seemed open. They walked around as if in a haze, ignoring the sea of humanity all around them.

A sea of humanity. That's what it felt like. It felt as oppressive and strange to Raim as the ocean had. And it seemed as easy for him to drown in it.

The only place he could compare it to was Kharein, and Aqben was nothing like Kharein. They passed through entire neighborhoods that were more downtrodden than anything he had seen in either Lazar or Darhan. It was squalor he could barely imagine. The streets were lined with the detritus of everyday life—rotting food, torn rags, hunks of twisted metal—and suspiciously dirty water ran in rivulets between the houses.

Raim's stomach twisted at the sight. He thought to Draikh: *Has the king seen this? Does he know?*

Draikh shook his head, and Raim knew he was just as shocked. "It would seem the king has other concerns."

Concerns other than his people?

Draikh shrugged.

It's like everything I thought Lazar would be … but it's worse. The South is cursed.

"You know they call the North cursed?" said Mei, and Raim felt startled, wondering if Mei could read his mind or somehow hear his thoughts. But she was reacting to his obvious disgust. "Because of the promise magic that binds you all," she explained.

"They don't knot here, do they? Like the Alashan don't," Raim said.

Mei shook her head. "It is only the North. The North is sealed by its promise magic. The sages did that."

"When they burned down Lazar." Raim had learned the story when he'd stayed with the Shan, Lazar's governors and the guardians of all knowledge relating to sages.

"Exactly. They burned down all knowledge of how sages were created. But they also sealed the North in the process. That's why there are the seven pass-stones."

Like the one Wadi owns, thought Raim.

"If you possess a stone, you may travel freely between the North and Lazar. And the Alashan are able to bring exiles from the North through the desert, to Lazar. Or to the South, as they brought Lady Chabi."

Mei's eyes appeared to mist over and her voice took on a dreamlike quality. "When we came out of the desert and entered the South, you cannot believe the welcome we received."

"You were with her?" asked Raim.

"Yes, I was part of the Council assigned to her protection. She was—as she is now—barely alive, a shell of her former self. The Council knew they could never keep her safe in the North, but here, we thought we would have a chance.

"Several events in the South fell in our favor. We found out soon after we arrived that King Song's father had just died after attempting to cross the Sola desert to reach Lazar. He too believed that capturing Lazar would be key to conquering the mysterious lands to the north and all their riches.

"Much of his army was wiped out. Many women lost

their sons and husbands. Faith in his dynasty's leadership was shaken, and his son—King Song—came to power.

"We on the Council knew that this was our chance to strike. The people were already in awe of us for surviving the desert crossing, a task that no Southerner had done in recent memory. We told them that one day a man would come who could restore the South to its former glory. We made King Song swear to help us, and we would—in turn—help him. He's been building an army, ready for you."

Raim gripped the reins of his horse even tighter.

"Are you starting to believe this?" asked Draikh.

Maybe. It seems like they have it all figured out.

"They do, and you do. This is going to be your chance," said the spirit.

As they rode further down the winding streets, the atmosphere changed again. Abject poverty had given way to a more prosperous district. There was a series of low buildings roofed with warm red ceramic tiles. The window frames were carved in intricate patterns, and every now and then there would be a perfectly circular door through which could be seen a serene garden just beyond. Raim had never seen anything so beautiful and peaceful, even despite the sheer numbers of people that must surround them. At one point, a woman stood in a doorway. She was dressed in a color so vibrant Raim couldn't remember seeing anything like it before in his life. The fabric shimmered and glinted, even though it was a cloudy day, as if it had been washed in silver or somehow woven from a Yun sword. The pattern—even the brief flash of it that Raim saw—was more intricate than anything he had seen Khareh wear. He thought she was stunningly beautiful—until he realized he had never even caught a glimpse of her face. The opulence of her clothes had blinded him.

"Where are we going, exactly?" Raim asked.

"To the Council home inside the palace. That is where we will find your mother."

"And what about King Song?" Raim's stomach clenched at the thought of meeting the king. *What kind of leader waits for an outsider to come and take his crown?* thought Raim.

"A weak one," said Draikh.

"King Song is with his army. We will take you to him as soon as we are finished at the Council. Once you are rid of your scar."

At that, Raim grew lightheaded. He couldn't really believe that he was on the brink of achieving the goal he had set out with. So many things had happened to him on this journey: mastering his sage powers, seeing—and leaving—Wadi, losing his brother. Through everything, his main purpose had loomed over him. He would never be able to do anything right while he was scarred as an oathbreaker.

Soon he would be an oathbreaker no longer.

When they pulled up in front of the palace gates, Raim was strangely disappointed. The walls were tall and imposing, painted bright red and thick enough for men to walk along the top of them—he could see the helmets of soldiers patrolling the perimeter—but they didn't seem to impart any of the glamor he had seen in fleeting glimpses of other parts of the city.

Draikh flew up to get a better view. "This palace is bigger than the entire city of Kharein," he said. That got Raim's attention. "If it doesn't work out, we'll get out of here—whatever your proposed destiny," Draikh added.

Raim's heart rate calmed. Draikh was right. Destiny or not, he would make his own decisions. That much he had learned.

After they were let through the side gate, they rode through a beautiful bamboo grove that seemed so at odds with the hustle and bustle of the city. It was an oasis of calm. At the far end of the grove, there was a low building, and it was there that Mei asked him to dismount. Raim did so, all the while craning his neck to take in his surroundings.

The building had the familiar curved roof he had been seeing everywhere in the South, but this was adorned with little carved stone animals creeping along the edge of the roof's wing. There was a sequence of animals—a tiger, a horse, a rat, a dragon—who were all working together to pull a cart.

In the cart lay the stone figure of a woman.

"Come inside, Raim."

He hesitated at the threshold. This was it. He had wanted answers, and everyone had told him that this was where he would find them.

He was ready to find them. He stepped inside.

RAIM

Draikh was the most agitated that Raim had ever seen him.
As they passed over the threshold and into the dark hallway,
he swirled around him like a mist. Raim raised an eyebrow in
his direction.

"This place is creepy," said Draikh.

Raim nodded. *I agree.* The stillness was unsettling.

The hallway was short, and led into a big, open room,
sparsely furnished. In the corner there was a small bench of
dark wood so rich and thickly lacquered it looked like solid
oil. It was topped with a bright red cushion.

A large picture of a beautiful waterfall hung on the wall,
a wash of delicate color. Raim had never seen its like before.
It was even more intricate than the most perfect woven carpet
he had ever seen. It looked like a window into another world.

Mei walked ahead. "She is in another room, across the garden."

The garden reminded him immediately of the water pagoda in Lazar, but it was much larger, with even more features. There was a pagoda here too, but it was perched high above the lake on a rock, which was cracked and full of holes like a sponge.

The pools of water here were perfectly still, and covered in water lilies. It was serene.

Mei registered his awe. "If you think this is impressive, you should see the king's garden."

"It's bigger than this?"

"It's his pride and joy. That, and his army, of course."

As they circled the perimeter of the garden, they passed by several rooms, all which opened onto the pond. The garden was the fourth wall for the entire building—it was like the palace had been built with a large hole carved in the center. Most of the rooms were empty, and all were sparsely furnished—though everything in them looked as if it would cost a vast amount of gold.

As they continued to walk through the garden, Raim noticed people watching him. They were all women, all dressed in the dark black robes even though it was blazing hot. They looked at him wide-eyed, and when he caught their gaze, they turned away as if embarrassed to be seen looking at him. Some of them even bowed their heads. Others nodded in a seeming show of support.

"They've been waiting for you," said Mei. "We all have. You're the one we have all been searching for."

Raim could feel the growing tension, the fact that they were getting closer. There seemed to be ever more women—more attendants—as they drew closer to where the sleeping Lady Chabi must be.

They approached the far side of the garden, and there was a broad outdoor staircase leading to a second level he hadn't been able to see from the other side. Women in the dark robes lined both sides of the staircase, and they all turned their heads to stare at Raim as he ascended.

When he reached the top step, he was made to stop by a black curtain, thick as night. Two women stepped forward to draw the curtain aside.

There, lying in state, was the Lady Chabi.

Raim almost didn't recognize her. She was older than the woman he had seen in spirit-form, her face lined with wrinkles. But of course she would be. The promise had been made sixteen years before. Sixteen years she had been lying like that, barely alive.

He approached the bed, but his every step was heavy. When he was close enough to reach down and touch her if he wanted, he stopped. He turned to Draikh. *I don't know what to do,* he thought. He looked back down at the woman who was his mother, not knowing what to feel. This was the woman whose decision had changed the entire course of his life.

But this was also the woman who'd believed in him enough to give up her soul to make sure his destiny came to pass.

"You must wake her," said Mei.

"I . . . I don't know how."

Mei was silent.

Draikh floated next to him and placed his spirit-hand on Raim's wrist. "This," he said.

Raim nodded. He unwrapped the strip of cloth from around his wrist, revealing the crimson scar to the room. The women recoiled. He could feel their visceral reaction even though he didn't turn around to witness it; he heard their sharp hisses and it made him wince. The scar looked disgusting even to a culture who didn't knot their promises.

He closed his eyes for a brief second, and when he opened them again, the spirit of Lady Chabi was in front of him, floating above her unconscious body. "You have to remake your promise to me. You have come so far. This is the final step."

He looked from her to Draikh. *Are you sure I should do this?*

Draikh smiled. "What have we come all this way for?"

Mei held out a length of promise rope, and Raim gasped. It was the same thin indigo thread that he had worn around his wrist. The same thread that had burned to form the crimson scar. "This came with Lady Chabi, to be used for this very moment."

Raim had nothing of his own to promise with—at least, none of his own promise string. So instead, he plucked a hair from his head—crude but effective. *This will have to do,* he thought.

He reached down and took her hand, and it wasn't as cold as he'd expected. In fact, it grew warmer under his touch. He held the piece of cord in a loose loop around his wrist, and then wrapped the hair beneath the string. He took a deep breath. "I … " He stopped, the words choking in the back of his throat. He looked up at Draikh, who gave him a firm nod. "I am Raimanan, descendant of Hao, the last true Khan of Darhan. I promise I will stop at nothing until I take my rightful place on the throne of Darhan and all the lands under Naran, as the Golden Khan. I promise that I will pursue this goal with single-minded intensity until I have fulfilled my destiny. I promise this, with all my heart." With each sentence, he pulled the knot tighter, and at each pull, his conviction grew. He *would* do this.

There was a flash of light, so bright it filled the tiny room and blinded Raim. He moved to pull his hand away from his mother's, but her grip suddenly tightened on his like a vice.

He stared down at his wrist in utter disbelief. The scar was gone.

In its place, the knot that held the new promise of his destiny.

Raim shook. He shook with relief and shock. His body was wracked with sobs, his muscles collapsed so that he slumped into a heap on the bed as the immensity of the weight that was *removed* from him suddenly hit him. He was free of the taboo. He had the chance to make everything right again.

Now, with this bracelet of honor—as opposed to the scar of fear—he could be a leader of people.

Maybe he was starting to believe it. Raim was no longer an oathbreaker.

49

WADI

She closed her eyes and let the heat wash over her.

She had missed this.

Oh, how she had missed this. How could she have forgotten?

When she breathed in deeply, the heat hit her in the back of her throat and the sand cleansed her nostrils. Even here, on the edge of the cliffs—not yet fully out into the desert—she could feel its power.

This was her home. When she had lived here with the Alashan, she hadn't known it. But now that she had been away, she could tell by the feeling in her bones. She felt settled. Her muscles were relaxed. Her breathing slowed. She recognized her feelings as the same ones that had shown on Raim's face when they'd reached Darhan from Lazar.

That air had been his. This air was hers.

Khareh came up to stand beside her on the edge of the cliff. Wadi half expected him to say something dismissive, but instead his eyes widened at the sight.

"Sola's great desert. Everyone told me it would be impossible to cross. But now, here we are." He passed her a drawstring sack filled with things she had asked for: water skins, dried meats, shelter, and a cloak similar to the ones used by the Alashan. She slung the sack over her shoulder.

The pass-stones had led her to this place. She had cast her mind out to reach the spirits concealed within the stones, and they had led her to a spot not far from where she and Raim had first parted in Darhan. Close enough that her chest ached from the ghost of her wound. Somewhere along these cliffs was a tunnel—a new entrance to Lazar. But Khareh wanted to experience one night in the desert first, and Wadi was happy to oblige. It meant fewer people might follow them, because—for now—they had the entire army with them.

Khareh turned to Wadi. "The entrance is nearby?"

She nodded.

"Then let's get started. I don't want to waste any more time."

Khareh moved toward their horses, his own still bearing the immense embroidered saddle that he loved to ride on. The beast held its head high—it was taller than any of the other horses in Darhan, ponies bred for stamina not speed.

Wadi had to stifle a laugh.

For all his intelligence, he really thought that he could bring that horse through the tunnels? That he could just

ride out onto the sand and conquer Sola like he had conquered Yelak? Maybe Khareh was just the human version
of that horse—too ornamental, too big, too needy for the
desert. The desert took everything you were, ground it up,
and spat it back out again. The more there was to grind,
the harder it tried. Khareh was a feast in the eyes of the desert. Wadi was barely a bite. She had grown up being tested,
ground down, hardened and shaped by the desert. She was
like a piece of sand glass—sharp and smooth at the same
time, a part of the desert, one of its creations. It couldn't
touch her; it could only make her better.

"Stop!" she said finally. "You can't. You can't go through
the tunnels on that animal—you'll kill it."

Khareh looked set to protest. Loudly. But instead he
threw his head back and laughed. "Of course not! See, this is
why I need you, Wadi. This is neither the time nor the place
for you, Brundi." He patted the horse on its dark neck.

Then he turned back to the group. "In fact, this is not
the place for human soldiers. Lars—I place you in charge of
my army. Should I fail to return, you must guard Darhan
against the Southern King. But it is not my intention that
he shall ever reach these borders."

Lars bowed in response. "We will be ready and waiting
for your triumphant return, my Khan."

"Good. Tell all your generals—I will be addressing the
army in a few minutes."

He stretched out his arms and his shadow flew him to the
top of the army's largest elephant, who stood at the front of the
ranks at the edge of the cliff, the desert spreading out behind

them. All the Darhanian soldiers were in front, thousands of men standing in silence, and behind them, yurts filled with women and children too young to fight but old enough to help the war effort.

Their fearless leader was about to set off to save them. And if he couldn't, then they would have to save themselves.

And even further back, Wadi knew, were the Chauk. The ones whose spirits were being used to fuel Khareh's spirit army.

Who was going to save *them*?

Wadi stood by one of the elephant's great feet, danger-ously close to the edge. She enjoyed it because she could feel the heat on her back, warming her.

Khareh stood, his feet wide apart, his arms on his hips, balancing adroitly. Wadi looked up at him. This was when Khareh was in his element. He shone here. And high up on the back of that elephant, he looked like the Golden Khan. He quite literally had the desert at his feet.

Were it not for everything he had done, he could be a leader the people could believe in.

His voice boomed out across the crowd as he cried out: "Soldiers of Darhan!" His words were echoed by generals, relaying his message out across the masses. "Thank you for your bravery! We have united the North; we have conquered Yelak and brought down the traitor Mermaden. Now we are facing another threat to our borders. The King of the South is coming! The heathens are coming to Darhan to take our land and enslave our people. But I will not let them. I am your Khan. I am your Golden Khan. And when I return,

Darhan will not only be free, but the most powerful nation on this earth!"

A cheer rose up from in front of Khareh, so strong that it almost knocked Wadi back off the ledge. As word spread down the field, more shouts rose up until it felt like the entire North was cheering for Khareh.

Wadi swallowed hard, more determined now than ever. She had to do something drastic if Raim was going to have a chance. Otherwise...

Something on the horizon behind Khareh caught her eye. At first she thought it might just have been light glinting off the helmets, or dust raised by the crowd beating their boots into the dusty ground. But it was neither of those things.

It was shadows.

It was Khareh's spirit-army.

As the spirit-army passed over the heads of the soldiers, she watched them cringe, bend their knees, and even keel over in an attempt to get away from the taboo. They cheered for Khareh, but they were also afraid of him. Afraid of the power he wrought through the shadows. Afraid of the scar that cut across his hand—and in a thousand other places beside that they could not see.

Even Wadi cowered as the spirits flew overhead. In a flash, Khareh was down from the elephant's back, sliding down the ladders with unnatural ease, and by her side. "Are you ready?" he asked, a twinkle in his eye.

Ready to enter the desert? She was born ready. She imagined it would take them a day—possibly more—to find a route down to the desert from the cliff. She shrugged a response to Khareh, who took that as affirmation.

He spun round to face the desert, on the very edge of the cliff. He stretched out his arms, holding out one hand to Wadi. "Shall we go?"

She didn't take his outstretched hand.

He took two steps forward anyway. And jumped.

The air thickened all around her as a steady stream of spirits whipped past, the entire army. They swept over her, around her, above her. She had to follow that? She grabbed her original pass-stone with her hand, held it tightly, and thought of Lazar and the mission that Dharma had given her.

Then she walked to the edge of the cliff, and continued walking.

50

WADI

It was hard to imagine that somewhere across the vast golden ocean, there was an equally vast army massing against Darhan. Wadi stared across the enormous dunes and half imagined that she could see the glint of sunlight off armor, spears shaking in the air, horses pawing the ground. It was exactly what she had warned Khareh against—no army could survive the desert, surely? But what about an army that had been preparing for this journey far, far longer than Khareh's army had? What if they had provisions, plans, access to water, and an unlimited numbers of soldiers?

What if all they needed to do was take Lazar? Then it would be an easier journey into Darhan.

She now felt that the Darhanian army, for all their training, wouldn't have a chance.

If an army scout from the South came and looked now, what would he see?

The two of them, standing on the top of a dune—Khareh still in his ridiculous crown, his intricately woven cloak wrapped over his shoulders, Wadi in her simple indigo tunic of the Alashan. And behind them, a dark swarm of shadows as far as the eye could see. Would the shadows look threatening to them?

"The desert. We are here at last. I feel like the gods have brought me here to this moment," Khareh said.

Wadi turned away, staring at the sand beneath her feet.

"Let's get on with finding the tunnel."

Wadi took him only as far as they could go while still keeping in sight of the dark line that marked the cliffs of Darhan. They continued to walk in the morning light; while Darhan was still visible, the sun was not at its full strength, and while they still had food and water in their bellies, they were strong.

Wadi felt the sun warm her bones, and relished the delicious burn of her muscles working hard to fight the sand.

To his credit, Khareh refused to show much discomfort, even though he must have been feeling it. The only concession he made was to remove his crown, which he passed to his shadow to carry for him. Sweat soaked his hairline, making his dark hair seem slick with oil. As he struggled just to put one foot in front of the other, he seemed to lose the hardness that defined his character in Darhan—the boy trying so hard to hold on to his newly won power. Even with the spirit-army behind him, Wadi saw the true meaning of

Khareh's journey. He was traveling all this way, on his own, to prove his worth.

There was something to admire in that.

When Naran reached her peak, Wadi said: "Stop. We will rest here before it gets too hot."

Khareh, however, kept on moving, plodding one foot in front of the other.

"I said stop!" Wadi repeated.

He spoke without turning his head back to look at her. "If I obey you, I won't be able to move again today. Or possibly tomorrow."

"That's the plan."

"Oh, good." Just like that, Khareh's legs gave out from under him and he collapsed to the ground in a heap.

"Not so easy, is it?"

"I could curl up in the sand here and die, if my entire country wasn't on the line ... "

Wadi chuckled, but then sobered. She was silent for a moment, then ran her hands over the sand.

Khareh leaned forward. "What is it?"

"Can you feel that?"

He spread his palms next to hers. "Feel what?"

Wadi was silent for a moment. "There! That."

"What?"

"Water." Wadi's eyes shone. "Deep below the surface. If we had a waterworm, we could access it." She breathed a deep sigh of relief because she could still remember how to read the desert, as easily as words on a page. Even more easily, maybe.

The desert didn't betray her, didn't carry secrets, didn't try to deceive or confuse her. It told her the truth.

She could feel the water surging through the sand, far below the surface, every granule beneath her legs vibrating the message. But then something jolted her out of her reminiscing. Khareh moved his hand so that it was over hers.

She looked up at him in alarm. But he wasn't looking back at her with desire—at least, not that kind of desire.

"Thank you," he said. "For showing this to me."

She snatched her hand away like it had been plunged in ice water and set about preparing her shelter for the day. Khareh watched her with his dark eyes, copying her every movement.

They rested through the heat of the day, and at night they started walking again. Wadi followed her instincts, guided by the pass-stones, which brought them back again toward the cliffs. Far above their heads, she could see a dark spot—the entrance to a tunnel.

Her hand moved to her pendant. She wasn't sure if she was imagining it, but it seemed like the stone pulsed with heat. *Yes, this is the place.*

"Is that the entrance?" Khareh asked. Wadi nodded.

"Then let's go."

RAIM

"My child, my son. You have made it to me."

Lady Chabi awoke, her eyelids fluttering, the words coming out as barely a whisper. The Council women behind him, including Mei, all made cries of astonishment as Lady Chabi shifted in the bed, trying to pull herself up to a sitting position.

Mei rushed forward and moved a well-stuffed cushion behind her mistress's back. "Lady Chabi of the Council, do you remember me? I am Mei. I have been your loyal servant ever since—"

"Ever since I had to leave Darhan." Chabi placed her other hand on the woman's cheek, although the movement made her wince. "Of course I remember you. So, have I made it to the South? Did you do everything I instructed?"

"Of course, my lady."

Relief washed over Lady Chabi's features. "Then we don't have a moment to lose. Get me out of this bed."

The long years lying still while her spirit accompanied Raim had atrophied the muscles in Lady Chabi's legs, even though the Council had tried their hardest to keep her moving and comfortable.

"Are you sure you don't want to rest longer, Lady Chabi?" In truth, Raim wanted to ask her some of the myriad questions he had on the tip of his tongue.

"Call me 'mother,'" she replied, her smile sweet.

Raim hesitated. He knew that his mother was originally Baril, but Loni and the other elders had raised him as a child of the steppes. The concept of "mother" and "father" rang hollow for him. He had been taught that his destiny was his own to carve out, and he felt far more affection toward Loni and even his mysterious grandmother Yasmin than he could toward this woman he had only just met.

Obviously he had been wrong about his destiny being his own, but he still left out the word "mother." It didn't feel right. "I just have so many questions," he said.

"My spirit will heal me quickly now that it has returned," Lady Chabi said. She inhaled deeply. "I will be strong soon; I can feel it. There will be time for questions later."

"Our most important duty now is to retrieve the pass-stone," said Mei. "Once we have that, we can join the king with his army at the edge of the desert. He has been waiting for you, Raim."

Raim nodded, swallowing hard. He stole glances down

at his wrist as the Council women fussed over Lady Chabi. He couldn't believe his scar was gone, just like that.

In order to move from the bed, Lady Chabi had to be lifted into a palanquin—a bamboo chair supported by poles—and carried by two of the Council women. Raim chose to walk alongside her. He even offered to carry one of the poles, but his mother refused.

They crossed an enormous courtyard paved in gray stone to reach the main part of the palace—a single-story, red-painted building that was the widest single building he had ever seen. The contrast between the red and gray made the place appear like a boat in the center of a dark gray sea: isolated, huge, and imposing. The roof of the building was tiled in gold—so much gold that Raim's jaw dropped at the sight. It glinted under Naran's rays, almost blinding Raim as they crossed.

Raim had always believed that the khans of Darhan were rich, with access to all the wealth they could want in the world. But compared to the king's palace in Aqben, they looked like paupers.

All around in the courtyard, Raim could see other men and women being carried in similar chairs as his mother, but the men who carried them wore nothing but a strip of cloth around their waists. He couldn't help but stare. "Are there many in Aqben unable to walk?" he asked Mei.

"No, they are just rich."

"Why would the other men carry them if they can walk? Or ride a horse?"

The woman frowned. "They don't have a choice. They are slaves."

"Oh—are they oathbreakers?" Raim asked.

She shook her head. "They are property. Slaves. They do their master's bidding."

Raim stopped moving at this point, forcing the entire group to come to a halt. "Why do they accept it?"

"They have no choice, Raim," said Lady Chabi. "Life is different here. You are in Darhan no longer." She signaled for her litter to start moving again, and Raim picked up his pace. But he kept glancing at the slaves carrying their masters around, and shook his head slowly. They didn't have slavery in Darhan. They had strict laws about oaths, they had exile, prisons, execution—but they didn't own people. They didn't own land, either. Raim could hardly be surprised that a people who enslaved their land did the same to their inhabitants. It sent a shiver down his spine. Maybe someone from the North would be a better ruler here.

He climbed the wide set of stairs up to the main building. Two carved beasts marked the entrance, one with a ball under its foot covered in curious markings. The other had a knot around its neck. Both the ball and the knot were made of gold. King Song certainly had cause to be called the Golden King if this display of wealth was anything to go by.

The inside was dramatic. Open flames, in carved-bone lanterns suspended from the far walls, lit the enormous throne room, and richly painted murals depicting great battles in colors brighter than he had ever seen before covered the walls. Incense smoke, from golden burners that hung underneath the lanterns, assaulted his senses, and he had only just walked in the door.

Hundreds of men in long red robes milled around, but in among them was something even more surprising—dozens of birds, flapping across the vaulted roof from post to post. Raim grimaced as he stepped in something white, soft, and squishy—it wasn't hard to guess where that had come from. Mei grabbed at his sleeve and pulled him back before he could step on any more bird droppings.

Beyond just the birds in the air, there were birds on the ground—enormous birds of midnight blue with long trails of green and purple feathers that fanned out behind them like cloaks. One of the birds hissed at him as he passed, and raised its "cloak" so it opened like a fan behind its back. The feathers seemed to have several hundred eyes on them, all judging him. Raim backed away several paces.

"The king has an obsession with birds of all kinds," whispered Mei, to both Lady Chabi and Raim. She raised an eyebrow and turned her nose up in disgust.

When Lady Chabi's palanquin dropped on the ground and she lowered her veil, the noise of hundreds of men chattering stopped at once. They all turned to stare at the woman, and then their gaze turned from her to Raim.

Then, heedless of the droppings on the floor, all the men dropped onto their knees. The first to rise was one of the fattest men Raim had ever seen.

"Dear gods," said Draikh. "Three Darhanian men could fit in that man's robe."

He wasn't far wrong.

"Lady Chabi, it moves me beyond my wildest imaginings to see you awake and in good health."

"This is Yuzi, my lady," said Mei. "He is one of the king's trusted advisers."

Yuzi turned his steady gaze to Raim. "And you are our savior from the North." Raim thought he caught a hint of derision in the man's voice. Suddenly he wished he had taken Draikh's advice after all and dressed in finery equal to this man.

"Be strong and announce yourself," said Draikh. "Take charge. These men will form your court one day."

"I am Raimanan of Darhan," Raim said, trying to insert as much confidence into his voice as possible. *I'm never going to convince them I'm anyone with my words,* he thought.

"So what, then, a demonstration?" replied Draikh.

Yes, let's do it. Something small, first. Let's see them sneer at this.

Raim closed his eyes.

The adviser coughed, impatient, and though his eyes were closed, Raim could feel the weight of the man's gaze upon him. But then he was the one with the power here. He felt the strength deep in his bones, as if it was about to burst out of his fingertips at any moment.

He stretched out his arms and thought of Oyu, who was more magnificent than any of the birds in the room. Draikh lifted him just a few inches off the ground.

He lowered him.

Raim opened his eyes.

The king's adviser snorted. "What was that? That was sagery?"

Raim stared at him. "No. *This* is sagery."

Raim reached out his arms, and as he did so, Draikh flew toward the flames in the lanterns lining the throne room. Draikh reached out to the essence of the flame, linking with it as he had done with the wind at sea, and brought it close. It happened so quickly that Yuzi had to duck to get out of the way, but not before the acrid stench of burnt hair caught on the air and a finger of smoke rose from the top of the man's head.

He squealed, but Raim hardly heard any of it. He was too busy concentrating on Draikh. That was the key. When they held concentration together, they were stronger.

The flames danced around Raim in circles, Draikh chasing after the flames, laughing.

"You know what this looks like, right?" asked the spirit.

Like I control fire and shadow.

"Have you seen their faces?"

It was then that Raim's eyes *really* opened. To shock, to fear, to awe on every man's face in the room.

His mother began to clap, in loud smacks that echoed around the throne room. "Now that you have all seen what my son can do, go—leave this place, spread the word that your savior is here. Your Golden Khan."

Mei signaled for the other Council women to pick up Lady Chabi's chair again. They brought it to the far end of the throne room, past the men streaming the other way, all leaving to share the news of Raim's arrival.

Raim followed behind the chair, trying to resist the urge

to run, jump, skip, anything. Excitement pumped through his veins. *That was awesome*, he thought to Draikh.

"I know, we can put on a good show when we want," the spirit replied.

That wasn't just a show. That was real power.

The palanquin came to a stop in front of a gilded altar, with a top of rich black marble. Inlaid in the very center of the tabletop was a round pendant, identical to the one Wadi had worn around her neck.

"Hidden in plain sight," said Lady Chabi. "Clever." She looked over at Mei.

Mei stepped forward and prised the stone out of its setting in the table. "No one—not even King Song—knows what this is worth."

"Then it is a good thing we know better." Lady Chabi took the stone from Mei and placed it around Raim's neck. "This belongs to you, my son. Now let us find the king and bring him his khan from the North."

52

RAIM

Back in Lady Chabi's quarters, Raim was given his own room, and a fresh set of clothes was laid out for him. The garments were in the southern style, cut close to his body but with vast sleeves that hung down to his waist, and fashioned out of expensive silk. Even as he pulled the soft material over his head, he felt gangly and out of place in the luxurious fabric.

Lady Chabi had asked to see him as soon as he finished dressing, but he procrastinated in his room, staring at his reflection in the glass. It was the first time he had been able to look at himself without seeing shame. He was no longer scarred.

It should have been a proud moment. But now that he was dressed in the fine robe, edges piped with gold and inlaid with jewels, his stomach filled with dread.

"You look like a khan," said Draikh. "Or a king, I suppose. You wouldn't catch Khareh wearing an outfit like that—though I do like the jewels."

"I look like a fool," Raim said out loud. "I can't fight in these." To prove a point, he drew his sword and almost sliced one of the flapping sleeves in two.

"If you want to be seen as a king, you have to act like one. You have to play the part."

Raim sheathed the sword and pushed the sleeves up over his elbows. They fell down again. "It's no use," he said. "I'm not anyone's king. I'm not anyone's khan. Coming here was a mistake."

"But your destiny . . ."

"Whose destiny?" Raim turned his back on his reflection, not wanting to look at himself anymore. "This woman I barely know told me I'm the descendant of a long-ago khan. So what? What about Khareh's right to rule? The warlords in Darhan agreed. He's been training for his duty his whole life. He was *born* for it."

"That's why you have me to guide you. I know everything that Khareh knows. I can advise you. That's part of your destiny. King and sage in one."

I did it, you know? He didn't want to speak out loud anymore, in case some of Lady Chabi's people were around. For some reason he couldn't explain, he didn't want her to know what he could do.

"Did what?" asked Draikh.

I released my own spirit after I washed ashore. I healed myself. Just a small cut, but I did it.

"That's great!" said Draikh. "If you can lend your power to mine, there will be no stopping us. You see? This is all part of it. This is all showing you that you're right to rule." Draikh's words were meant to fill him with confidence, and Raim puffed out his chest. But it still didn't feel right. He couldn't picture himself ruling a nation. Protecting a ruler of nations, yes. If that couldn't happen, then the alternative life he saw for himself was rescuing Wadi, escaping to the steppes, and never returning.

"You can't do that," said Draikh. He floated at eye level with Raim, not allowing their gazes to separate.

"I know that," said Raim.

There was a knock outside his door. "Yes?" answered Raim.

"The Lady Chabi is here to see you," said Mei.

Raim walked over to the door and opened it. Lady Chabi's palanquin swept into the room.

She cast her gaze over Raim's clothing. "Very good. The king will prefer to see you in Southern clothes, I think. Put me down now," she said to her ladies. They helped her over to a chair in the corner of Raim's room. "Now leave us."

When all the women were gone, Raim didn't know what to say or do. His skin crawled as Lady Chabi stared at him intently. She lifted a hand to her forehead and rubbed her temples. "I have been asleep for such a long time, Raim. Waiting for this moment. They tell me that my spirit has been with you for all these years. But I don't remember any of it. Tell me—since you are no longer an oathbreaker, why do you have a shadow? If you were a sage in the same manner as Hao, you would not have a shadow like that following you around. It would come from within."

Raim swallowed. "I am not like Hao. You don't remember anything from your time with me as a spirit?"

"No," said Lady Chabi. "Spirits are not people, my son. They are sent out to guard promises, and if they are strong enough, they can interact with the physical world. But they are a product of a single moment in time. That is why I am old and weak, and the spirit version of me you saw was young and healthy." She smiled ruefully. "I miss that time. So tell me. How is it that you have this shadow?"

"When I broke my vow to you," Raim said, "the vow *I didn't know I made*—" He was unable to keep the anger from his voice then. He took a moment to compose himself. "It happened when I was in the middle of making an Absolute Vow to my best friend. Prince Khareh."

Lady Chabi's knuckles turned white on the arms of her chair. "What?"

"That's the reason your spirit said that she couldn't reveal herself to me. In case the spirit of Khareh learned your plans."

"Quite right, too! I can't believe...does that mean that he is here now? Khareh, blood of the usurper, is in this room with us?" She stared wide-eyed at the shadow.

"He is not Khareh. He is Draikh. He came to save me. He is my best friend and this is the part of him that would rather be with me than doing...whatever it is the other part of him is doing in Darhan. Khareh is not the same person I knew. Draikh is."

Lady Chabi studied him intently. "But you are ready to

do your duty. To fulfill your end of your destiny, and take up arms against Khareh."

"Yes. Except ... I cannot harm Khareh myself."

"Why not?" she said, too sharply.

"Because something else happened out in the desert. The bird that follows me is a garfalcon. He swallowed my promise knot to Khareh and made my Absolute Vow to him permanent. I can't break it. I *can* bring down Khareh's spirit-army. I can be a sage. I just cannot harm Khareh myself. No matter how much I might want to."

"Then it is a good thing we have an army behind us. Mei tells me that the Southern King has been preparing his army, but he is growing impatient. He knew he would need to wait the sixteen years from your birth for you to reach your Honor Age, and obviously there was a delay in getting you here. But no matter. You are here now. And, my son, we are going to make you a khan, shadow or no shadow. Now rest. You will need all your strength for the journey ahead."

53

RAIM

They rode out of the city, and Raim surprised himself by how comfortable he felt surrounded by the crowds of people. It was as if his mind no longer could be shocked by big changes. The magnificence of the palace made everything else pale in comparison.

His mother did not ride with the rest of the troupe. She traveled in a carriage—perhaps the only thing that Raim was not impressed by. Although it was gilded and richly inlaid with jewels, and clearly signaled enormous amounts of wealth, it did not compare in size to the Khan's great royal yurt drawn by seven oxen. Still, the Khan had the steppes as his "road," whereas here they had to travel on narrowly defined pathways barely big enough for the carriage itself, let alone if someone traveling the other direction needed to pass it. Not that they encountered many people traveling in the opposite direction. Most saw the Council's convoy and fled to get out of the way.

It only took them three days to reach the army outpost. Any spare moments when they stopped he divided between lessons from Mei and his mother on how to act in front of King Song, and testing with Draikh the limits of their new power. Soon, Draikh could sustain a wind for over an hour and could turn the smallest spark into a roaring fire. Not that they ever needed to camp. Every night they found a large enough town with an inn to house them. Raim wondered if there was anywhere in the South that wasn't inhabited by so many people.

Late at night, when everyone was asleep, Raim blocked his thoughts from Draikh and practiced his new skill. But every time he thought he was getting somewhere in unlocking his own spirit from inside his body, he either passed out or failed completely. He didn't come close to healing himself again. On the second night, he cut himself deeply with his dagger, to see if the additional pain would force the spirit out of him. It didn't work. He had to break down the walls he'd put up and ask for Draikh's help.

Draikh didn't say anything as he stemmed the blood flow and healed the wound, but he knew what Raim was trying to do.

Raim was snapped out of his daydreams by Oyu's sharp cry in his ear. They were nearing the top of a vast hill, and he nudged his horse forward so he could see down into the vast valley below.

It was his first look at the Southern King's army. Now

Raim knew the true meaning of awe. He gazed down and saw a shimmering stain of iron and flesh marring the entire valley floor. Just beyond it, barely visible on the horizon, he saw seemingly empty space that glowed yellow: the desert. Bright red standards—the color of King Song—flew from the central column of soldiers, but there were others there too: of armies brought together from across the South, all joined in the campaign to conquer the North.

There was no way they would all get across the desert. Raim just could not imagine it.

Halfway down the path to the valley floor, there was a vast tent set up with a view over the armies. King Song's military headquarters. It didn't have the sturdy set-up of a yurt, but it would suffice. A soldier—one of the king's guardsmen—came out of the tent and gestured to Raim.

"The king has been waiting for you."

"He should have sent an entourage out to greet us," said Lady Chabi.

"He wants to meet you on his territory," said Draikh. "Classic power establishment tactics. Don't let him see you sweat, and don't let his petty mind-games get to you."

Raim said nothing. He cracked his knuckles and readied himself. He didn't know what to expect from his meeting with the Southern King.

He dismounted.

"You go ahead of me," said Lady Chabi. Raim followed the soldier into the tent.

The inside was brightly lit with torches and seemed bigger than it had from the outside. There was a large table in the center, covered by an enormous map with polished tokens on it representing the king's different armies. There was a stretch in the center that was painted gold, representing the desert. There were almost no distinguishing features on the desert, not until it ended somewhere arbitrarily at the other end of the table. Above that, stuck on like an addition, was the North.

"Do not bow to him," Draikh said in his ear. "You are his equal."

The king stood observing the table, and only looked up when Raim coughed to signal his arrival. He stared at Raim for several long moments, his eyes scanning from the tip of Raim's new leather boots to his dark blue tunic with its ridiculous sleeves to the gold-edged turban around his head. The Council had not spared any expense in dressing Raim for the occasion.

"You are Raimanan." It wasn't a question, but a statement.

Raim didn't reply, but observed the king in turn. He was surprisingly slight, especially compared to some of the advisers Raim had met, and his face bore the lines of age—or of great stress. He had a long thin moustache, the ends of which drooped on either side of his small mouth and tickled his chin. It reminded Raim of the seadragon.

The king nodded, making his moustache shake. "I take it you have seen the army outside?"

"Yes," Raim said.

"And you are impressed?"

Raim raised an eyebrow. "I have never seen an army its equal," he admitted. "Of soldiers, that is."

"I have been building that army for sixteen years. Ever since I took my place as king. All I have been waiting for is the one who can show me a path across the desert. That one, I presume, is you." He craned his neck over his shoulder. "Since you are here, does that mean that the Lady Chabi is awake?"

"She is outside," said Raim.

"I am here," said a voice from behind them. Lady Chabi had managed to walk into the tent. She had been right—she was healing faster than normal. She moved forward and placed one hand on the king's map table to steady herself. "King Song, we meet at last."

Raim noted that Lady Chabi didn't bow to the king either.

"My lady—you are beautiful. It is an honor to see the high priestess of the North awake at last. When your Council said that in sixteen years, someone would come, I wasn't sure whether to believe them. And yet here he is. As you can see by this army, I have fulfilled my end of the bargain. You needed my army, and I have provided it."

"And now I present you what you need: Raimanan," said his mother. "He is ready."

"What I need is a *khan*," said King Song. "Instead you have brought me a boy, as green as a rice paddy in spring. I have heard tales of the new northern khan, tales that would frighten the feathers off a vulture! You are telling me that this boy will help me defeat him, more than my army? Pah. I'm not so sure, Lady Chabi, that you have fulfilled your end of the bargain."

Raim's first thought was: *He's right.*

"You're a sage," said Draikh. "Act like it."

Raim nodded. He lifted his arms and Draikh flew around the tent, sending objects soaring around the room. The king looked terrified and ducked beneath the table. His guards drew their swords but didn't dare approach Raim—fear was written on their faces too.

"Stop, please!" said the king.

Raim lowered his arms, and the objects fell to the ground with a clatter. "I may be a boy, but I am also a sage," he declared. "And you need me. Khareh-Khan is a sage too, with an army that will devour yours like a swarm of behrflies no matter how many men you throw at him. He doesn't just have an army of men. He has an army of *shadows*. I am the only one who can stop him."

There was a fluttering of wings outside the door, and Draikh said, "It's Oyu. He's outside."

Raim opened the curtain and the bird flew in, coming to rest on his shoulder.

The king stared at the bird. "Is that a garfalcon? My word, I have never seen such an amazing creature. Maybe it is possible to make a khan out of you after all."

54

WΛDI

She could see the indent where she needed to place the pendant. The problem was, an enormous boulder was blocking the entrance. She placed both hands on the stone and looked up. The boulder loomed over her, almost twice her height.

"Is the tunnel behind there?" Khareh asked.

Wadi nodded. She ran her fingers over the pendant. The stone pulsed with power against her chest, and she was both compelled and repulsed by it. This was definitely the right place.

"Move back," Khareh said.

Wadi took a few steps backward. A swarm of haunts flew over and began to move the boulder. It took more and more of the haunts to do it, but eventually the rock began to shift.

A cool draught blew onto both Wadi and Khareh from

deep inside the tunnel. She relished the coolness, although Sola's dry air quickly sapped it away.

When there was a big enough gap to fit through, Wadi squeezed herself inside and Khareh soon followed suit. The walls dripped with moisture, so surprising after the desert. She tried to imagine what the route might have been like when trade and commerce were freer between North and South, when Lazar was the center of activity. When the Alashan ruled the desert without worrying about shepherding Chauk, when there were more oases, places of rest—an easier life than the one they lived now.

She didn't think it involved wandering through a dank tunnel.

Had the sages known the trouble they would cause by sealing the tunnels to Lazar? Could they have predicted the way Darhan would falter—isolated and stunted in its growth? They had broken the natural movement of the world. Could they have predicted this new power struggle between a young boy who wanted more, and another who didn't know better?

She could ponder those kinds of questions later. For now, there were even more pressing threats to the world—a threat from Khareh, and a threat from the Southern King. Only Raim stood in the middle, able to do what the other two couldn't: lead without cruelty.

Raim could do it.

She just had to help him along a bit.

She gripped the outer edges of her pendant and said a prayer to the spirits she knew resided within. *Let us get there quickly. Let us not be too late.*

Timing was crucial. If they arrived when the Southern King's army was in sight, she wouldn't be able to tear Khareh away from the attack. They had to get there beforehand, so she could have enough time to coax Khareh through Lazar's main gates.

They traveled through the tunnel for what seemed like hours, negotiating three junctions on the way. At the fourth crossroads, Wadi made her request as she imprinted her pass-stone into the rock: *Bring us outside the gates,* she thought. The spirits controlling the tunnels showed her the way. Sometimes she tried to speak with them, but they never answered other than to direct her to Lazar.

She stumbled on a slippery rock underfoot. Khareh reached out and caught her arm. "Are you all right?" he asked.

"Fine," she said, snatching her arm away. But her movement was sluggish.

"We've been going for too long," said Khareh, noticing her fatigue. "We need to rest. Eat something. The haunts don't need a break, but we do."

Reluctantly, Wadi nodded. Her eyes were drooping shut with tiredness, and she would need all her senses alert if she wanted to outwit Khareh. "Just a bit further along, we should find a storeroom. We might be able to find supplies there—if we're lucky."

"I'll go on ahead and have a look," said Khareh.

Here, just the two of them, it felt so much more natural. Almost easy.

"Found it!" called Khareh a few moments later. "Although

there's just some weird-looking plant. The dried meat doesn't look like it would be good to eat."

Wadi smiled despite herself. "It's Jarumba root," she said. "You can chew it and it will quench your thirst."

Khareh took out a sharp folding knife and sliced two rootlets off the plant, taking care not to nick the main stem. Wadi was impressed that he knew how to preserve the plant. She took the root and chewed it, savoring the refreshing taste that tickled across her tongue.

Her first conversation with Raim had been about Jarumba root, she remembered. She had been distrustful of him, of course—he had been Chauk, even if at that point he hadn't been followed by a normal shadow. But she had also been excited. She could see the fire in Raim's eyes, and she'd wanted to get to know him despite herself. And although she loved the Alashan like family, she felt cut off from Darhan. Raim had just been a convenient subject to practice her Darhanian language skills on. Then she'd ended up losing her heart to him.

"What are you thinking about?" asked Khareh.

"Nothing," Wadi replied, but her eyes flicked to Khareh's spirit-guard before she could stop herself.

"Oh, you're thinking about Raimanan, aren't you? I wonder where he is. I wonder if I will ever see him again," said Khareh, staring down at his boots.

I know where he is, thought Wadi. *We are going to him now, don't you see?* But she wouldn't say the words aloud.

When Wadi didn't reply, Khareh continued. "How much longer do you think it will take?"

They had passed through four gateways. Three to go.

"One more night, I imagine."

"Good. I only hope that the Southern King hasn't beaten us to it. It will be much harder for us if we have to lay siege to the city of Lazar than if I can take them out in the open. In the desert, my army can descend on them like behrflies. The city will be harder."

"The tunnel will take us to the outskirts of Lazar, not inside the city walls itself. That way you can see whether the Southern King is inside or not."

"Great." Khareh jumped up, rubbing his hands together and looking more alive by the moment. He walked up to Wadi and placed both hands on her shoulders. He looked her straight in the eye. "Thank you for coming back."

"Don't thank me yet," said Wadi.

"Wadi, can I ask you something?"

She made a noncommittal sound. Tiredness was beating down on her like a hammer on stone. Still, Khareh continued. "Why did you save me, that night Mhara returned? I was beginning to think you would have done anything possible to kill me. You could have let her finish the job. But you didn't."

No, but I should have, she thought. Out loud, she said, "I don't know. But I suppose, I would rather you were in charge than the Southern King."

She had meant to lie to Khareh, but she was surprised to realize those words were true. It didn't matter, she reminded herself. Neither of those options would come to pass.

She bit down on her tongue before she could say more. She couldn't risk breaking the trust he had misplaced so fully in her. That trust might save Darhan. It might save the world.

That was worth more than her conscience.

"Well, thank you," said Khareh. "I wouldn't be here without you."

She knew he meant it.

55

RAIM

The ride out to the army's front line that evening was exhilarating. Raim had never experienced such an atmosphere before. The closest he had come to a real army had been Khareh's, when he'd skirted the lake at Pennar. Any warfare he had participated in as a Yun apprentice seemed like nothing but tiny raids compared to this.

The Southern army consisted of many different groups, all joined together under King Song's banner. Raim could distinguish them by the different colors and styles of their dress. Some wore armor similar to Darhan's: thick leather jerkins over long tunics, with loose trousers underneath. Others looked strange to Raim's eye, the men wearing full-body suits of armor, unwieldy and uncomfortable. Raim hoped they would take them off before they entered the desert or else they risked boiling in their chosen clothing.

As they neared the front line, there was another group of soldiers—the largest unified group Raim had seen. The majority of these men had no shirts on, just loose black trousers tied around their waists with string. They each bore an intricate tattoo on their right shoulder. Most of them looked strong, but Raim spotted a few whose emaciated bodies made him wince. Many of them turned their faces to look at him as he passed, their expressions impassive.

This is the king's front line? They must be his elite warriors, thought Raim.

"I wouldn't be so sure of that," said Draikh.

"Who are these men?" Raim asked the king.

"These? My secret weapon," said the king with a sour smile. "They are slaves from the western islands, and the fiercest fighters you will find anywhere."

Raim's brow furrowed, his mouth set in a grim line, but the king didn't seem to notice his expression darkening.

Instead, King Song spread his arms wide, gesturing to his entire army. "For generations, the kings of the South have wanted to make this crossing. Our libraries are full of tales of the great trading outpost Lazar, its greatness and richness, and of all the lands above the vast desert with their immense resources. Those resources could feed my people in times when we cannot grow enough food ourselves. And I am going to be the one to do it. Because of you."

Raim tore his eyes away from the slave army. He felt determination settle in his stomach, but he would address that later. For now, he still needed the king. "Your father attempted to cross once," he said, remembering Mei's story.

The king frowned. "It took years to recover from my father's attempt. Do you know how many lives we lost? Countless. Men and their animals, great soldiers and generals lost to the sands. My father took the largest army the South had ever known—until now—into the desert, and came back with only a handful of men.

"You can only imagine how they survived at all. My father was driven mad by the experience. The desert took his sanity, as well as his power. A usurper took over the throne and banished me to live with the other survivors. It was the most stupid thing he could have done, however, because those survivors told me all I needed to know. They spared me no details. How they wandered through that godsforsaken desert with dreams of finding the trade city, and instead found nothing—nothing!—but sand on top of sand on top of heat on top of death.

"Do you know how long it takes before an army of that size becomes desperate for water? Days. Hours. And even those who carried some water with them grew heavy in the heat and collapsed.

"They ate the animals first. Drank their blood and tried to suck water from their flesh and organs. Some even claimed to see shadowy figures on the other dunes—the savages that live in the desert—but despite their cries for help, no one ever came. But still, they were a good, loyal, army. For them, giving up was as hard as going on. They subsisted on the belief that if they walked far enough then one day, surely one day, they would come across the city, which had water in abundance ... or at least an oasis." The king fell silent.

"But they never did?" prompted Raim, after a period of silence.

"They never did. My father sent out smaller scouting parties to look for routes, but none of the scouts ever returned. He thought maybe some of them had found the city and chosen not to return. But that was only until he came across their bodies. He could only identify them by their weapons and standards. Their bones had been picked clean by flies, and bleached in that short space of time by the sun."

Raim shuddered. He remembered behrflies as well as anyone.

"That was when my father and the dregs of his soldiers turned back. But by then, it was far too late. His reign was in tatters, much like his army. So now it is my turn. I must avenge him."

Draikh spoke in Raim's mind: "Sola be damned, he looks determined."

I know, Raim replied. Aloud, he said, "But I don't understand. You have your throne here. Why risk crossing the desert again when your father experienced such disaster?"

The king's eyes swept over the vista in front of him. They had reached the very front of the his vast army.

"Because, young Raim, where my father failed, I shall not. The South is as strong as it has ever been, and it can be stronger still. I have been preparing for this moment for sixteen years. My armies have been training in the desert day and night. They can subsist on the smallest ration of water possible, and we have camels loaded with empty pots, ready to be filled with water and buried for the reserve battalions to drink from. I will have a constant supply of fresh soldiers to feed my campaign. I have learned from my father's mistakes. I only had to wait for one thing: you.

"I will establish you as khan in the North. In return, you will bring the Alashan to our side, yes? With their ability to find water and navigate the desert, we will reach Lazar. Show us through the desert, young Raimanan."

Raim's fingers tightened their grip on his reins. "I will," he said. He dismounted from his horse, swinging his leg over the saddle.

He couldn't help but shudder as his boots hit the sand. He was back in the Sola desert.

56

RAIM

Raim stepped out onto the golden sands glittering in the moonlight, and he almost gave up then and there. Could he really be doing this? About to head out into the desert, on the way back to Lazar? Only Oyu seemed happy about it; the bird had taken off across the sand almost as soon as Raim gave him wing. Oyu could bury himself in the sand to stave off the heat. Humans weren't so lucky.

Things were different this time, though. He was no longer marked as an oathbreaker. He stared down at his wrist—adorned with a promise knot, not a crimson scar. And this time, he knew what he had to do to fulfill his vow. Part of it meant that he find the quickest route to Lazar, and with enough water to supply an entire army. No easy task, but one he thought he could manage. But only if he could find the one group of people capable of knowing the perfect route.

The Alashan.

Wadi's face drifted to the forefront of his thoughts, as it had done many times before. He wouldn't be doing this if it wasn't for her, and they could be together again if he succeeded. This was the final leg of this journey. And the quicker he could do this, the better.

He walked out onto the first dune, his head held high.

"My, how things have changed, right, Raim?" said Draikh.

You're telling me.

"Do you remember what to do?"

He thought back to what Wadi had taught him, about how the Alashan could be summoned. Well, summoned wasn't exactly the right word, as the Alashan had no masters. But they could be "called."

Whether they answered would be up to them.

Behind him, he could feel the king's eyes on his back, awaiting some kind of miracle.

The miracle for Raim was just remaining upright as he walked out further into the desert. He had almost died—not once, but several times—out here on these dunes.

"This time, you are stronger," said Draikh.

True. He clenched his fists. The Alashan. He needed to focus.

He walked away from the king and the army. He walked until he could almost imagine that he was alone. All the while, he talked to Draikh.

Do you trust him?

"The king? Not at all."

He doesn't want to make me Khan.

"Maybe he does, maybe he doesn't," said Draikh. "He wants to make you a vassal at best, like one of Khareh's warlords, or to kill you at worst. To kill you would be my guess."

Raim stopped in his tracks. "Then why—" He cut himself off, remembering how far sound traveled in the desert. *Why are we helping him?*

"We're not. He's helping us. Let him bring his army, let him believe that he can get the better of you, but we know the truth. We are ten steps ahead of him."

Raim dropped to the ground. "Here. This is as good a place as any."

He dug his hands into the sand, running rivers of it through his fingers. He pushed at the sand, digging deeper, until he had created a crater for himself. In the crater, he drummed out a rhythm with the flat of his hand, in the closest pattern he could remember to the one that Wadi had taught him.

The Alashan read the vibrations in the sand and interpreted them. That's how they found Chauk wandering through the desert; from their uneven rhythms, their staggered footsteps, they could tell the presence of someone unfamiliar, scared, and desperate. He knew they would have felt the king's army, even though it was camped at the very edge of the desert. The sound of all those heavy footsteps would carry miles on the sand. He only hoped that over their roar, his little message would get through.

He sat there, drumming and repeating all night, until the sky lightened. Then he stopped and hurried back to the camp. He was not prepared to wait out the daylight hours in sight of Naran if he didn't have to.

His mother was the one waiting for him at the edge of the camp. "Did you manage it?"

Raim shrugged. "We will find out soon enough."

Lady Chabi's eyes followed Oyu as he swooped and hovered in the sky. She reached out and grabbed Raim's arm. "You must not tell the Southern King about your Absolute Vow, or who your shadow is. He will not trust you if he finds out."

"I won't," said Raim.

"Does the spirit hear all your thoughts?" asked his mother.

"I know how to block him, if I choose. He taught me that trick."

"I see."

Draikh swooped down, sending Lady Chabi stumbling back a step. "The question is, does *she* trust *you?*" Draikh asked Raim.

Raim didn't know the answer to that.

They didn't have to wait long for the Alashan. Raim was eating in the small tent the king had given to him as a temporary home when Draikh burst through the walls, buzzing with excitement. Raim followed the spirit outside, and that's when he saw several figures silhouetted against Naran's dying rays. They were moving quickly, in the method they used when hunting Chauk.

"Is that them?" the king asked, striding over to Raim.

"I think so."

"Then let us get started!" The king turned to his generals. "Get the troops ready to move. Remember, every man is to carry his own water, and if he forgets, it is his life that is forfeit."

They bowed and hurried off.

"Wait," said Raim. "The Alashan will ask for a trade in order to take us to Lazar."

"A trade?" King Song said. "How about, in exchange, I won't enslave them. They should be honored I am sparing their lives after what they did—or should I say, *didn't*—do for my father's army!"

"If you do not offer some kind of trade, they won't help you. They will just disappear into the desert and your dreams of reaching Lazar will quickly come to an end."

"Fine. What do you suggest?"

"Give them something they find hard to get here. Give them bolts of fabric that you use to make your tents and robes. Give them weapons. Tools. All the things they have to trade with Lazar for."

The king snapped his fingers, and one of his generals hurried off. "Done. Is there anything else before I head off to speak to the savages?"

Raim grimaced. "I would avoid calling them that to their faces."

But the king had already stomped out of earshot.

57

RAIM

Maybe Sola had been hearing Raim's prayers after all. The Alashan that had arrived were his old tribe, led by Old-maa. He would have recognized that old, wizened face anywhere.

Raim hung back while the king negotiated his trade, and the Alashan agreed to lead his army through the desert. Two of the Alashan were to take an advance group to prepare the water stations for the rest of the army. The advance group used camels to carry quantities of large empty pots. Once the Alashan found an underground spring, they would use it to fill the pots, burying them deep underground so the water inside would not evaporate in the searing heat.

From the moment the advance party left, the king was insatiable. The sun was setting and he didn't want to waste a single second. Horns blared out from the front lines, echoing further back as other trumpeters relayed the signal. Raim took the moment to rush out to greet his former tribemates.

Mesan grinned widely to see him, and they embraced. Mesan had been Raim's second in his fight to join the Alashan—a hand-to-hand duel against Wadi. It was a duel Raim would have lost were it not for the interruption of the horrendous behrflies. He and Mesan had been close ever since.

"What are you doing here?" Raim asked. The Alashan language came out clumsily in his mouth. He supplemented the words with hand gestures, so that anyone listening in would have trouble following them.

"Old-maa could not bear to travel our old routes, not after losing Wadi and the disaster we faced after bringing the Chauk to Darhan. Old-maa took the tribe to the southernmost part of the desert. There are no Chauk here, but we had enough waterworms to sustain us. Still, not all of us in the tribe were happy with Old-maa's decision to abandon you and Wadi. Many of us wanted to return to the North. That was why, when we heard the call we had taught you, we knew we had to respond."

"I thank you for that," replied Raim.

The army began to move, an enormous centipede crawling across the earth. They followed the Alashan through the dead of night, not stopping until the barest streaks of dawn appeared on the horizon.

Raim knew how to spot the signs now, so he wasn't surprised when one of the Alashan stopped in his tracks and sounded out a high-pitched whistle. The noise was picked up by the army lookout nearby, and he raised a trumpet to his lips and blew hard, the sound echoing out of the desert.

"What? Already?" The king clambered down from the camel he had been riding. "How can it be time for us to stop? We've only just started moving—and it is still dark! We are never going to get to Lazar at this pace." He walked up to Raim and jabbed a finger at him. "You! Tell them we need to move more quickly! We can't just stop and start. There must be hours of night left."

Raim stared up at the sky. "Not hours. But enough time for the entire camp to prepare their rest for the day, just as you must."

The king threw his arms up in the air. "Ridiculous. How many more days?"

Raim raised an eyebrow at Mesan and did some subtle signing with his hands. Once he got the response, he turned back to the king. "Mesan says it will take a week."

"Not good enough. Tell him we don't stop until there is light on the horizon. Or I will send slaves ahead to prepare the way, so help me gods." King Song spun on his heel and walked back toward his tent. The king, at least, had shelter carried for him wherever he went.

Raim's eyes stayed on the king as Lady Chabi rushed out to talk with the Southern ruler, their heads close, hands gesturing across the dunes.

"You like this king?" asked Mesan.

Raim shrugged. "We share a mutual goal."

"And you are certain about that?"

"He can't get rid of me until we reach Lazar. And neither

can I, for that matter. For now, I have to work with him. I need his army."

Raim walked with Mesan to reach the Alashan camp, set aside from the rest of the army. It was the only place where he felt truly accepted. Even with his mother, he felt uncomfortable. He wondered if that was normal.

Old-maa, who had once revelled in his departure, allowed him into their circle—as much warmth of feeling as he had ever received from her. As the Alashan set up their homes in the traditional way, laying bolts of cloth on top of a semicircle of rattan walls, he relished the routine. They were welcoming him as part of their tribe. Realizing this both comforted and terrified him.

"Behind you," said Mesan, and then he walked away. Raim turned his head and saw his mother heading in his direction. He looked up at the sky and saw that he had a while before needed to be under his shelter.

"Raim, you should come and stay in the king's tent. He has servants on rotation who will be using fans to keep us cool."

"Slaves, you mean."

She leveled her gaze. "For now, we must abide by the king's rules. When you are king, you can make your own rules and abolish slavery if you would like. But anyway, there are documents you should read to prepare you for your throne..."

"Let me stop you right there," said Raim. "I can't read. Not well, anyway."

Lady Chabi's hand flew to her lips. "What? You are my son, you are a son of the Baril, you should've—"

"I was raised on the steppes just like anyone else. When you abandoned me, no one knew who I was. My grandfather took me in, but why would he teach me to read? He made sure I knew how to fight, how to hunt, how to mend my bow. Important things. Wadi was beginning to teach me to read, but we ran out of time."

"Oh, Raim." Lady Chabi's eyes filled with pain and disappointment. It was not a welcome look.

"I need to set up for morning, and so should you. I'm staying here." Raim turned his back on her. He felt the sands shift beneath his feet as she walked away.

Did you see that, Draikh?

"I saw."

That look in her eyes. She knows I'm no Khan. No matter what Mhara and Aelina said about my destiny. You can't just go from soldier to Khan overnight.

He stilled his mind. He would need all his concentration if he was to survive the day.

RAIM

They continued for another night and day, until the third sunrise when they came to the first watering hole, marked with bright flags. It was a welcome sight, as Raim's water-skin was running dry. He imagined it was the same for the others, and worse for those who hadn't rationed their sips.

The advance party had filled enough clay pots to refill the skins of most of the army. The storage points stretched across several dunes, and soldiers were instructed to dig them up from underneath the sand. Mesan and three of the other Alashan used their waterworms to open up more channels for those that were unable to fill from the buried pots.

Raim was glad they had been trained to move on little water, and on rations of Jarumba root. They would need as much stamina as possible to reach Lazar, if Khareh was there. Each night seemed longer than the next as King Song pushed them to the very edge of their limits.

The king and Lady Chabi seemed to have avoided Raim ever since his admission that he couldn't read. He wondered if Song knew. Likely it would only confirm the king's suspicions about him: that he was not ready to be a leader.

"We'll have to be careful," said Draikh. "If King Song doesn't see you as a necessity, he might see you as a threat. Something to be rid of as soon as possible."

You know so much more about this political stuff than me, thought Raim.

"As long as I'm telling you, what does it matter? You learn quickly and I can tell you everything you need to know."

A loud cry disturbed Raim just as he was ready to settle beneath his Alashan cloak. Draikh hissed in his ear. "Quickly."

What is it?

Draikh didn't even have to reply. A sharp crack filled the air, followed by a scream.

Raim jumped to his feet and ran toward the noise.

A young boy, not wearing a cloak to shield him from the sun, cowered in front of the king, red lines striped across his back. The king wasn't holding the whip, but one of his guards was, sweat dripping from his forehead. A dark stain was spreading across the sand—a tipped-over waterskin leaking its contents.

Already the heat was rising in the air, sapping Raim's strength, but with everything he had, he flung himself in front of the boy. "What are you doing?"

"Move aside, boy. He is nothing."

"If he is nothing, then why are you beating him?"

"He is my slave. I can do as I please with him."

Lady Chabi rushed forward, grabbed Raim by the arm, and then turned to face the king. "Your Highness, he doesn't understand. They don't have slaves in Darhan."

"That's right. We don't need to enslave children to hold our power." Raim drew back into fighting stance. "Now stop beating him."

In response, several of the king's guards jumped up and drew their swords, pointing them at Raim.

"You think you can fight me barehanded, boy?" said the king, and he threw his head back to laugh.

He didn't laugh long. Within a flash, Draikh swirled against two of the guards, disarming them and giving one of the swords to Raim, the other to himself.

"Let the boy go," Raim said, his voice like gravel.

"Raim, don't do this," said his mother, her voice pleading.

"Listen to her, Raim. I know you might be a sage, but I am a king—and a king is always prepared." King Song snapped his fingers and two of the soldiers emerged from the tent. Raim held his sword firm, even as the pit in his stomach opened as wide as a gorge.

"It's bad. I can't do anything to stop it," said Draikh. "Not without killing everyone."

Then Raim saw what Draikh meant. The two guards dragged behind them a prisoner, a dagger at the prisoner's throat. It took everything in Raim's power not to throw down his sword at the sight. It was Tarik.

"Yes, Mother Sea brings me many gifts," the king said.

"Now, if you or your blasted shadow move even an inch with those swords, I will slice his throat."

The point of Raim's sword quivered, and then lowered.

"Better. And I will have none of that when I am the Golden King. You can rule your pitiful lands in the North, but you will always answer to me. Do you hear me, Raimanan?"

I hear you. But I will not listen.

Aloud, Raim said: "Give me Tarik."

"I don't think so," King Song replied. "I think I'll keep this one as a little collateral. Take that boy if you want him, he's nothing to me. But this one"—he gestured at Tarik—"stays with me until we reach Lazar."

Oyu screeched and circled overhead, externalizing the frustration that Raim felt. The king looked up sharply at the sound, his eyes following the garfalcon's movements. Then he looked back at Raim.

"What is that?" The king spoke each word slowly and deliberately. His eyes were focused not on Raim's face but lower, at his chest. Beside him, Lady Chabi's face had drained of color.

Raim grit his teeth and looked down. In the commotion, the ties of his robe had come undone, revealing the tip of the black scar of permanence representing his Absolute Vow to Khareh.

I don't care what the king thinks of me, Raim realized with a shock. *I'm going to be the Khan. I don't need his permission.*

He grabbed at his tunic and ripped it open, baring the scar in all its glory. Oyu let out another screech, but this time it didn't sound pained—it sounded triumphant.

"This is the source of my power," he said.

The king's jaw dropped. "Is it an oath?"

"An unbroken vow," Raim declared. "The strongest kind. This is the vow that will make me the Khan. Don't you forget the bargain you made with the Council, or I will make you pay for your treachery." He spun round, grabbed the slave boy by the tunic, and—without waiting for the king to protest—headed back to the Alashan.

Lady Chabi moved to follow, but the king stopped her. Raim thought that she would follow anyway, but instead she stayed back with the king. She even placed a hand on his arm and moved him away.

What is her plan? Raim asked Draikh.

"I don't know. But I don't like it, whatever it is."

WADI

They rested at opposite ends of the cavernous storeroom, facing each other. Wadi shut her eyes, but her heart beat so loudly in her ears that she couldn't sleep. She didn't know if she had the guts to do what Dharma wanted her to do.

If Khareh suspected her plan, he would not be merciful with her.

She must have fallen asleep at some point, because in what felt like barely a second later, Khareh was gently shaking her shoulder.

"Come on, Wadi. We've rested for long enough."

She sat up, embarrassed that she'd slept for so long and that Khareh had been forced to wake her. She wiped the sleep from her eyes and shook her head quickly to awaken her senses.

"We don't have much further to go," she said, leading

Khareh into the main tunnel. Her stomach turned, and she had to grip the wall next to her.

"Wadi?" Khareh's voice was filled with concern.

"Sorry," she said, between gasps of air. "It's the shadows. The haunts. I have never been so close to so many of them." The tunnel was so thick with shadow the torches she and Khareh carried were barely able to cast any light in front of them.

"Do you know what I see when I look at them?" asked Khareh. "I see faces. Hundreds of faces. Faces that will help me to victory."

Wadi couldn't look.

She steadied herself. Then she gestured for him to follow, and they headed down the tunnel. They came to the next doorway quickly, and with the turn of her pass-stone, Wadi let them through.

"You can get rid of those stones soon," said Khareh.

Wadi let herself smile. "Yes, only two more turns left. But I was rid of my stone once before, and somehow it still comes back to me. My destiny is tied to these stones, I fear."

"I won't let it stay that way," said Khareh.

Wadi shrugged. "In a way, I want it to. I want to help. It's not right that all those people are stuck in Lazar, with no way of returning to their homes and families even after their oaths are forgotten. It's barbaric. The sages didn't think of that when they sealed the tunnels."

"No, they didn't. They also prevented any trade between the North and South. Darhan has suffered because of it."

Wadi searched Khareh's face for any hint of a malicious

plan, but he seemed genuinely concerned about the barrier to progress.

The sound of rushing water filled the tunnel, and Khareh's eyes grew wide as they passed a natural window in the rock. He leaned against the edge and peered down at the sight of the massive underground river that coursed its way deep under the mountains, and eventually through Lazar.

They were further downriver than the enormous cavern she had taken Raim through, not so long ago. Here, they were closer to where the waterworms were bred. In fact, only a few steps later, they came across one of the breeding caves. Khareh stared in amazement at the millions of little eggs sitting in shallow pools of water. They seemed to glow with their own supernatural light, illuminating the caves in the darkness.

"Only a few worms will actually make it out alive," said Wadi. "But they breed all these eggs, in case. It's a delicate process. The Shan have to make sure they capture the worm right at the moment it hatches. If they don't, it will try to drink up all the water in the cave—including all the eggs that are around it—and make itself explode."

"Incredible," said Draikh. "I've heard of the Shan. Garus was one of them."

Wadi nodded. "They are led by an old man named Puutra-bar now. They style themselves after the Baril, hence the "bar" ending."

"And this is how the Alashan find water?"

"This is what they trade for, yes. They get waterworms in exchange for giving oathbreakers safe passage across the desert and bringing them to the city. But they would rather not have to trade with Lazar at all."

"So the Alashan would welcome it if I opened the trade routes between Lazar and Darhan again?"

Wadi nodded. "They would welcome it if they no longer had to transport Chauk through the desert. Too many have died needlessly. We do not find them all." She paused. "We are almost there."

At the final turn, the atmosphere between them changed. They could both sense the heat rising in the tunnel. It would have felt oppressive if it hadn't been so exciting. They were reaching the end of their journey.

Even the spirits that guarded the tunnel seemed impatient to let them through. "This is the final gate," said Wadi. "Maybe you want to go first?"

He stepped past her and turned the final corner of the tunnel. "Wadi... it's magnificent."

She stepped out behind him. Her heart stopped in her chest and her breath caught. It was possibly the most wondrous sight she had ever seen. They were high up in a cliff, looking down through a window onto the entire desert. The sun was just setting, bathing the dunes in a red-orange glow. Unlike before, Wadi could see steps cut into the side of the cliff, steps that would lead down to the path into Lazar. And she would be able to find that path and bring Khareh to it. She had the navigational instincts of the Alashan. It was in her blood to be able to find Lazar and negotiate the mysterious avenues of the desert.

Something glinted on the horizon, catching the light and reflecting it. Wadi shielded her eyes against it.

"What direction is that?" asked Khareh.

"It's ... south," said Wadi.

"That's what I thought. That's the Southern King's army. They're almost here."

"The entire army?"

"They must have had help. Maybe it's one of your tribes?"

"The Alashan? The Alashan wouldn't help anyone through the desert. Unless ... "

"Unless they had a great-enough trade."

That wasn't what Wadi was going to say. She was going to say *unless they had Raim*. But she nodded. Let Khareh think that.

"Then we have no time to lose. They look only a day's march away. That means we have to be ready for them."

"Khareh?"

"Yes, Wadi?"

"Claim the city of Lazar as your own. Even without all the pass-stones, you are a sage. They will need protecting."

"They will accept me as their leader?"

She nodded. "I can help convince them."

"And you would do that?" he asked.

Her throat turned dry. "Of course," she managed to choke out.

"Well then, Wadi. Take me into Lazar."

"As you ask, Khareh-Khan."

RAIM

He had marked the exact place where Tarik had been held prisoner.

There was no way that the king was going to get away with threatening him and holding his brother prisoner. So Raim decided to do the unthinkable. It filled him with fear and went against everything he had ever known about desert survival, but it was the only way. He was going to rescue Tarik, but he was doing it at the height of day, when Naran was at her peak.

Even opening his eyes at this time of day felt unnatural. But Mesan assured him that he could do it. The Alashan managed it on rare occasions—they trained for it, learning from experience how to move in the heat of the day—and now Raim was going to attempt a daylight run without destroying his body in the process. His eyelids peeled apart, squinting in protest at the bright light. Even the slightest exertion—just blinking—caused beads of sweat to appear on his forehead. His mind screamed at him that this was wrong, but he kept going. He stretched his legs, keeping every movement slow and smooth so as not to disturb the others around him. The king was hidden away in his tent and the soldiers around him were all sleeping, their heads completely covered by their cloaks, masking them against the sun.

Being awake while everyone was asleep was strange. They resembled more a sea of rocks on golden water, pebbles on a beach, than an army.

Draikh, Raim reached out to the spirit.

"I am here."

Are you feeling strong?

"I'm ready to kick some southern backside, if that's what you mean."

Good. Raim held his arms out and Draikh lifted him off the ground. That way he wouldn't make any vibrations that might signal his approach. Together, they flew over to Tarik's prison tent. Raim held his breath as he flew past the guards, but no one moved a muscle. Sweat poured from his face, and he wiped his eyes with his upper arm. Draikh dropped him down by the tent, and Raim swiftly pulled up one of the pegs anchoring it into the ground. The bottom edge of the tent rippled and Raim froze, his muscles tensed, wondering if anyone inside the tent had seen.

He waited for one second. Then another.

No movement. He breathed a quick sigh of relief, then

dropped down to his belly. Slithering like a sand-snake, he made his way into the tent.

It took a moment for his eyes to adjust to the dim interior from the brightness of the outside. The air inside the tent was incredibly humid, made sticky and wet by the breathing of its occupants. Raim much preferred to be outside, where at least the air was dry.

In the far end of the tent, there was a cage, like something Raim might use to trap rabbits on the steppes. Cramped inside the tiny space, folded up like a scroll, his wrists wrapped in chains, was Tarik. On the opposite side of the tent, two guards were asleep, curled up under their Alashan-like hoods even though they weren't directly outside.

"Surely one of them should be awake," said Draikh.

Gods, who wouldn't fall asleep in this tent? Even I feel drowsy and I've only been in here for a few seconds.

Still, Raim didn't want to hang around to see if one of them might stir. He crept over to the cage. He didn't want to wake Tarik the normal way, so instead he used a tip that Mesan had taught him. He poured a drop of water from his water bottle onto a strip of cloth and placed it on Tarik's wrists. His brother's skin was almost searing to touch, and Raim worried that he might be suffering even beyond being kept in the cage. If he had been in a similar condition to Raim when he'd been washed up on the shore, he would have needed serious treatment. He doubted the king had given it to him.

Tarik's eyes fluttered open. He stared wide-eyed at Raim's face and momentarily recoiled, but relaxed when he recognized his brother. Raim put a finger against his own lips, then slipped a piece of Jarumba root out of his pocket. He passed it through the bars, and Tarik bit down on it eagerly. His eyes rolled back in his head as if he was experiencing some kind of ecstasy.

"Tarik, where are the keys to the cage?" Raim whispered. He held up the thick lock that held the bars together. He could maybe hack through it with brute force, but that would attract far more attention than he wanted.

"The guards," Tarik said. "The one on the left has the keys to the cage, the one on the right has the keys to my chains."

Raim bit his lower lip. Of course the guards had them. He mouthed "just a moment," then crept along the perimeter of the tent until he was close enough to reach out and touch the first guard. He signaled to Draikh to go around to the other the guard.

He took a deep breath.

One of them opened his eye a fraction, then opened his mouth to cry out. Raim quickly snapped the edge of his hand against the man's throat, and the guard slumped to the floor.

Draikh was far subtler, pressing down on a pressure point on the other guard's neck until he too slid from sleep into unconsciousness. Raim took the keys from around the guard's belt and rushed over to Tarik. In a few seconds they had the lock undone, and Draikh passed over the second set to undo his wrists.

"You can't stay here," said Tarik, his voice full of urgency.

"No, I realize that—but once I get you to the Alashan camp, the king won't be able to punish me. He still needs me, and I him, but I'm not going to let him bully me."

"No, it's not that," said Tarik. "It's the king and the

Lady Chabi. The king offered to make her his wife and Queen of the North. They're going to use you to destroy Khareh's spirit-army, but then they will destroy you. Your mother has no love for you, no matter what she has said."

Raim reeled from Tarik's words. "How—how can that be true? The destiny—the blood of Hao? The Council?"

"What is a destiny but words, and what is blood but liquid? Your mother was never truly loyal to the Council; she only wanted power for herself. Why do you think she is your mother? She located the bloodline of Hao, and then wanted to make herself a part of it. And when she was on the brink of losing everything, she made the reckless decision to force the promise on you as a baby. Why would she do that? She did it to save herself. But then she needed you to wake her from her sleep."

A movement from outside the tent, like a loud thump, made them both jump. "I will explain it all later," Tarik whispered. "For now, we need to get out of here…"

He was too weak to move very far, so Raim supported his brother's weight across his back. *Draikh, can you carry both of us?*

"For a short period."

Do it, please. The Alashan are waiting on the outskirts of the camp.

They'd barely taken two steps outside the tent when Oyu screeched a warning cry. Raim stopped in his tracks. From behind him, a deep voice resounded. "What are you doing?"

It was King Song, the Lady Chabi, and several alert soldiers—slaves—who'd dropped their fans and taken up swords instead. Raim had to hand it to the king. He looked wide awake and, if he was suffering from the heat, he wasn't going to show it.

"Stand up to him," said Draikh in his mind.

"I'm freeing my brother," Raim announced, pulling himself up to his full height. "You have no right to keep him locked up in a cage like an animal."

"I have every right. The Lady Chabi and I have been discussing this matter. You are not the savior I was promised. You are no khan-in-waiting; you are an arrogant boy with a few paltry tricks up his sleeve and a weak shadow. I needed someone to destroy the young khan in the North and his shadow army—and now I hear you cannot even do that. Your mother told me the truth. She told me that scar on your chest is a promise to the northern khan. That means you are nothing to me."

Raim couldn't help but look at Lady Chabi in that instant. Her face was pale but determined. So Tarik had been right.

"I'm sorry, my son," she said. "If you hadn't made that Absolute Vow, maybe things would be different. My spirit obviously knew the truth. And I needed you to come here to wake me. But now I will be Queen of the North."

The king smirked. "Together we will rule your blasted land, and I will take your wretched people and make them my slaves. Just what they deserve."

Draikh?

"I'm on it." Draikh swooped at the nearest guard, disarming him and throwing the sword in Raim's direction.

But this time, the king just laughed. "You might have been

told about my obsession with birds. Well, I happen to know a thing or two about garfalcons, even though I thought they were just a legend. It's something I suspected when I first saw that scar on your chest. Now, how about we prove my theory?"

In one swift motion, the king drew a bow from behind his back, and several of his guards did the same. They pointed their arrows at Raim.

Draikh? What do I do?

"I'll protect you!" Draikh swooped back toward him. But then the shooters changed direction, aiming their arrows at Oyu, who was circling the air above them. They let fly all at once.

"No!" Raim and Draikh cried at the same time.

Draikh changed direction and flew up to Oyu, solidifying in the air, trying to knock Oyu out of the path of the arrows. He deflected several of them, taking the points into his own form, which knocked him down. But one of the arrows hit true, burying itself deep in Oyu's body. The garfalcon tumbled out of the sky, black feathers flying in every direction, until he hit the desert with a sickening thud.

Raim tore at the skin on his face, his throat forming an inhumane sound of grief. That's when an arrow hit his own chest and he was knocked to his knees.

As he fell, he caught sight of Lady Chabi, the bow in her hand pointing at him. He looked down at his chest in shock. But even as the blood blossomed out of the wound, all he could see was that the tattoo of permanence, the scar of his Absolute Vow, was gone.

"I'm sorry, my son," Lady Chabi repeated, her words just

reaching him through the veil of pain that descended over all his senses. Behind him, he could hear his brother's voice saying "no, no, no" over and over again.

He fell forward, just managing to turn sideways with a last show of strength to stop the arrow burrowing any deeper.

Darkness descended. He welcomed it.

RAIM

Come back to me.

He could picture Wadi's hands making the symbol for protection. He tried to reach out to touch those hands, but his limbs wouldn't respond no matter how hard he willed them.

Come back to me, she said again.

I'm trying.

"I can't heal you anymore. It won't be enough." A voice broke through the fog of his mind. Khareh's voice. "You have to do it, Raim. Can you hear me? Raim, you can do this."

No, not Khareh's voice. Draikh's voice.

I don't know how. His thoughts were weak, ill-formed things.

Draikh seemed to pounce on them like a wildcat. "You're

there! Do it. I know you can. Do it for Wadi. Do it for vengeance. We can still stop the king! It's not too late."

It is too late, he thought. But a tingling sensation ran through his body, concentrated in his chest. He drew away from it, the pain suddenly becoming too much. *It hurts, Draikh.*

"I know it does, Raim. But just a little more. It's working, I promise you. The Alashan are all here. They will help you. You just need to heal."

"What's happening to him?" Now Raim heard Tarik's voice. "Look at his wound! It's smaller, I'm sure of it."

A damp cloth was pressed to Raim's forehead, and the coolness of it helped to clear his mind. If he could hear Tarik now, it meant he was getting stronger. He focused on the tingling sensation again. *Separate,* he willed his spirit. *Heal me. Make me strong.*

Searing pain made his body convulse, but it was a different kind of pain from the initial wound. He panted, but he wouldn't let it stop. *Water, I need water.*

Instantly, water poured over his head and dripped into his mouth. Tarik cried out.

"You're doing it!" said Draikh. "Keep going!"

He pushed and pushed.

"There! The wound is healed. You can open your eyes now. You can stop."

Come back to me, Raim said, and this time he was talking to his own spirit. He felt himself become whole again, and the tingling ended.

"Gods, Raim, you've really done it."

He had healed himself. He felt power surge through him, felt his spirit lingering just beneath the surface. He would be able to draw it out as easily as breathing now. The tingling returned, but he welcomed it. He knew what it represented. He felt unbeatable. Invincible.

He opened his eyes. He saw Draikh, weak and near-transparent. Through him, he saw the shocked look on Tarik's face.

"You moved the water from the bowl," Tarik said, his mouth gaping like a fish after ever sentence. "Your wound just healed. Was that your shadow?"

"In a way," said Raim, not sure how to explain what had happened. He rubbed where the arrow wound had been with his hand. It itched like the ghost of a wound, but there was barely even a scab there.

"You did a better job than I could ever have done," said Draikh. "I'm proud of you."

"The king," Raim said aloud. "Where is he?"

Tarik's face darkened. "After the arrow, we all thought you were dead. The Alashan took you away, and they gathered Oyu's body too. The Alashan left the camp then, moving too quickly for King Song to keep up. But I don't think he cares. We are so close to Lazar now, he can see the line of the mountains."

"How long have I been out? Are we too late?"

"That depends on how strong you are," said Tarik.

"I'm strong enough for this," replied Raim.

"Then you must leave at once. If you move now, you can catch up with them."

"We must do more than catch up with them," said Raim.

"We have to overtake them." Out of the corner of his eye, he saw Mesan standing in the corner. He caught his gaze, and the man nodded once.

Raim turned back to Tarik. "Thank you for all that you've done."

"Thank you, brother, for saving me." Tarik pulled Raim forward, touching their foreheads together. "You can do this. And when you are done, I will write a full account of your journey, so that all may know the truth."

Raim stood, and was glad to see his legs held beneath him. "King Song will pay for what he did to Oyu, and for all that he is planning to do." He followed Mesan outside.

There was only one mystery left. *Draikh, I thought once Oyu was gone, you would disappear too?*

"You can't get rid of me that easily." Draikh chuckled. Then his tone turned more serious. "You have never been an oathbreaker to Khareh, Raim. I didn't appear to you because you broke an oath. I appeared because *Khareh* broke his vow. And I couldn't stand for that. I chose to stay with you."

"You are the part of him that I would follow to the ends of the earth," said Raim.

"Right, so now let's destroy the Southern King and make you a real khan."

Once they got outside, Raim was shocked to see that Mesan had abandoned his cloak completely. He only wore his lightweight tunic; it covered the majority of his torso, but the cloak was an Alashan's pride and joy. It was their moving shelter. Still, Mesan motioned wordlessly for Raim to abandon his, which he did so with great reluctance.

"We will move faster this way," Mesan said with his hands.

Raim dropped his cloak without any more hesitation. He looked up at the sky, where Naran was still high overhead. "We still have many daylight hours left while the army won't be able to move. I want to go as quickly as we can."

Raim's stomach chose that moment to growl loudly. He was about to ask for Jarumba root, but Mesan held up his hand to stop him. "No, don't eat anything. You must be as light as possible. Let's go."

Mesan was one of the best at moving during the daylight hours. Raim tried his best to copy his sleek, undulating movements, but it was almost impossible to be as efficient as he was. Mesan took him on a meandering path that followed as closely as possible the shadows that the dunes cast in the desert. Even then, those shadows were but narrow lines of relief—the sun seemed to remain overhead for much longer than it ought. They were so close to the center of the desert that the sun made the air feel as thick as water, and each beam felt like a current drawing him backward. Raim struggled for every breath, and every step felt like torture. Every so often, Mesan would slow down and repeat for Raim the mantra of moving in the desert: to keep his limbs as loose and liquid as possible, to keep his mind empty of anything except his destination, to try to force his mind away from the fact that his skin felt like it was roasting alive inside his lightweight tunic.

What kept him going was that horizon. The mountains were drawing closer, and that meant that Lazar was closer too. Just a taste of Jarumba root…

"Don't think about food," said Draikh.

How about water?

"Don't think about that either!"

How about you just stop talking about it, then maybe I will? It would soon be worth it, though. If he could reach the city before King Song did, he could prepare them. *How are you feeling? Are you strong?* he asked.

"I'll be ready," Draikh said.

If Raim wanted the rightful Golden Khan to be in power, then he would have to go out there and fight for it himself. No more waiting for others to clear the path for him.

All of this had been started by Lady Chabi: a woman who had never had his best intentions at heart. All she'd wanted was power.

Raim knew what he wanted: to get back to Wadi, to Loni, to Dharma, and to the land that he loved. The new knotted bracelet around his wrist felt more like a betrayal than the scar ever had. No matter what vows he made, he would always choose to defend the ones he loved at all costs. And right now, a threat was coming to his lands, and he was the only one who could stop it.

Or maybe Naran had just gone completely to his head.

"I hope you're making the right decision. I wish you'd let me know what it was."

Raim kept his mind carefully guarded. *You know I can't do that.*

"Just don't do anything stupid."

What, like sneaking past the army of the man who tried to

kill me, in the middle of the desert, in the middle of the day, toward the person who is my sworn enemy?

"Well, anything *more* stupid."

I'll try.

Focus was his main goal now. Focus, and the thin blur of mountains on the horizon that was steadily growing thicker with every swerve they made through the sand.

"You do know that I might be able to summon water out here, if we move to a spot where I can sense the underground river more easily," said Draikh.

Just those words in his head made Raim's mouth yearn for water. In any other place, his mouth might have filled with saliva at the thought—but here it was just full of dust and sand. *Why would you torture me by saying that?*

"I just meant—"

No. Raim cut him off more sharply than he meant to, unable to keep control of his temper in the heat. *I need you to do nothing else but focus on getting to full strength.*

"Fine," said Draikh. "Just know that I could help you."

The thought was so tempting. He could ask Draikh to lift him up and take him to his destination, but that would defeat their purpose. Draikh needed all his strength—every ounce of it—for what Raim would soon want him to accomplish.

Too quickly the sun dropped behind them, and they doubled their pace. Raim knew that the king would not let his army rest until they reached the mountains of Lazar. Every time he felt like flagging, he remembered just what the price would be if he failed. He wished he'd realized his mother and the king's treachery earlier. Then maybe Oyu would still be alive. It was too late to think of that now, so he had to be quicker.

He kept his head held high, though the muscles in his neck felt the strain. They were almost there.

Is there any sign of Khareh's army?

Draikh lifted up into the sky. "I can't see anything, just more desert."

How is that possible? I thought... Raim felt his heart constrict in his chest and he struggled to control his breathing. *What if he hasn't come? What if something happened to him already? What if...*

"Wait. I think I see something. Up there, on the mountainside."

Raim looked up, following the direction that Draikh was pointing. Then, for the first time in hours, he stopped moving.

The loss of momentum caused him to drop to his knees.

Mesan snapped his neck around, not stopping his own movements—only slowing them. "You can't stop here. You must keep moving."

Raim let Mesan help him to his feet again, and somehow he willed his legs to keep moving. But he couldn't tear his eyes away from the mountain.

Pouring out of a yawning cave entrance high up the mountainside was a river of spirit energy, so thick he could hardly make out individual spirit-forms. It looked like a shimmering, silver waterfall, one that curved in on itself and back into the mountain.

There was only one person on the earth who commanded that many spirits: Khareh. Khareh had brought his spirit-army to face King Song's army. The person who commanded that spirit-army would easily be able to defeat the Southern King and take the throne of the Golden Khan—ruling over the North and the South.

Khareh might wear the crown and be the Khan. But, Raim remembered, part of his own spirit led the army.

Then something sent him into a tailspin of panic once again. The spirit-army was heading back into the mountain. That meant that Khareh *wasn't* preparing his army to meet the Southern King's.

It meant that he was about to enter Lazar—and lose his spirit-army for good.

Raim forgot about the heat. He forgot about the sun. He forgot about how hard it was to move in the desert. Before Mesan could raise a cry to stop him, Raim burst into a sprint. He yelled for Draikh. And with a running leap into the air, he allowed himself to be caught by Draikh, and together they flew as fast as the spirit could fly toward the path that would lead to Lazar.

WADI

The first time she'd traveled this passage between the cliffs, she had been running toward the city, away from the Alashan. She'd had an insatiable desire to see Lazar, a desire driven by her pass-stone, and yet she'd been filled with dread.

This time, she felt almost the exact same emotions. A drive that led to excitement. A fear that led to dread. Except this time, she was not alone. In fact, if she dared to look behind her, not only would she see Khareh in his impressive costume, his crown perched back on top of his head, his green velvet cloak around his shoulders, but behind him she would see the shadows of his spirit-army fill the rest of the narrow crevice, as far back as her eyes could see.

But she did not turn around. She kept her eyes focused forward.

They reached the first courtyard, with its two gigantic figures standing guard—one in an expression of sadness, the other in an expression of horror. They passed the gong, which still lay on the floor from when Silas-yun had broken it into pieces. She stepped over the shards and walked straight up to the massive gate on the far side. She pounded on it with her fist, the action barely making a sound.

But she knew that someone would hear it.

She banged once more, as hard as she could, for good measure, and then she turned around.

A wave of nausea came over her at the sight, and her knees felt weak. There was so much power in front of her under Khareh's command. But she forced herself to remember: the only real power here was Khareh and his original spirit. The spirit part of Raim had never been to Lazar. Wadi thanked all the gods for that fact. The haunt didn't know what was to come, and couldn't warn Khareh what she had planned.

She had expected Puutra-bar or another member of the Shan to appear at the top of the gate, but he didn't. A small door, carved within the larger, opened off to one side. Her heart jumped to see the familiar, white-bearded man appear on the threshold. He appeared equally surprised, stopping in his tracks when he saw Khareh and his army and letting out a squeal so undignified that Wadi almost laughed. Until she thought about how scared Puutra must be.

He was already shutting the door, so Wadi cried out, "Puutra-bar! It's me."

The door opened again by an inch. "Wadi?"

She nodded. "I have brought with me the Khan of Darhan. He has come to declare himself khan of this city, and his first act will be to protect you and the rest of the Chauk from the approach of the Southern King."

Khareh walked over, and to Wadi's surprise, he dropped into a small bow to the old man. "With my spirit-army, I am unstoppable. Accept me as your leader without any quarrel, and I will not let your city or its people come to any harm."

Confusion wriggled across Puutra-bar's face.

"Tell me you will welcome him, Puutra? The people of Lazar have no choice." Wadi was careful to keep her voice neutral, and Puutra studied both of them for what felt like an endless second.

Then he returned Khareh's bow. He raised an eyebrow and said, "We are a people subjugated by our own demons, my Khan, but if you are offering us protection, then we will take it—as we can provide none for ourselves. Please, let me open our city walls, and you can enter to own what is rightfully yours."

"Thank you, Puutra-bar," said Khareh, his voice solemn. Puutra retreated back behind the door to signal the opening of the gate. There was a loud creak, and slowly the huge doors opened.

Khareh put his hand on Wadi's shoulder, and she had to control herself not to jump a mile in the air. "That was easier than I expected," Khareh said.

Wadi did not trust herself to speak.

They waited until the gates were fully open, and they looked up to see the entire city of Lazar gathered above the walls, peering at them just as they had when Raim had entered before.

Wadi took the first step forward. She turned back to Khareh and extended out her arm. "Are you ready?"

RAIM

He swam through spirits.

Draikh had dropped him at the entrance of the crevice in the mountainside that led to Lazar, and from there he had been running through the sea of haunts. They did not impair his movement at all, but it was disconcerting. He tried to keep his focus ahead, unable to look any of the haunts in the eye.

Faster, faster.

Raim willed himself to move. He wasn't too late yet. Not if the haunts were there. He needed Khareh to have his spirit-army still.

He skidded out into the first courtyard, and his heart stopped when he saw the gates were open.

He saw Wadi, her arm outstretched, standing inside the gates of Lazar.

He saw himself—spirit-Raim—behind Khareh. He caught the haunt's eye and saw the panic in his face.

He saw Khareh take a step.

He let out a cry that echoed off the crevice's high stone walls:

"No!"

WADI

Wadi held her breath.

Khareh stepped through the gates.

There was a loud cry from across the cavernous entrance. Wadi's jaw dropped as her eyes took in Raim—the real Raim—who burst from the passage opening shouting a long, drawn-out "NO…"

Even the sudden appearance of Raim, though, could not hold her attention for long, not with Khareh standing there. After he passed through the gates he seemed confused for a moment—not only from Wadi's sudden expression of surprise, but from the shock of hearing Raim's voice—and so he hadn't fully registered what was happening.

"Wait. Where are they going?" said Khareh finally. He looked up, and the color drained from his face. His spirit-army had followed him into Lazar, but as they crossed the threshold, they flew into the sky and disappeared. One by one, his power drained away, lost up into the sky.

"What's happening?" asked Khareh. "Wadi? What is happening?" He jumped into the air as if he could catch the spirits and hold them to the ground. "No! No, they can't! I need them."

Waves of relief and guilt and happiness and fear swept over Wadi, threatening to overwhelm her. She didn't know whether to feel joy at what she'd accomplished or terror at the potential consequences. This was what she wanted. But it clearly wasn't what Raim wanted. She didn't understand.

When she spoke, her voice shook. "Khareh, you have come to Lazar, the home of the oathbreakers. As you pass through these gates, your oath is fulfilled. The spirits may forgive you, or they may not. It appears that every single person you betrayed, in order to gain a haunt for your spirit-army, has chosen to forgive you."

Even as she spoke, Wadi watched as more and more of Khareh's spirit-army disappeared, until a final whoosh of spirit energy rushed through the doorway and there were no spirits left. With one exception: the spirit of Raim.

"You betrayed me," said Khareh. He'd never looked so young in all the time that Wadi had known him. He stared at her with wide eyes. "I trusted you."

"You shouldn't have," Wadi whispered. But now she couldn't tear her eyes from Raim, who approached the pair with a look of thunder upon his face.

65

RAIM

"You." Raim ran at him then, all thoughts of using Khareh's strength against the Southern King gone from his mind. All the words he'd planned for this moment were gone too, lost in a swirling ocean storm of rage. Raim collided with Khareh and his crown flew off his head, crashing to the ground.

Spirit-Raim, the only one of Khareh's haunts to remain, leaped to Khareh's defense. But Draikh was also there, and more than a match for him.

Raim's fury added power to his punches, but also made them swing wild. Khareh ducked and dodged, avoiding the full brunt of the assault, and eventually landed one of his own kicks on Raim's stomach, knocking the wind out of him. Raim didn't care. Even as his stomach complained and his lungs struggled for air, he grappled for Khareh's leg, grabbing it and twisting it around.

Khareh dropped to the ground with a thud, but with his other leg kicked out and brought Raim to the ground too. They wrestled there, Raim unable to shake the anger that fueled his every movement.

"Stop!" cried Wadi. "This isn't you!"

And Raim knew that she was right. He pulled back and scrambled to his feet, dropping his fists just in time for Khareh to land one last blow on his cheek, which sent him flying into the ground.

He tasted dirt and blood.

"Raim!" he heard Draikh's voice in his mind.

Let him finish me, thought Raim. *I don't care.* He dared one last glance at Wadi. She was in fighting stance too. But she wasn't looking at him. No. Her last fierce words hadn't been for him at all. They'd been for Khareh.

Khareh was breathing heavily, his cheeks flushed red. "The wolf is here for me again, Raimanan. The wolf is here, and this time you've not come here to save me. Look at me. I have nothing anymore." He opened his hands, palm out. His clothes were ripped and caked in dirt, his crown cast aside on the ground, one of the jaguar fangs cracked.

All the eyes of Lazar were on them, and Raim steeled himself for their scrutiny. He forced himself to stand up, the rush of blood and pain making him woozy. But his mind was clear, and the familiar tingling sensation ran across his body, healing his every wound. He saw Khareh's eyes go wide as the cut on his cheek closed with Draikh nowhere near.

"When we were children—after I saved you from that wolf—you became my friend," Raim panted. "I knew you, and I knew you'd have done the same for me. But now? Now I don't know you. All I see is the person that maimed my sister, that killed his own uncle, that betrayed his land and his people by becoming this... this oathbreaker khan. And you have all this power because of me. Because I was stupid enough to entrust you with my vow to protect you—that vow meant everything to me. But now I have the power to take it all away."

Raim's resolve broke then. *I don't know if I can go through with this.* He flicked his eyes to Wadi.

Wadi, who had given him strength since the day he'd met her.

Wadi, who gave him the confidence that he could be a leader. *The* leader, if he wanted it.

Wadi, who nodded at him ever so slightly, her eyes never leaving his. She knew what he was about to do, and she approved. That was enough for him.

He faced Khareh again. His former friend stood stock-still, apart from the rise and fall of his chest as he breathed.

Raim took a deep breath of his own. "I was told, once, by someone much wiser than you or me, that what is past is past, and we make the best of what we have now. And so, despite the fact this goes against every fiber of my being, despite everything I believe... I forgive you, Khareh. I forgive you for what you did to Dharma."

As soon as the words left his mouth, Raim watched as Spirit-Raim moved in front of him, a shadow separating the two former best friends. Then the spirit floated forward, slowly fading, until he and Raim were one again.

Power surged through Raim's veins once more, and, for the first time in a long time, he felt whole. Khareh looked down at his hand, and the scar that had lived on his palm—the scar of his broken vow to Raim, the scar that had started it all for him—was gone.

Khareh stretched his hand out, then curled it back into a fist and stretched it again. But the scar had truly disappeared. "Thank you," he whispered to Raim. "I feel so free now."

The crown lay on the ground in between them, and to Raim it seemed to pulse with its own life and power. It would be so easy for him to pick it up and take it for his own, as maybe he was meant to do.

But that was not what he wanted.

He looked at Khareh. "The Council told me I was destined to rule Darhan. They dedicated their lives to make sure the bloodline of Hao was restored. This crown ... it's in my blood."

Khareh nodded. "I know of Hao. He was a legendary khan. I had no idea you were his blood."

"Neither did I," Raim said. "But I don't know the first thing about leadership. I don't have plans for Darhan. I have followed people blindly, made bad decisions, been lied to and deceived. But through it all, one person has been there to guide me."

He turned to Draikh. *You.*

Draikh shook his head. "It was all you, Raim."

You know that's not true. You have been with me every step of the way.

Raim clenched his fists. He looked back at Khareh. "And although I hate—*hate*—what you did, and who you are now, I know that's not who you really are. You lost the best part of yourself when you decided to break your vow to me. But now that part—Draikh—is stronger than you are. He is the one who should rule Darhan. Not you as you are, and not me."

Wadi stared at him with wide eyes. "No, Raim, you haven't seen the things he's done. You don't know the whole story. You can rule on your own."

Raim couldn't look at her then, or else he risked losing all of his conviction. He kept his eyes on Khareh and tried to keep his voice firm. Steady.

"You've been preparing for this your whole life!" he said. "If you were whole, if you could make the right decisions, you would be a great leader. The right leader."

"But I can never be whole," said Khareh, holding a hand over his heart.

Raim mirrored the gesture, placing his hand where his Absolute Vow had once been a tattoo of permanence. "Because you cannot forgive me and make yourself whole again, the way I forgave you?" he asked.

Khareh nodded.

"You need Draikh. Without that side of you, you are not a good khan. But with him...you would make our nation great. I know it. With him, I believe you are the right person to lead Darhan."

There was a sharp intake of breath. Raim's eyes darted

to Wadi, and then to Draikh. Both could not conceal the shock on their faces. He'd never even dared to think the words he'd just said, in case Draikh could sense his intentions. Now, having said them out loud, he knew that he was making the right choice.

"Raim, what are you doing?" Wadi's voice reached him. He looked over at her and mouthed the words, "I'm sorry."

He turned back to Khareh and bowed his head, plucking a hair from it. It wasn't much—it was crude—but it was something.

"I don't deserve this," said Khareh, his voice shaking.

"Raim, are you sure about this?" said Draikh, his voice rattling through his mind. "I'm not sure I'll be able to stop her. I won't be able to hold her back."

Try your best, Draikh, thought Raim.

Raim stared at Khareh. "Maybe you don't deserve this. But you can spend the rest of your life earning my forgiveness—and the forgiveness of Darhan."

He reached out and tore one of the long threads from the base of Khareh's tattered green cloak. "I, Raimanan of the Moloti tribe, promise my life to you, as the true and rightful Khan of Darhan. My word, and my life, are yours. This is my Absolute Vow." He slipped the knot around his neck.

An anguished scream filled the air—and Raim was immediately transported back to the day he'd first promised his life to Khareh, after his Yun duel. The moment he had become an oathbreaker. The scream came from the spirit of his mother, the Lady Chabi, just as it had before.

Raim's promise knot bracelet burst into flames again,

and this time the shadow *did* appear, along with the scar. He looked over at his mother, the haunt who lived within the knot. It had only been days since he'd remade this promise to her. But now he was willing to break it, and intentionally—to do what was right for Darhan.

When her cry came to an end, in her hand was her spirit-blade.

"No, Lady Chabi!" Draikh flew into action, diving through the air at her to protect Raim.

Khareh and Wadi jumped too, shocked at the sight of Raim's flaming wrist.

Raim could see the anger in his mother's eyes as she plunged forward to bury the spirit-knife deep into his chest.

But this time, he was ready for her.

66

RAIM

His spirit spread out of him, but this time he was in control of it, not Khareh. Spirit-Raim was stronger than the haunt of Lady Chabi, and his spirit-hand was on her arm, stopping it before she could push the knife any further.

"Remove my scar," said Raim and his spirit in unison, their voices firm.

"Never," she said. "You will be scarred as an oathbreaker for the rest of your life—just as you deserve."

"The vow was false."

"You made the vow; you broke the vow."

"I would never have made it if I had known your plan to deceive me. The first time I made this vow to you, I was too young to understand what was happening. You forced it on me. The second time, you deceived me—and eventually tried to kill me. That breaks any conditions of the vow I made to you. You don't care about my bloodline—you care only about taking power for yourself. And as I am in Lazar, I have fulfilled the conditions of an oathbreaker. You can remove my scar. I'm asking you nicely—remove it. Or the moment I see you in the desert, I will remove *you*."

Lady Chabi let out a scream of frustration. "This is not over," she said, but even as she spoke, she rose, flying up into the sky. As she left, there was a bright flash of light and the scar around Raim's wrist was gone.

He was truly free of all his vows. There was only one thing left now.

"You know she only did that because her body would have collapsed without its spirit again," Draikh said. "She was undone by the power of that oath. She'll probably still try to kill you the moment she sees you."

I know, said Raim. *I'll deal with that later. But for now, you know what you need to do.*

"Are you sure you want me to do this?"

It's the only way. I won't lose you, will I? Raim couldn't hide the momentary thread of panic in his voice.

"You won't be rid of me that easily," Draikh said with a wry grin. "I'll always be close to the surface." Then he headed toward Khareh, disappearing until they were joined again. Draikh and Khareh. The dream and the reality. Together and whole.

Raim prayed it was for the best. And he would be there, always watching, in case it wasn't. That was a vow he intended to keep.

No more spirits were left in the courtyard. A buzzing reached his ears, and he realized it was the sound of hundreds of Lazar voices talking all at once about what they had seen.

He turned to Wadi. Hurt and confusion was written all over her face. "What did you just do?" she asked.

He took the few steps that separated them and gathered up her hands in his. She didn't resist. She ran her hands along his wrists. "You're no longer an oathbreaker," she said with a small smile.

"No, no I'm not," said Raim, and he could hardly believe it.

"But you're still an idiot. You've given him everything."

Raim was shocked as Wadi's eyes filled with tears. He could only guess at what she'd seen that would make her feel so strongly. "The Khareh you knew is not the Khan now," he said. "The Khareh *I* knew is."

Khareh dropped to his knee. "It's true, Wadi. I can see every reason why you would hate me, and I will do everything in my power to make it up to you."

"I was meant to be Yun, Wadi," said Raim. "That was my destiny—the one *I* chose. I know that now."

The word "Yun" seemed to bring fresh horror to Wadi's face.

"What is it?" Raim asked, stricken that he had caused Wadi more hurt.

"Raim, I have something to tell you. The Yun warrior Mhara was going to kill Khareh. But I saved him. I … "

Raim felt his heart stop for an instant. Then he felt the power of the oath he'd made. The vow to protect Khareh.

"Then I guess you did my job for me," he said. "Mhara was her own woman. She had her own vows, her own duties. She would not have hesitated, even if I had been at Khareh's side. That was one of the reasons I respect—respected—her so much. Her destiny was her own."

Their moment was interrupted as Puutra-bar came running over. Raim wanted more time to speak to Wadi, to explain his decision, but the old man's tone spoke of something even more urgent than answers.

"We are all in great danger," Puutra said. "We sent out a scout after we heard that the Southern King was approaching. The king is now here. He can't find the entrance to Lazar, but it's only a matter of time—he's prowling the cliffs. He's close, and if you don't hurry, he will find us."

"Then this is your first duty as the Khan," Raim said to Khareh. "Let's go out and finish this Southern King. He will learn that he can't bring an army to Darhan and not face your wrath." Raim picked up Khareh's crown and brushed the dirt from it. "You will need this."

Khareh took it from him and held it out in front of him as if the base was dipped in poison. "I still have a problem: I have no army."

Raim nodded. "I know. But I have a plan." He turned then and grabbed Wadi's hands. "Do you understand what I did?"

She shook her head. "I don't think I ever will."

He pressed his lips to her hands, then released them. "Soon, I'll be able to explain everything. But for now—please take us back to the desert," he said. "You're the only one who can."

Wadi hesitated for a second, and then nodded.

As they walked through the thin crevice—Wadi and Raim first, Khareh just behind—they could hear King Song's screams echoing off the sheer faces of the cliffs, as clear as if he was standing five feet away from them: "Raim! Come out here, Raim. You can't hide from me. I will find you and kill you and raze your entire city to the ground!"

Raim stopped when Wadi signaled that they were about to turn the final bend to reach the desert. He turned to Wadi.

"I don't know if my plan is going to work. If it doesn't, call on the spirits of Lazar, using the pass-stones like only you can. Seal this passage. Don't let the king and his army through. Don't let them reach Lazar. Even if it means leaving us out there."

"How about you just don't fail?" she said, her voice trembling.

"I'll try," he said.

Then he turned to Khareh. "Ready?"

They turned and walked out to meet the Southern King together.

67

RAIM

King Song seethed with barely concealed fury. His entire body trembled with it. Just behind him stood three of his generals, their faces dark, hands on the hilts of their swords. Worse still, the generals were guarding the Alashan, their hands bound behind their backs. Mesan was among them, the bright red egg of a bruise growing on his cheek, his lip split and bleeding.

And behind them, in a long straight line as far as the eye could see in the dying light of the sun, was the rest of the army.

When the king saw the two boys exit the thin crevice in the cliff face, he threw his head back and laughed. Raim let the sound wash over him. Beside him, he heard Khareh take a sharp breath at the sight of the king's army. But Raim was not scared. They walked forward until only a few feet separated them from the king.

"*You* are the northern khan I've been hearing so much about?" the king said when he finally stopped laughing. "You?" His eyes combed over Khareh's ludicrous crown, his green cloak—and, by his side, Raim in his borrowed clothing from the South, now in tatters from his journey through the desert. "And where is the so-called shadow-army I've heard so much about? Or did you crawl out of your dark tunnel like a cockroach to turn your lands over to me? I am the Golden King, and the desert is mine. The North is mine."

He turned to Raim. "And you. You were exactly what I thought you were: dirty, oathbreaking scum from the North. I should never have listened to the Council when they said they would bring me a hero from the North, but it was the only way I could cross this infernal desert. And I should certainly never have listened to that treacherous mother of yours. She's disappeared, abandoned me. Abandoned both of us, it looks like."

The king's words about his mother made the hair stand up on the back of Raim's neck. Khareh opened his mouth to say something, but Raim jumped in first. "King Song, this is your chance to surrender to Khareh-Khan. If you do, you may return to your lands to govern them as you always have. We will have several demands that will need to be met, of course. No more slavery. And free trade routes between the North and South."

"I hope your plan is a good one," Khareh whispered to Raim.

"Don't worry," Raim whispered back. "I made a vow to be your Protector, and I intend to keep it."

Khareh looked at the Southern King. "Go home, Song. We're making the choice easy for you. The North is not yours for the taking."

King Song's eyes threatened to bulge out of his head. "You would give orders to me? You are nothing but a boy with a crown and one friend. I am a king. I have an army of thousands. I don't have to listen to you. If you do not move, I will crush you."

"I am nothing but a boy with a crown, that is true. But you underestimate the power of my friend."

At that, Raim closed his eyes, leaned his head back, and stretched out his arms. He called his spirit to the surface, where it coiled like a snake about to strike. Like a layer peeling away, his spirit spread from his body. He was a sage of the highest order, using his own spirit as the source of his power. His spectral form flew straight up into the air, following the line of the cliff, and as he did so, a handful of sand by his feet flew out behind him.

The sand buffeted against the king's clothes. He wiped it away, perplexed.

Then Raim's eyes flew open and he directed all his energy at the king. His spirit whipped up the sand in front of the king until it was a whirlwind in miniature.

King Song took several steps backward. "You think a little sand will stop me?" he bellowed. Then he raised a horn to his lips and blew it hard—the signal for his army. They began to rush toward the cliffs, a thousands spears lifted at once, and the desert shook with the sudden approach of men hollering for victory. They wanted to make Raim and Khareh flee to safety in Lazar, where they would pursue them until the end. But Raim had no plans to move. And Khareh stood solid as a stone beside him.

Raim sent his spirit flying out across the desert, picking up more and more sand in his wake. It looked as if a curtain of sand was lifting up out of the desert—a wall built from thousands of tiny grains. The spirit spun the grit around, so that the walls became more like tornados: whirlwinds of sand that were about to hit the Southern King's army with all the force that he could muster.

"Do not falter!" the king shouted, and he blew the horn again. Raim couldn't tell if his words or the horn had an impact on the sand-battered soldiers—the great golden wall absorbed all sound in the thunderous roar of its own making.

The sand hit the soldiers as they were running, and their battle roars turned to screams. As Raim fed more power into his spirit, the sand gained momentum, building into a fierce maelstrom that devoured everything in its path.

"Are … they … running?" Raim's voice was strained and stilted. His eyes had closed again from the effort, but his eyelids twitched as if they were under great strain. He felt his lips move, speaking unheard words. Every real word required a lot of effort—effort that he didn't have.

"They're dropping their weapons!" Khareh said, and Raim could hear it too. Swords fell to the ground as the sand, each grain as sharp as a shard of glass, ate away at every inch of exposed flesh on the soldiers' bodies—starting with their hands.

"They're turning back!" said Khareh, unable to disguise the glee in his voice.

"No!" yelled King Song. "Keep coming! Keep coming! Make it to the cliffs!" But even if they'd wanted to, the army could not obey. The men covered their heads with their cloaks, disorientated, confused and in pain. The only relief came from turning back, away from the storm.

Inside the whirlwind, the friction of the sand in the air set the king's tent alight, and flames joined the sand and the wind. The heat grew unbearably intense, and smoke thickened any air that was left to breathe.

"Just a little more!" shouted Khareh to Raim.

Raim squeezed his eyes shut even tighter. The storm that raged in the desert grew even stronger as his spirit summoned even more sand, engulfing the army. They turned and fled, sprinting back across the sand as fast as they could run. "Retreat!" came the cry from further back, but it was unnecessary. Every soldier was abandoning his post, and soon there was nothing left in that stretch of desert but the bent and broken blades of dropped swords, and the bodies of the men who had succumbed to the sand.

"They've stopped," said Khareh, and at that Raim broke his contact and opened his eyes. The wall of sand dropped like the final gasp of a waterfall, and his exhausted—but triumphant—spirit came back to join him.

Immediately, Raim's spine straightened and a new light came into his eyes. He had done it. He really was a sage— and without a single broken oath in sight.

Somehow, the king was still on his feet in front of them,

his armor beaten and bent, his rich garments ripped to shreds by the sand, his skin blistered and burned. His army had abandoned him; even his generals looked defeated. The Alashan had huddled together, making themselves as small as possible in the storm. Helmets, swords, and shields littered the ground around the broken king.

Khareh took a step forward. "Song, this is the end. Turn over your army and your lands to my command."

Raim was drained from raising the sand. His muscles were weak; his spirit exhausted. It took all his concentration merely to remain on his feet. And so he was almost too late to see the knife.

King Song snarled. "Never." He whipped back his cloak; in his hand, he held a sharp silver dagger. He stabbed the blade at Khareh.

"Draikh!" Raim screamed.

The spirit burst from Khareh in time to shove Khareh aside. The blade sliced harmlessly through the air. Draikh and Khareh rejoined, but by now Khareh had had time to draw his own sword, and it plunged into the king's side.

Song dropped to his knees. "I have failed," he said, and those were his final words.

King Song's generals were in shock, but when Khareh turned to look at them, they instantly dropped to the ground in the lowest bow they could muster.

One dared to lift his sword above his head, and he said the words: "Our swords belong to you, now. You are our king."

WADI

"Raim!" Wadi couldn't stand it anymore. As soon as she'd seen the storm of sand die down, she'd rushed out of her place in the crevice. She had seen the danger as the king thrust a blade toward Khareh, and she'd seen the exhaustion in Raim as he called for Draikh prevent it. She had never seen a storm rage so fiercely in the desert—not in all her years of living there—and Raim had controlled it. No wonder he was so tired.

She ran up to him and threw her arms around him. She felt his body collapse into hers, and she broke his fall as he slumped onto the ground. She held his body close to hers and buried her face in his hair.

"Wadi, you're here," he said, his voice weak.

She pushed him away, enough to look into his eyes. "You've made Khareh the Golden Khan of Darhan and the

South. There will be many you will have to convince of this decision. Including me," she said in a low voice.

"I know. And that is why I will be at his side, making sure he doesn't make the same mistakes. But I trust him. I trust Draikh."

"I hope you're right," she said.

"Help me stand?" he asked. Wadi put his arm across her shoulders, and together they stood and faced Khareh.

Khareh came over and clasped Raim's hand. "We've done it."

Raim nodded. "The South is yours now. You are the Golden Khan. You can claim it."

"Yes. The South is mine. But I have one last thing to do first. Can you stand on your own?"

Raim nodded again. Wadi unhooked his arm from around her shoulders, but she did not move from his side. Her body was still tensed in high alert from having Khareh so near. She didn't know what Khareh was going to do, and she didn't trust him. Not even Raim's trust in him could convince her to—not yet.

Khareh reached out and grasped Raim's hand. "Raimanan, I want to release you from your Absolute Vow to me."

Wadi saw Raim's hand tighten around Khareh's, felt his shock as the words hit home. She placed her other hand on his upper arm, steadying him as he took a shaky step forward. "What?" he said.

Khareh bit his lip, a moment of hesitation, before continuing. "You must choose to agree, of course. But I don't want you to protect me anymore." He held his hand up to stop

Raim from interrupting. "Only do this *if*, in exchange, you agree to knot your allegiance to me as Khan of Darhan, in my place." He lifted his crown from atop his head and held it out to Raim, gripping it by one of its jaguar fangs.

Raim's eyes grew wide. He didn't reach out to take the crown. "I ... I don't understand."

Khareh gestured to his new generals. "I have a new land to rule now. And if what you say is true about the slaves, then I have a lot of work to do to change things there. And I have so much to learn about the South—knowledge that can help improve life in Darhan. You know it's always been my dream to visit Aqben. If I want to be the true Golden Khan, then I have to rule equally over the South as the North. And to do that, I have to go there and understand the people."

Raim seemed lost for words. "But I'm not ready. I'm not a khan."

Khareh raised an eyebrow. "There's a part of me that says different."

For a moment, Khareh's face flickered, and Wadi caught a smile on his face that she had never seen before. It was kind and mischievous all at once.

Raim seemed to recognize this other side of Khareh.

"Draikh?" Raim said. The tension seemed to leave his body and a smile appeared on his face too. "You'll love it in the South. Get them to show you their boats—they're so different from the ones on Lake Oudo—although I don't suggest a long journey on one."

"I will. And don't worry about leadership. You will have

Wadi with you. I don't think you could ask for a better person to help you remember what's most important."

Wadi raised her eyebrows at Khareh's praise, and he laughed. Then he flicked his eyes back to Raim. "So ... do you accept?"

Raim swallowed hard. "I do." He reached behind his neck and lifted the knotted promise over his head.

"Raimanan of the Moloti tribe, I release you from your Absolute Vow to me," said Khareh, holding onto one side of the necklace.

"Khareh-Khan, by your will and yours alone, I am no longer your Protector," Raim replied.

Only the knot began to smoke and dissolve in front of Wadi's eyes, leaving behind the piece of thread and the strand of Raim's hair. They tied them together again, in a loose knot, and spoke the new words:

"Now, Raimanan of the Moloti tribe, will you make a vow of fealty to me, your Golden Khan, as the Khan of Darhan, to be my honored vassal, and to watch over the homeland of my birth in my stead?"

"I vow that I will, and that you will always have my loyalty, Khareh-Khan, the Golden Khan, leader of the known world." Raim's voice was steady as he spoke, and Wadi squeezed his shoulder in encouragement. They pulled the knot tight.

"With you looking after Darhan for me, I know my homeland will be safe. In a year, you must come back here to Lazar to meet with me again, and I will share with you everything I've learned from the South! We'll make Darhan great," said Khareh.

"We will," said Raim. He finally reached out and took the crown from Khareh's hands.

Wadi felt her heart soar. This was what Raim was destined for. When Raim had pledged to once again be Khareh's Protector, she'd thought all her hard work had been for naught. She thought she had failed Dharma—and failed Darhan. But now, Raim was Khan, and Khareh was heading to the South.

A groan came from one of the Alashan, and Wadi remembered herself. She rushed forward, sliding a knife out from the sheath at her belt, and sliced it through their bindings. When she reached Old-maa, she hugged the old woman tightly. She felt her stiffen at the affection at first, but then she relaxed. Wadi smiled until her cheeks burned. She'd missed her old tribe so much.

Raim turned to Mesan. "Are you all right?"

Mesan nodded. "The king did not take too kindly to me helping you escape. But that doesn't matter now. That was quite the storm. I don't know how you did it, but I have never seen anything like that in all my time in Sola's grasp." Wadi helped to interpret his rush of language.

Raim clasped his shoulder. "Will you help Khareh return safely through Sola to the borders in the South? Then you and the rest of the tribe will be free to travel as you choose."

"Of course," said Mesan. "It is the least we can do for you both."

Wadi stepped up and embraced Mesan too. "Thank you."

Khareh turned to Wadi, his deep black eyes boring into hers. "Look after Raim for me, won't you?"

"Always."

Wadi hooked her arm through Raim's, and they watched as the Alashan led Khareh and his new generals back across the dunes—to find the remnants of King Song's army and claim his place on the Southern King's throne.

RAIM

The city of Lazar welcomed Raim and Wadi with open arms when they returned from the desert. Puutra-bar came rushing out to greet them through the main gates, and the eyes of the citizens of Lazar still peered down from every angle. This time, Raim felt no fear or trepidation.

This time, Raim was no oathbreaker. He was a khan.

"We could hear the sand storm from everywhere in the city," the old man said, his voice trembling. "We thought Sola had taken you all."

"No," said Wadi. "It was Raim who summoned it. Or should I say, the Khan of Darhan did."

"What's this?" asked Puutra, one eyebrow rising.

The crown felt heavy in Raim's hands, but he gripped it tighter. He would strip it of its jaguar skull once he got to Darhan, but the emerald green he would take on as his color. "It's true. Khareh has given me Darhan while he heads to the South to establish his rule there. I will be his general, guarding the lands in his name."

Puutra placed a hand on Raim's shoulder. "You will be a good ruler, Raim. You were born for this too. You are a sage, and now … you are a khan as well."

Raim fought back tears that pricked behind his eyes. "Thank you, Puutra-bar."

"I suppose you will be returning to your homeland," Puutra said. "The people of Lazar thank you for saving us from the Southern King. We will lead you to the tunnels. Of course, you will need a pass-stone."

"Oh," said Raim. "I almost forgot." Underneath his tunic, where his new promise knot to Khareh now sat, he also bore the pass-stone that Lady Chabi had given him. "This belongs to Lazar."

At the sight, Puutra's eyes lit up and Wadi gasped in shock. A feverish murmur spread like wildfire through the crowd above them. "Where did you get this?" Wadi asked, helping him remove it over his head.

"A final gift from Lady Chabi," Raim said. "Maybe the only useful thing she has ever given me." He leveled his gaze at Wadi. "I feel like things aren't over with her. She will be back."

"I know," said Wadi, in a voice that was barely a whisper. Then she revealed the three pass-stones she had in her posses-sion. "That brings our total up to five, counting the stone in Lazar," she said. "Two more out there. Two more, and then the route from Darhan to Lazar can be opened for good."

Raim nodded. "When we reach Darhan, I will make it my priority to hunt down the remaining two stones. But for now, I have my first declaration to make as Khan." He raised his voice and tilted his head back, so that it was clear he was addressing the entire population of Lazar. "Anyone who wishes may accompany Wadi and me back to Darhan, to return to your tribes. Sola knows, you have earned it. Or you may stay, under the continued leadership of Puutra-bar and the Shan, and help rebuild this city to its former glory."

Some chose to stay. But a large majority decided to make the journey with Raim and Wadi, and Raim was glad. He remembered the rush of relief and comfort he'd felt after arriving back in Darhan. He could imagine others feeling the same way.

Seeing the people of Lazar gathering their humble possessions to join them, Raim brimmed with pride. Wadi smiled at him too, a bright, beaming grin he hadn't seen on her face since they'd spent time together in the desert.

"And you thought no one would want to follow you. But look at them now," she said.

He turned and stared. These were people who were no longer haunted oathbreakers—just men and women who longed to return home, to the people who had forgiven them. And now they had that choice. Wadi took Raim's hand in hers and squeezed it tight.

"Let's go home," said Raim. "We have a nation to rule."

epilogue

DHARMA

She could not see him, but she recognized the pattern of his steps, the weight of his presence, just outside the tent walls. But, of course, she had seen this moment coming in her dreams. She just hadn't known exactly when. She tightened her fist around the piece of cloth she'd been mending and bit her lip in anticipation.

Light fell on her face, the warmth of it tingling her cheek, as the curtain to the yurt swung open.

No words were spoken. He simply rushed in, all muffled cries and swift-moving air, and gathered her up in his arms. She allowed herself to collapse against him and threw her own arms around his neck. He smelled like sand and fierce heat, overlaid with grass and rain. He wasn't long from the desert.

They broke apart, and she could sense him smile at her.

She lifted her hands to his face and traced the line of his cheekbones, the bridge of his nose. Then she remembered herself. She bowed her head. "My Khan," she said.

He laughed. "Dharma, it's just me. Your brother."

She wrinkled her nose. "I know who you are, silly. You've come with a task for me."

He hesitated.

"It's all right," she said. "It's no burden. In fact, it's almost done."

She dropped her hand from his face to his shoulder, then drifted down his arm until she found his hand. She took it and indicated they both should go outside. She led him around the back of the yurt, and she could feel the footsteps of many others following them—their grandfather, Loni, and the girl, Wadi. She knew this place so well, she walked as confidently as if she had full use of her vision.

"Let me see the knot," she said, holding out her other hand.

"Here you are," he said after a moment. He leaned forward so she could feel the weight of the knot in her hand. She could feel the importance of the vow: Raim's pledge of allegiance to Khareh, the Golden Khan—not as his Protector, but as one khan to another. Then, she snapped her fingers.

At her command, two of her best weavers stepped forward, carrying between them the project that she'd been working on for a long time—a secret project that not even Loni had known about. She could tell by their shocked silences that they saw what she had done, and were taking it all in.

"This is the story of your vow," she said. "It's all woven in there. All that was needed was this final piece." She stepped up to the intricately woven rug and ran her hands over the fine webs of fibers, finding the space in the very center where she'd left a hole for the promise knot itself. The whole story would now center around that knot, each scene depicted as she had seen it in her visions.

"Dharma ... " Raim's voice broke with emotion. "It's perfect."

Dharma knew what he was looking at. She knew every knot in the carpet by heart, as well as she knew the ridges on the backs of her hands and the comfort of her grandfather's embrace. Still holding Raim's hand, she brought it up to touch the first panel, the first part of the story, which she could see so clearly in her mind's eye.

There, woven in threads of browns, golds, and greens, the colors of the earth, was Raim. He was sitting in the crook of an old, cracked tree, one leg dangling in the breeze, his head leaning back against the trunk.

ACKNOWLEDGMENTS

Second books are tough, and I couldn't have reached this point without support from all corners. Many thanks are due to my agent, Juliet Mushens, for her friendship, care, and attention. The team at Random House Children's Books, especially my editor, Lauren Buckland, copyeditor, Julia Bruce, and publicist, Harriet Venn, have been absolute rock stars. In Canada, thanks go to Amy Black, Pamela Osti, and Lindsey Reeder at Doubleday Canada for creating such an amazing reception for these books over there. Lastly, I am endlessly grateful to the Flux team (including Brian Farrey-Latz and Sandy Sullivan) for bringing this duology to life in the USA.

Thanks are also long overdue to Tanya Byrne, Kim Curran, James Dawson, Will Hill, Laura Lam, Tom Pollock, James Smythe, Team Mushens, and the Lucky 13s, for understanding in ways that only other people on this mad journey can. To my family and friends—and everyone who came out to support my first book—your support means the world to me, and I am the luckiest girl in the world because of it.

But the biggest thanks of all goes to Lofty, who shares in all my mad adventures—both fictional and real.

Photo by Marte L. Rekaa

ABOUT THE AUTHOR

Amy McCulloch is a Canadian author and freelance editor living in London, UK. She was bitten by the travel bug at an early age while accompanying her parents on buying trips around the world for their oriental carpet business. It was this love of travel that inspired her to set a novel in a hot desert location. (Moving to freezing Ottawa, Canada, where her first winter hit -40 degrees, might have had something to do with that too.) She studied Medieval and Old English literature at the University of Toronto.

Connect with Amy on Twitter: @amy_alward or visit her website: www.amyalward.co.uk.